HER MOTHER LEAN
LOWS. THEY HADN'T
OR WHAT HER MOTHE

Fay reached across to st
"What will happen to me?

Her mother moved he
nightstand. "My cards," she said, her hand floating weightlessly
down onto the bed.

Fay found the Tarot cards at the back of the drawer,
wrapped in the old blue scarf they had been wrapped in for
seventy years. She placed the cards in her mother's hands,
and the old woman unwrapped them carefully, then slowly
but deftly tied the scarf loosely around her neck.

Fay cut the cards and dealt them, calling out their names.
"Death, Justice, the Sun, the Falling Tower, the Wheel of
Fortune, the High Priestess, the Hanged Man."

Her mother thought a minute. "That's good. There's a
man. I want you to have a man."

"I don't know if I remember how," Fay said.

"There may not be marriage, but there *is* a man. This man
will not be a problem for you. Lizzie will."

"What about Lizzie?" Fay asked.

"Don't be fooled into thinking you can keep her safe."

"I can try."

"She's not safe, Fay," her mother said. "She wasn't born
safe. If you could find a way not to love her, that would
protect *you*, anyway."

"None of us is safe, Mother."

"Oh yes," her mother said. "You are safe. You are perfectly
safe. Your only misfortune is that so many of the people you
love are not safe at all."

"If they stay with me, will they be safe?"

"No, my love."

THE FORTUNE TELLER
by Marsha Norman

"SWEEPS THE READER FROM PAGE TO PAGE . . .
THE FORTUNE TELLER CREATES REAL SUSPENSE,
THE KIND THAT BUILDS TO SUCH TENSION THAT
YOU HAVE TO FORCE YOURSELF NOT TO PEEK
AHEAD AND READ THE LAST PAGE."
—*The Providence Sunday Journal*

THE
FORTUNE
TELLER

MARSHA NORMAN

BANTAM BOOKS
TORONTO · NEW YORK · LONDON · SYDNEY · AUCKLAND

This edition contains the complete text
of the original hardcover edition.
NOT ONE WORD HAS BEEN OMITTED.

THE FORTUNE TELLER

A Bantam Book / published by arrangement with
Random House, Inc.

PRINTING HISTORY
Random House edition published May 1987
Bantam edition / May 1988

ISBN 0-553-27284-5

Published simultaneously in the United States and Canada

Bantam Books are published by Bantam Books, a division of
Bantam Doubleday Dell Publishing Group, Inc. Its trademark,
consisting of the words ''Bantam Books'' and the portrayal of
a rooster, is Registered in U.S. Patent and Trademark Office
and in other countries. Marca Registrada. Bantam Books,
666 Fifth Avenue, New York, New York 10103.

The author gratefully acknowledges
Dorothy and Wendell Cherry

1:00 A.M.

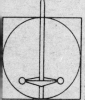

FAY MORGAN NEVER HAD ANY MONEY. HAD NEVER had any money, in fact. But, then, she'd always *known* she'd never have any money, and that helped, really it did. More than you'd think.

The other thing Fay had always known was what was going to happen. Where things were. Who was coming into who else's life and when. And why.

What little money Fay had, she had earned by selling these powers of location. The police department would pay five hundred dollars to find a suspect. Widows would pay half that much to discover their little doggies asleep under the porch. Then, of course, there were ordinary people, brokers and teachers, lovers and clerks, who would pay fifty dollars an hour for Fay to read the Tarot cards, or their palms, or the looks on their faces and tell them where *they* were.

It was a good life, and a good enough living to raise a daughter. A daughter who wouldn't have to tell fortunes for a living. A daughter who would have a better life. A girl named Lizzie, who was nineteen now, lithe and lush-haired.

Lizzie had asked about it one night, how it worked.

"All I do," Fay had said, "is tell people who they are."

"Don't they know that?" Lizzie asked, getting ready to go out.

"They like to get a second opinion," Fay said.

1

Lizzie bent over to brush her hair. "But what about fate?" she asked, upside down.

"Fate is just . . . fate is what happens to people like you," Fay answered.

"Like me?" Lizzie asked, from under her hair.

"No, hon." Fay smiled. "Like them."

Lizzie straightened up. "Don't I have any fate?"

"You're fifteen," Fay said. "What happens to fifteen-year-olds is they grow up."

Lizzie nodded. That suited her fine. She threw the brush on the bed, left for the dance, and never asked about it again.

But the work would always be something of a mystery to Fay. People were rarely surprised by what she told them. In fact, the less surprised they were, the more impressed they were by her genius.

But, Fay would say, it doesn't take a genius to know what's going to happen. The same things happen to everybody. Our children grow up and leave us, and our friends die. Our families hurt us, then help us, then hurt us again. We find our work, we lose our selves, and we spend what little time we have wondering where it went.

It takes a genius, Fay would say, to live in spite of what we know; to be, despite our friends and families and our own best efforts, alone.

Most days, though, Fay would counsel, it will be all right to be alone.

This story is about one of those other days, when it wasn't all right at all. The day the Devil came and took Fay's daughter away.

THERE ARE SEVENTY-EIGHT cards in a Tarot deck. Four suits of fourteen cards each, Swords, Cups, Coins, and Wands, and twenty-two picture cards called the major arcana, the big mysteries. Fay's mother told her she could learn these picture cards by associating them with people she knew, but it had taken nearly forty years to meet them all.

The Juggler was a boy she loved and lost when he kept going to school and she didn't. The Hanged Man ran the mission at the corner, the Pope ran numbers for the mob. Naturally, she'd married the Fool, Lizzie's father, and though

Fay didn't know where he was today, she was sure he was *still* a fool, God bless him.

Justice was Arnie Campbell, just about the best detective on the force and Fay's lover now for years.

But she'd never met the Devil. Oh, sure, she knew mean people, liars, schemers, and cheats. But it takes more than mean to be a Devil. The Tarot's Devil is a special horror. He is the leering genius of evil. He is willful and proud, vengeful, haughty, greedy, and cruel.

What does *he* care if everything goes to hell? Suits him fine. He lives there.

The exact picture of the Devil depends on which Tarot deck you're using, but the basic elements are always the same: He has a hog's body, a crocodile's head, wings, hooves, horns, and a snake coming out of his stomach.

But he also has luscious breasts and a stiff penis. Which is exactly how you know he's the Devil. He can do it all himself, thank you. He doesn't need anybody for anything. He is endlessly and successfully self-absorbed.

The five-cent version of the card's meaning is destruction through black magic. But, depending on where the card appears in a reading and the skill of the reader, it can mean evil forces are gathering, or maybe you're just believing anything anybody tells you these days, and, honey, they're all lying.

A generous reader, trying to make you feel better, might caution you about being seduced, or tell you not to make any decisions right now. Not Fay. She'd ask who it was who wanted your soul, find out if you wanted to sell it, and then make sure that at least you got a decent price.

The card has, however, another meaning. Yes, the Devil can come after *you*, but you can also go to the Devil. In the classic portrait, he is pictured with two slaves, lesser beings, humans who look like goats.

These slaves are the card's way of warning you that if you use magical powers for selfish ends, you will wind up enslaved by those powers, chained securely to some whipping post in the underworld.

Magical powers like spells and chants? No. Magical powers like somebody trusts you and you betray that trust, or somebody tells you something in good faith and you use it against them, or somebody loves you and you lock them up and refuse to let them go when the time comes.

The Tarot is very clear on this. Not for spells and chants are you damned, but for ordinary abuse of extraordinary things.

FAY HAD BEEN about to close when they came. At one o'clock in the morning, anybody else would have seen three college boys in tuxedos, all pretending to be drunk. But Fay recognized the Devil right away. He was the one in the middle. Glossy black hair, a smooth tanned face, and a carefully withheld smile. He was easily the best-looking man she'd ever seen outside the movies.

The boys were having a great time. They'd probably told themselves they were doing the town. What they really wanted to do was get laid, but in the meantime, they'd get their fortunes told. Maybe the fortune teller would know whether they got laid or not.

The Devil leaned against the window while his friend Phil, brave with brown hair and glasses, sat down at the table.

She handed him the cards to shuffle. "What do you want to know, Phil?"

The cards were too big for him to shuffle comfortably. But then he wasn't going to be real comfortable here anyway.

"I don't know." He sat up straighter. "You tell me," and laughed.

"Cut the cards in three piles to your left," she said.

He could do that.

"What's the matter with your neck?" she asked.

"Nothing!" he said, grabbing the sore place.

"It's all right," she said, wishing he would relax. "It'll go away in another day or two. Why don't you try sleeping on a different pillow?"

"It never bothered me before," he said, massaging his neck now, wondering what else she knew about him.

She collected the three piles and dealt seven cards off the top in an arrangement known as the Magic 7 Spread.

"Maybe if you didn't go to bed drunk," she said, "you could find a more comfortable position before you passed out."

"Good idea," he mumbled.

The Devil was standing by the record cabinet now. "Who's this?" he asked, pointing to a picture of Lizzie at the piano in a blue satin dress and straight brown hair, five years old.

"One of the kids in the neighborhood," Fay said, and looked down at the cards.

But he'd found the other pictures, so he knew Fay was lying. There was Lizzie on the first day of junior high, Lizzie on the debate team, Lizzie on the black stallion at the riding stable, Lizzie going to the prom, Lizzie at graduation, and Lizzie on the beach.

Lizzie on the beach was the one, of course. Fay knew what he was thinking. Marry me, be my wife. Big house. Lots of servants. Take you away from all this. Show you the world.

He picked up the picture of the little girl at the piano. His laugh was haughty and mocking. "Who made the dress? You?"

Of course she had made the dress, and what damn business was it of his? It fit, didn't it? The seams were flat and smooth, weren't they? Nobody else at that recital even *had* a long dress.

Lizzie hadn't wanted to wear it. Cried about wearing it. Fay told her the reason nobody else wore a long dress was their mothers didn't care how they looked.

"No, Mother," Lizzie had said, "their mothers all know what you're supposed to wear. Just regular clothes, Mother."

Well, how was Fay supposed to know that? She thought Lizzie should look nice, that's all. The lessons had cost a lot of money, and the trips to the lessons had taken a lot of time. Lizzie was good on the piano and Fay was proud.

O.K. So the dress was Fay's celebration. The dress was a dress she, Fay, would want to wear if she could play the piano. What of it? It was a nice dress. And no, Lizzie didn't play very well that day, but it wasn't the damn dress, it was just too hot in there.

"I can't concentrate with you standing there," she said to the Devil. "Do you mind sitting down?"

"Yeah," Phil said, turning around to him, "I've got my life on the table here."

"Where would you like me to go?" the Devil asked.

Fay didn't know what she could use on him that would work, that would drive him away, but there had to be something. Why wasn't her mother still alive? She would know exactly what to do.

Phil was getting anxious. "What do you see?" he asked, tapping the table.

Fay was grateful for the interruption. She laughed and looked at the cards. "Not much," she said.

Phil didn't like that. "Not much future?"

Fay glanced up at his face, but it was there too. "Sorry." She smiled.

But Phil wasn't going to settle for that. He knew he had a future. If worse came to worst, he could buy one.

"You're lying," he said. "Tell me what you see."

"O.K.," she sighed. "You'll do all right in school, not great, but good enough to get out, then you'll go home and work for your dad. You won't like it much, but it pays well."

She pointed to the Queen of Wands. "Then you'll marry Joanie and have two boys. They won't look a thing alike, but that's because"—she paused—"one of them won't be yours."

Phil played dumb. "Who's Joanie?" he asked.

Fay looked up at him. "She's tall, athletic-looking, nice teeth, bad feet." She paused again. "Right?"

He tried to laugh again. "You're just making this up," he said.

"No," Fay said, "I'm just making a living."

Phil couldn't stand it any longer. "O.K.," he said, "so I already know Joanie. Who's the guy she has the thing with?"

His friends laughed.

"Phil, that's years and years from now," Fay cautioned.

"I want to know," he said.

Fay picked up the Valet of Cups. "Joanie's a runner, right?"

Phil nodded. "Cross-country."

Fay was sorry to have to tell him. "She joins a running club. It's the man she gets her shoes from."

He was a lot sorrier than she was. "Like a coach, maybe?"

Fay picked up the deck again. "Maybe. I really don't know. What's the matter with her feet?"

"They're flat," Phil said, his anger rising. "I'll call her as soon as I get back to the dorm."

"And say what?" Fay asked.

"And break up with her!"

"Don't do that!" she said, and she dealt three more cards for a little more information.

He twisted in the chair. "Why shouldn't I call her? You want me to waste the next forty years of my life?"

She winked at him. "It's not a total waste, hon."

Phil bounced back fast. "You mean something good happens to me?"

Fay smiled at the new cards on the table. "Well, of course it does. One of your boys wins a spelling bee in the fifth grade."

Phil's mouth dropped open. "That's the good news?"

Fay picked up the cards and put them back in the deck. "No," she explained. "The good news is you work during the day. You don't have to go."

Phil stood up, buttoned his coat, grinned, and looked around the room. What a lark, huh? He took a deep breath. He couldn't believe how sober he was all of a sudden.

The Devil slapped him on the back, walked over to the window, pulled back the curtains, then turned to face Fay.

"Do you know what's going to happen to *you*?" he asked.

Fay stood up. There was no point in kidding herself about it. "I get robbed," she said.

His black eyes glistened. "When?" he asked, letting the curtains fall from his hand.

"Later on tonight," she said.

Phil was beginning to recover from his future now. He didn't like the sound of this robbery business.

"What you sitting around for?" he said. "Get out of here! Lock the place up tight, take your money and go."

Fay shook her head. "So they can catch me with all my money in my purse? So they take my keys too, and my credit cards, and my picture of my mother?"

"So they don't hurt you," Phil said.

"No," Fay said. "I've been fooling with the future for a long time. It doesn't help to run from it."

Phil didn't understand.

"You run right into it, that's what you do," Fay said.

"So you just have to sit here and wait for it?" he asked.

"That's how the future works," she said easily. She liked this boy.

"I don't know," he said slowly, putting his hands in his pockets.

"You haven't been there." She finished his sentence for him.

He laughed. "That's what I was going to say."

She laughed with him. "No kidding."

FAY WANTED THEM to leave now. Lizzie was due home anytime. Actually, she was due home sometime ago, but you didn't have to read the tea leaves to know your child would come home later than she said.

In fact, reading the tea leaves was the only thing Fay had never tried, though she knew if that was all she had to go on, she could probably come up with *something*. She wouldn't charge for it, though.

The idea of charging for any of this was uncomfortable for her. It wasn't really a skill, not something she learned or worked hard to get good at. She'd just always had it. By the time she was in the fourth grade, none of her girlfriends would play cards with her. It wasn't fair, they said. Fay always knew who had the Old Maid.

By the time she was in high school, she had learned that not everybody wanted to know their boyfriend was standing them up, or that they were going to choke on their driver's test. Everybody *did* want to take her to the local trotting track, but she almost never had a date for the movies. Even if the people were made up, Fay knew what would happen to them.

So, because she wanted to make friends, and wanted to keep them, she dismissed it, this talent of hers, until one other August night, hot like this one, and about this time of night too. Lizzie was about a year old then.

They'd buried Fay's father late that afternoon. Everybody had gone to the country for the funeral: Fay's two sisters, their husbands, their babies, and Fay's husband—Lizzie's father, Ed.

The service had been fine. The preacher gave the details of her father's life, raved about how he had served his country in World War I, and explained that he'd met his bride in someplace called "the old country." Then he said how kind he was to his animals, how proud he was of his mustache, and how sick he had been for so long.

Fay looked at her sisters, both of them wearing hats, and suddenly knew what was going to happen.

They would all go home to dinner. But after dinner, the sisters and their families would leave. Then Ed would look at Fay and say it was time for them to go, too.

Fay would say, "We can't go. I can't leave Mother by herself."

Ed would say, "Well, she can't live with us, if that's what you mean."

And, of course, that would be exactly what Fay had meant. They'd argue about it until two o'clock in the morning, but neither of them would give in. Ed would leave, go back to their apartment in the city, and Fay would never see him again.

She and Lizzie would stay with her mother, pack up the house and sell it. Then the three of them would move back to the city together, where her mother would tat and crochet for four more years until she died of pneumonia, which would set in after she broke her hip falling on the sidewalk. Fay wouldn't marry again, and her mother would always be a lot madder at the others for leaving than she ever would be grateful to Fay for taking her in.

At the time, as Fay was sitting there in the church seeing all this, she simply couldn't believe it would happen. It was too crazy, too contrived, too detailed to be true. So she put it out of her mind, looked over and smiled at Ed, then squeezed Lizzie's hand.

But four years later, when her mother died and everything had worked out exactly as she had seen it that day, Fay rented the little apartment down the street from the police station and hung up the sign that said FORTUNE TELLER.

FAY WAS WORRIED about Lizzie now. Not that the girl had ever given her any reason to worry, but then, she wasn't home, so there wasn't any reason *not* to worry either.

Phil had asked if he could use the bathroom, the Devil was looking at the show clock in her afternoon paper, and the third boy was scratching his palm.

"It's almost two in the morning," she said, when Phil came back into the room. "It's time for you to go."

But they didn't know where they were going next, so Phil just walked over and joined the Devil, who was now trying to find a nightclub that had a late late show.

Rudy, the third boy, sat down at her table.

"No, no," she protested, "no more. I'm closed."

"I used to play the flute," he said quietly.

"You still do," she said, turning around to check on Phil and the Devil.

He looked up at her. "I don't like it," he said.

"I know that." She grasped his shoulder lightly. "I'm tired, hon."

"Should I quit?" he asked, turning his palms up for her to see.

This boy had a problem all right. A big one. Wearily, she sat down across from him and reached for his left hand.

"You play well," she said, feeling for the Mounts and sensing the overall strength of the hand. "How can you be so good at it and not like it?"

Rudy didn't answer.

She looked up at him. "You need to call home," she said.

He was alarmed. "What happened?"

"How long has it been?"

"I don't know. A month, maybe."

She found his eyes. "Do they send you money?"

He was really worried now. "Yeah, they do. But I got it yesterday."

"Good," she smiled. "Call them up and thank them."

But he didn't want a lecture on family courtesy, he wanted the answer. "I want to quit," he said.

"Your father wouldn't like that." She picked up his other hand.

"He wants us to go on tour."

"And you can't figure what's in it for you, is that right?"

The boy nodded. "Right."

Fay was studying the hand for real now. "Look here," she said, "see this space between these two lines? See how small it is in your right hand?"

She looked up at him, just to see if he had his eyes open, which he did. She was genuinely puzzled. "You had the makings of a real ham, but you're not. How come?"

His hands started to shake. "I don't know."

"What did he do to you?"

"Who?"

"Your dad," she said, matter-of-factly.

And then she saw it.

And he saw she saw it, and tried to pull his hand away, but Fay held on.

"I'm so sorry, hon," she said, much more softly. "What happened to him? Something terrible happened to him."

"It was an accident," the boy said.

"But you were driving?" she asked.

"Yeah," he whispered.

"But he's not dead, Rudy," she said. "I can see he's not dead."

"He's in a wheelchair," the boy said. "And he has a bag, you know, a colostomy thing. But he plays every day. He's still good, you know, still feels it and all, but . . ." Rudy couldn't finish.

"I see," she said. "You don't want to be the other half of his freak show."

It hurt him to hear it, but she was right. "Yeah," he swallowed.

Fay rubbed the top of his hand, patted it. "He's good, isn't he, your dad."

The boy smiled as his eyes watered. "He's great."

She turned his hand over, this time knowing exactly what to say. "How many months is the tour?"

He was relieved to answer a question with a number. "Six," he said.

She traced the Life line to its base and showed him. "See here? You have to go. I see . . . trouble ahead if you don't." Then she squeezed his hand and placed it back on the table. "What's six months, huh? Not very long, really."

He spread his fingers wide and stretched his hand. "I guess not," he said. And then he made a fist and stared at it. "Hell, the army could take more than that and they wouldn't even ask."

Fay stood up. Where was Lizzie, anyway? She wanted these boys to leave before the girl got home, but she *did* want her home.

"So!" Rudy turned to his friends and clapped his hands. "What's up?"

Phil showed him their choices in the paper, while the Devil took one more look out the window. Fay wasn't the only one who wondered where Lizzie was.

She stood perfectly still and tried to send a message to her daughter. "Stop at the police station," she said to herself. "Go see Arnie." She didn't really expect it to work, but she had to try something.

When Lizzie was little, Fay had worried that someone might just walk in the door one day and scare her, or hurt her, or take her away. So she rigged a sort of alarm system on the inside of the door. She sewed hundreds of tiny bells on red felt strips, then hung them on either side of the door. When it opened, there was no missing it. This was not the wind. This was somebody there. Not a frightening sound, you understand. More like—well, like hundreds of little bells ringing.

"And when you hear these funny bells start to ring," she told Lizzie, "you run like hell and lock yourself in the bathroom." Fay didn't know if other mothers taught their daughters to lock themselves in the bathroom, but it made the little girl feel better, so who cared?

Just then, as the Devil was folding up the paper, and Phil was counting how much money he had left in his wallet, as Fay was watching every move the Devil made, and Rudy was wondering if there were a Burger King on this street, the doorknob turned and hundreds of little bells started to ring. Lizzie was home.

FAY RUSHED TO the door. She knew what she had to do. Catch Lizzie before she walked in. Send her up the street to get Arnie. Arnie had to get a look at this Devil so he'd know who they were chasing when Lizzie left with him.

"Hi," Lizzie chirped.

"I'm not through yet, hon," Fay said quickly, pushing the girl back out on the sidewalk. "Can you go get Sergeant Campbell for me?"

Fay blocked the Devil's view with her body.

"Who's in there?" Lizzie asked.

The Devil moved to the window and pulled back the curtains.

"I tried to call Arnie," Fay said through the crack in the door, "but they keep putting me on hold."

Lizzie craned her neck to see who pulled back the curtains. He didn't look so dangerous. He looked pretty good, in fact.

"What's going on?" Lizzie asked.

"I'm all right," Fay said. "Just go, huh?"

"Sure," Lizzie said, shrugging her shoulders. "No problem." She liked Arnie. Maybe it was some kind of party for him.

"Thanks," Fay said and closed the door, then watched the girl as she walked up the street.

Fay didn't like this solution, but it was her only choice. If she forced the boys to leave, Paul—the Devil's name was Paul—would just forget his scarf and come back for it sometime later when Lizzie was there alone. Then they'd disappear together and Fay would never find them. No. She had to watch this meeting and find out where Paul was taking her. Then, of course, she had to find a way to stop him.

2:00 A.M.

WHEN LIZZIE GOT TO THE POLICE STATION ON THE corner, she found Arnie on the phone to his bookie. She was glad to see him, a rough-edged, handsome man slouched over his battered desk, the racing form spread out in front of him. He looked a little used this time of night, but not used up, not by a long shot. Arnie Campbell could be tired, hungry, mad, beat-up, and broke, and still get the job done, whatever it was.

"What's the spread on the Cubs?" Arnie asked the bookie.

Lizzie took off her Yankees baseball cap and shook out her mass of black hair.

He covered the mouthpiece with his hand. "Great hair," he smiled. "Where's your mom?"

"At home," she whispered, pointing down the street.

She kicked off her old sneakers, then pulled off the baggy black jumpsuit and stuffed it into her dance bag.

"Nice," he mouthed, as the silky black dress she was wearing underneath slipped over her hips and down her long, slim legs.

"Thanks," Lizzie said, retrieving her black stiletto heels from the bag and stepping into them. Owing to years of dance class, she could change from a dark cloud to Queen of the Night in less than thirty seconds. Or go the other way if she was coming home late and didn't want any trouble on the street.

"O.K.," Arnie said into the phone, "I'll take the Orioles and four, the Mets and eight, and five hundred on Thunderhead to place in the fifth."

Then he hung up the phone, shoved the racing form and reading glasses into his desk drawer, stood up, and reached for his cigarettes.

"What's up?" he asked, sensing, somehow, that it wasn't a murder or anything serious.

"I don't know," Lizzie said, taking his arm. "Mom wouldn't let me in. She told me to come get you."

Suddenly, his whole manner changed. Apparently, anything having to do with Fay was serious. "Was somebody with her?" he asked.

"All I saw were three guys in tuxes," she said.

He held the door open. "So what is it?" he asked, trying not to frighten the girl. "You think they stole the tuxes?"

"Maybe they did," she laughed.

"Where'd you say you went?" he said, as they started down the street.

"I didn't."

"But you had a good time, right?"

"It was O.K.," she said.

Actually, it had been more than O.K., but she knew better than to tell him about it. Arnie Campbell didn't know Mozart from Moby-Dick, and didn't want to, either.

Lizzie wondered if her Mom was still screwing Arnie. She didn't mind, either way, but she would like to know. She probably was. Lizzie figured if you once loved this man, nothing on earth could make you stop.

Arnie took her hand, gave it a gentle squeeze, and they walked the rest of the way without talking.

BEFORE LIZZIE AND Arnie got back, the Devil had picked up, looked at, and laughed at every doodad, knickknack, and whatnot in the room, including Fay's jar of clear-glass marbles.

"Crystal balls," she explained, then watched carefully to make sure he didn't steal one.

He thought the lampshade made of postcards was maybe

the ugliest thing he'd ever seen. He asked if she'd been to all those places.

She said the lampshade was there when she moved in.

He played with the fringed black shawl on the table and wondered what had happened to the fringe.

"It's just worn off over the years," she said. "People, you know, sit there and braid it while I shuffle the cards." She paused. "Like you're doing."

Then he asked about the bears. One hundred onyx bears, sitting on chessboards, also onyx, which had been given to her by a client who had paid her in onyx.

The client had told her he had a garage full of old school desks, a fabulous collection of geodes, and a safe full of Green Stamps if she'd rather have those, but she wouldn't. Lizzie liked the bears.

"What I'd like to have," Fay had told the man, "is some of the cash you buy this stuff with."

"But I never have any cash," he said.

But she knew he had money coming. He had the longest, deepest Fate line she'd ever seen. She could wait.

The Devil asked where the bears came from, but Fay didn't want to tell him. He said they were funny. She said yes, they were.

And then Arnie opened the door and walked in, flashing his badge.

The boys stood up, scared to death. This was a man who got what he wanted.

"Fay?" Arnie said. "It's a little late for you to be open, isn't it?"

"I've been telling them to go," she said, looking at the boys. "But they haven't been hearing me."

"Let's go, folks," Arnie said, "fun's over," and opened the door for them.

Lizzie slipped in behind him as quietly as she could.

Phil spoke up in their defense. "She said she was going to be robbed," he said, pointing to Fay.

Lizzie couldn't help laughing. "And you thought *you* could protect her?"

"No," the Devil said to her. "We were waiting for *you.*"

Lizzie stopped laughing. *They* weren't waiting for her. He was waiting for her.

"How did you know I'd show up?" she flirted.

"We prayed," he said, in his softest smirk.

Fay was right. It was all over. All they'd had to do, these two, was see each other.

Lizzie backed away and started rearranging the bears on the chessboards. She had nothing more to say to anybody but him. The Devil took Phil's arm and walked toward the door. He had to get rid of these kids and get back here.

"It was great talking to you," Phil said over his shoulder to Fay.

"Yeah," Rudy said. "Thanks."

"If I were you"—Arnie caught the Devil's sleeve as he walked through the door—"I'd take those cufflinks out of my shirt and put them in my pocket."

The boys stepped out onto the sidewalk, and Arnie closed the door behind them.

But as soon as he saw Fay's face, he knew the boys weren't the problem.

"What was that all about?" he asked.

"I'll tell you later," she said, and turned to Lizzie. "Where have *you* been?"

Lizzie was still fooling with the bears. "You tell me," she said, and laughed as though it were a joke.

Fay looked like she had been slapped.

But Lizzie was right, of course. Fay did know where she had been.

"Come on, Lizzie," Arnie said, trying to stop this squabble before it got started. "Answer your mother, huh?"

Lizzie turned around. She hated it when Arnie corrected her, but he was usually right about it. "I went to hear Ashkenazy at the Philharmonic. Want to see the stubs?"

"Till two o'clock in the morning?" Fay asked.

"I met some friends," Lizzie said.

"What friends?" Fay pushed.

"Mother," Lizzie pleaded, "you don't know them, so what difference does it make?"

Arnie wanted out. Fay could be such a witch. So the kid went to a concert. Isn't that why Fay paid for all those music lessons all those years, so the girl would go to concerts? Lizzie was ready to leave home. Why didn't Fay, who knew everything else, know that?

"You girls don't need me for this," he said. "I'm going back to work."

Fay grabbed his arm. "Please don't go."

"Have to." He grinned, leaning down to kiss the top of her head. "I need the money."

"Isn't there somebody else down there?"

"Oh, sure," he said, "but he's answering the phone."

"So can't he call if he needs you?"

"Sorry, love," he said. "I have to listen to the radio." He waved to Lizzie. " 'Night, angel."

Lizzie blew him a kiss and Fay walked outside with him.

"I'm sorry," Fay said.

"It's O.K.," he said. "Just let her alone. She'll be all right." He put his arm around her. "She's a good kid."

But it would take more than a hug to comfort Fay. "She's going to leave me, Arnie."

"Honey," he said, as gently as he could, "she's got to. She's all grown up."

Fay looked away.

"You did a great job. You should be real proud. She's going to do great things out there. Make you even prouder."

"No, Arnie," Fay said. "She's going to leave me for that boy in the black hair, Paul. She's not going to do anything except what *he* tells her to do."

"Fay"—he reached into his pocket for a cigarette—"she just met the boy!"

"You don't believe me."

"Sure I believe you," he said, staring at the building across the street. "I believe everything you say. But she could do a whole lot worse, Fay. He's got some money anyway. Let her go."

"Arnie, I'll never see her again!"

"You'll see her."

"She'll be ashamed of me. She'll never come back."

"She'll be back."

"He's the Devil."

That did it. "Good night, Fay," he crooned, and walked away. He wasn't mad, but he walked as though he might be.

He shouldn't have stayed this long. He really did have to listen to the radio. He hadn't wanted to tell Fay yet, but there was something real strange going on out at the fairgrounds. Something that could involve her, before it was over.

* * *

WHEN ARNIE FIRST made detective, they moved him downtown, but he didn't like it there. The coffee was made by
somebody who thought coffee was bad for you, and the water
cooler burped. Arnie liked his water out of the faucet, so he
came back to this neighborhood and stayed. The deli was
cheap, the shoe repair was fast, and the firehouse was a good
place to pick up extra cash playing cards. Then, too, Fay
Morgan lived here.

When he worked days, Arnie would go down to Fay's for
lunch. She was never busy at lunchtime. At lunchtime, people were still trying to figure out the future for themselves.
Only after work did they give up and see a professional.

The first summer Lizzie went to ballet camp, Arnie took
Fay fishing. He had a little cabin, and a little boat, and a big
sweater for her to wear at night. He liked fishing well enough,
but that wasn't why he went there. He kept this cabin, year
after year, because he liked to catch rainwater in a tin bucket,
take the bucket to the porch, and shave outside.

"Always get a better shave out here," he said. "Good
water. Good light. Fresh soap. Makes a big difference."

She nodded.

He liked her to watch. He had thought about marrying
her, but he knew he'd never be as important to her as Lizzie
was. That was the way it should be, but it wasn't how he
wanted to be married. So he never asked. And she never said
anything about it.

Their first job together had been almost fifteen years ago
now. Arnie's brother owned the butcher shop next door to
Fay. Middle of the day one day, somebody came in and shot
him. Fay would've seen the whole thing, but she'd taken
Lizzie to the pediatrician.

Father June, from the mission, had gone down to the
butcher shop to borrow some bratwurst for lunch. He saw the
blood, found the body, then ran back to the station house and
grabbed Arnie out of his chair.

The killer didn't take any money, didn't even mess the
place up. It was weird. Arnie couldn't tell whether the blood
on his brother's apron was from the bullet wound or from the
steaks and chops he'd been cutting up when he was killed.
The crime unit would know later it was lamb's blood, but
Arnie wouldn't ask them.

Arnie went into the back room and threw up. He would've

checked this room eventually, of course, but as he raised his head from the sink and wiped his mouth on a spare apron, he saw the handprint on the back door.

Apparently the killer had slipped on a wet spot on the floor and grabbed hold of the meat-bloodied cutting table to keep from falling. When he'd pushed open the back door to escape, he'd made one perfect red print of his left hand.

The department ran a check on it, but came up with nothing.

Arnie hadn't met Fay before, but he'd seen the palm-reading sign in her window. It was worth a try, he figured. So he walked down to her parlor, knocked, then opened her door. She was reading; Lizzie was beside her.

"Are you Fay?" he asked.

"Yes," she said, standing up and smoothing out her dress.

"I'm Arnie," he said.

He still wore a uniform then, so he didn't have to say he was a cop.

"I'm Jack's brother." He motioned toward the butcher shop. "Next door?"

Fay already knew who he was. She had seen the crowd when she came home, and another detective had already been in to see her.

"I'm so sorry," she said. "I've just been here a couple of weeks, but he seemed so nice."

"He was O.K.," Arnie said. "He was my brother."

"I'm sorry," she repeated. "Is there anything I can do?"

He was a little nervous. "I saw your sign," he said, hoping she would read his mind.

"Yes?" she said, having not a clue.

I'm sorry," he said, turning around. "This was a bad idea."

"No, no," she said. She knew she made people nervous. "You saw the sign and you thought . . ."

"Well, look," he said, not knowing how to say it, "this sunuvabitch who killed my brother left a palm print on the back door."

"Was it his left hand?" she asked.

Now he was really nervous. "How did you know that?"

"Just a guess," she said, trying to make it seem like one. "He probably had his gun in his right hand, that's all."

He wished he hadn't come here, but he couldn't leave now without insulting her. "O.K.," he said. "Come on." He started for the door. "Bring your stuff."

"I don't need any 'stuff,' " she said, "but I can't leave Lizzie."

Arnie stopped cold. He was a detective. His brother was dead. What was he supposed to do with a five-year-old?

"Bring her with us," he said. And he walked over to the playpen and picked Lizzie up, picked her way up—Arnie was a big man even then—and followed Fay out onto the street.

They walked through the police barricade and into the empty shop next door. He stopped in front of the meat cases, where steaks and chops were turning gray.

"Somebody ought to eat this stuff before it spoils," he said.

"Why don't you call the mission?"

"Good idea," he said, walking to the phone. "I'll call them right now."

He shifted Lizzie slightly in his arms. "Go on back," he said, pointing toward the other room. Arnie didn't want to go in there again just yet, so he called headquarters and told *them* to call the mission.

When he came in, she was staring at the palm print.

"Well?" he asked. Lizzie was asleep on his shoulder.

"It's pretty messy," she said. "You didn't see his other hand anywhere, did you?

He didn't think that was funny. But on some other day he might.

"O.K.," he said, turning around. "Thanks anyway."

"No," she said, motioning for him to come look. "He was real short. Does that help?"

"Well, he had to be short," Arnie grumped. "Look where the hand is on the door." He turned back toward the front room.

"And lazy," she said.

Arnie stopped. "Lazy?"

"And young," she said. "A kid, maybe. He's either not lived very long, or not lived very much. He's been sick, though, so that could account for it."

Arnie took a step toward her. "He's a kid?"

"It's the fingers," she said. "See how short they are?"

He came close enough to see for himself now. "That third finger's not so short."

"Well, it's longer than the rest of them, but that's because he's a gambler."

"Come on," he said. "You can tell from his hand he's a gambler?"

"I'll show you," she said. "Put your hand up beside it."

He shifted Lizzie to his other arm and put his left hand up beside the killer's print. She had to laugh. Arnie had that same long third finger.

"You're a bit of a gambler yourself, aren't you?"

"Well," he said, "I'm not getting through life on my looks."

"You could," she said, turning back to the hand.

He didn't want to hear that. He cleared his throat. "So we're looking for a sick, kid, gambler."

"Yes," she said. "Know any?"

He didn't answer.

"How old was your brother?" she asked, just to keep him talking.

"Older than me. Forty, I think."

"Did he have any children?"

"Just one," he said. "Bobbie."

"I'm sorry," she said. "This must be awful for him. How is Bobbie doing?"

Arnie knew he shouldn't tell her, but for some reason he wanted to. "Bobbie doesn't know it yet," he said. "We can't find him. But he's not home much anyway."

"Neither was this one." She pointed to the hand. "See how straight that Life line is? This kid doesn't know where home is. A real drifter."

Arnie nodded.

She went on, almost as though she could see the boy. "He's real emotional, though. He has terrible crying jags, then fits of hysterical laughing. But he gets all out of breath and you think he's going to die right there in front of you. Like—" she stopped and looked again. "No, not like anything. Asthma. The boy has asthma."

"Are you sure?" Arnie asked. "Asthma?"

"I'm sure," she said. "And I could probably tell you when he got it, but that would be showing off."

She expected Arnie to laugh, but he didn't.

"What else?" he asked.

She bent down for a closer look. "O.K. He's careless. He drops things. But this is the problem right here."

She pointed it out to him, but he wasn't looking. "See how small his little finger is?"

Arnie didn't answer.

"He thinks nobody loves him anyway, so what's he got to lose? My mother used to say you could stretch fingers like this, just by pulling on them whenever you thought about it. Even if it was you that loved you, that would be better than nobody, she'd say. The future's not over yet, right?"

When she stood up and turned around, Arnie was staring out toward the front room and stroking Lizzie's hair. Fay didn't know when he had stopped listening. He was lost in some other day. Any other day.

"I guess we should go," she said.

"I'm ready," he said blankly.

Arnie walked her back to the house and took Lizzie into her bedroom to finish her nap.

"Can I make you some coffee?" Fay asked when he returned.

"No thanks," he said.

But he didn't seem to be in a hurry to leave.

"She's a sweet kid." He motioned toward the room where he'd left Lizzie.

"She'd better be," Fay said. "She's all I have."

"Do you have plans for dinner?" he asked, sitting down without even realizing he had.

Fay didn't think he'd make it to dinner. If he closed his eyes for even a moment, he'd be asleep on his feet. But far from being nervous about a stranger in the room, she suddenly felt quite safe. She even liked the apartment better with him in it.

"Why don't you go in and lie down," she said, nodding toward her bedroom. "I'll wake you when it's time for dinner."

He stood up. He knew he should leave, but his feet just wouldn't move.

"It's all right," she said quietly. "I won't bother you."

He rubbed the brim of his hat between his fingers. "How do you know I won't—"

"Won't what?"

"Won't sleep through dinner," he said, looking down at her.

"I'll wake you." She smiled.

He nodded, turned, and walked into the bedroom. Fay followed him at a respectful distance and closed the door.

Inside the bedroom, Arnie sat down on the bed and took off his shoes. Jesus God.

He took off his pants and coat and hung them over the chair. Bobbie had killed his dad.

He folded up his holster and put it on the seat of the chair. He couldn't believe it, but he wasn't surprised. Maybe he'd even seen it coming, but nobody thinks things like that will really happen. Not even policemen. Not in their own families, anyway.

He eased back onto the bed. What could he do about it now? Nothing. Nothing, that is, except catch the kid and put him in jail for the rest of his life.

Arnie closed his eyes. He had never done this before, collapsed like this. He didn't know who she was out there, or where he was in here, or when he'd ever wake up, and he didn't care to know any of those things. He only wanted to sleep.

He slept straight through Lizzie's nap and Lizzie's dinner. After Lizzie was back asleep again, this time for the night, Fay opened the door, just to check on him.

She knew too, that it was his brother's own son who had killed him. She didn't know how she knew, but she was glad she hadn't said anything. That was his to say. He was the detective.

Now, standing there watching him sleep, she remembered seeing the sign on the door of the butcher shop. The funeral was tomorrow. Suddenly she felt such love for him, this man in her bed. What was his name? Arnie?

The room was dark except for the night-light she left on for Lizzie. She closed the door quietly behind her, tiptoed over to the bed, and leaned down to wake him, though by now he was fully awake and watching the whole thing.

"Arnie," she whispered, "do you want some dinner?" She leaned over and kissed him on the forehead like an old love.

He took her face in his hands and pulled her mouth gently down to his.

It was a sweet kiss.

She sat down beside him.

"Where did you come from?" he whispered, stroking her arm.

"Oh, you know," she smiled, patting his chest. "The front room."

"I guess we're not very busy tonight, are we," he said, finding her hand and squeezing it.

"I guess we're closed," she said.

Then he reached up to kiss her neck, then her mouth, and then, together, they sank back onto the bed.

There was no small talk. There was no talk of any kind. Nobody asked for directions, nobody gave them. There were common courtesies, yes, but no modesty to speak of. This was simply necessary.

He took hold of her like life itself. He wanted some answers here, some proof that it was worth it, some proof that it was possible. That he could go on. Live. Start over. Have something besides all this goddamn pain all the time. See something besides how ugly everything was. Love somebody.

She reeled from his desperation, but clung to him. She found the rhythm of his rage and lost herself in it. This was not a man she knew, and Fay was not a woman he'd spent years learning to love. This was a man fighting death itself, and a woman who was not afraid to watch.

When it was over, he lay beside her, still without speaking. In a few moments, the tears came from behind his eyes, where they had been hiding, and crept down his face, hoping to get away before anyone saw them.

When Fay saw them, she got out of bed and left the room, giving him all the darkness she had for cover.

He came out a little later, and though he was fully dressed, he wasn't quite ready to talk yet.

"I'm sorry," he said.

"For what?"

"I promised you dinner."

"I ate with Lizzie."

And then he saw the cheese sandwich she had made and left for him on the table.

He picked it up and took a bite. "Please don't say anything," he said.

"About what?" she asked.

"About Bobbie," he said. "About Bobbie killing his dad."
He nodded toward the butcher shop. "I have to find him. I
don't know where he is. But I want to be the one who finds
him."

"Your bookie might know."

"Yeah," he said, as he swallowed. "He probably would."

He lifted the sandwich to his mouth for another bite,
then stopped and put it back on the plate.

"What's the matter with me?" he asked. "What do I
mean, I want to find him? I don't want to find him! What am
I going to say to him?"

He put on his hat.

She picked up the sandwich, walked him to the door,
opened it, and handed the sandwich back to him. "You'll say
you're sorry," she said quietly. "You'll just say you're sorry."

And a month later, when Arnie found Bobbie five hundred miles from home, dirty and broke, that is exactly what
he said.

LIZZIE HAD ALREADY changed from the silky black number she
had worn to the concert into a pink sundress, in case Paul
came back.

Fay stood in the bedroom doorway. She wondered what
Lizzie was wearing under that little sundress, but she also
knew the answer: not much.

"You don't need a sundress," Fay said. "The sun went
down a long time ago."

"I'm just trying it on," Lizzie lied in a cheery voice.
"How does it look?"

"You better take a sweater," Fay said, leaning on the
doorjamb for support. "It's cool on the river."

Lizzie was never really surprised when her mother knew
where she was going, but she liked to pretend she was. It was
a game they had played for a long time. So long that it was
almost fun.

"Am I going out on the river?" Lizzie asked.

Fay nodded. "Paul is coming back for you," she said.
"He has a boat."

"That's great," Lizzie laughed, changing into her crepe-
soled flats. "A boat is great on the river."

Fay clasped her hands in front of her. "I'm sorry I screeched at you a while ago, I was worried, that's all."

"You weren't worried," Lizzie said. "You just don't like me to go out."

"I want you to go," Fay said, "I just want you to come home when it's over."

"No," said Lizzie, "you don't want me to go at all."

Fay was quiet a minute. "The dress looks great," she said.

"Thanks," Lizzie said, putting a rubber band in her pocket in case she needed it to control her hair in the wind.

Fay took a few steps toward her, hoping to make up.

"Mother"—Lizzie took her hand—"if he were going to hurt me, you'd know, right?"

"Right," Fay said.

"So he's not," Lizzie said. "So don't worry, O.K.?" She reached out and stroked her mother's hair.

Fay didn't like Lizzie to do that. It made her feel like a pet, like a cat. She backed away and made herself talk.

"He's very smart," she said. "Very smooth. And he's going to be wild about you."

"Thanks," Lizzie said, wondering if her mother knew *when* Paul was coming.

Fay could feel his presence at the front door. "There he is right now."

Lizzie walked past her and into the hallway, but she didn't see him.

"Where?" she asked.

"He dropped his car keys," Fay explained, following Lizzie into the living room.

And then they both saw him, standing outside the window, putting his keys back in his pocket. He was alone now, and even better looking, Lizzie thought.

"See you later," Lizzie said, kissing Fay lightly on the cheek.

"Have a nice time," Fay said, as pleasantly as she could.

Then Lizzie turned, flashed Paul a ready smile, and left.

As Fay locked the door behind them, she was proud of herself. She hadn't said one wrong thing. Well, all right, maybe she *had* said a wrong thing. She didn't always know what the wrong things were. But she hadn't screamed, anyway.

She went to the record cabinet to get the deck of Tarot

cards she used for family matters, then sat down at her table
and shuffled them.

"What's going to happen to us?" she asked, cutting the
cards three times. "To Lizzie and me," she added, reassem-
bling the deck and dealing seven cards off the top.

In the Magic 7, the first card indicated the past. It was
the seven of Coins. Oh boy. Coins never meant money when
Fay was reading for herself, so it was some other valuable
thing she was about to lose. Guess what that might be, huh?

Next card. The present. The Valet of Swords, a young
person. Boy or girl? Girl. Lizzie. Next card. The immediate
future. The six of Swords. She already knew that too. Journey
by water. Why was she even doing this?

Quickly, she turned up the rest of the cards. The fourth
card was the three of Coins. A sale? She was selling her
child? Come on. So maybe it's the other interpretation, an
old association can help now, but who? Arnie, maybe. Her
mother?

She turned over the fifth card.

"Jesus Christ," she whispered.

It was the nine of Cups. The wish card. There was only
one meaning to this card: You get your wish.

Fay was suddenly very cold. What wish? That Lizzie not
leave? No, the girl was already gone. That the Devil died?
Yes, she'd probably wished that, all right.

"Calm down," she said, talking out loud now. "Turn the
cards."

The sixth card would show who was against her, or if not
who, exactly, what their qualities were.

The Knight of Swords. This was too much. A dashing,
headstrong young man? No kidding.

She hesitated a moment before turning over the last
card. This was the end of it, the outcome of the situation, and
there it was. The King of Coins.

"So his dad's a banker," she said. "So I'm beat. Lizzie
goes off to count his father's money."

She looked at the spread as a whole now. Coins and
Swords. Money and Conflict.

The wish card bothered her. Could it be something she
had wished for in the past, maybe? Like for Lizzie to have
everything she herself had never had? Sure. What was wrong
with that?

She picked up the three of Coins. Had she wanted her daughter to be rich? Wanted it so that she, Fay, could be rich? What if she did? If there was that much money, what was wrong with sending Mom some of it?

She turned to look out the window.

What if the cards were talking about Lizzie and not Fay? Was Lizzie about to lose something, have some dark and secret wish come true? Lose her self, maybe, a self she didn't know what to do with anyway? To a headstrong young man and a banker?

Suddenly Fay felt the same fear she'd seen on the faces of her clients over the years. If there's bad news, and I can't do anything about it, *don't tell me*. If there's bad news, and I *can* do something about it, but I blow it so it happens anyway, but now it's my fault, *don't tell me*.

Fay wished Arnie would come back. But he'd come when he was ready, she knew that.

Should she call Gail?

She started for the phone.

No. She stopped. Gail and Marvin had taken little Beth to the fairgrounds tonight, so they'd be exhausted by now. Fay looked at her watch; it was almost 3:00 A.M. Anybody in this time zone would be exhausted by now.

She stared out the window. The building across the street had been condemned last week. The windows were boarded up and people were being evicted. The sign on the front said the wreckers were coming at the end of the month.

The place is already a wreck, Fay thought. What's left for them to do?

And then, just as she was wondering if anything in the refrigerator would help, Arnie's face appeared on the other side of the glass.

3:00 A.M.

"LET'S WALK," ARNIE SAID, AS SHE OPENED THE door for him.

He wasn't taking a break. She knew it. Something was going on.

"Are you still on duty?" she asked.

"I sure am," he said. "And so are you."

She waited while he stopped to light a cigarette. There was something he had to tell her, but he didn't know where to start. If it was a new case, she'd have to turn him down this time. She could hardly go looking for some suspect while her daughter was out with the Devil.

Arnie threw the match in the trash can, then picked up the lid from the ground and jammed it back on as hard as he could. The garbage men were going to have trouble with that lid in the morning. They might have to take the whole thing, can and all, or leave it here, trash and all.

"Looks like we've got a strange case in the works," he said, finally.

She knew that someone was missing. "Who is it?" she asked.

He took her hand. "It's Gail's little girl," he said. "Beth Wilkins."

Fay stopped cold. "*My* Gail?"

"Your Gail," he said. "Her Beth. Come on. Keep walking."

Fay couldn't keep walking. Gail was the only friend she had.

"Arnie!" she protested. "We can't just walk around the block while Gail—"

"She isn't home yet," he said. "She's still down at headquarters. There isn't anything for us to do now but walk."

She turned back to look at Gail's building, but all the lights were out.

Arnie grasped her hand, more firmly this time, and pulled her around beside him.

"I'll tell you what I know," he said, "but it isn't much. I stationed one of our guys at the apartment in case Beth shows up there."

"Beth couldn't get home by herself, Arnie. Beth is five years old."

"That's what I told the Chief," he said. "But you know how he is."

She forced her feet to move. "Just tell me what happened, hon."

He shook his head. "It's real simple. Gail and Marvin took Beth to the fair. Gail paid for the cotton candy, but when she turned around to hand it to Beth, Beth wasn't there."

"When was this?" Fay asked.

"Gail thinks it was about nine o'clock. But it was midnight before all the other parents were standing at the information booth."

Fay stopped. "All *what* other parents?"

He nodded. "I told you it was strange."

"How many parents are we talking about, Arnie?"

He took a long drag on his cigarette. "Twenty, thirty, maybe. And the last count on the kids was somewhere in the twenties. Twenty-four, maybe. I forget."

"You forget?"

"O.K.," he admitted. "I didn't listen. It's a lot, though."

Fay was frantic. "So what are you doing? The police, I mean."

"Checking," Arnie said.

"Checking with whom?" she demanded. "There isn't anybody left at the fair now except the freaks and the farmers."

"Right," he said. "They're waking up all the freaks and farmers, and asking if anybody saw anything."

"I think we better go over there," she said.

"I think we better just keep walking," he said. "Did you get all patched up with Lizzie?"

"Gail's Beth is gone?" Fay asked, still not quite able to take it all in.

"Beth is gone," Arnie said.

Fay shook her head and walked on. She knew better than to try to *see* where Beth was. That was the movie version of what psychics did. Real psychics needed real information first.

And the only real information this psychic had was about her own lost daughter.

"So did Lizzie leave with that boy or not?" Arnie asked.

"Yes," Fay said, "she did."

"Did they say where they were going?"

"They didn't have to."

Arnie knew what that meant.

Fay had seen it, all right, as clearly as if she had been there, as plainly as if it had been projected on a billboard in front of her. Full color like a billboard, too, plus wraparound sound like a film. Faster, though. A flash forward.

"They're on a boat," she said. "On their way to another boat, a bigger boat. The biggest boat I've ever seen."

"A ship?" he asked.

"A yacht," she said.

Then she saw the flags on the big boat. Weather flags maybe, but another country's flag, too. Fay didn't know which country, though; she didn't know much about flags. Lizzie's dress was whipping around her legs, her hair was blowing wildly in the wind. She was wearing the Devil's tux jacket and eating a bagel.

Fay had to laugh. The girl had stopped for a bagel. The Devil was smiling. The moon was out.

"Why did you come with me?" the Devil asked Lizzie.

"Oh, I don't know," Lizzie said. "I wasn't ready to go to bed yet."

"Well," he caught her hair in his hand, "you just let me know when you are."

Fay turned her head and they were gone.

Arnie put his arm around her shoulders. He didn't know what to call these trances of hers, these sightings, but he knew when she was having one. He thought, though he wasn't really sure, that when she saw something, something happening somewhere else, there was a slight drop in her body temperature. Her hands became very limp, her whole body grew still, her breathing was very deep. The real sign, though, was that the part of her he liked to think of as her, as Fay, was gone.

When she came back, he tried to speak very softly. "Lizzie will be all right," he said.

"We'll see," she said.

He laughed. "I just wish I had a boat to take *you* out on."

Fay was lucky to have this man, and she knew it. "I like these walks," she said.

"I do too," he said.

She particularly liked these walks this late at night. She liked to catch the night changing into the morning. She could feel it turn. Clocks had nothing to do with it. Clocks had it all wrong, in fact. So did the calendar. The way Fay saw it, the day should begin at 4:00 A.M. and the year should start in September.

LIZZIE'S FIRST DAY of school had been the first and only day Fay had used the 8mm movie camera that one of her clients had given her. She learned that day that however annoying it was to see the future before it actually happened, it was even more irksome to see the past the way it really was.

She'd taken Lizzie to the school for registration the week before, presented her birth certificate, and proved she'd had her shots. Then she found Lizzie's classroom, and introduced the girl to her teacher.

"You're a single mother, Mrs. Morgan?" the teacher asked, looking at Lizzie's papers.

Fay didn't like that question. "Do the other kids have more than one?" she asked.

The teacher didn't like that answer. But then she noticed Fay's address, and it was really something to worry about. Only welfare people lived there, hookers, robbers, and bums.

"And what do you do?" the teacher asked.

"I'm a fortune teller," Fay said, wondering if that was above or below a stripper in this woman's view of things.

"I see," the teacher said. "How interesting."

Fay looked at the woman's signature on the blackboard. It wasn't that she lacked imagination, just that she only imagined the worst.

"I'm not a prostitute," Fay said, "if that's what you're thinking."

The teacher coughed. Lizzie dropped Fay's hand.

"Of course not," the teacher said. "But even if you were, that wouldn't affect the quality of instruction your daughter will receive here."

Lizzie walked to the door. She was ready to go.

The teacher smiled at the little girl, promising to provide a welcome relief from the nightmare the poor thing must live in.

Then she turned back to Fay. "I like to have as much background as I can on the children."

"Her background," Fay said, joining Lizzie at the door, "is just fine."

Fay was sure Lizzie didn't know what a prostitute was, so she didn't discuss the teacher's conversation on the way home. They didn't talk at all really, except Fay did say how much fun it was going to be for Lizzie to find out who else was in her class.

But when the first day came, Lizzie said Fay could walk her to the school but she wanted to go up the driveway and in the door by herself. She said she remembered where the classroom was, and she was a big girl now.

That's when Fay thought of the camera. If she couldn't actually *have* the experience, she could at least see it whenever she wanted.

Once they'd crossed the street, Fay handed Lizzie the little sack lunch with the pimento-cheese sandwich and the two dill pickles wrapped in wax paper, and said how nice Lizzie looked. Then Fay promised to get back here in two minutes if she had to. For any reason, she said. When the warning bell rang, Lizzie said she'd better go because she didn't want to be late and have to sit in the back.

Fay kissed her, stepped back, and let her go.

Lizzie started up the walk, then turned to her mother, smiling and waving. That was Fay's cue. She put the camera up to her eye and pressed the button. She followed Lizzie all the way to the steps, then tried to keep her in sight as the other kids, most of them with their mothers, all of them worried about being late, crowded around the little girl and pushed her up the stairs.

By the time Lizzie got to the big wooden doors, Fay had lost her completely. She took the camera from her eye and found herself quite alone on the sidewalk. The second bell rang, and the custodian closed the doors from the inside.

Fay looked at the camera, then looked at the doors, then hoped like hell the pictures came out, because she sure had missed it if they didn't.

The pictures did come out. But how could Fay know the batteries were low and the camera was shooting in slow motion? She couldn't. And neither could the projector, which played the film back at normal speed.

So Fay's permanent record of Lizzie's first day of school was of her daughter running up the walk with that choppy, old-time-flickers motion. Not walking. Running as fast as she could. Lizzie couldn't wait to get away from her, it looked like.

The brave smile and sweet wave Fay thought she remembered were projected on the screen as the giddy, glad-to-be-rid-of-you gestures of a pint-sized prisoner making her first escape.

Lizzie thought the pictures were funny, and asked to see them again and again.

Fay gave the projector and the screen back to the mission, and threw the camera away.

FAY AND ARNIE had walked almost a mile now. As they came around the corner, back on their own street again, they saw an ambulance with its light flashing and a fleet of police cars massed in front of Gail and Marvin's building.

When Fay didn't start running toward the ambulance, Arnie knew she must know something.

"Well?" he asked.

She shook her head. "They didn't find Beth."

Arnie stopped at the curb to talk to one of the other detectives, while Fay made her way inside to talk to Gail.

"It's more than Beth," Gail said, when Fay finally found her in the little girl's bedroom. "It's like the Pied Piper, it's like maybe thirty, forty children missing. All of them from the fair, all of them about Beth's age."

"And you didn't see anybody?" Fay asked.

"Nobody," Gail said. "She just disappeared."

"Where's Marvin?"

"Still at the fairgrounds," Gail replied. "I think. Trying to help or something. But there isn't anything for him to do now, is there?" She rubbed her eyes. "I don't know why he isn't here. He likes to be," she faltered, "where it's happening, I guess."

"Did they talk to the guard at the gate?" Fay asked.

"I don't know." Gail was going through Beth's closet now, flipping the little dresses quickly, but looking carefully at each one.

"That won't help, hon," Fay said.

"No, no," Gail explained. "They need something that smells like her." She looked down, almost embarrassed by what she was about to say. "But I keep her things so clean. She doesn't wear anything more than once. I don't know if I have anything here that . . ."

Fay finished the sentence for her. "Anything that smells like her."

"Yes," Gail said, grateful for the help.

"Give them a pillowcase," Fay said. "Nothing smells more like kids than their hair."

Just then Arnie came into the bedroom, holding a list of the children's names. He went directly to Gail and put his arms around her tight.

"I'm real sorry, Gail," he said.

"Thanks," she said, patting him on the back and squirming free. Gail wasn't ready to be held yet.

Fay took the pillowcase off Beth's pillow and folded it into a square. She stared at the picture of Beth on the dresser, all done up like Humpty-Dumpty for the day-care center's Easter party.

"They didn't find anything at the fairgrounds," Arnie said. "Marvin's on his way back right now."

Gail took the pillowcase from Fay and pressed it to her face.

Arnie turned to Fay. "How can forty kids just vanish?"

"They can't," Fay said, sitting on the little girl's bed. "Somebody took them."

"Yes, I know that," he said. "But who? And for what?"

Gail sat down in the rocking chair, still holding the pillowcase.

Fay wished she could talk to Arnie alone, but she didn't want to leave Gail right now, so she had no choice. "What did the guard at the gate say? Did he see anything funny?"

"Like a panel truck rolling out the gate, you mean?"

"It has oranges on the side," she said.

"*What?*" he asked.

Fay shifted slightly on the bed. "It's a fruit truck. The kids are in a fruit truck. There are oranges painted on the side of the truck."

"Are you sure about this?" he asked. But he knew she wouldn't have said it unless she was sure.

"Yes." She glanced at Gail. "It's a tractor trailer with oranges painted on the side."

Arnie started for the door, suddenly feeling new energy course through him. "Good." He patted her on the shoulder as he passed. "That's a start."

By the time he hit the stairs, he was running. Maybe Fay was right, maybe she wasn't. But she was right often enough to check it out.

Gail got up and walked to the window. "I just don't understand," she said softly.

Fay came over and put an arm around her friend. They looked out the window together, hoping there would be something to see, but there wasn't.

Arnie was talking to the chief of police, who had just driven up. A photographer was taking pictures of the front of the building. Two police cars were pulling away from the curb, apparently in pursuit of Fay's lead. And three girls from the strip joint were leaning on squad cars talking to the cops.

Finally, Gail spoke again. "Is she going to be all right?"

Fay waited a moment before answering. Gail wanted the truth. "I know she's all right for now," Fay said. "Does that help?"

"Sure it does," Gail said, nodding. She folded her arms across her chest. "Some."

FAY HAD MET Gail one day about five years ago, when Gail walked in off the street, sat down at Fay's table, and asked if Marvin would ever be any fun to live with.

Fay had looked at her palm, showed her the strong psychic line just above her wrist, and told her she could make a decent living telling fortunes. But Gail already made a decent living writing not-so-decent greeting cards.

She showed Fay one she'd just written. The front of it said, "A DAY IN THE LIFE OF A RESPECTABLE MAN," and the inside was perfectly blank.

So Gail already knew the good times with Marvin were over, but she had no idea what to do about it. So she just kept writing the greeting cards, but they were getting sicker and sicker.

The company that bought nearly everything she wrote was beginning to refuse them. One of the latest rejects said

LIVING WITH YOU IS NEVER EASY,
BUT I'M STILL HERE BECAUSE

(turn the page)

I KNOW HOW MANY MORE OF YOU
THERE ARE OUT THERE, AND IT
WOULD MAKE ME FEEL REAL STUPID
TO GET A DIVORCE, MEET SOMEBODY
ELSE, FALL IN LOVE, AND FIND
MYSELF STUCK IN THIS SAME SHITTY
MARRIAGE ALL OVER AGAIN.

Fay read the Tarot cards for Gail, saw the Moon in a dangerous position, and took her up to the deli for lunch. On the way, they passed the warehouse across the street from the mission, and it occurred to Gail to buy it.

"Marvin needs a project," she said.

They had had little Beth to save their marriage, but it hadn't worked. Gail said she thought maybe they could save a building instead, so they bought the warehouse across the street from the mission and converted it into loft apartments, which were rented to painters, some of whom could paint, but all of whom had to prove to Marvin that they had outside income.

It had worked out pretty well. Gail and Marvin were still

married, and Fay and Gail had become friends. Still, every time Fay read the cards for Gail, the Moon came up somewhere.

The Moon is maybe the unluckiest card in the whole deck. Worse than Death even. Death is a breeze compared to the Moon.

The picture on the card is of two towers, seen only in the dim moonlit shadows. A road passes between the towers, and two dogs, one white and one black, bay at the moon. A scorpion crawls in a small pool of light.

The card warns that the darkness is not empty, that there is someone, something, there. Stop now, it says. Listen carefully. That is not just the wind you hear. You may hope those are not footsteps behind you, but they are.

People smiled when the Moon card showed up. It didn't scare them the way the Death card did. People thought the Moon must be a promise of some romantic encounter.

But the Tarot held with the old notion of the moon, which saw it as cold and bleak and dead compared with the sun. If you had your choice, you should take the sunny, rational, right-handed, active male road to wealth and power, rather than the moonlit, emotional, left-handed, passive female route to confusion at best.

Over the years, Fay had realized that people loved the moon because they were a lot more interested in deception than they were willing to admit. People do believe the lies they are told. People do tend to trust because they want to, not because they have a reason to. And people do think that if they avoid the truth, it might change to something better before they have to hear it.

Yes, maybe we do want to be seduced, want to be deceived, Fay would say. Seduction and deception do require that someone spend some energy on us, notice things about us, lavish a certain kind of attention on us.

But we also love the moon because we, too, have things to hide. Maybe we don't look so good ourselves in the all-revealing light of day. In the moonlight, we can be heard and not seen. We can say who we are and present no physical evidence to the contrary. For this opportunity to deceive, we willingly pay the price of being deceived ourselves.

What Fay said about the Moon card depended, of course, on where it was in the spread. If it showed up in the past, it wasn't so hard to tell people they had been deceived. If it indicated the forces against them, she could simply tell them to double-check their information, or be wary of any advice they received right now from neighbors or friends. When the Moon was in a position describing their powers, Fay would warn them that they were fooling themselves about something, and they would have to pay for it eventually. Rarely did she say, You are lying to me—but that was the case, more often than not.

When the Moon was in the fate position, or the final outcome position, well, what was there to say? Could she say, You're not safe? Yes, sometimes she did. She told people to take themselves out of their situation if they could, or keep an eye out for an escape, if they couldn't leave immediately. Whatever you do, Fay would say, don't put yourself in someone else's power; and don't count on being lucky, because it's just not in the cards.

Fay had said that to Gail over and over again. This was not, however, news to Gail.

When Beth was just a baby, Marvin had bought an old clapboard house near a big park in the city. It was just an ordinary three-story disaster, but Marvin, blind as he was, saw something in it. They spent every penny they had restoring the house, and moved in.

Marvin's experts had told him the furnace in the basement would last one more winter. He believed them, because in a year he could afford a furnace. His geothermal wells would really be gushing by then, wouldn't they?

But one morning, when the milk froze around his cornflakes, Marvin had to admit his experts were wrong. Something had to be done. He consulted his home-repair manual and decided to replace just the blower on the furnace. He would do the work himself.

"Save money," he said, "nothing to it."

Gail was too cold to complain.

Marvin bought all the parts, got the thing installed, and came upstairs that night in complete triumph, except for the fact that he looked like there'd been a cave-in at the mine.

The house did seem warmer, though. Maybe this would work after all. They went to bed and slept straight through without having to get up once for another blanket.

But the next morning, Gail woke up sneezing. That

wasn't so strange, really; she often did that. But that morning, every sneeze blew great gusts of black powder out into the room.

What the hell? she thought, and put her feet down on half an inch of black powder on the floor.

"Oh my God, Marvin!" she said, looking around the room, beginning to understand the size of this calamity. Every surface in the bedroom was covered with soot. Walls, curtains, rugs, everything. She turned on the light, but that didn't help much. The lampshade was black, too. She shook Marvin and he sat up in a cloud of dust.

"What's the matter, honey?" he said.

"It's your goddamn blower," she said, getting out of bed and wrapping her gray robe around her. "You didn't clean out the vents or the ducts, did you. You just went to bed, didn't you. You saved us so much money doing it yourself, didn't you. Well, congratulations, Marvin. Your goddamn new blower just blew two hundred years of soot onto every fucking thing we own." She picked up her hairbrush from the dressing table and was beginning to attack her hair when she remembered.

"Beth!" she screamed. She threw down the brush, and ran down the black hallway, leaving a trail of footprints for Marvin to follow if he dared. She opened the door and by now her hands were black too, just from turning on the lights. She took one look and stopped. She put her hand to her heart to stop the pounding. Beth was all right. There she was, safe and warm in her crib. There was her little black face, nestled peacefully in her little black blanket, her little black arm around her little black bear.

Gail walked slowly across the room to the chest of drawers, and took out a clean white diaper. Praise God for chests of drawers. She leaned over and carefully dusted off the child's face, then brushed her fine blond hair and wiped off her round little hands. There wasn't any point in waking her up, was there? What was there to tell her? Maybe by the time Beth grew up, they would have forgotten about this morning.

Gail walked over to the window. She had planned to stare out and cry, but of course the window was solid black too, so she couldn't see a thing. She took a deep breath and drew a big circle in the soot on the pane. Then she calmly wrote the word HELP inside the circle, in mirror writing, in the fervent hope that someone—anyone—out there would see it.

The Moon was Gail's card all right. She was not safe, luck was never on her side, and Marvin always did the wrong thing.

4:00 A.M.

 GAIL WONDERED WHERE MARVIN WAS. NOT THAT she wanted him home, or wanted to talk to him, just that she didn't want the rest of her family lost, too.

She started for the kitchen. She needed something else to think about. "How's Lizzie?" she asked Fay. "Want some coffee?"

"She's fine," Fay said. "She's out."

"At four o'clock in the morning?" Gail asked.

Fay followed Gail into the kitchen, hoping they weren't going to have a conversation about Lizzie.

"Well," Gail said, smiling now, "it's about time, I guess."

"About time for her to come home?" Fay asked.

"No," Gail said, "it's about time for her to find somebody."

"Somebody found *her*."

"Decaf or real coffee?"

"Decaf," Fay said.

Gail turned around, terrified. "You can't leave me!"

"I'm not leaving you," Fay said. "I'm right here."

And to prove it, she sat down and started folding a stack of newly washed napkins.

Gail was silent.

"O.K., O.K." Fay smiled. "Real coffee."

Gail was a little ashamed of herself now. She tried to

laugh. "You can have decaf if you want. I just don't want you going home to bed."

"Real coffee," Fay said.

"No, it's all right," Gail said. "We'll both have decaf."

She measured the coffee into the filter. "So tell me about this boy of Lizzie's."

Fay cleared her throat. "His father's a banker. They went out on his boat. That's all I know."

"But he's gorgeous, right?" Gail asked, thinking maybe it would help if she lived in Lizzie's life for a while.

"Oh yes," Fay said. "Black hair, black eyes, lean, tan, rich. The works."

"I had a thing with a gorgeous man, once." Gail poured the water into the coffeemaker. "An actor. But he didn't work much, so we played all the time. He made me laugh. Great in bed. You know."

"I know," Fay said.

Gail turned on the coffee machine. "I was so dumb," she said. "I thought all that fun wasn't enough."

"I know," Fay said again.

Gail got two cups down from the cabinet. "I don't even know where he is now." She opened the refrigerator and reached for the cream. "I wish I did."

"What would you say to him if you saw him?" Fay asked.

"I don't know," Gail said. "Just . . . 'I'm sorry I was so dumb,' I guess."

"How long ago was this?" Fay wanted to keep the conversation going.

"A long time."

"So," Fay said, "if you did see him, or run into him somewhere, he'd look older now."

"Right," Gail said, and laughed. "Would that make me feel better or worse?"

"Oh, much better," Fay lied.

And they both laughed, and shook their heads. And Gail sat down across the table from Fay and appeared, for the first time all night, to relax a little.

THE TAROT'S NAME for the ups and downs of fate is the Wheel of Fortune. It looks a little like a Ferris wheel at a carnival, or a spin-for-dollars wheel on a TV game show, or a clock, or the paddle wheel of an old riverboat, or the little wheel that hamsters run on between meals. We say we invented the wheel, but all we really did was tame it, put it to work, make it look like fun.

It's almost impossible to be around a Ferris wheel without looking at it. The children scream and clutch their cotton candy, their feet kick wildly and their stomachs are suddenly all goofy inside them. It is fun, yes? It's a ride, right? The Tarot would certainly agree that it's a ride, all right.

The picture on the card is an eight-spoked wheel; its axle is a great column, on top of which sits a sphinx holding a javelin. Two creatures climb forever along the edge of the wheel. In most decks, it is Anubis, the genius of good, who clutches one side of the rim and rides to the top. Typhon, the bad guy, is carried under by the turning of the wheel. In a moment, though, all the good in the world will be ground down, and the evil one will rejoice on top. This is how things go, the Tarot says. But we all know that.

It is no accident that there are eight spokes in the wheel. Eight is the Tarot's number for justice. Justice is done when the wheel turns and balances things out. One trip around is coming full circle. Stars come around, and spring comes around. And human lives, in time, come around.

The ancients believed that time itself was a circle. A few of the more calculating ancients even thought the same people were born and the same events occurred every 36,000 years or so. Circular time was comforting. If you had an idea, it was sure to be one you'd had before, so there was no reason for you to be afraid of it. If you lost something, you were bound to find it again; and if you had ever been happy, you would feel that way again someday, so you might as well relax and enjoy your depression.

Scientists have proven, of course, that time is a line, not a circle. Today they can even prove that time moves forward. This means that there can be progress, that humans, as a group, can get somewhere. But it doesn't make us feel as good as when we believed we'd have another chance at things, another go-round.

When the Wheel of Fortune card came up in a reading, Fay would look at the other cards in order to know where the client was on the wheel, which direction he was going, that is. She thought the bottom half of the wheel was submerged in water, so that you really couldn't breathe under there. She'd seen something like this in a movie, some torture device, she thought, where the poor victim was tied to the wheel and turned around and around until he talked or drowned. Even if it wasn't a torture device, the Wheel of Fortune was, at the very least, exhausting.

For Fay the question was, Did the Wheel of Fortune revolve endlessly by itself, quite oblivious to the despair and the joy it delivered at every turn? Or was it more like the ones hamsters run on, turned by the action of the people on the edge?

There certainly was something about being on the bottom that forced you up. But there was also something about being on top that pushed you over and dragged you down. What that was exactly, she didn't know.

Fay thought the rim of the wheel was more like a circular ladder, with rungs to grab hold of as you climbed up, and rungs to hold on to as you plunged down. The figures in the picture on the card do have claws instead of hands. Is it this clawing that turns the wheel of life? Is grabbing the only way to get around?

Can't you just walk through life appreciating what is there, taking only what comes to you naturally, and letting things, like years, simply go by? Maybe you can. People do it. Maybe they are the lucky ones. Some people can just look at a giant Ferris wheel, they don't actually have to ride it. For some people it is enough just to watch other people take a spin.

What the Tarot says is that once you grasp the wheel, once you reach out for even one rung of it, you are caught. You'll reach for the next one just to stay on, then the next one to get higher, and so on, until you reach one rung too far and over you go. You'll get on the thing and forget it's a wheel.

But it *is* a wheel, and you're going down. You hold on tight, grasping whatever security you can find. You try not to listen to the squeals of joy from the people behind you, or the agonized howls of those further ahead, and finally you reach the bottom. Your head is bursting with the blood pooling in it, and gravity is pulling you with a force that seems irresistible.

You are easily five times your normal weight. It would be so simple to let go. But if you let go, then where would you be? Alone, weightless, drifting in the vast empty space that surrounds the wheel. You have no idea when you would ever touch anything, or anyone, again.

But even at the bottom, you can't just hang on. If you don't move, the people behind you will crawl over you, trample you. You feel them shoving you already. They will push you off if you don't move.

You can let go and drop off, or you can get on with it. So you force one claw open, you summon a strength that is made of nothing but fear, and reach for the next rung. Reach, with some blind faith that the next rung is there. Reach, out of some vague and distant memory that this is a circle.

You go. You reach. You feel it. There. You grab it! You've got it. You bring your other hand up. It's a little brighter here. You feel a little lighter now. It's O.K. Keep going. You're moving easily. You shake your head. You laugh. You yell back to encourage the others, you take one hand away and wave to your mother. You're coming up all right. You're almost there. It's terrific up here! The view is incredible. One more step and you're at the top. Nothing to it. Take it!

You're there! You made it! Everybody sees you. They love you. They thought you were finished, but you showed them, didn't you? You can stand up straight now. You hold both hands over your head in triumph and the crowd cheers. You did it. You're at the top. Enjoy it. Everybody in the whole world wants to be you. You try not to make them feel bad about it, but what is there to say? You worked hard, and you won. You've got it all! Everything you ever wanted.

You take the next step with your feet, no hands, just to show them how easy it is, and suddenly, you stop. You keep smiling, of course, but is that foot you just moved a little lower than the other foot? It is. Shit. What does this mean?

Put your hands down, that's what it means. Stop congratulating yourself and get hold of this thing. Grab the next rung.

And which way are you looking now? Down. You're looking down. This thing is a circle. You're on the way down again. Goddamn this thing.

Could you have avoided this fall? If you hadn't been standing there grinning and having your picture taken, could you have seen it coming and protected yourself? Certainly not, if the wheel turns by itself. And if the wheel is turned by the action of the people on it, then no, the scrambling of the others behind you trying to stand where you are would have pushed you over.

The only way to stay on top would be to shrink so as to occupy as little space as possible, then carefully take one step backward over and over again, suffering the knocks and curses of the others climbing past you to the top.

There wouldn't be much room, and you'd be afraid most of the time. And although you *would* appear in all the photographs of everybody else in *their* moment of glory, you would probably be looking at your feet. People on their way by would ask you what you'd done lately. "Staying on top" wouldn't seem like enough of an answer.

No, hard as you tried, you couldn't stay on top for long. Somebody would push you, or maybe you'd just give up and go around again.

Who made it a circle is a good question, but not anywhere near the point. The point is nobody asked you to get on it. You wanted something else, right? Something more than you had. Well, this circle is what else there is to have. Get off it if you can't take it, and hang on if you can't let go.

Some people do try to escape by jumping off while they're at the top. Actually, this is harder than you might think, requiring an actual jump rather than a simple letting go. But they do it, because they think they can beat the wheel that way. And maybe they can, for a while. But eventually, they realize the emptiness that surrounds the top of the wheel is more or less the same motionless void that surrounds the bottom. And wherever you are in the emptiness, you can still see the wheel, towering, gaudy and bright, far above everything else, like the Ferris wheel when you drive by the fairgrounds on the expressway late at night.

Gail hadn't noticed the Ferris wheel when she left the fairgrounds in the police cruiser. If she had looked back, she would have seen that it had stopped for the night. A terrible sight, a dead machine. On the Tarot's Wheel of Fortune card, there is a warning about this. The sphinx at the top of the wheel, holding the javelin, can stop the wheel at any moment, catch you and hold you wherever you are in the cycle. And when this wheel stops, you fear it will never turn again.

Fay looked at Gail now, and wondered what good would be intense enough to seem like the other side of the wheel from having your child kidnapped. And what had Gail ever done to deserve this?

Not that anybody ever deserved anything like this, of course, but what had Gail ever reached for, to trap her on the wheel, this wheel which had turned and caught her now? Nothing.

Well, she *had* wanted a little girl. Was that all it took to start this wheel moving? One hand, extended in the direction of one, so-far-faceless, unborn child? Yes, Fay admitted reluctantly, sadly, it was. It happened all the time.

AS GAIL WAS rinsing her coffee cup in the sink, she heard his footsteps and froze. Marvin was coming up the stairs two at a time.

"Gail!" he shouted from the front door. He sounded frantic, as if he'd carried his barbells up the stairs and was about to drop them if she didn't get there in time.

"What is it?" she said, running, Fay followed her down the hall.

"They found the truck!" he shouted.

"Where?" Fay asked.

He was talking very fast. "It's just like you said!" He slapped Fay on the back. "One of the guards saw a truck with oranges painted on the side!"

He slung his jacket over the chair, and flipped off the John Deere tractor cap he wore at night for fun.

He was so proud to be the one to tell them. "The guard thinks it left at midnight!"

Gail looked away.

But Marvin moved around so she could see him again. "Gail, they've got every highway patrolman for two hundred miles watching for the thing! They're bound to spot it sooner or later."

Fay spoke for Gail. "So they didn't actually *find* the truck."

"No," Marvin said, rubbing his hands on his pants. "Just a matter of time, though."

Fay shook her head. He was behaving like a junior varsity cheerleader.

She spoke slowly, hoping to calm him down, get him to take this seriously. "So all they really know, Marvin," she said, "is that somebody else besides me saw the truck. Is that right?"

Marvin sank into the chair. "Yeah. I guess so," he said. He thought it was better news than that.

Gail tried to cover her disappointment. "Want some decaf?" she managed.

"No thanks," he grinned. "I had some coffee and donuts with the boys," he said.

"What boys?" Gail asked.

"The police."

"I see," Gail said. "The boys." And she walked back down the hall to the kitchen.

"Is Arnie still out there?" Fay asked, pointing to the street.

"He went back to the station," Marvin said. "He said he'd call if he learned anything, and he wants you to stop by before you go home."

"Thanks," she said.

He planted his hands on his knees and leaned forward in his chair. "How did you know about the truck?" he asked, eyes wide in amazement.

"I don't know," she said, "I never know."

"Well, do you know anything else?" he asked.

"They're not going very far," Fay said, turning for the kitchen. "I don't even think they're on the highway."

Marvin jumped up and flew to the phone. "That's great!"

Fay left him talking to the police, and found Gail at the sink, her face buried in a wet washcloth.

"If you're all right," Fay said, "I better go."

"Please," Gail said weakly. "Don't leave me with him."

"You just stay in the kitchen," Fay said. "I'll tell Marvin to stay out there."

"He's having *fun*," Gail said.

"I know it looks that way," Fay said, "but that's how men handle a thing like this. They run. They make calls. They keep moving so it can't get them. They don't mean any harm by it. They just can't help it."

Fay gave Gail a hug.

"I want him to sit and cry with me," Gail said. "I want him to be somebody else, somebody who could make me feel better."

"I know. If I could change him for you, I would. But I can't. All I can do is go find Beth. O.K.?"

Gail stepped backward and turned on the water. She was mad all of a sudden. "What are you going to do," she asked, "read the cards?"

"I don't know," Fay replied simply. "I don't know what it will take."

"I'm sorry," Gail said. "I'm sorry I said that."

"It's all right," Fay said. "You just rest now."

In the living room, Marvin was hanging up the receiver.

"I think you should stay near the phone," Fay said to him. "Gail isn't in any condition to answer it."

"Good idea." He picked up his cap from the floor.

"And I wouldn't wear your cap."

"Yeah." He opened the closet door. "It looks a little funny, I guess."

"Yes," she said, "it looks like you're having a good time."

He pitched the hat up on the closet shelf and closed the door.

Fay knew she made him nervous. And she knew why. Marvin was afraid Fay would know what he was thinking before *he* did. But she couldn't help that.

FAY SHUT THE door behind her. She liked hallways. Always had. Even when you loved the people you'd been to see, it was such a relief to leave.

She had to find Arnie now. And maybe Lizzie was home. But as she grabbed the newel-post at the top of the stairs, she stopped cold. There it was, the whole thing. She saw it all. She stood there, paralyzed, and watched.

Lizzie and Paul were on the big boat. So were a lot of other people. All dressed up. Dancing. Drinking. Paul's mother was in white, beads all down the front in little roses, with curling vines of beads wound around her hips. No, not beads. Pearls. Ten or twenty thousand dollars' worth of pearls. Maybe more.

And food. Oysters on ice in a brass cart and a special waiter, his hands red with cold from shucking them. Somebody carving something. Rare, whatever it was, and black bread to go with it, and a bowl of whipped cream. Couldn't be whipped cream. Horseradish. Whipped.

Paul and Lizzie were dancing. Lizzie looked better than any of the other girls, no money or not. They could be skating, they were so smooth together. Everybody else had to work at dancing; they got hot, bumped into each other, smiled too much. Paul and Lizzie belonged together. They . . . fit.

They left the dance floor. They were talking with his parents, now. Lizzie liked the pearls; she wondered if the dress was heavy.

"So heavy," his mother said, "that Pierre guarantees I'll lose three pounds just wearing it." She laughed.

Lizzie knew not to ask who Pierre was. Chances were she'd meet him soon enough without asking. Paul and Lizzie walked out onto the deck.

"Where does he find these orphans?" Paul's mother asked, after they'd left.

The moon was still out.

Wait a minute.

This boat was moving. Moving fast. Too fast not to be going somewhere. The other people were gone. The party was over. This boat was under way.

Where were they going? Altantic City? Bermuda? Some island not on the map?

Fay saw Lizzie's cabin. It was already stocked with the clothes Paul's mother always provided for his girls. All Paul had to do, Fay realized, was find somebody the right size.

Where was he taking her?

Paul and Lizzie walked to the back of the boat, the stern.

"It's the Red Sea," Lizzie said, watching the huge wake curl and foam behind them.

"What Red Sea?" he asked.

"You know," she said. "Moses. He raised his arms and the Red Sea parted." She raised her arms and Paul slipped into them.

"In the movie?"

She laughed. "And the book."

"I love your hair," he whispered.

"It's Mother's," she said. "It's gypsy hair." And she folded her arms around him.

"Who *are* you?" he asked.

"Nobody," she said.

He kissed her.

She liked it, laughed and pulled one end of his bow tie. It fluttered up, all undone, then settled down smoothly against his shirt.

This is what you pay for in a good tie, Fay thought, as she watched.

Then Paul lifted Lizzie up to sit on the railing, stepped between her legs, and kissed her hard.

FAY RAN DOWN the steps to the street. The police would simply have to find these missing kids without her. She had to find Lizzie, and Arnie had to help her. Alert the coast guard, rent a speedboat, catch up with the yacht, and get Lizzie away from that boy.

She crossed the empty street and walked quickly to the police station. She hated to think how she must look by now, but she was glad she didn't know.

Arnie was alone in the duty room, waiting for her.

"Boy, am I glad to see you," he said, standing up.

"Arnie . . ." she began.

"Look at this," he interrupted, unfolding the front section of the early edition of the newspaper on his desk.

The headline read:

27 CHILDREN ABDUCTED FROM STATE FAIR

and, underneath, in smaller type:

LOCAL PSYCHIC ON THE CASE

Spread across the page, in rows, were the pictures of twenty-five of the children.

Fay sat down. Thinking about missing children was quite different from seeing their pictures in the paper.

"Where are the other two children?" she asked. "I thought you said there were twenty-seven."

"The other two are the Mayor's," Arnie said. "He kept their pictures out because he hopes maybe the kidnapper doesn't know they're his kids. He doesn't want the ransom to go up because of them."

"Poor man," Fay sighed. She liked this mayor, Peter

Ewing; she had known him for a long time. "Does Peter have
any enemies?" she asked.

"We thought of that," Arnie said. "Not a one. The unions
are happy, the businessmen are happy; hell, even the Republicans are happy. He's a hit."

"Well, then, what about his wife?" Fay asked. "Isn't Vi
on some abortion thing? Some Planned Parenthood, or pro-
choice committee or something? She's always on TV about
something. Isn't that it? Abortion?"

"I don't know," Arnie said. "But what does that have to
do with a kidnapping?"

"Maybe it's Vi they want to punish."

He shook his head. "You just don't like her," he said.

"No, I *don't* like her, but they're her kids too, aren't
they?"

"This doesn't have anything to do with abortion, Fay, it's
a kidnapping," Arnie said, standing up.

She nodded, but she wasn't at all sure Arnie was right
about that.

"Anyway," Arnie went on, "Vi is out of town. Speaking
at some convention somewhere."

"Saying what?" Fay asked.

"You're going in the wrong direction, Fay. All I wanted
to tell you was the Mayor called here looking for you. He said
if there was anything you needed—"

"I can't work on this case, Arnie," she said.

"You have to," he said, folding up the paper and putting
it under his arm. "There's one kid recovering from bronchi-
tis, one who's on an anticonvulsant . . ."

"No," she said, "I can't. All I can think about is Lizzie
and Paul. All I see is the two of them."

"It's not the same thing, Fay." Arnie greeted the new
sergeant coming on duty. "Lizzie and Paul are two nearly
grown-up kids doing what we'd all like to be doing right
now."

He opened his desk drawer and pulled out his shoulder
holster. "These other kids are babies in the hands of some
real weirdo who's doing God knows what to them."

"Lizzie is my baby," she said. "We have to find her."

He strapped on the holster. "Lizzie will come home all
by herself."

"No," she said. "That boat is going somewhere. He's taking her somewhere."

"Honey," Arnie said flatly, "I can't go find Lizzie because she's not breaking the law." He picked up his keys. "This creep, this maniac with all these kids, *he's* breaking the law. He's who I have to find, not Lizzie."

Fay shook her head. He didn't understand.

"I'm glad Lizzie's out with somebody," he said. "I hope he's the best she's ever had."

"He'd be the first, Arnie." Fay folded her arms across her chest.

"You don't know that."

"I do know that!" she snapped.

"All right, Fay," he said. "Fine. Do you want her to be a virgin all her life?" He started for the door.

Fay whirled around in her chair. "Where are you going?"

"You'll see," he said. "Come on."

She spun the chair back. "I told you. I'm not working on this case."

"Fine, then," he said, coming up behind her, touching her gently on the shoulder. "You're not working on this case. You're just taking a ride with me. Remember me?"

She covered her face with her hands.

"Now what's the matter?"

"It's not a man."

"Who's not a man?"

"The guy who stole the kids. It's not a man."

He sat down across from her. "It's a woman?"

"There's something about a church . . ."

"What church?"

"And girls."

Arnie couldn't keep up. "Is the truck at the church?"

But she didn't answer.

"Girls or women?"

"Girls."

"All right, then. Let's go," he said, standing up.

"Go where?"

"Go see the man who'd know about a group of all-girl, anti-abortion religious fanatics," he said simply. "Isn't that who we're looking for?"

She shook her head. He was amazing. Even when he didn't seem to be listening, he never doubted what she said.

She stood up. "If I find these kids for you, will you find Lizzie for me?"

"Fay," he said wearily, taking her arm and leading her toward the door, "this is twenty-seven kids. I'll do whatever you want."

"Say it again," she said. "I want a real promise."

He held the door open for her. "You find these kids and I'll find Lizzie."

"O.K., then," she said, and stepped out onto the street.

As the door closed behind them, he stopped a moment and looked at the moon. "We're in the wrong business, Fay," he said. "Everybody's in bed but us."

"We'll get there," she said.

He unlocked the unmarked car. "I hope you slept well last night."

"Why is that?" she asked.

"Because," he said, starting the engine and shifting into gear, "the Chief says the kidnapping statistics all say the same thing. If we don't find these kids in twenty-four hours—"

"—we don't find them," she finished.

"Yeah," he said, pulling away from the curb. "Ever. We don't find them, ever."

5:00 A.M.

FAY HAD MET THE ELEGANT YOUNG MAYOR DUR-
ing his first campaign. He was walking her
neighborhood in a yellow windbreaker, knocking on doors and introducing himself. She
looked at his palm, saw his Mount of Mercury and the star on
his Head line, and told him he would win.

"So I can quit all this walking and talking?" He laughed.

"If you want to," she said.

"But I like it!" he said.

"That's why you're going to win," she said. "The other
man doesn't want to do the work, he just wants to be the
mayor."

"How do you know that?"

She smiled. "Trust me," she said. "I know these things."
She laughed out loud. "In fact, all I do is know these things."

"Can I use that?" he asked.

"Sure," she said.

And he did. He brought a camera crew down to Fay's
parlor, and they went through the whole scene again on film
for an ad. The Mayor won the election, and the ad took the
top national advertising award, in the political category that
year.

Fay met Peter's wife, Vi, at the big victory party after
the election. But Vi Ewing was not a woman you'd ever really
know. If you tried to get close to her, all you would see were
the details of the surface.

Fay was a big star at the victory celebration, entertaining

the troops with a little Tarot numerology. When you add up the numbers corresponding to the letters in a name you get a key number, which indicates one of the Tarot cards—which, she said with a wink, was the sum cosmic total of everything that ever has or ever can happen to you.

At one point in the party, the Mayor's wife flew by and perched on the arm of Fay's chair like a parakeet, chirpy and bright but not likely to light there for long. She gave them all a big smile, and said, Wasn't it fun to know somebody special like Fay, and wasn't the ad worth all the trouble it caused everybody.

One of the young volunteers said Fay was doing numbers, and why didn't Vi let Fay do hers? Vi was trapped, but she was used to that.

"Is Vi your full name?" Fay asked.

"No, but that's what everybody calls me."

"All right, then," Fay said. "V is six and I is ten. That makes sixteen. The Fallen Tower."

"Oh, that's no fun," the Mayor's wife said, "do my whole name. I'm sure I have something better than that."

So Fay added up all the letters, including Vi's maiden name, the middle name she never told anybody, and the real first name on her birth certificate, and it still came to sixteen.

Not wanting to seem afraid of some voodoo nonsense, and not wanting to insult this woman whose endorsement had been so good for them, Vi asked Fay what the "infernal" tower meant anyway.

"But that would take so long," Fay said, knowing what she would have to say if she were forced to.

"Go on," someone shouted from the group. "We dare you." Nobody could back down now. Not at a victory party, anyway.

"O.K.," Fay said. "It's like the Tower of Babel in the Bible."

"I like the Bible," Vi cooed. Then she looked at the group and added quickly, "I like the Torah too, of course." She looked back at Fay. "That's like the Tarot, I guess, isn't it? I like them all, is what I'm saying. Go on."

"Well," Fay said, "there's something in your life built out of lies. Out of nothing but selfish ambition."

"I'm not ambitious," Vi said. "I just want the right people to be where they should be."

Fay tried to be careful. "The people who live in Falling Towers—well, they sit up there and look down on everybody else."

"Not look down," Vi corrected. "Bring people up to where we are. Where we all *should* be, I mean."

"Right," Fay said.

And the Mayor's wife shouted a little "hooray" and some of the people in the group clapped.

"The danger is," Fay went on, "that one day while you're looking over the wall and having a great time—you know, throwing things off the wall just to see how long it takes before they hit the ground—"

"That sounds like fun," the Mayor's wife said. "I used to do that from a hill at my old daddy's farm."

"One day," Fay went on, "lightning could strike and the tower could fall, and because you're up there on top of it, so could you."

"What a wonderful game," said the Mayor's wife. "How long did it take you to learn it?"

Fay knew she should stop, but she couldn't. "It isn't just lightning, though. Sometimes the tower crumbles from within. All because of the lies. The lies simply won't stand up."

"I don't lie," the Mayor's wife said, defending herself with practiced cool. "How could I lie? The press can find out anything, you know. Anyway, what would I have to lie about?"

"Sometimes it's crumbling already." Fay looked at the group. "People lie about that, you know, like a woman whose marriage is ending, who gets all involved in some social issue . . ."

The Mayor's wife stood up and motioned to someone that she would be there in just a moment.

The group was listening, so Fay went on. "But that only puts more stress on the original tower, makes it crumble faster."

"I wish I could hear the rest of this," Vi said, standing up, "but you know how parties are."

She shook Fay's hand. "Thank you for all you've done for my husband."

Then she turned to the group. "I think this one should have her own TV show, don't you?"

The group applauded, and the Mayor's wife breezed back into the crowd standing around her husband.

At the time, Fay had felt a little humiliated, a little done in by her own faith in herself, and a lot relieved there was always the bathroom to go to in moments like that.

But now, as she drove through the sleeping city with Arnie, going she knew not where, she shuddered to think about the Mayor's wife and the Falling Tower. Was this kidnapping what the cards had seen that night? How many of these children would the tower take with it when it crashed?

Fay tried to look out the windows, tried to think of something else, tried to rein in her racing mind. No, she insisted. No. She would rather reject everything she knew about the cards, find other ways to explain why they had been so right so often, than believe they actually had prior knowledge of something as terrible as this.

But it wasn't the cards, was it? The cards didn't know anything, not by themselves, anyway. It was she, Fay, who knew things by looking at them.

But that was even worse. Had Fay really known that night that this woman, Vi Ewing, was going to fall? It couldn't be. What lies could Vi have told to unloose a horror the size of this one? There weren't any lies that big, were there?

No. Vi couldn't be responsible for this. She must be an innocent victim, just like all these other parents.

But Fay knew there was a lie of some kind behind this thing. Some tower was coming down, all right. Right on top of all of them.

SOMETHING WAS BOTHERING Arnie, too, Fay sensed. He hadn't said a word since they left the police station. Maybe he didn't know if he could really find his informer in the middle of the night. Maybe he was just tired. Or maybe she'd made him mad making him promise to find Lizzie.

He pulled into the parking lot of the bus station and got out of the car, still without saying a word. She followed him, but there wasn't anything to see. Just the empty bus lanes and the empty benches beside them. Somebody had left a suitcase in one of the garbage cans.

Arnie walked over, picked it up, shook it, then jimmied the lock with his pocketknife.

"Is this where he lives?" she asked finally.

"Where who lives?" he asked, opening the suitcase.

"The man you're looking for," she said.

"Sure is," he said.

Fay wasn't convinced.

The suitcase was filled with old shoes, a whole family's worth. Arnie picked them up, pair by pair: battered wingtips; ragged sneakers; red pumps, one of which was missing its heel; four pairs of once-white baby shoes; and yellow plastic cowboy boots that might fit a teenage girl.

Arnie shook his head. Something about the suitcase made him feel worse. He slammed it shut, pitched it back in the trash can. Then he took Fay's hand and led her toward the door of the bus station.

"Is that how you know where he is, that suitcase?"

"No," he said. "That's just somebody's whole life they threw away."

"Is something the matter?" she asked carefully.

"I don't know." He opened the door to the waiting room. "Stay here."

He walked over to the rest rooms, disappeared into the men's, came out and went into the ladies'.

"It's late," he said, coming back to her. "Let's get some coffee, huh?" He nodded toward the coffee shop on the other side of the station. But Fay could already see through the glass that it was empty too, except for the man behind the counter. Whoever Arnie was looking for wasn't here.

"We can't just stop and have coffee, Arnie," she said, trying to help. "How about the produce mart? Maybe that's where they stole the truck."

But he didn't want any help. "I need some coffee, Fay," he said, opening the door. "I can't go any further till I get some coffee. It won't take long."

Fay didn't like it here. "The produce mart is a perfect place to hide an orange truck," she said.

"I'm a policeman," Arnie said. "I have to have my coffee when I say so." He opened the door. "And my donut. I want a donut."

"O.K., O.K.," she said. "We'll get you a donut."

But that wasn't all Arnie wanted. "And I'd like to go to bed," he grumped. "And get up and go fishing. And fry some catfish in an old black skillet and have a few beers."

"Anything else?" she asked, beginning to understand what this was about.

"Yeah," he said, sitting down at the counter. "I'd like to walk around the lake with you, and hear the birds. I like birds." The words were coming easier now. "I'd like to live outside with the birds. I'd like to spot a blue warbler up in the top of some tree, then take you back to the tent for the rest of the afternoon."

"That sounds good," she said.

"Two coffees, two donuts," he said to the waiter who shuffled toward them.

"Toast for me." Fay was trying not to watch Arnie too closely.

Arnie unzipped his jacket and reached for the sugar, so it would be ready when the coffee came. He shook his head. He picked at the spout of the sugar container, scraping away the crystals.

"It's real simple, Fay," he said finally, staring straight ahead. "I don't want to find these children."

"You don't want to find them hurt or dead, you mean."

He took a deep breath. "I don't find people any other way, Fay."

They sat silently, as though they didn't know each other, while the waiter set the coffee in front of them, filled water glasses from the faucet over the sink, and replaced Arnie's spoon, which had something vaguely green on it.

When the waiter left, Arnie took a sip of his coffee and sat up a little straighter.

"I could do other things, you know. I could drive a bus, or teach car repair, or hang wallpaper. I could paint fucking doghouses is what I could do."

"Arnie, Arnie," she said, "it's all right. The kids are all right."

"No, Fay, they can't be all right. Why kidnap them if you're not going to hurt them? Ten dollars says tomorrow we get a message, telling us which garbage can they stuffed the first one in."

This was a conversation they'd had over and over again, and there never was anything for her to say at the end of it. Arnie simply didn't like criminals. He liked that they were off the streets for a while, but he didn't like being with them on the way to the jail. He didn't like driving them downtown. He didn't like their talk. If he'd known he'd have to spend so much time with them, he'd never have set that first foot in the police department.

"Let's just go home, then," she said. "You can come back to my place and sleep for a few hours anyway."

"I don't think I could sleep."

"All right, Arnie." The waiter came around to refill their cups. "What do you want to do?"

"I want you to marry me," he said, lighting a cigarette.

She turned to face him. She thought he was joking. But no, Arnie was quite serious. As serious as she'd ever seen him. If there was any emotion in his face at all, it was something you'd have to call hope. Why was he doing this?

He took her hand and stared down at it. "I want us to move away somewhere. Wyoming maybe. A friend of mine out there says they haven't had a killing in his county for eight years, except two cocaine dealers nobody knew anyway. He told me you never need a key to your house, and the only time you even have to lock your car is when you go into town during tourist season."

"Marry you?"

He shifted in his seat. "O.K. You don't have to marry me if you don't want to. But come out there with me. Come out of here with me."

"Arnie, what would I do in Wyoming?"

"Don't they have a future in Wyoming?"

"Sure they do, but I don't know anybody there. It would take me years to—"

"O. K.," he mumbled. "Forget it, then." He took out his wallet and put a five-dollar bill on the counter.

But that wasn't what she'd meant. "I don't want to forget it, Arnie, it's just that I . . ."

He tried once more. "I want you with me, Fay."

"I *am* with you," she said, and stroked his face lightly. "I'm right here."

He pulled away. "I don't want to live someplace where they steal children from the fair."

"We'll find them."

"Yes," he said. "We will. And then I'm going away."

He turned around on the stool. His face was set. For the last twenty years, leaving the police force had seemed impossible. In the space of one conversation it had become inevitable.

"I can't leave Lizzie, Arnie," she said.

He stood up. "I thought you said he was taking her somewhere. That boy. Paul."

"He is," Fay said.

"So what are you going to do? Sit here and wait for her to come back?"

"We're going to find her," Fay said. "You promised me . . ."

"Right," he said. "I did. We'll take her with us. She'd like Wyoming."

But Fay knew that Lizzie would never go to Wyoming. "Can I tell you tomorrow?" she asked.

"Sure," he said. "Tomorrow is fine."

"Where are we going now?" she asked, standing up too.

"I'm going to the men's room," he said. "Want to come?"

She sat back down. "No."

He smiled and patted her on the shoulder. "O.K.," he said. "I'll be right back."

She smiled at him. He was all right. The coffee had helped. The conversation had helped. He could go on now.

AS FAY TURNED to watch Arnie walk away, she saw that the coffee shop wasn't completely empty after all. A drunk was slumped over in the last booth.

What she didn't know was that this particular drunk hadn't had a drink in fifteen years. He was calling himself Dr. Goodlife now, and was actually doing a fair amount of good recycling the neighborhood bums by teaching them to refinish furniture.

"Wake up, buddy," Arnie said to Dr. Goodlife.

"God bless you, brother," the slicked-back head said as it raised up from the table.

"It's me, Arnie."

"God doesn't care what you call yourself, my friend. He knows who you are."

"Open your eyes, Doc," Arnie said.

"You open your heart, I'll open my eyes," said Dr. Goodlife, his hands clamped around his Bible on the table. "I don't want to see you, son, till you've seen the last of drink."

"It's Detective Campbell, Doc," Arnie said.

The doctor opened his eyes. "Got a dollar for some coffee?"

"Sure," Arnie said, and motioned to the man behind the counter. "I'm looking for some girls." He sat down. "Some church girls."

"How many you need?" the doctor asked, searching his pockets for the paper clips he played with since he quit smoking. "Methodists, Baptists, bowlers, ball players, what?"

"I think it's a new church," Arnie said. "Something private. Weird maybe. Sick maybe. Tough, young. The kind that can drive a truck."

The doctor found a toothpick in his pocket and stuck it in his mouth. "Lot of girls drive trucks now, Campbell," he said. "Farm girls always did, of course. Then there's army girls. Girl bus drivers could drive a truck easy, I guess. If they had the truck. How big a truck we talking about? Lot of trucks in and out, you know. Gotta get things place to place. It's a big country, America."

"Have you seen a truck with oranges painted on the outside?" Arnie asked him, remembering now how much work this man could be.

"Maybe I did."

"Where was it?"

"I guess it was in Florida," the doctor said. "I used to live there, you know. Years ago. Nice place. Gets pretty hot, though. Lot of Cubans. I probably saw an orange truck there sometime, wouldn't you think?"

Arnie thought he was waiting for money, but he didn't know how much money the doctor's information was worth. The coffee arrived.

"Drink your coffee," Arnie said. "There's no rush. I'm just sitting here waiting for the sunrise."

The doctor took a sip. "You hear about those kids?"

Arnie laughed. "Drink your coffee, pal," he said, and got out his wallet.

Arnie thought about asking Fay to come over, save him some money and just read the doctor's mind. But when he looked back at her, she seemed to be counting the little boxes of dry cereal. That wasn't something he wanted to interrupt.

"Do you know where they're keeping the kids?" Arnie asked.

"Make it real easy on you if I did, wouldn't it?" The doctor grinned.

"Do you?"

"No."

Arnie tried again. "Do you know who the girls are?"

"Bad girls."

"Yeah, I figured they might be," Arnie said. "Why did they steal the truck?" Arnie asked.

The doctor shook his head. "You ever sit with a bunch of kids in a car?"

"No."

"Never shut up, kids. Got to keep 'em in a truck, I guess, if you're gonna have any peace, you know."

"How much do you want?" Arnie pulled out what money he had.

The doctor waved away the money. "The church is at Ninth and Oak," he said. "They've got a sign out front with Jesus hanging upside down from one foot, tears running up his face, blood running up his shirt. Not a Xerox or anything. Looks like they did it with crayons."

"Where's the truck?" Arnie asked again.

"What do you want the truck for? You're looking for the kids, right?"

"Right."

"Can't keep kids in a truck very long."

"Yeah," Arnie said. "Thanks. How much do you want, Doc?" Arnie extended his money.

"I don't want any money." The doctor lowered his voice. "I want you to find those kids. And chase those girls out of that church."

"Girls or women?"

"Girls."

Arnie stood up. "I want to give you something for this."

"Uh-uh," the doctor said. "Some other time." He opened his Bible. "Some other life, you can buy me a drink."

Arnie put a ten-dollar bill on the table. "You ever been to Wyoming?" he asked.

"Cold out there," the doctor said, turning to Revelations.

"Lot of animals," Arnie said.

"Sounds right."

"Well, if you ever get there," Arnie said, tapping the table, "look me up."

Arnie walked back to Fay, and raised her head from the counter.

"Let's go, love," he said.

She brushed her hair out of her eyes. "Go where?"

"You were right about the girls. And the church is at Ninth and Oak. Come on."

Once they were out the door, he walked so fast that Fay could barely keep up with him.

"Who was that man?" she asked. "Are the kids all right?"

"He doesn't know."

"Are the kids at the church?"

Arnie opened the door for her. "He doesn't know that, either."

"They can't be," she said. "If that drunk knows where the church is, then a lot of people know where the church is, so it wouldn't be a safe place for the girls to come back to, would it?"

"He's not a drunk, Fay," he said, starting the engine.

"I'm sorry."

"It's O.K." He knew she was tired, but he needed answers now. "Doesn't one of your cards have a guy hanging upside down from a tree?" he asked.

"Yes," she said, "the Hanged Man. Why?"

Arnie sped out of the parking lot. "This church has an upside-down Jesus in the front yard." He paused at the red light, then ran it.

"He isn't Jesus in the cards," Fay said. "He's just anybody."

"What does it mean?" he asked.

"It doesn't mean anything," she said.

"I *know* it means something," he insisted.

"Arnie." She patted him on the knee, hoping he would slow down. "It's probably just some old hippie who burns incense and flips through the coloring books at the mystical bookshop."

"That's right," Arnie said. "It's done in crayons. Tell me what it means."

"Are you taking me home or am I going with you?" she asked.

Arnie wasn't sure he wanted her along. With any luck, this could be dangerous. But he realized he needed her.

"You're coming with me," he said.

He picked up his radio and called headquarters for backup at the church. He could see it all. The truck would be parked in the alley, empty. He'd find the kids all huddled up in the nursery, tied together maybe, and the kidnappers upstairs preparing their statement for TV. He'd arrest the weirdos, rescue the kids, take Fay home to bed, and quit the force in the morning.

Fay saw it quite differently. Nobody was at the church. The kids were all split up now, not in the truck anymore. The truck was gone, but not empty. Somebody was working in the truck, making signs. Posters. Pictures. Pictures of the kids, and writing. Like a traveling exhibition, a McDonnell Douglas van that teaches school kids about jet engines, the kind you walk through, look at what's there, and come out the other end.

She couldn't tell him that, though. It didn't make any sense.

He turned at Oak Street and slowed down, making a mental map of it. Frame row houses, a welfare hotel, and a deserted foreign car repair place, its new location painted on the window. One new building, mid-block, Something-or-other for the Blind. And on the far corner, a bar with blinking neon martini glasses over the door.

He pulled up in front of the church. It was a low white frame building. The faded lettering over the door said it had been erected in 1940 and was, at that time, a Pentecostal tabernacle. It didn't look erected, though. It looked as if somebody had lowered a tin roof onto a double-wide mobile home.

"I think you better stay in the car for now," Arnie said. "I'll come get you if there's—" He saw the backup cruiser pull in behind him, and got out of the car without finishing his sentence.

"I'm fine," she said to the silence. And then she locked all the doors and cracked a window.

FAY WATCHED AS Arnie and the other two detectives approached the upside-down Jesus in the front yard, then proceeded to the front door. They found it locked, and split up to find another way in.

Could Arnie really be serious about moving to Wyoming? Could he really be asking her to choose between him and Lizzie?

She couldn't think about it. Not now, anyway. She stretched her legs out across the front seat, folded up her jacket and placed it between her head and the window. Maybe she could sleep for a while.

But that was not to be. As she closed her eyes, she saw

Lizzie and Paul standing beside his parents at the railing of the boat.

"I'm glad you could stay," Paul's mother said to Lizzie.

Staying? Staying what? Fay thought. Overnight?

"I hope you found everything you need," the honey-haired woman said.

Fay saw the guest room. There was not a human alive who could actually *need* all those things. Little lizard-skin pillboxes, tortoiseshell trays of dusting powder and perfume, smooth ivory bowls filled with sherbet-scented soaps. indications, Fay noted, of how the endangered species got that way.

"Yes, thank you," Lizzie replied. "It's lovely."

Lovely, Fay thought. Since when did Lizzie say lovely? By morning she'd find the stewards divine, and the air delicious. By lunchtime, she'd be calling people darling.

"Will you come inside, or stay here?" Paul's mother asked them.

"Here," Paul said, laughing at her for even asking.

"Cook will be awake, if you need anything," she said, and swept off through the door.

There was that word again. Need.

Paul pulled a thin cigarette from his coat pocket, put it to his lips, lit it, inhaled deeply, and passed it to Lizzie. Fay wasn't surprised. Marijuana, she thought. Did people *need* marijuana?

Lizzie took the joint from him happily. Fay waited for her to cough. When she didn't, when Lizzie seemed to know exactly what she was doing, on this boat, with this boy, with that dope in her lungs, Fay opened her eyes, sat up, and bolted out of Arnie's car and onto the sidewalk.

But then where was she? Staring at the upside-down Jesus stuck in the front yard of some tacky white church at six o'clock in the morning. And, for the moment, that was exactly where she wanted to be.

6:00 A.M.

FAY WALKED INTO THE YARD AND STARED AT THE hanging Jesus. The Tarot card on which the drawing was based did not always mean bad news. Sometimes, when it showed up in a reading, she would simply tell the client, "Oh, you're all right. Your life is just upside down right now." Or she might ask if there was something they'd left hanging. Or if there was something the matter with their left ankle. If there were other clues confirming some recent escape, she would say, "You caught yourself just in time, didn't you?"

"What do you mean?" they'd ask.

"You know what I mean," she'd say. And they'd laugh, and tell her the story.

Sometimes she'd get hold of a real martyr, like the preacher who ran the mission at the corner, or somebody's mother. The question was always the same. Why don't my children appreciate what I did for them? I gave them my life. Why don't they love me?

The answer was always the same, too. Nobody likes a sacrifice.

"If you sacrifice everything for your children," Fay would say, "they'll only end up hating you for it. It's an unpayable debt. Sacrifice makes people mad."

Fay didn't know why sacrifice made people mad. But then, nobody had ever made a big sacrifice for her, so she only knew one side of it. Except for Jesus, that is. The preacher who ran the mission at the corner told her Jesus had died for her sins. That would qualify as a sacrifice.

"What sins?" Fay asked. "Who has time to sin anymore?"

"He died to save you, sister," the preacher said.

"I didn't ask Him to die for me."

"You didn't have to ask," the preacher said. "That's how much He loves you."

"He can't love me," Fay said; "He doesn't even know me."

"Oh, He knows you," the preacher said.

"Prove it," Fay said.

"He died for you, didn't He? Would you die for somebody you didn't know?"

"He doesn't know me!" Fay screamed.

"O.K." The preacher gave up. "He doesn't know you. But that doesn't keep Him from loving you."

"Well, I don't want anybody loving me who doesn't know who I am."

"You can't stop Him," the preacher said.

"I don't *want* it," Fay said.

"It doesn't matter if you want it or not. He loves you."

Fay knew when she was beaten. She gave the preacher five dollars for the mission and walked off.

But now, as she looked at Jesus' face hanging upside down on the poster, she understood about sacrifice. She knew exactly why Jesus did it. For the same reason she did it.

But Fay didn't want to be paid back for her sacrifice. She just wanted Lizzie to love her. No. Not even that, if she didn't want to. Just . . . What?

Nothing, Fay thought. I gave her my life because I loved her. All I wanted to do was show her I loved her.

But did I love her too much? Fay wondered. Tell her too often? Did I make her feel bad because she could never love me as much as I loved her? Maybe I did. Maybe I drowned her in it. Maybe I rained that love down on her so hard, for so long, that now all she wants is to live in the desert, where she has to go out and look for water, where she has to work for it, where, most of the time, when she thinks she sees it, it's only a mirage. She wants to feel *lucky* to find it, kneel down on the ground and praise the Lord for it. Oh boy.

Fay thought about Jesus again. His sacrifice had back-fired, too. He died on the cross for the sins of the world, but then the people decided, since it was already paid for, they might as well go ahead and sin.

It was true. Sacrifice made people mad.

ARNIE HAD FOUND an open cellar door around the side of the church. Deciding not to wait for the third police car, which was on its way with the search warrant, he took off his shoulder holster and slipped inside.

The cellar was more of a cave, really; more like a hole the church was dropped into, filled with rocky ooze and muck, with pools of water in particularly low places. It smelled like snakes. Arnie wasn't at all sure that there was a way to get upstairs from here, but in the beam of the flashlight he saw a ladder. He sloshed over to it, then noticed the trapdoor directly overhead.

The whole place felt like a rodent playground, particularly the ladder, the rungs of which, Arnie was sure, the rodents were using as a latrine.

He took his first step up. It seemed solid enough. He held on with both hands and stepped up to the second rung, but not for long. It cracked right in two and Arnie fell seat first into the slime.

"Goddamnit to hell," he said, and heard something climb the wall to get away from him.

"That's right, you little bastards, run." He drew his feet up under him, so he could get up without putting his hands in the goo.

He tried the first rung of the ladder again, then took the big step to the third rung, then the fourth and hit his head on the ceiling. This was not what he had in mind when he joined the force.

He braced himself on the ladder and gave the trapdoor a hard shove with both hands. It opened with a loud crack and slapped over on the other side. Arnie waited a moment, in case anyone was around to hear the noise, then climbed the next two steps so that his head was poking up through the floor.

The air in the room was stale, and smelled vaguely of old paper. There was a slight hint of chlorine that made no sense at all to Arnie, but he hoped it was enough to kill whatever germs he'd breathed in the swamp. He wiped his flashlight on his pants and brought it up to floor level.

Directly in front of him was a pane of glass. He took another step up the ladder, turned around, and realized he was in some kind of box. What was a box doing at the front of a church?

Ah. O.K., he thought, it's a baptismal tank.

Arnie wished, just for a moment, that he was ten years old, fidgeting in the front pew on some hot humid night, bored by the sermon and mad at having to sit there, when all of a sudden some guy poked his head up through the bottom of the empty baptismal tank and took a look around.

There was a painting on the back wall of the tank. Jesus at the river baptizing a little girl. It was pretty sentimental stuff, but it made Arnie feel better to see Jesus right side up.

Arnie climbed up the stairs on the other side of the tank, and out onto the slightly raised floor that was probably the pulpit. He did a quick sweep of the main floor with his flashlight.

"What the hell?" he said, under his breath.

There were no pews. There was no altar. There was only a lectern with a projection screen set up beside it, and tables. Metal tables, maybe twenty of them, covered with white tablecloths, with some funny metal pieces attached to the foot of each table.

Feeling a little more comfortable now, he walked over to the tables for a better look. The tablecloths were made of paper, and the tables weren't real examination tables like in emergency rooms, but they would do in an emergency, he thought. The metal pieces at the end were stirrups, for women's feet during deliveries and pelvic exams.

Shit, he thought, Fay is right about this whole thing.

The last thing Arnie wanted to do was get in the middle of a war about women's things. Women's things were too messy for him—the blood, the milk, the water breaking, the afterbirth, the whole thing. Women were comfortable with mess, he knew. Not men. Men liked death better.

There was a knock at the front door.

"Yeah," he called. "I'm all right."

"We've got the warrant," the other detective said. "Open up."

He walked to the front door, slid the bolt out, and opened it slightly. When he turned back around to the church, he saw the muddy path he had left on the floor.

"Whatcha got?" Heller asked, stepping inside.

"Tables," Arnie said. "Some kind of clinic."

"Can't be," said Heller, walking on in. "There's no medicine."

Heller was right. Even if they kept the medicine locked up, there would at least be trays of cotton swabs and gauze around.

Fay walked up behind the two detectives. It didn't feel so bad here. Girls had been here, all right, but not bad girls. Nice girls. Girls like Lizzie.

"What do you think?" Arnie asked her.

She had to laugh at him. "I think you shouldn't have gone wherever you went to get whatever that is all over you."

"Yeah, I know," he said. "Did you see the Jesus?"

"Yes," she said. "It's a Tarot card, all right. Just an ordinary Jesus wouldn't have those coins falling from his pockets. As far as I know, Jesus didn't need pockets."

"What do you make of this?" Heller asked.

She backed away. She needed some air. "I don't know. It looks like a classroom to me."

"Yeah," he said, disappointed. "Me too."

"I have to call downtown," Arnie said to Fay. "Do you want to stay here?"

"I need to sit down," she said. "Can I sit on the steps out there?"

"Not with the print team coming, hon," Arnie said. "Why don't you come back to the car and wait there?"

Fay remembered seeing a rocker on the porch of the house next door. "Do you think I could go next door and sit on that porch?" she asked.

"Nobody there to ask," the young detective said. "I rang the bell. Nobody home."

"Go ahead," Arnie told her. "We'll be about twenty minutes."

The young detective loaded his Polaroid with a new pack of film, Arnie and Heller left for the cruisers at the curb, and Fay stood there quietly, listening to the camera clicking.

There *was* something else here, some other memory. Not the person at the lectern, though. Someone very small.

No, not small. Short. No. Sitting. Someone sitting. Sitting in a wheelchair.

She shook her head. She was too tired to do this. The man in the wheelchair probably came here for the laying on of hands. Then he probably got up and walked home after the service. That wasn't any help at all.

She turned quickly and left the church. All she could do here was get out of the way.

WHEN FAY STEPPED outside, it was morning. She took her first gray breath of air and saw Lizzie and Paul asleep on the deck of the big boat, lying on a double air mattress, covered with a beige comforter. The ocean sunrise was there too, but they didn't know it yet.

Paul pulled himself up on his elbows and turned to look at Lizzie, her hair shimmering in the early morning light. He walked over to the railing. And Fay had to admit nakedness actually seemed natural in the morning. She even liked her own body in the morning. But his—well, his was perfect. It was Apollo, or David, one of those.

His back was surprisingly muscular for a man who did no work that Fay knew of. Maybe he got those muscles by playing all day. Tennis. Something like that.

Paul stared out at the water, at the light frosting the tips of the waves. It was the hour of dolphin spray and sea sprites, of soaring terns and mermaids, when blue and pink were simply shades of silver.

He climbed onto the prow of the boat and unwrapped the flag. It unfurled easily, then flapped briskly, eager to rid itself of the creases of the night. Lizzie was awake now, watching him.

"Nice morning," she said quietly, when he was on the deck again.

"Nice night," he said, and just stood there letting her look at him.

She sat up, brushing her hair away from her face. Fay hadn't seen Lizzie's breasts for years now. Paul was remembering them too.

"Don't get up," he said. "I'm coming back."

"Good," Lizzie said, and pulled the cover away to show him the rest of what he remembered. She rubbed her fingertips along the inside of her thigh, maybe unconsciously, maybe not, maybe reminding him where he had been, maybe just remembering, herself. She shifted slightly, as if to get more comfortable.

He sat down beside her, eased his hand up to meet hers on her thigh, then let it slip between her legs.

Lizzie shifted again, and his fingers traced some invisible line up her stomach to the little hollow between her breasts.

"This is a sweet place," he said.

"It is?" she said.

"Yes."

"You mean on the sea?" she asked.

"No," he said.

Lizzie leaned back and Paul moved on top of her with the same smooth motion he had displayed on the dance floor. Fay couldn't see Lizzie anymore now, only Paul. Only his back rising and falling, Lizzie's arms around him, her hands pressing him to her, playfully at first, then settling into a rhythm that was young, yes, but felt oddly familiar to Fay. Lizzie wasn't a beginner after all.

Didn't they worry that someone might come up here and see them? No. Wasn't this what the morning was for? Yes. Wasn't the sea the oldest lover of all? Yes. Yes. Yes, Lizzie was whispering.

"You," Paul said, "you are . . ." He couldn't finish his sentence. He gave in easily, naturally to the ecstasy, as though it were his birthright.

Fay wiped her eyes. She hadn't wanted to see this. Didn't want to know it. But there it was. Paul lay quietly on his back, and Lizzie nestled under his arm, her hand resting peacefully on his chest.

As Fay walked across the yard of the church, Paul pulled the cover back up over them, and they slipped back easily into the sweet sleep of little children.

LITTLE CHILDREN, FAY thought, turning back to the church for one more look. Where are these children? Not in that church; she was sure of it. They'd never been in there.

She continued on across the yard and up the cracked concrete steps of the peeling yellow house next door. It certainly did look empty. The grass had given up years ago,

he front screen hung from one hinge, and the cobwebs
outside the front windows were more closely woven than the
curtains hanging inside.

But as soon as Fay sat down in the rocker on the porch,
she felt it. Someone was watching her. Someone inside this
house. Her shoulders quivered from their eyes on her back.
It could be anybody, though, or anything. It could be bats.
Or somebody who'd died here. Fay had learned long ago not
to jump to conclusions about these watchers when she felt
them.

She sat very still. If they watched long enough, she
would be able to tell where they were, anyway.

The gaze settled between her shoulder blades. She felt a
flush spread over her back. They were alive.

It was hard not to move, particularly hard in a rocking
chair, but just a little longer now and she would know where
they were.

There. She felt it. Just a slight prick, then a tingle. She
caught it as if it were a fishing line and held it inside her,
then she followed the beam back and up to the eyes behind
the blinds in the upstairs window.

She didn't understand. Was this watcher in a chair? The
eyes were barely as high as the windowsill. And then she got
it. This was no hermit in a wheelchair. This was a child.

"Arnie!" she screamed, and tore down the steps. "Arnie!
Quick!"

The policeman from the church came out of the door,
and Arnie raced up from his car.

"What is it?" he shouted.

She stumbled on the clawing roots of a tree in the front
yard, and fell into Arnie's arms.

"What *is* it?" he asked.

"There's a child in that house," she said, pointing behind
her. "Second floor. All the way to the right."

The other detective shook his head. "I knocked for ten
minutes," he said. "If there was anybody there . . ."

"So maybe she's locked up," Arnie said. "You stay here
with Fay. We don't have a warrant for this place either."

As Arnie ran toward the house, the detective turned to
Fay. "How did you know that?"

"Let's see if I'm right, first."

"I think I better help Arnie," the detective said.

"No." Fay grabbed his arm. "I think you better do what Arnie told you."

Arnie slit a hole in the screen of the rear door with his army knife, and flipped up the hook. Then he jimmied the lock and drew his gun, just in case Fay had missed seeing who else was in this house.

The kitchen counters were covered with a thin coat of dust. There was no food whatsoever, except for a grape gumdrop under attack by an army of ants on the kitchen table. Arnie made his way to the hall, found the stairs, then wondered, as he started up, where the hell the ants thought they were going to take that gumdrop.

They'll give up, he thought. They'll just pick at it until it's gone. Or maybe they'll each take a bite and run it home to the kids. But some of them would probably swallow their grain of grape sugar by accident on the way. And the rest of them would probably forget they even had kids and eat it on purpose. Ants can't be very smart, he thought. With their mouths full, they probably can't remember a damn thing. And then he wondered how smart he was to be thinking about ants all this time.

There were no lights on anywhere in the house, but as his feet hit the upstairs hall floor, he heard the voice.

"Mommy?" It was a girl. "Mommy?" she cried.

Fay was right. Arnie hurried to the door.

"Is somebody in there?" he called.

Tiny feet pattered toward him across the floor and stopped. Arnie bent down to what he guessed was her level and spoke through the keyhole.

"Hello, little one."

"Hello," the child answered softly, and Arnie heard her turn around and lean back against the door. From the sound of the hello, she must be sucking her thumb.

"What's your name, love?" Arnie said.

"Shelley," she said. "What's yours?"

Arnie guessed she was about three. "My name is Arnie," he said. "Do you know your other name?"

"Yes," she said, sounding so proud.

He had to laugh. "Well, Shelley, my sweet, what is it?"

"Chambers," she said.

Arnie pulled the list of missing kids from his back pocket.

She was on it, all right. Shelley Chambers. Only the list said she had a sister, Susan, who was also missing.

"Shelley?" Arnie asked. "Is anybody in there with you?"

"They went away." Arnie could hear her fumbling with the doorknob.

"O.K. now, Shelley," Arnie said, putting away his gun. "You have to listen real close, O.K.? I've come to take you to your Mommy, but the door's locked."

"When is Mommy coming?" she cried.

"As soon as I get the door open, we'll go see Mommy."

"It's me, Shelley," she said.

"I know it's you Shelley, and this is me Arnie, and I have to break the door down now, O.K.?"

"O.K."

"Good." Arnie stood up. "Now why don't you go over to the window and see that lady on the porch."

Shelley didn't answer, but he heard her moccasins scuffing across the floor. He only had a second before she'd return. He rocked back and crashed into the door, grabbing it as it gave way, ending up on his knees in the middle of the room, his hands prickling from the splinters.

But when he looked up, there she was, a blond, curly-haired cupid cowering in the corner.

"You broke the door." She pointed.

"I wanted to see you," he said. "Doors are easy to fix."

"Where's Mommy?"

Then he saw the other one, on the bed. Or what looked like another one. A pile of blankets. Something like a foot at the end.

"Who's that?" he said to Shelley, jumping up.

"It's Susie, silly." She took her thumb out of her mouth, padded over to her sister and pulled the blankets back just enough for Arnie to see that Susie was breathing.

"What's she doing over there?" Arnie asked.

"She's sleeping," Shelley said. "But we don't want to wake her up, because she'll cry and we'll get upset."

Arnie walked to the bed. "We won't get upset," he said, picking up the child in the blankets. "We haven't heard anybody cry in a long time."

"Why not?"

"Because I don't have any children," he said, taking Shelley's hand.

"Why not?"

"I don't know." Arnie led her out into the hall.

"Why not?"

"I never thought about it, I guess."

"Why not?"

He was relieved when Susan woke up and started crying and they couldn't talk anymore.

They got to the stairs and Shelley came down them backward, then flapped toward the open door as if she had always lived in that house. Arnie knew without a doubt that this was the best morning's work he had ever done.

SHELLEY'S PARENTS ARRIVED outside the house in ten minutes, followed shortly by an ambulance, the crime lab team, a dozen or so police cruisers, the Mayor, the Chief of Police and about fifteen neighbors who had nothing better to do than stand behind the police barricades and try to guess what was going on.

The department was checking all the houses on the street now, hoping to find the rest of the children. Fay didn't think they would, but there was always a chance. They'd asked her if she'd go sit on every porch, door to door, but she'd said no. There wasn't *that* much of a chance.

"I wish you could have seen Shelley's face when I broke down the door," Arnie said, as he walked Fay to his car. "I wanted to just grab her up and—No." He stopped. "The person I wanted to grab up was you."

"I'm real glad," she said. "I'm real . . ."

"You're real tired is what you are," he said. "But you ought to be real proud, too."

"I am." She tried to smile. "It's just that . . ."

"Fay," he said. "We all know you can't find the rest of them this easy. We're just happy to get started, that's all."

"I don't want to talk to the press."

"You don't have to."

"I don't want to talk to the girls' parents either," she said. "I just want to hide."

He put his arm around her. "You don't have to talk to anybody but me."

"I know that sounds weird," she said, "but . . ."

"Who cares what it sounds like?" he said. "You found the girls, so you get what you want."

"Thanks." She tried to smile, but it didn't feel right yet.

"Just lock the doors and scoot down in the seat," he said, putting her in the car. "They won't even know you're here."

But as soon as Arnie shut the door, the Mayor appeared at her window. Peter Ewing was lean and fit, but this morning he was holding himself up with will, not muscle. He hadn't been to bed either. He couldn't even imagine it until his boys were found.

"Fay," he said, "I can't thank you enough for—" He stopped, seeing the exhaustion on her face. "Are you all right?"

"I'm fine," she said. "I just need to be quiet."

"Do you mind if I come sit with you a minute?" He motioned toward the driver's seat.

She did mind of course; then she saw his eyes. Always, before, they had been eager to see what happened next. This morning they were shadowed by the fear that they had seen it all before.

"You're sure you're all right?" he repeated, getting into the car.

"Yes," she said. "I'm fine. It's just . . ."

"What do you think it means?" he asked. "Are they all spread out, the kids? Hidden away like this all over the city?"

"Yes," she said. "I'm afraid they might be."

"What should we do?" he asked. "What if I went on TV and asked everybody to check the empty houses on their streets?"

"That's worth a try," she said.

"Good," he said. "I taped the announcement as soon as I heard."

She shook her head. "If you'd already done it, why did you ask me?"

"I thought you might know some reason why I shouldn't, that's all."

"No," she said wearily, "I don't know a thing."

"But you found these two, didn't you?"

"Yes." She turned to look out the window. "But I can't promise I'll be able to . . ."

"I know, I know," he said. "All the same I'd like to tell you what my sons were wearing."

He couldn't help it. He was trying to be the Mayor, trying to be concerned about all the missing children, but not for one second could he really forget that two of those children were his.

"Let me see your hand," she said.

"You can see my boys in my hand?" he asked, wiping his palm on his pants.

"If your boys are in your brain, they're in your hand."

"Fay," he stuttered, "I didn't mean to put you to work here. I just wanted you to know that if you need anything, even to be left alone . . ."

"This is what I need," she said. "What we both need. Let me see your hand."

It would be rude to resist her now, so he turned on the interior light, gave her his right hand, and hoped one of his aides would come looking for him soon.

"This is your Heart line," she said. "This one at the top." She saw the island on the line right away, but she couldn't talk about that yet.

"These little feathers pointing down are disappointments in love, early in your life. One major one, here, see? How old were you? Twenty?"

"Yes," he said. "You're right." He tried to laugh. "I thought I was over it, though." He was very nervous now. "Not so, huh?"

She smiled. "You like to be in love. You like to be married."

"I guess so." He noticed Arnie's radio and wondered if a police operator somewhere was monitoring the conversation.

"You do," she said.

"That girl I loved," he said, quietly, "she barely spoke English."

"Where were you?" Fay asked.

"I was in the Peace Corps in Africa." He paused. "Avoiding the draft."

"You should've come to see me before you went," she said. "I could have told you travel was no good for you."

He didn't laugh. "I could've died from loving her. I ate what she ate, swam where she swam, slept where she slept. I *should've* died from it, gotten one of those tropical diseases and died. But I didn't. I escaped. But I've been sick ever since from losing her. I feel it every day, somewhere in me."

He tried to get back to the story. "I taught her what little English she knew," he said, "but the more she learned"—he played with the turn signal—"the more she wanted to go speak English with somebody else. Somebody who didn't know how she learned it."

"Yes," Fay said. "That happens."

"Tell me about the boys," he said. "Are my boys all right? Do you have any idea where they—"

"Here they are," she said. "These two little lines over here, those are the boys." Then she spotted something else. Good news. "Peter, there's another child here." She smiled at him.

He tried to pull his hand away, but she grasped it more firmly.

"It's not for another three years," she said, and felt him relax a little. "But it's . . ."

"What?"

"It's somebody else, another relationship, another woman. Another marriage, I think."

She glanced up at him, suddenly wished she hadn't gotten into this, released his hand, and tried to make light of it. "There's nothing to be ashamed of. You haven't met her yet."

"I can't be married again." He laughed, rubbing his hands together. "It would ruin my career."

"Peter," she laughed. "Romance is on the way." She patted his knee. "Cheer up."

They sat in silence for a moment, neither of them quite knowing where things went from here. She had already stumbled across more information than she felt entitled to know. But she had to ask him about that island on his Heart line.

"Look at your right hand," she said. "There's a little circle on your Heart line. Do you see it?"

"Sure." He was holding his hand up to the light.

"We call it an island," she said. "And islands on the Heart line mean a loss, an emotional loss."

"Not the boys," he said, his eyes wide with fear. "Please not the boys."

"No," she said, "I don't think so." But of course she wasn't sure of that. "Is there anything else you know of that could . . ."

"It's Vi," he said, staring out the front window. "It's not the boys. It's Vi. It's over between us."

"I'm sorry, Peter."

He shook his head. "I'm sorry I sat down here," he said. "I was feeling pretty good before. Two kids found, twenty-five to go."

"Feeling good?"

"O.K.," he admitted.

"I could be wrong," Fay said.

He shook his head. "If I lose Vi, I'm finished as a politician."

"I don't think so," she said. "Once you get past that island, everything's going to be a lot better. Work *and* life. I promise."

"Thanks," he said, wishing he could believe her.

She spoke softly, knowing that he needed to be comforted. "Your hand is like a road map of your brain," she said. "An island begins to form as soon as you know you have to protect yourself. If the island is there now, then I'd say you were ready to deal with it, whatever it is. It can't . . . hurt you now."

He nodded, hoping she was right.

"Our brains," Fay went on, "are smarter than we are. All they want to do is help. And all we have to do is stay out of their way."

"I didn't know this would be so personal," he said, reaching for the door handle.

"I don't know why you're complaining." She grinned, trying to sound unconcerned. "All I told you was your boys are fine and there's someone new coming into your life. Most of my clients would pay double to hear that."

"I have to go," he said, stepped out of the car, closed and locked the door, then straightened his tie, motioned to his driver, and walked around to Fay's window.

"Thanks again for finding these girls."

"Your boys are O.K. All the children, they're all O.K. I know it. They're just lost."

"I hope so," he said.

"Trust me," she said, grasping his hand and squeezing it tight. "I know these things."

He smiled. "That's better. That's what I wanted to hear."

Fay nodded and watched him walk toward his car. What

Peter Ewing needed right now was to be the Mayor again. But what he had to do first was go pick up Vi at the airport.

Fay took a deep breath. Did she really know the children were all right? Yes. They were sleeping. But would they be all right when they woke up? That she didn't know.

"Ready?" Arnie opened his side of the car.

"I didn't even *see* you," Fay said.

"I know," he said. "I waved, but you were—"

"Lost," she said. "Are we ready to go?"

"We sure are," he said. "It's about time, too, don't you think?"

"I think we're late."

"O.K. Then we'll hurry." And he turned on his flashers and siren, and blasted off down the street.

7:00 A.M.

 ON HIS WAY TO THE CAR, ARNIE HAD PICKED UP the special edition of the newspaper. As they drove, Fay unfolded it and looked at the front page. The banner headline read:

27 CHILDREN ABDUCTED FROM STATE FAIR

"Want me to read this to you?" she asked him.

"Sure," he said. "If there's anything new in it."

But there wasn't. The main story had quotes from the Security Chief at the fairgrounds, the Police Chief, the Mayor, and the parents. There was a list of hot-line numbers and a statement that the city had posted a reward for information leading to the arrest of the kidnappers or the recovery of the children.

There was a companion piece in the next column about two children who got off the school bus a year ago and never made it home, and a background piece further down, about missing persons nationwide.

Then across the bottom of the page were the pictures of the children. She had seen the pictures earlier this morning, but looked more closely this time. One little girl was taking a shower under a garden hose. The heads of two little boys were poking out of a tent in their backyard, and one chubby boy was sitting in Santa's lap in a department store. None of them were old enough to read the story and learn what had happened to them.

She glanced at the weather forecast, found it wasn't going to rain today after all, rolled the newspaper back up, replaced the rubber band around it, and remembered Lizzie's fourth birthday party.

Fay's mother had been quite withdrawn then, crocheting in her room for ten, sometimes twelve hours a day, her rocker thumping like a heartbeat, her lap covered by the ever-lengthening white tablecloth.

Lizzie was afraid of her granny and wouldn't go in the room. There was, she said, a bad smell in there. Fay kept asking Lizzie why didn't she go sing for Granny. Lizzie said Granny didn't know any of her songs. Fay said, "You could teach them to her," but that only made Lizzie cry and grab the bottom of Fay's dress.

In truth, Fay wasn't sure how much the old woman could hear anymore. What she hoped was that her mother *could* hear Lizzie singing in the bathtub, but *couldn't* hear her say that Granny smelled bad.

Lizzie's birthday was on a Saturday that year. Fay had invited her sisters and their families to the party. She wore a red flowered dress and spiky black heels, and served fried chicken and mashed potatoes, Lizzie's favorite. The cake from the bakery was dry and grainy, but everybody said it looked good. Fay had asked them not to put those ridiculous green leaves around the roses. She said there wasn't a single thing in the whole of creation that pasty-colored green, but the baker forgot and put the leaves on anyway. More leaves than ever, Fay thought.

Then came the presents. The sisters brought clothes for Lizzie, both of them thinking Fay had no taste in clothes and that's why she and Lizzie looked like gypsies. The cousins brought dollhouse furniture and one of the brothers-in-law promised to build Lizzie a dollhouse for it as soon as he got a free Saturday.

Finally, there was only one present left, a long box wrapped in giraffe paper and tied with a yellow bow. Lizzie looked up at Fay in wild delight and said she already knew she didn't have one of these because she'd never gotten a box like this before. The joy on the child's face, the sheer ecstasy of anticipation, was unlike anything Fay had ever seen.

Children are funny. They actually believe they are going to get something they want. They can't imagine *what* they might want, of course, but they *know* it's in there. It's something they'll jump up and down about, something they'll run around the room and show everybody, something they might feel slightly bad about the other kids not having one of, but, finally, something that will make them feel loved and understood. Children think that presents are for *them*, that their parents know who they are, and know how to make them happy.

Lizzie tore into the box. She threw off the lid and ripped away the tissue paper and there it was. A brown umbrella with a little dog head on the handle.

Fay saw it happen, saw Lizzie pull the shade between them. The hopelessly disappointed little girl, crying behind her eyes, stood up, held the thing out for the relatives to see, and said, "It's an umbrella."

Fay didn't know why she had thought a four-year-old would need an umbrella, much less want an umbrella. Lizzie thought it was fun to get wet. What did she need an umbrella for? So she could be a little grown-up? Lizzie had no idea, until that moment, that she would ever *be* a grown-up. But now she knew. And from the look on her face, the idea didn't appeal to her.

Maybe Fay gave Lizzie the umbrella because she, Fay, wanted a new umbrella. Or maybe because what Fay knew about life then was that it rained a lot.

Anyway, it was a bad idea. Fay saw that now.

But then, as they were all diligently admiring the umbrella, and trying to convince Lizzie what fun it would be to have one, they heard Granny's door open. No one had expected to see her, much less to see her walk into the living room, but walk she did, carrying a package under her arm.

As Granny creaked into the room, Lizzie backed up and tried to hide behind the piano.

"This is for her," Granny said, pointing to Lizzie. "It's her birthday."

"Isn't that nice of Granny," Fay said, prying the child's fingers off the piano bench. "I wonder what it could be."

"Thank you, Granny," Lizzie said, like a well-behaved little robot.

"Open it!" Fay said to Lizzie, trying to show enough enthusiasm for both of them.

"You open it," Lizzie begged.

"No, you," Fay said. "Granny worked real hard to get you something and everybody wants to know what it is."

Lizzie accepted the package. She sank down on the floor and began to open the box. But she was much more careful this time. She worked very slowly, hoping to postpone the sight of another gift until, say, next year, when she was older, when she could handle it better.

Granny didn't watch her. She seemed content enough just to sit in the rocker one of the cousins brought out from the bedroom. It was such a shock having the ancient woman with them that nobody knew quite what to do. What could they say to her? How is your room? No. They couldn't even say they were glad to see her because they weren't at all sure they were.

Lizzie lifted the lid off the box. There was no tissue paper in it, there was only another box, a cheap red plastic box.

"What is it?" Lizzie asked, looking up at her mother for help.

"Well, I don't know," Fay said, in her cheeriest voice. "Let's lift it out and see."

It was too big for a lunch box, but it was about the right shape, Fay thought. But it had some moving parts inside, some of which were moving by themselves already. Fay hoped it wasn't broken; the party was in enough trouble without that.

"Here," Fay said, showing Lizzie the latch on the side of the box. "You open it."

By now, Lizzie wasn't resisting her at all, but was simply going along because she was the little girl, and this was what little girls did on their birthdays. She popped the little plastic flap open and raised the lid.

And then she shrieked, "It's a record player!"

She jumped up and nearly hugged Granny to death. "A record player! I've never had a record player! Now I can listen to records!" And just like that, Lizzie started singing one of those songs kids make up out of sentences: "I've got a record player, I've got a record player." She danced around the room holding her skirt out and kicking her legs up as high as they would go.

"You have records too," Fay said, finding them taped to the inside of the box.

"I want to hear it!" Lizzie squealed, and went over to hug Granny again. Everybody clapped and said they wanted to hear it too. Granny looked up from her crocheting and said what she wanted was some bourbon.

So, as Lizzie held on to the arm of Granny's chair, rocking her faster than the old lady had ever gone in her life, Fay started playing the records. They heard "The Animal Supermarket," "The Three Little Pigs," "Little Red Riding Hood," the ABC song, and "Twinkle, Twinkle." They listened to all the records twice, in fact, before the rest of the family remembered wherever it was they had to go that afternoon.

After they left, Granny continued to crochet and Fay sat on the floor with Lizzie until bedtime, wishing somebody would tell her what she was supposed to learn from this.

The next day, she subscribed to the Record-of-the-Month Club for Lizzie, and their life was changed forever. Fay's made-up stories had been just fine for a baby, but now Lizzie could fly with the Eagle and the Thrush and cheer for Dumbo, puzzle over the Grasshopper and the Ants, and imitate the Queen Ant's firm but fair voice.

In another year Lizzie could identify numbers, so she didn't need Fay to tell her which record was the beginning of "Cinderella." And the year after that, Lizzie found books. Night after night, year after year, Fay would see Lizzie sitting across the room with a book, but when people are reading, you never really know where they are.

Fay didn't know what had happened to that little record player. But she knew what had happened to Lizzie that day, and knew that it was irreversible. And she knew, finally, that Granny could hear absolutely everything.

"HOW LONG DO we have?" Fay asked Arnie, as they parked in front of his house.

"Till somebody needs us someplace else," he said. "We should take a nap if we can."

"Arnie, how can we take a nap?"

"Easy." He grinned. "Pull the shades." He turned off the engine. "Come on."

Fay yawned in spite of herself.

Arnie lived on the top floor of a white frame row house in an area called Germantown. When he first moved in, he agreed to paint the green shutters once a year instead of having his rent go up. But every year after that the landlady had added one more chore to his list, reasoning that if he lived there for six years, he would be paying six rent increases, not one. After ten years, the landlady didn't see any reason to keep the ladders, hammers, and paint in her apartment when Arnie was needing them virtually every weekend, so he moved everything up to his place, and now he lived in what looked like a one-bedroom hardware store.

Fay liked being there. She liked the sawdust he swept into the fireplace, and the screwdrivers standing with the knives and forks in the drain rack beside the sink. There was a can of turpentine on the floor in the shower, and in the bedroom were two sawhorses on which his paint-spattered drop cloths hung, folded and serene like prize quilts.

He unlocked the front door. "When we get upstairs," he said, "we'll make a pot of coffee and call Lizzie. If she's not home, we'll get the Chief to post somebody at your house to watch for her." He collected his mail from yesterday. "Then we'll drink the coffee, take a shower, and go to bed."

"Have you see a big Indian anywhere?" she asked, following him up the stairs.

"A big what?"

She saw it quite clearly. "There's a big Indian somewhere, like a sign, only 3-D. A statue."

He picked up the newspaper outside his apartment. "An Indian?"

"It's plastic, I guess; or wood maybe, like a tobacco-store Indian."

He opened the door, pitched the paper onto the hall table, and walked into the kitchen. "Sure there is," he said. "At that Indian Point Shopping Center, out in the south end. Big Indian. Thirty feet tall, maybe."

There was no place for Fay to sit down in the kitchen, so she leaned against the refrigerator as he filled the old percolator with water. She had given him a Mr. Coffee coffeemaker for his birthday one year, but he never used it. He said the coffee didn't smell right unless it perked.

"That's it, then," she said.

"It what?"

"That's where they're going to set up the orange truck."

He lit the burner under the coffee. "They're going to drive the truck to a shopping center?"

She nodded, picking up the phone.

"And do what?"

"I don't know," she said, dialing. "Park it, I think."

He looked at the pot, listened to the hiss and static of the water as it began to feel the heat. He had to have a break here. He didn't want to know about the orange truck. Not now, he didn't.

Fay hung up the phone. "Lizzie's not there," she said.

"I'm going to take a shower," he said. "You watch the coffee. When it starts to perk, turn it down."

Fay nodded, she knew a little about coffee herself, and patted his arm as he passed her.

But just as he hit the hallway, the telephone rang. He looked at it, swore under his breath, and picked it up.

Fay looked down at the floor. She had helped him lay this tile. They had done a great job. This green and gold tile was the best thing about this kitchen.

"What do you mean, where am I?" Arnie shouted into the phone. "I came home to take a shower! What's the matter, did everybody else quit?"

Arnie covered the phone with his hand. "It's the Chief," he whispered. "He wants to talk to you."

Fay shook her head.

"She's going to cost you plenty on this thing," Arnie said to the Chief.

"How much?" the Chief asked.

"She'll do it for ten thousand," Arnie said.

"Ten thousand dollars?" the Chief said. "How about a hundred dollars an hour."

Fay had never heard Arnie negotiate her salary before.

"Christ Almighty," Arnie said. "She's working twenty-four hours a day. She'll cost you ten thousand in four days. Better take the flat fee, Chief."

"O.K.," the Chief said, "ten thousand."

"And another thousand for each kid she finds alive," Arnie said. "You can get that back from the parents."

"I can try," the Chief said. "Do you know where she is?"

"No." Arnie winked at Fay. "But I know how to find her."

"O.K., then," the Chief said. "I'll see you both down here in an hour."

"No," Arnie said. "It'll take me till nine o'clock to find her. Meet us at the Indian Point Shopping Center at nine."

"Why there?" the Chief asked. "Does she know something?"

"She knows everything," Arnie said. "Did we pick up the orange truck yet?"

"No," the Chief said.

"O.K.," Arnie said.

Fay was trying to get his attention, but he knew what she wanted.

"Punch up the harbor list for last night," Arnie told the Chief.

Arnie heard the Chief getting the list up on his computer monitor. Fay walked over to listen.

"Got it," the Chief said.

"Get to the private boats. I'm looking for a big yacht that left last night about three o'clock."

"Yeah," the Chief said, "here it is. God Almighty, this is a big fucking boat. *Mia Querida*'s her name. But it's not scheduled to sail till tomorrow night."

"They could've left early, I guess," Arnie said.

"Does this have something to do with the kids?" the Chief asked.

"Just check it," Arnie said. "I want to know everything there is to know about that boat."

"They don't have to tell us where they're going, you know. It's a private citizen. They can go wherever the hell they want."

"Find out where they're going," Arnie said. "Find out who it belongs to. And get a warrant ready."

Fay mouthed a thank-you to Arnie, and walked back into the kitchen. If Arnie did leave, she would miss this place. She would miss the morning light in this kitchen. Not that it streamed in, or flooded the room or anything. It seemed, well, almost amused to be here, tickled by the trick it had

pulled to get here, stealing around the neighboring house-
tops, ducking under the trees, jumping to the roof of Arnie's
building, then sliding down and slinging itself in this window
right at the last minute. If Arnie left, she would miss him,
too. But how could she go so far away? Could she go? She
couldn't go. Could she?

"I love you," he said, coming back to find her.

"I know," she said, turning around.

"Come here." He opened his arms.

And as the coffee started to perk, they wished, as neither
of them had ever wished before, that everything would just
stop, that they could hold each other forever like this, in a
space just wide enough for one embrace, with the cabinets
and the appliances standing guard against time and the world.

"I need a shower too," she said, finally.

Arnie released her and turned around to the broom
closet. "I think I've got another bar of that, what is it, Dove
soap," he said. "Yeah." He smiled, finding the soap. "I sure
do." He held it out to her. "I don't want to force you, though."

"Force me to take a shower?"

"Force you to make love with me."

She looked at his face. It was a ragged face, eyebrows
going gray and eyes a little red around the edges from the
night, but a handsome face, easily and happily male. He
never thought about his face; it was just another thing he'd
always had, like long arms. He wouldn't know what to think
about it. She did.

"You watch the coffee," he said, turning the burner
down. "You'll know when it's ready by the smell. Just take
the basket out and turn it way down. I'll be out by then."

And he walked down the narrow hallway to the bathroom, leaving Fay holding the soap.

FAY STOOD THERE a moment, then reached for the phone to
call Gail.

But before she could pick it up, the phone rang. Was it
going to be one of those days? she wondered. Those days
when she knew every goddamn thing one half second before
it happened? She hoped not. Those days seemed so long.

"Hello," she said.

The voice on the other end was frantic. "Fay, thank God

I found you," Gail cried. "They called me! The people who took Beth. They just called me!"

"Jesus Christ," Fay said. "What did they say?"

Gail was hysterical. "They said I would have to work to get her back. They said there wasn't any other way to wake people up. They said if I wouldn't help, I'd never see Beth again. They said they were serious, they were going to win this thing once and for all, and then the whole country would thank them."

"Just what did they tell you to do, honey?"

"Wait for another call, they said. I told them I'd do anything."

"That was exactly right, Gail. Did they say what this thing was they wanted to win?"

"No." Gail's voice sounded hoarse.

"All right," Fay said. "Did you hear anything in the background?"

Gail blew her nose. "I guess it was a phone booth, but I don't know, I just—"

"Breathe, Gail," Fay said. "Nice deep breaths."

"I'm sorry," Gail said. "But that voice just . . . I don't know. It made me mad, it made me sick."

"Breathe, Gail," Fay said. "Beth is obviously all right or they wouldn't have called you. They need you for something. So until they get what they want from you they're not going to hurt Beth."

Gail wanted to believe that. "O.K., O.K. I'll try." Gail cleared her throat and made an effort at normal conversation. "Did Lizzie get home all right?"

"No," Fay said. "I mean, she's all right, but she didn't come home."

"Did she call you?"

"No, but I've been with Arnie all night, so that helped. You stay by the phone, like they said, and I'll call you as often as I can."

"Where are you going to be?" Gail asked.

"I don't know," Fay said. "But I'll call you. Or if you need me, the police can always find Arnie."

"O.K.," Gail mumbled.

"It's all going to be all right," Fay said. "You'll do what they want, and they'll give Beth back."

Gail managed a broken "Thanks, Fay," and hung up.

By the time Fay got to the bathroom, Arnie was already in the shower, balanced on one foot, his other leg bent up so he could soap his calf, the water beating down on his back and running over his neck and ears in slick streams.

"That was Gail on the phone."

"What?" he asked, scrubbing his foot, massaging the big toe that had bothered him since last summer when he had dropped a can of creosote on it.

"The kidnappers called Gail." She sat down on the wicker clothes hamper under the little window.

He turned off the water and slid open the door. "What did they want?"

But she waved him back into the shower and shouted over the noise of the water. "They don't want money," she said. "They want the parents to do something."

"Do what?" Arnie asked, rubbing the soap between his hands to work up a good lather, then squirting the soap back into its metal dish.

"They didn't say. They're going to call them back later."

"Sons of bitches."

A cloud of steam was forming on the ceiling, and Fay could feel her hair frizzing at the ends. Arnie sudsed his chest, neck, and under his arms. Then he reached for the soap one last time to wash his face.

"Would you hand me another shampoo, hon?" he asked, spitting soap bubbles as he talked.

Fay went to the closet and picked out the shampoo from among the tubes of caulking compound and Superglue. As Arnie opened the shower door, a puff of steam escaped and swirled around her. She put the shampoo in his hand.

"That the right one?"

He nodded. "Thanks," he said, and closed the door.

The misty cloud picked up a faint medicinal scent.

"God, this feels good," he called to her. "Want to get in here with me?"

She shook her head and sat back down on the hamper. He stood directly under the water now, rinsing his hair first, then turning around to rinse his face and the rest of his body. When the soap was gone, he just stood there, letting the water pound him.

"Great," he said. "Just great. Best thing in the world."

"It's seven-thirty, Arnie," she said.

"Christ!" He turned off the water, opened the door, and stepped out onto the rug. "Good morning," he said.

"Feel better?" she asked.

He reached for a towel. "I look pretty good for an old man, don't you think?"

"Why do you think I'm sitting here?"

"Don't blame you a bit," he said, and wrapped the towel around his waist. "Did you try Lizzie again?"

"No," Fay said, stepping out of her shoes and taking off her dark stockings.

"Why not?"

"She's not there, Arnie."

"How do you know unless you call?"

"I know."

"Want me to call, just in case?"

"No," she said. "Thanks." She unbuttoned her blouse and walked out of the bathroom to find a hanger for it. "Lizzie's not a virgin, though. You were right about that."

"Of course I was." He reached blindly for the hand towel.

"How did you know?" she asked, coming back in wearing her half-slip and bra.

He dried his face, hung the towel back up neatly, turned to her, and sighed with pleasure. He slipped his hands under her bra straps and eased them gently down over her shoulders. "I know Lizzie's not a virgin," he said, "because she's got your body. And young men"—he let his fingers trail along the lacy edge of her bra until they came to rest on the clasp between her breasts—"young men"—he undid the clasp, eased the bra away, and cupped her breasts in his hands— "young men," he whispered, "are not so different from old men."

"I don't know why you keep calling yourself old," she said, as she stepped out of her slip and panties.

He opened the medicine cabinet to get his comb. "Because old people don't work," he said, looking in the mirror. "If I'm old, then I don't have to work." He ran the comb through his wet hair. "All I have to do is catch fish and get laid."

"Well, you don't look old," she said.

"Go on," he said, opening the glass door for her. "Get in the shower. I'm getting older by the minute."

She smiled. He was getting *something* by the minute, that was obvious, but it wasn't older.

Fay stepped into the shower. Arnie blew her a kiss through the door, and went to the kitchen for his coffee.

FAY KNEW SHE would never enjoy a shower the way Arnie did, the way men did. Women, she thought, women just get clean in the shower. Men *play* in the water. It's no trouble for men to get wet. That's the difference. It's fun. Men and children.

Lizzie was awake now, Fay could feel it. She didn't even have to shut her eyes this time. They were standing in the boat's galley. Not Lizzie and Paul. Lizzie and Paul's mother, Mrs. . . . What? What was her name? Ah. Honey. God. Honey. Lizzie was watching Honey crack eggs into a fine old copper bowl.

"What does your father do?" Honey asked, handing Lizzie a wedge of Parmesan and a grater.

"I don't know," Lizzie answered. "He ran off."

"Oh, I'm so sorry."

"That's all right," Lizzie said. "We weren't all that crazy about him."

Lizzie was lying. They'd been wild about her father. Both of them. Wild about him.

"Careful of your fingernails, darling," Honey said, reminding herself to buy a food processor for the boat. Lizzie put the cheese down on the counter and stepped out of the way while Honey finished the job correctly.

Fay was desperate to know where the boat was going.

"Where are we going?" Lizzie asked.

"Oh, didn't Paul tell you?" Honey asked. "California."

"Aren't we going in the wrong direction?" Lizzie laughed.

"Darling," Honey said patiently, "you can't go the other direction by boat. It's almost solid land the whole way."

"Yes." Lizzie smiled. "So I've heard."

"How long do you think you'll be with us?" Honey asked, turning the heat on under the omelet pan.

"Is there any way for me to get off?"

"If you were desperately ill," Honey said, pressing a buzzer to call the steward, "we could call the coast guard for a helicopter. But the last time we had to do that, they said we'd have to pay for it from now on."

"Well," Lizzie said brightly, backing out of the narrow room toward the stairs, "so far, I feel just fine."

Fay washed herself quickly and turned off the water. That was enough. The girl was gone. Happily gone. Gone off on every girl's kidnap fantasy come true. Somebody will come get me, it goes. Somebody who knows I don't belong here. Somebody who knows what I really want. Somebody who has nothing to do but play with me. Somebody who never says no. Somebody fun.

FAY WALKED OUT of the bathroom and into Arnie's bedroom.

"Feel better?" he asked from the bed.

"Lizzie isn't coming back," Fay said, opening his closet and pulling out the blue cotton robe she gave him last summer. "They've sailed for California."

"The Chief said the boat isn't scheduled to leave till tonight."

"They left." Fay said. "She's gone."

"Do you want me to call and check?" he asked, putting the newspaper on the night table and reaching for his coffee cup.

"No."

"She'll be back," Arnie said. "I promise. She's all right."

Fay nodded. She'd said the same thing to Gail.

She had to try to think about something else. "I don't know why you don't like this robe."

"I do like it," he said. "It's just that I don't wear robes. But if I'm ever sick, I'll be real glad I have it, love."

She walked over to the window. "I always give people the wrong things," she said, wrapping the venetian-blind cord around her finger. "For years I've given you these . . ."

Arnie was friendly but firm. "Fay," he said "we love the things you give us."

She turned to face him. "But why don't I know what you want? I know all this useless stuff, like a lady shows up for a reading and I know she hurt her back that morning falling off a ladder in her closet, but I don't know what Lizzie wants for her birthday, or what you want for your birthday, or what you and Lizzie *don't* want for your birthdays."

"Please, Fay," he said, extending his hand to her.

"What, hon?" she asked simply, dropping the cord and turning around to face him.

"Please come love me. Please don't worry about birthdays or Lizzie right now. Just let me have an hour, or half an hour, even. You have the whole day to hate yourself if you feel like it. I just have this one hour and then I have to go back to work. Please," he said, "I need you."

She walked toward him, slipping off the robe.

"That's better," he whispered.

They had loved so long and so well that sometimes, like now, just looking was enough to bring them to an aching readiness. But this long love had also taught them how to wait, how to linger in the memories of other nights, other days, other afternoons. His eyes fell from her face to her slim neck and smooth shoulders to the fullness of her breasts. He approved as her nipples rose to meet his gaze, their tawny coral still a miracle of coloration to him.

Just looking, he could taste them. It was summer; there would be a hint of salt this morning, and a trace of soap, then finally, in the shadows under her breasts, he would find the warm scent of camellias, a fragrance she had used for so long her skin would yield it now, even fresh from the shower.

"What are you looking for?" she asked, easing one knee up on the bed.

"Oh, you know," he said, accepting her breezy invitation, his eyes sweeping the widening triangle between her thighs. "Peace of mind."

She smiled. The list of his answers to this question was as long as their love. She took his cock in her hands and stroked it, peacefully at first, then more deliberately until it swelled in her hands.

He began to float, moored only by his manhood. He was a boy, a boy in a dream, feeling the sun's pulsing heat as it began to burn its way through the morning haze. Her fingers circled him languidly, urging the flesh to tighten further still.

He reached for her, for something to hold on to, for her arms, then her waist, and pulled her gently forward. "Ah," he gasped, the sudden silkiness of her skin registering in his brain like an electric shock.

"Yes," she breathed, slipping down over him into the heat and the wetness that was no longer clearly his or hers.

"Please," he said, "I need a few of my brains for the rest of the day."

"No you don't," she said. "You like this, remember?"

"I remember," he said.

He knew what she was going to do now: glide up and then down, her hands planted on his shoulders, her body luring him away from his mind, his past, his life, and into his own pulsing heartbeat. He loved the sound of it, the lapping, tidal rhythm of it.

He opened his eyes to watch. His lips parted slightly, no longer under his control, and he looked into her eyes, and directly, he thought, down into her heart. She knew him so well, how could he not love her? He blinked, as two quick tears filled the outside corners of his eyes. He didn't know why that happened, but he didn't mind it. Just that it was out of place. We can't cry over this. It's not the last time, it's just another morning together.

He pulled her down to lie on top of him, then wrapped his arms around her, rolled over, and lifted himself high above her. He paused a moment.

"Do you want to start over," he asked, "or shall I go on?" She didn't answer him. She never did. And he always took that to mean he should go on. It was a silly question, but one he enjoyed asking.

Fay felt him relax, heard his easy, assured sigh, and knew he was going to take his time here. Sometimes there was an urgency he made no effort to control, but today he would leisurely drive her up to the edge and then quite good-naturedly push her over. If there were an accrediting organization for this, Arnie would be a life master.

His was not the giddy agitation she remembered in young men, or the noisy exhortation, the somber preparation, endless narration, or frenzied determination she had, unfortunately, shared with others. With Arnie it was all effortless, uncomplicated pleasure. He was a born lover, a natural in bed. It seemed like something he'd always known how to do. He never consciously showed off his skills. He may not have even known he had them. He was just perfectly at home between her legs. In fact he was so goddamn comfortable with it all that sometimes Fay half expected to hear him start whistling.

She shifted slightly under him and felt a tongue of fire

race between them as her movement forced him deeper inside her.

"God, you feel good," he said, and lowered himself onto her. She wrapped both legs around his waist. "I could do this all day," he said.

"I know," she whispered, licking the beads of moisture from his neck.

"I don't know why anybody ever does anything else." He brushed his tongue behind her ear, then skimmed up along her temples, as though nothing were going on below, as though they were just beginning. And then he found her mouth, slipped his tongue under hers, circled around to her throat, and dared her to breathe. She knew there was no going back now, and knew that he did not want her to wait for him.

For all the things Fay saw in her life, her visions in bed with Arnie were her favorites. She'd never told Arnie about these accompaniments, but guessed he was probably doing the same thing. When he didn't want to come, he'd told her, he thought about laying roof tile. So it was reasonable to assume that when he *did* want to come, there was also something he thought about.

She saw herself leaning back against the railing of a boat. It was night, there was a moon. There was another boat, a little way off in the water. There was a man standing at the railing of that boat. He saw her. She wore a loose gauze robe which fluttered in the soft breeze to disclose her bareness, which robe was tied only at the neck, which tie she loosed as he watched.

Her hand stirred on her thigh, then drifted in open suggestion across her pale skin to comb lazily through her thick chestnut ruff.

Another man, her companion on the boat, emerged naked from the shadows, or from the cabin—she never quite knew where he came from, or who he was, even. He brushed the robe away from her hips and spread her legs with his hands.

The man watching from the other boat lit a cigarette, signaling his attention. But her own was now drawn sharply to the throbbing flesh suddenly thrust into her from the darkness. She gasped from the insistence of the entry, the immediate, unyielding demand.

She grabbed the railing with both hands. She couldn't breathe, she couldn't see, she could only gulp the black air and utter cries of surging need, cries that were clearly heard by the man on the other boat. The ringing in her ears pitched higher and higher, the pressure coursing from its white-hot center, ripping up her spine, clawing at her neck, and finally stabbing through the back of her brain to find the hairbreadth trip wire and detonating a massive explosion, blasting and shattering a brilliant blue star into the empty black sky of her mind. Its particles shimmered silently for an instant, then floated weightlessly out into the universe.

Arnie stroked her hair gently, brushing the wet curls around her temples back into place.

"Was that nice?"

She didn't answer. She was still trying to get her breath.

"It was nice to watch," he said.

"It was nice, Arnie," she said, relieved to find that she could still talk.

"I don't think I'll come today," he said. "I'll come tomorrow."

"What if we can't be here tomorrow?" she managed.

"No," he said, "I want you to stay till tomorrow. Stay right here till tomorrow." He rose up on his hands so she could breathe more easily. "You won't be bored, I promise. We'll take it real easy, like we're screwing for charity and we get a thousand dollars an hour."

"Oh, you think you can last another hour, do you?" she asked, with a little laugh.

"I do."

She put her fingers in her mouth, then stroked her nipples, pulled them toward him like an offering, and watched his brain give way, watched it run for cover as his eyes took in the sight below him.

He watched as long as he could, until his eyes glazed, until his head was spinning, until he released his control, his driving hips no longer restrained, no longer considerate and masterful but loosed to their fury, wild in their rush toward the quivering, wondrous satisfaction he claimed so regularly.

And in the quiet that followed, a cool morning breeze blew across them. He kissed her cheek. She smoothed his forehead, then wrapped her arms around him tenderly.

"How old did you say you were?" she asked.

"I forget," he said.

"Well, that's all you forget."

"Is that a compliment?" His eyes were still closed.

"It is."

"Thanks."

"You're welcome," she said. "Anytime."

"How about tomorrow?" he asked.

"Tomorrow is good," she said.

"All right, then." He sighed, easing himself up, then over to rest beside her on the bed. "It's a date." He found her hand, squeezed it, and they drifted into a familiar double sleep they both knew would be the last luxury of the new day.

8:00 A.M.

THE MAYOR WAS WAITING IN HIS LIMOUSINE ON
the tarmac when Vi's plane landed. The other
passengers didn't understand why they had
to wait while she got off first, but they'd
watched enough movies to be mildly intrigued by the scene.
Through his car window, the Mayor looked at their heads,
framed in the portholes, as they followed her down the ramp
and over to his car. When Peter realized he was watching
them instead of his wife, he wondered what that meant.

An aide opened the car door for her, and she sat down
without saying anything. He leaned over to kiss her, but
before he could get there, she reached for the button to close
the window behind the driver.

The Mayor sat back as the window sealed them in. He
wanted to hold her, he wanted to be an ordinary man in pain.
But she was never very receptive in the morning. Maybe
he'd start off with the good news. That should make her feel
better, he thought.

He rolled his newspaper into a tube and tapped his knee
with it as he talked. "There's wonderful news," he said, as
they drove off. "Fay Morgan just found the first two."

"You don't mean that fortune teller," Vi said.

"That's her," he said. "One of the other mothers is a
good friend of hers. She got right on it."

Vi was not pleased. "Peter, for God's sake, can't we do
better than a fortune teller?"

"Vi, she found two of the children already."

"What are the police doing?" she snapped. "Shuffling her cards for her?"

"Vi, Vi," Peter said, "they're doing everything they can. But Fay thinks—"

"I don't want to hear what Fay thinks," Vi said. "I want you to find my boys." She opened her purse. "How much money would the city pay?"

"As ransom, you mean?"

"Yes, as ransom," she sighed.

He thought a moment. "I don't think the city can pay anything. If the kidnappers ask for a ransom, we'd have to pay it ourselves."

"You're the Mayor!" she said.

He wished he had sent one of his aides to get her. Let somebody else fill her in on the details before he saw her. He could've been waiting at his desk, she could've come in, closed the door behind her, and walked into his arms.

"The city can't pay a ransom, Vi," he said. "I wouldn't even ask."

"What about the other parents? Do they have any money?"

"Maybe the kidnappers don't want money," he said.

"What else is there, Peter?" she asked, wishing he would wake up about all of this.

They rode for a while without saying anything. The Mayor wanted to ask her how her speech went, or how the flight was, or even if she'd had breakfast yet. He wanted to ask questions for which there were answers. He had been expecting her to cry, but now he was beginning to fear she wouldn't.

Finally, he forced himself to talk. "I have to tell you what Fay thinks because you might get a question about it from the press."

But Vi still didn't want to hear it. "You never should've gotten involved with that woman. All she wants is publicity for herself. It's my boys who are gone, but who's getting all the attention? She is."

"She found two girls!" he said. "Isn't that *worth* some attention, Vi?"

"All right," she muttered, reaching in her purse for her hairbrush. "What does Miss Fay think?"

"She thinks it's about abortion," he said. "And that you might be the real target of this whole thing. She thinks they want to force you to take back your position on abortion, and admit that it's a crime. Make a public statement or something."

"Well," Vi said quickly. "I could have told you that." She brushed her hair.

"What do you mean?" he asked.

"We've been expecting something like this," she said.

"Who has?" he asked, not following her at all.

"We have," she said, "in the movement. We're targets. We always have been."

"You haven't been in the movement long enough to be a target."

"No." She smiled. "But I have a position now."

"What position?" he asked. "Did something happen at the convention?"

"I'm your wife," she said. "Remember?"

He remembered all right. His staff had talked to him several times about her pro-abortion stand. It could hurt him in the next campaign, they said.

But he had known it was no use asking Vi to abandon it. Sure, he wished she'd adopted some other cause, like handicapped children, or Meals-on-Wheels, but he couldn't ask that, either. So he simply told her that he couldn't go with her when she spoke on the subject, and he couldn't co-sign the letters of appreciation she wrote to abortion clinics.

He was, in fact, pro-abortion himself. That is, he believed it should be available to women who needed it. He knew there were families who couldn't afford more children, and teenagers who were too young to be mothers, and any number of other situations where lives would be saved by it.

But abortion was a hard thing to fight for in an election. It was hard to pound the lectern and campaign for it. He admired the people who did, but he couldn't. He just hoped the Supreme Court would stay strong about it. The truth was, he thought, nobody likes to think about it, nobody wants abortion to be necessary. It makes you kind of sick to think about it. And it makes us sad that we don't have enough money or space or time or love for all the children we make, but the fact is, we don't. Better not to have them than have them grow up knowing there really isn't any place for them.

Abortion is for the Supreme Court to uphold, he thought. Politicians have to get elected, have to represent *all* the people; they can't always say what they believe. But the

Supreme Court only has to say what's right. They can protect
the option of abortion in the name of freedom, in the understanding of human error, in the faith in a second chance.
Only the Supreme Court can ensure the safety of the women
of this country. Everybody else is just too human.

The Mayor's limousine turned off the expressway now
and headed for City Hall.

"Did you fire him yet?" Vi asked.

"Fire who?"

"That aide who lost my boys."

"Vi," he said, "I can't fire him without letting the kidnappers know that two of the children are ours."

She turned on him in shock and anger. "What did you
say?"

He unrolled the newspaper, and showed her the twenty-
five pictures. "I kept Kevin and Kerry's names out of it," he
said. "We decided it was—"

"*Who* decided?"

"The staff and I decided—"

"Why didn't you tell me this last night?" she screamed.

He tried to talk calmly. "We didn't really decide till—"

But she wouldn't let him finish. "You mean I'm supposed to *pretend* my boys are in school today?" She was wild
with rage.

He looked at her. "Yes," he said.

She couldn't believe it. She just couldn't believe it.
"Don't I have anything to say about this at all?"

"I could be wrong, Vi, but I just don't think it's a good
idea for the kidnappers to know who they have. It will be
easier to get all the children back if it doesn't get political."

"It's political already, Peter."

"Well, I don't have to give them the platform," he said.

"You don't want to give *me* the platform," she said.

"Or you either," he said. "That's right. I want to try to
keep this as ordinary as possible, an ordinary, terrible crime.
And the city is going to solve it, get the children back, and
punish the criminals, not because they took the Mayor's
boys, but because they took the city's children." He paused.
"I'm asking you to go along with us as long as you can."

"You're not asking," she said, "you're telling."

"Well," he said, and thought a minute. "Yes. I guess I
am."

The car pulled into the alleyway that was the Mayor's private entrance. The guards at the street saluted, the sidewalk was lined with photographers. Two aides opened their doors, and the Mayor and Vi, having nothing further to say to each other, got out of their respective sides of the car.

FAY WAS AWAKE, but she hadn't decided what to do about it yet. Her eyes opened, found they were not able to stay open by themselves, and closed again slowly. Arnie was still snoring quietly, lying on his side facing the wall. She considered getting up, but there really wasn't anything to do in Arnie's apartment. He didn't subscribe to any magazines, or have any plants she could water, or cats she could feed. There wasn't any juice in the refrigerator, and she couldn't make any phone calls without waking him, so what was the point of getting up?

She rolled over and curled around him. He moved slightly, apparently aware of her presence on some level, but not, she realized as he resumed snoring, on any interesting level. So she turned back to her side of the bed, opened her eyes again, and stared at the ceiling.

And though she didn't want to see Paul and Lizzie, there they were, or there he was, anyway, waiting for her on the deck of the boat, his loose white shirt and khaki shorts just the thing for a beautiful day at sea.

"You didn't tell me we were going to California!" Lizzie said, grinning as she came up the stairs.

"You didn't ask," he said. "But once I saw you last night, I couldn't leave without you. Who knew where you would be when I got back?"

"I'm kidnapped," she said, picking up her shirttails and tying them in a knot above her waist.

"A slight deception, I'll admit," he said. "But I'm weak."

He motioned toward that silver-haired man reading a stack of telexes that had come through during the night. "Dad wanted me on board. Maybe because it's a new boat, but there really isn't that much for me to do." He stroked her hair. "If they bother you, we can just let them fly home from St. John's or someplace, and take it the rest of the way by ourselves."

"Do you live in California?" she asked.

"They do, some of the time."

Lizzie smiled. She enjoyed this slippery talk. "Where do you live, Paul?"

"Oh, you know," he smiled. "Wherever."

"Are we going through the canal?" she asked.

"Yes," he said. "But we'll stop in Bermuda, maybe, and St. John's to see people, and possibly St. Martin's too, but I doubt it. Dad doesn't like it there much anymore."

"Why not?" she asked.

"I don't know. Something about a woman, I think."

"What if there's a storm?" Lizzie asked.

My question exactly, Fay thought.

"If there's a storm," Paul said, leaning over to kiss her forehead, "we'll go inside."

"What does your father do?" Lizzie asked.

"He reads his mail and makes calls."

"Is that what you're going to do?"

"When I grow up, you mean?"

She laughed. He shook his head.

"I'm not going to grow up," he said. "Hungry?"

"Starving."

Paul took her arm and escorted her toward the stairs to the top deck. His father put down his papers, smiled at Lizzie, nodded to Paul indicating his approval of her, and followed them up.

Fay closed her eyes and felt a little dense for not seeing the resemblance before.

Lizzie's father wouldn't grow up either. No wonder Fay was afraid of this boy. When somebody you've lost to once before shows up again, you can't help but be afraid.

ED, LIZZIE'S FATHER, had been lean, like Paul, and smooth. He moved like a skiff skimming the water on a cloudless day. He danced like a dreamer and loved as if the world owed him his pleasure and his only obligation was to share it.

Fay was not what you'd call popular in high school. She didn't look like the rest of the girls. Her hair was wildly out of control and her mother refused to let her cut it. She already had a woman's body, but it didn't fit the girls' clothes that were handed down to her. She was ashamed of it. Ed Conley would change all that.

The night they met it was late fall, and she was seventeen. She didn't remember why she'd gone with her religious sister to the church youth group's hayride, but it was probably as simple as not having anything else to do.

She saw him right away, standing a little apart from the crowd. The other boys were gathered around a black Corvette convertible parked in front of the church. They inspected the tires, and one boy cleaned the rearview mirror with his shirttail. Two of them bounced the rear bumper and whistled in awe of something they called the suspension. They pressed their faces against the windows and drooled at the black leather interior. Then stood back up and giggled about how it wasn't a good car for a drive-in, but who'd want to go to the movies when you had that car to ride around in?

The kids didn't know who it belonged to, but Fay guessed it must be Ed's. She watched as he watched them. He was keeping his distance from these youngsters.

The hayride truck was parked directly behind his Corvette, but the other kids were staying well clear of it. They wouldn't even look at it, much less lean on it as he was doing. The old farm truck waited, mysterious and forbidden, like something they had to be invited into by the adults, like some shifting and not altogether safe bed.

Yes. They were all going to jump into bed together, but not until the counselor said to. They were going to climb up into the hayloft in God's name. But who knew whose name they would be calling when they came down again.

Most of these kids had grown up together in that church, learned their Bible verses together, presented Christmas pageants together, and given themselves to Christ as a group when they were eleven. Now they were fifteen, sixteen, some of them seventeen, and God was no longer who they wanted to be one with.

Fay asked her sister who was the dark-haired boy leaning up against the truck.

"He's a hood," her sister said.

"I can see that," Fay said. "What's his name?"

"I don't know," the sister said. "Ask Miss Thompson."

"Who's Miss Thompson?"

Her sister looked at Fay in utter despair. Why had she brought her along anyway? Was she going to ask stupid questions all night?

"Miss Thompson," the sister sighed, "is the head of the youth group. Over there. Wearing the scarf." And she walked away from Fay to join the other girls.

Just then, Miss Thompson saw the truck driver come out of the liquor store across the street, where he had gone, he said, to buy cigarettes. She waved to her co-leader, the new young assistant minister—new to the church, that is, but not new to Miss Thompson.

Years ago, when his team won the state basketball championship, she'd cut his picture out of the newspaper and stuck it in her mirror. She'd seen him again during college, when the Christian Athletes set up a booth on the beach in Florida. He was beyond her now, having married a girl from somewhere back East, but she was not beyond asking for his help with this hayride.

With the truck driver assisting, the minister lowered the tailgate of the big old truck. Miss Thompson checked the kids' names off the list as they climbed up into the hay. Fay managed to get behind the unknown hood, so she could hear his name.

"It's Ed Conley," he said, as Miss Thompson looked at her clipboard. "But I'm probably not on your list."

"Well, you sure are now, Eddie," Miss Thompson said brightly. "How did you hear about us?"

"The preacher knows my dad," Ed said, grabbing one side of the truck.

"Do you know anyone else here?" Miss Thompson asked.

"No," he said, putting one foot up on the truck. "But it looks like I'm about to."

"Well, wait a minute," Miss Thompson said, turning him around to face Fay. "This is Fay Morgan. She doesn't come with us as often as she should, but we like her anyway."

"Fay?" Ed asked. "That's your name?"

"Yes," Fay said.

"I like it," Ed said, and put his hands around her waist and lifted her up into the truckbed. Then he jumped up himself, easy as a cat, and led her to the far corner, knowing that the minister and Miss Thompson would sit at the back to make sure nobody fell out.

"Are you going to be warm enough?" he said, tugging gently at the thin sleeve of her blouse.

"I don't know," she said. "Is it going to get cold?"

"It might," he said. "You let me know."

"What will you do?" she asked. "You can't give me your jacket because you're not wearing a jacket."

Suddenly, she was shoved into him, as two girls standing in front of them held hands and flopped down in the hay on the count of three.

"If it really gets bad," he said, putting one arm around her, "I'll steal one of *their* jackets for you." And he pointed to the windbreakers and junior varsity letter jackets the well-prepared boys' mothers had reminded them to wear. They both laughed. These other people were children, they were not. Ed was comfortable with that knowledge, even casually proud of it. Fay felt very calm all of a sudden. She'd known she didn't belong here, but it took this hoodlum to show her why.

As the truck pulled away from the curb, the singing started. Neither Ed nor Fay knew any of the hymns or camp songs, but it didn't bother them to listen. When they stopped for traffic lights, people in cars would roll down their windows and clap for this beat-up choir truck, and wish they were kids again. Then they'd turn around and tell their own kids to shut up in the backseat and think how much nicer other people's children were.

At one point the truck took a corner too fast to suit Miss Thompson, and the girls squealed as they were all thrown across the truck onto the boys. Fay's head fell against Ed's chest; he wrapped both arms around her, pulling her on top of him under the cover of the pileup.

The young minister stood up at the back of the truck. "Anybody hurt up there?" he called. Then he saw that the tangle of bodies was straightening out by itself, thanks to good manners and all those years in church. He leaned back against the slatted sides of the truck and decided to ride standing up for a while.

Miss Thompson didn't want him to think she was just going to roll around in the hay like a teenager, for God's sake, so she stood up beside him.

"Who are those two?" he asked, noticing Fay and Ed curled up next to each other in the corner.

"He's new," she said, and remembered what the senior minister had told her. "His dad's a drunk. She's Doris Morgan's sister."

"Do you think I should go sit with them?" he asked, suspecting that some liberties were being taken up there.

"If they like each other," Miss Thompson said, patting his chest to reassure him, "we'll have two new regulars, won't we?"

The minister looked down at Miss Thompson. He didn't blame her for wanting to touch him, he just hoped it was all in the spirit of Christian fellowship.

Suddenly, one very thin girl in pigtails asked the new minister if there were any mice in the hay. He said there probably were a few, but they were little ones, and everybody screamed. Two of the boys shouted that they saw one and started burrowing through the hay to catch it. All Miss Thompson could think of to get control of the situation was to start singing. So she launched into a chorus of "Since Jesus Came Into My Heart." She knew they couldn't resist that, and she was right. Pretty soon the burrowing boys were doing no more than sneezing, and everybody else was singing.

The truck bounced off the main road and onto the gravel path that led back through the truck driver's fields. Somebody spotted the bonfire, and kids stood up all along the sides, watching as they approached the glowing spot in the middle of the pasture.

Fay started to stand up, but Ed pulled her further back into the corner. "I sure am glad you're here," he whispered.

"Me too," she said. And he squeezed her closer to him, turned his head toward her, and brought her lips to his for an easy kiss. Nobody saw, because they were all watching the bonfire. Nobody, that is, except Fay's sister, who was horrified.

Later, around the fire, while Miss Thompson passed out marshmallows and the truck driver showed the boys how to whittle the end of a stick into a point, Fay's sister let her have it.

"I saw you kiss him," she snorted.

"*He* kissed *me*," Fay said.

"You liked it. I saw you like it."

"It was your idea for me to come here," Fay said.

"It wasn't my idea for you to start necking with a greaseball," her sister said, full of contempt.

"I'm not necking and he's not a greaseball," Fay said.

"Don't you know what people say about him?" Doris asked.

"How do you know what people say about him?" Fay asked. "While ago, you said you didn't know him. Now you're telling me you've heard people talk about him. Make up your mind, Doris."

"They say terrible things about him," Doris said, "but that's nothing compared to what they're going to say about you."

"I don't care what they say," Fay said. "I don't like them anyway."

"I'm going to tell Mother," Doris said.

"Fine," Fay said. "Tell Mother. Then I'll never have to go to church with you again."

Doris realized there was no point in talking to Fay anymore. If Fay wanted to ruin her reputation with a hoodlum, that was fine with her. Fay wasn't aware that she had a reputation to ruin. She was only aware that Ed was waiting for her back by the truck.

"Want to have a smoke?" he asked.

"I don't smoke," she said, "but I'll wander off with you, if that's the idea."

"That's the idea." He grinned.

"Why did you come here?" she asked him, as they headed for a clump of trees.

"My dad's drunk tonight," he said. "I like to get my car out of the driveway when he's drunk."

"I *thought* it was your car," she said. "How did you get it?"

"I bought it," he said.

"Well, I didn't think you stole it," she said.

"Somebody else stole it," he said. "I bought it from them."

Fay was quiet a moment, trying to sort out the ethics.

"It takes a lot of work to keep it running," he said.

"Is that what you do, work on cars?" she asked.

"It's good work," he said.

"I didn't say it wasn't."

"I'm not used to talking so much," he said.

"We don't have to talk then," she said. "It's all right."

"Do you want a ride home?" he asked.

"Yes," she said. It was easy to say, it was all she could say, all she would say for six years.

On the trip home in the truck they had their spot in the

corner again, but by that time the new minister had had enough of Miss Thompson's fellowship, and sat down. Right next to Ed, in fact.

Ed and the new minister talked about basketball, but all the time they were talking, Ed had his hand down the back of Fay's pedal pushers, between her panties and her skin, and she didn't dare move or everybody, including her sister who was sitting directly in front of her, would see it. It wasn't that he did anything, exactly. It was that he knew where he was. And if Fay had ever thought that nobody could stay interested in her round little behind for twenty minutes, well, she was wrong.

When the truck reached the church, Fay told Doris that Ed was taking her home, and that was the last real conversation the sisters ever had. Doris didn't come to the wedding, even. Over the years, Fay heard from their mother that Doris was praying for her, but Fay never knew precisely what Doris was asking for.

When Ed unlocked the door of the Corvette in front of the church, seven boys gasped. The one who'd cleaned the rearview mirror nearly fainted. But Ed took no notice of them. He sat down behind the wheel, reached across to the glove compartment, got out the gray-tinted glasses he wore to protect his eyes, handed an extra pair to Fay, started the engine, and tore away from the curb, leaving the boys and girls dumbstruck on the sidewalk.

That Fay slept with him that night was a given. The surprise was that he called her the next day, and the day after that, and there wasn't one day from that night to the night of her father's funeral when she didn't want him. Want to be around him, want to look at him, want to go to bed with him. When she got pregnant, they got married. He said he didn't mind. He said he always figured he would marry.

So yes, Fay knew about men who wouldn't grow up, and she wished she could tell Lizzie, warn her. But she knew Lizzie wouldn't listen any more than she had listened.

A man like this is so wildly attractive, so maddeningly alive, that he is absolutely irresistible. In the Tarot deck, he is the Fool; he sits, depending on the deck, either at the beginning or the end of the picture cards. When these major arcana cards are placed in a circle, describing, as the Tarot sees it, the journey we all must take, it's clear we're all going to love at least one fool in our lives, and it's probably both the end and the beginning.

In the picture on the card, the Fool, like a hobo, carries a sack tied to a stick. They leave you, these men, but they never said they were staying, never said they were committed, or purposeful—or responsible, even. All they want is to have a good time. And what's wrong with that? Nothing, except you begin to wonder how interested *you* are in having a good time. You begin to think you might not even be capable of having a good time for very long, and there's plenty wrong with that.

The joy of being with these men is the giddy return, through them, to a child's world, where there are no clocks and no claims on your time, no clothes to be kept clean, and no consequences to be considered. Days and nights are filled with the silliness, the spontaneity, the conspiratorial privacy, and all the breathless secret pleasures of life in a tree house.

Girls, as we know, are rarely allowed in tree houses, so the invitation, when it comes, can't be refused. You're curious at first, and then giddy about the prospect of actually belonging. It can take quite a while before you realize you don't know what you do up there all day. When you ask what else there is to do besides play, well, then you see the other side of these men.

They don't always come home, and they won't ever apologize for it. They won't help around the house because they like it all messed up. They won't work very hard because they don't want to get trapped by success. And they won't work at the relationship because it's not supposed to be work, it's supposed to be fun. If you don't want to play with them, they don't mind. But that isn't going to stop them from playing.

Somehow, they make you feel very old, these men. They turn you into their mother.

On the Tarot card, a cat is nipping at the Fool's pants legs, pulling them down to expose his bottom. He is walking toward a fallen obelisk. When he gets there, the crocodile hiding behind the obelisk will eat him. You can see that he's walking blind and bare-assed right into the mouth of destruction. But *he* can't. He can't see the crocodile. You know the outrageous stupidity of simply following the road. You know he's making a terrible mistake. But he thinks, God save him, he's having a good time.

You have to tell him. You have to warn him what's ahead. But when you do, he leaves you. He strolls out of your life as aimlessly and happily as he wandered into it.

This card always troubled Fay when it came up in a reading. What is a mistake compared to the other evils the Tarot cautions against? What's the matter with a little light-hearted folly now and then? What is life without it?

Should she try to keep people from making mistakes, from being foolish? Was it even possible? Weren't people going to make mistakes no matter what she said? And what was a mistake anyway?

Was it a mistake to marry that black-haired boy whose arms were lean and strong? No. She would have been a fool not to fall for him. Was it a mistake to get pregnant? Not if the baby grew up to be Lizzie, it wasn't. If it was foolish to love him, then she would give her very soul to be foolish again.

People could survive mistakes, and Fay didn't want to face a world without fools. She wished, in fact, she knew more of them. She wished she had one to call up right now. She wished Arnie would wake up and say something silly. She wished she could laugh and laugh and forget herself and everything else in the company of one exquisite fool.

FAY GOT OUT of the bed, found a blouse she'd left in Arnie's closet, and got dressed. She wanted to believe Paul was just a Fool, but he wasn't. He was the Devil. He wouldn't return Lizzie when he was finished with her. He would finish her off and move on.

Arnie stirred. "What time is it?"

"Quarter of nine," she said, going into the bathroom to brush her hair.

"My God." Arnie jumped out of bed. "Why didn't you wake me? We have to meet the Chief at Indian Point at nine."

"What if there's nothing out there?" Fay asked. She wanted to go to the harbor, see for herself if the boat was there. Find Lizzie.

"Look, honey." Arnie was throwing on his clothes now. "Nobody expects you to take us directly to these people. Every cop on the force is on the lookout. They've got the computer going crazy looking for parking tickets in front of the church, or anything that could be a lead. But I happen to believe that your hunches or instincts or whatever the hell you want to call them will get us there faster. If you say there's something about Indian Point, then we'll go there. And if it isn't there, then I'll just assume it went away while we were asleep."

He followed her into the bathroom, where she was trying to tame her hair. "I'm buying you breakfast either way, whether we find something or not, so what have you got to lose?"

"Lizzie," she said.

"I'll call right now," he said.

But suddenly Fay stopped brushing her hair; the brush had caught in a thick tangle, her eyes were caught by something in the mirror. "One of the kids is sick," she said.

He rushed back in the room. "What?"

"Asthma," she said. "One of the kids has asthma." She grabbed the edge of the sink. "Call headquarters. Tell them to alert the emergency rooms. He'll die without help."

Arnie raced to the phone. Fay closed her eyes. Her head hung limp as she clung to the sink. Why couldn't she see something good? Wasn't there anything good to see?

Fay found Arnie at the phone and motioned that she had something else to tell him. "They'll bring the boy in and leave him somewhere."

Arnie nodded. "He's on the list of missing kids, all right. All I had to say was asthma. His name is Timmy Willis. They're calling the parents right now. Anything else?"

"Blue shoes," she said.

Arnie spoke into the phone again, then listened and gave Fay the thumbs-up sign. "Blue shoes. That's our boy, all right."

"Tell them to hurry," she said quietly.

"O.K.," he said into the phone. "That's it for now. Every hospital in the city."

Arnie hung up and reached for Fay's hand. She looked so weary. Whatever she had seen had hurt.

"They wouldn't let him die, would they?" she asked.

"No, Fay, they wouldn't." He stroked the back of her hand. "Death in the course of a kidnapping is murder one."

"Arnie, they're not worried about *that*!" She pulled her hand away.

He went to the bedroom and closed the window. "Oh, I imagine they *are* worried about that."

She didn't like the tone of his voice. "Arnie," she said, "if they were worried about being punished, they'd never have done this in the first place."

"Well," he said, strapping on his holster, "I guarantee you they're thinking about it now."

"I don't think so," she said.

He stuck his badge in his pocket. "Then they don't know what they're up against," he said.

"The police force rides again," she said.

"You're damn right."

Fay felt a sudden chill. She spoke slowly. "And what will you do with these people, kill them?"

"If they hurt those children we will. You bet your ass we will."

Fay forced her head up. "He's not breathing, Arnie. Timmy Willis stopped breathing."

Arnie stopped cold. "Jesus Christ, Fay, are you sure?"

She stood up. "I'm sure."

"Let's go then," he said, handing her her purse. "We don't have another minute."

She wasn't ready to move yet. He took her hand.

"I'm sorry I got a little, you know, whatever."

"Coplike," she said.

"Yeah," he said.

"O.K.," she said. "Let's go."

Calling Lizzie would have to wait. Finding Lizzie would have to wait. Maybe Arnie was right. Maybe Lizzie would come home by herself. She wasn't a baby. Timmy Willis was a baby. And Timmy Willis was dying.

9:00 A.M.

WHEN THE DEATH CARD CAME UP IN A READING, Fay never said it meant a death. It did, of course, but if she said that, people always took it the wrong way, people overreacted to the word.

The card itself, not so coincidentally numbered thirteen, shows a skeleton reaping a harvest of heads, feet, and hands that have sprouted from the earth. He swipes a scythe across the field and smiles. The smile is because the Tarot is not talking about death in general, or about the death of a person, but rather the death of a project, a partnership, a way of thinking, a way of life. This Death, says the Tarot, will be the beginning of a transformation, the first step toward some new life.

"Something is coming to an end," Fay would say. Then she would look at the other cards to see how soon it would happen, then at the face of the client to see how much of a surprise it would be.

"Don't be afraid of it," she would say. "Things have to end. Things die to clear new space for other things. Just think of death as good housekeeping," she'd say. But that never went over very well.

"All right, then." She'd try again. "The thing about the future, death included, is that it's nothing new. Maybe, at the beginning, it was just a look on your face, or a difference of opinion. But it accumulated, like interest on a savings account, until finally there was enough of it to do something with. That's when you started calling it the present. When it keeps growing until there's so much of it you can't even begin to control it, then you'll call it the future. But there was a moment, way back there, when the future was a speck so tiny you didn't even notice it, or didn't take notice of it."

People didn't like that explanation either. It made them feel guilty, or dumb, for not doing something while there was still time.

"Well, look," she'd say finally, "whatever this is that dies on you, it's going to leave a vacuum. Nature abhors a vacuum. Something will fill it up."

"Yeah," they'd say, "like pain."

"Maybe," she'd say. "But maybe not as much as you think."

"Yeah," they'd say. "Maybe more."

Fay didn't know who said "Nature abhors a vacuum." Whoever said it was dead, though; she knew that much. Nobody said "abhor" anymore.

Finally, Fay would give up. "What is it?" she'd ask. "Your marriage?" That was a pretty safe guess these days.

"I don't know," they'd say.

Fay knew that meant yes.

"When is his birthday?" she'd ask. And when they told her, she would flip through the big red book of astrological tables to find out who the husband was.

Fay didn't know why the star tables were as accurate as they were. And it didn't matter to her. She used them because they helped. She didn't know why the cards worked, either. But then, whoever said that nature abhorred a vacuum probably didn't have a clue why *it* worked. It just did. And that was enough.

As soon as Fay had some feeling for the husband, she could see whether the ending the cards predicted was the end of the marriage, or just the end of this particular period in the marriage. Sometimes, in a marriage, people were simply going to school, taking an advanced course in some special area of the relationship. When the course was over, there would be a final exam, and then, a vacation. People already knew this about their marriages. Fay just helped them remember it.

A Death card meant a change, that was all. People don't like change either, but they like it better than death. What Fay believed, but never dared to say, was that a change required a death. She would love to meet the client she could say that to. Starting at that point, they could really get somewhere.

Fay's mother had understood that. "I'm changing," she had said. What she was doing, Fay knew, was dying. But "changing" was, as far as her mother was concerned, exactly what was happening. She'd changed before, and had always liked who she'd become, so there was no reason to be afraid of this one.

It had been months since her mother had sat in her rocker, longer than that since she'd crocheted. It was winter, and lying there on the bed her mother would, as she described it, "take little trips." She would leave her body under the covers and "go places." Fay would come into the room and nearly die herself, looking at the seemingly lifeless form beneath the sheet. Her mother warned Fay to check her pulse very carefully before calling the coroner. She didn't want her body carted off to the funeral home, then have her spirit return to the bedroom and not be able to find it.

Fay asked if that wouldn't be a way to cheat death after all, to have your spirit on the loose, with its bags checked conveniently in the locker downtown.

"No," her mother had said. "People don't pay any more attention to spirits than they do to old ladies."

"I would," Fay said.

"I know you would," her mother said. "But you've got your own life to lead now. I've taken up enough of it. It's time for me to go."

"Do you know what's going to happen to me?" Fay asked.

"I always have," her mother said.

"I know," Fay said. "Will you tell me?"

It was nearly dusk outside. What little light remained in the day filtered through the lace curtains, making rosette shadows on the bedspread. The walls receded into the darkness as Fay sat quietly, her chair pulled up close to the bed.

Her mother leaned back against the pillows. They hadn't talked about the coffin, or what her mother wanted to be buried in. But her mother had never slept on tufted pink satin, and she'd never, that Fay knew of, slept in her clothes. Fay wished, when the time came, that she could slip both mother and bed into a big cedar chest, eyelet covers and all.

Fay reached across to stroke her mother's withered hand. She could see the bones clearly, and knew that the skeleton which had, until recently, been in hiding, was about to shed its skin and emerge. It was waiting patiently for the pumping and gurgling to slow and then cease, for the rising tidal chest walls to fall for the last time, for the blinking electrical circuits to dim and flicker out.

And then, the last messages from the world received and filed, its work would be finished. The windows would be closed, and the white skeletal form would lie alone in the silence, in the creeping chill, in the red becoming black. The skeleton's length and form would be the only remaining evidence of the life it had upheld.

"What will happen to me?" Fay asked again softly.

Her mother moved her hand toward the drawer of the nightstand. "My cards," she said, her hand floating weightlessly down onto the bed.

Fay found them at the back of the drawer, wrapped in the old blue scarf they had been wrapped in for seventy years. They smelled faintly of camphor now, from the little vials and pots of salve her mother also kept in that drawer.

Fay placed the cards in her mother's hands, and the old woman unwrapped them carefully, then slowly but deftly tied the scarf loosely around her neck. Fay knew then that her mother was through taking her little trips; her spirit had found whatever it had been looking for, and was now content to help her over this next little rough place in the road.

Her mother handed the cards to Fay to shuffle, which she did, fighting back the tears that formed at the sight of this nearly bald white-haired woman in a long-sleeved white cotton gown, lying perfectly still with a never-washed, never-worn-but-wearing-thin blue silk scarf looping lazily at her neck.

"You have a great gift," her mother said, "and you'll start using it soon." She patted Fay's arm. "Just be sure to charge a lot of money." She smiled. "It's the only way they'll believe you. And don't tell people it's a mystery. Tell them it's a trick. Tell them they could do it. Tell them anybody could do it."

Fay couldn't answer, but cut the cards and dealt them, calling out their names. "Death, Justice, the Sun, the Falling Tower, the Wheel of Fortune, the High Priestess, the Hanged Man."

Her mother thought a minute. "That's good," she said. "There's a man. I want you to have a man."

"I don't know if I remember how," Fay said softly.

"There may not be a marriage," her mother said, "but there is a man."

Fay liked the idea of a man. Lizzie was getting old enough to be left with a sitter for an evening, and Fay missed the smell of a man. She missed how a man could pretend to know where he was going, and by pretending, get there.

"This man will not be the problem for you," her mother continued. "Lizzie will. But he'll help you take your mind off Lizzie."

"What about Lizzie?" Fay asked.

"Don't be fooled into thinking you can keep her safe."

Fay saw the Falling Tower but answered anyway. "I can try."

"She's not safe, Fay," her mother said. "She wasn't born safe. If you could find a way not to love her, that would protect *you*, anyway."

"None of us is safe, Mother."

"Oh yes," her mother said. "You are. You are perfectly safe. The world is your home. You know where everything is, where everything goes. Your only misfortune is that so many of the people you love are not safe at all."

"If they stay with me, will they be safe?"

"No, my love." Her mother made an effort to smile, as her eyes blinked open, then closed again. "Look at *me*."

Fay's tears fell freely now. Her mother was right. She had thought that by taking the old woman in, she could save her, she could keep her from falling on the ice, or prevent the pneumonia Fay had seen coming when her father died. And now she saw she couldn't. Finally, fearfully, she was watching her mother die. She was, she realized, about to lose her mother's life.

"Are you crying, Fay?" her mother asked, her eyes still closed.

"Yes, I am," Fay said.

"I'm sorry that you're crying," the old woman said slowly. "But I hope it makes you feel better."

And when Fay looked up, her mother was dead.

Fay reached for her mother's wrist and felt for a pulse, but she knew she wouldn't find one. After a moment, she lifted the lifeless palm to her lips and kissed it. Then Fay stroked her own face with her mother's hand. It was what her mother would have done if she could, what her mother had always done when Fay was sad. Smooth her hair back from her temples, slip her hand gently up to her forehead, feel for a fever.

With her mother's hand, Fay brushed her tears away, accepting the tender consolation granted so freely by those who are unable to help.

When Fay could stand up, she did, and left quietly, leaving the lights off in the room. Soon enough, someone would come in, need to see, and turn the lights on again. Fay and her mother didn't need them.

FAY'S TIP ABOUT Timmy Willis had gone out to all the squad cars, all the hospitals, all the walk-in clinics, and directly to the Mayor's office. The news wasn't released to the press, but they knew it anyway because they monitored the police radio.

Madonna Willis phoned Timmy's doctor to make sure he was available, and Ted came home from his real estate office to wait with her. Timmy was Madonna's red-haired elflike son from a former marriage. Ted had wanted to adopt the boy, but Timmy liked his real dad, a minor league pitcher with a fiery temper and a mean curve ball.

The call came in to police headquarters from dusty old St. Vincent's Hospital way out on the Brownsville Pike. A brown Ford station wagon had driven up to the front door and deposited Timmy Willis on the steps. Bobbie Jenkins, who had been sitting behind the reception desk for forty years, looked up from the Donahue show on TV in the lobby, saw the stricken boy, picked up the house phone first, and then activated the new automatic-dial function for the Emergency Medical Service. Even from the window, she recognized the symptoms: status asthmaticus. Her own mother had nearly died from an attack of it.

She was talking to the EMS when two orderlies and a

young intern rushed across the lobby. Several people waiting there tried to get out the door with the men in white suits, but Bobbie barked at them to back off. If they hadn't moved, they would have been run down by the inhalation therapist pushing his wobbly cart faster than was safe for either one of them.

What St. Vincent's had in the way of an emergency room was not much more than a first-aid station for the staff. All they could do was keep Timmy alive until the ambulance got there.

The orderlies brought Timmy inside and laid him down on the wide countertop right in front of Bobbie. They clamped the oxygen mask over his little blue face, and Bobbie reached over and squeezed his hand.

The young intern remembered that aminophylline could cause convulsions if the dosage was too high. Or was it theophylline? Or were they the same thing? Adrenalin should be safe enough, he decided, and called for an IV hookup.

Bobbie thought Timmy didn't look as blue as he had on the steps, but she worried it might just be the light. Then she heard the siren, and saw the ambulance racing around the circular drive to the front door. Two police cars followed, and a photographer jumped out of a black Honda that came in the driveway the wrong way.

The people in the lobby were wild with excitement. They felt like extras in a hospital show on TV.

While the EMS men transferred Timmy to the ambulance, the police asked Bobbie to describe the car. Did she get the license number? No. Could she describe anybody in the car? No. Well, did she remember how many people there were in the car? Two, maybe. Which direction did the car go? That way. How long ago was it? Ten minutes. Did she remember *anything* about the car? It was brown. What color brown? It had a strip of wood down the side of it. Any bumper stickers? Don't remember. Anything in the back window? There was something on the aerial. What? Like a little pompon. What about the paint? It was dirty. It had mud flaps on the wheels. All the wheels? Just the back.

Bobbie lit a cigarette. The administration had told her not to smoke at the desk anymore, but this was a moment when any smoker smokes, regardless.

The photographer had snapped about fifty shots of every-

thing, from Timmy on the stretcher to the begonias in the
concrete urns on either side of the steps. Now he wanted a
picture of Bobbie with the intern. She drank the last of her
grapefruit juice and put her cigarette out in the empty can.
The intern and the two orderlies stood behind her chair—the
photographer wanted a good view of the countertop—and
they all smiled.

The ambulance arrived at Duncan Memorial at 9:20, and
Timmy's doctor was there by 9:30. But Madonna and Ted
were caught in a traffic jam caused by construction on the
freeway. It would be the longest half hour either of them
ever spent in a car, and after this was all over, the first thing
they would do was sell that Subaru.

By the time Timmy's doctor found him in one of the
treatment rooms, the little elf was not only breathing, he was
crying. Seeing his doctor made him feel a little better. And
the doctor had thought to bring along the old yellow teddy
bear he kept in the office for the kids to hold on to. The
doctor was afraid Timmy might not recognize him, but he
knew the child would remember the ragged bear.

The other patients in the waiting area just outside the
treatment rooms had no idea why so many police were hanging around. They didn't seem to be sick. All they were doing
was bothering people for change for the candy machines.

Fay, sitting in the coffee shop at the Indian Point Shopping Center, didn't know Timmy had recovered. But she did
feel a little better. She thought it was the coffee.

THEIR BOOTH IN the coffee-shop window provided a perfect
view of the monstrous Indian. Fay figured his loincloth to be
at least five feet wide. She doubted if he was anatomically
correct underneath it, but she couldn't help wondering about
that. His nipples and boots were brown, his eyes were yellow, his hair black, and the blue streaks on his face were, she
guessed, somebody's idea of war paint. Otherwise, of course,
he was red. Fay was glad there weren't too many real Indians
left in this part of the country.

"Who do you think we're looking for?" the Chief asked
Fay when their breakfast came. "Are they here anywhere? I
mean, are the kids hidden in the shopping center?"

"No," Fay said.

Arnie stopped the Chief before he could say it. "Don't ask her how she knows."

"O.K.," the Chief said. "Who are they?"

"It's ordinary people," she sighed.

"Ordinary people don't steal children," he said. "It has to be nuts. Religious nuts."

"Maybe," Fay said. "But they don't look like nuts. They look just like us. That woman"—she pointed across the coffee shop to a middle-aged woman wearing a beige polyester pantsuit—"that's what they look like."

"But what do they want?" the Chief asked. "Why haven't they called us with their demands?"

"They will," Fay said. "They've got twenty-five children to take care of. They're busy."

The Chief didn't like her attitude.

"I don't think they'll hurt the kids," Fay said. "On purpose, I mean. I think if you do what they say they'll give them back."

The Chief put down his fork, looked at Arnie, and then at Fay. He tried not to sound mad. "Pardon me, Miss Morgan, but I'm not paying you ten thousand dollars to tell me to go along with these people."

"Don't pay me, then," Fay said. "I have three clients today who do care what I think. I'll just go home and see them." And she tried to get past Arnie in the booth.

"Fay," Arnie said, easing her back into her seat, "we have to find these people. If they get away with this thing, we'll have kidnappings twice a day."

"I'm *trying* to help you," Fay said. "You're just not listening."

"Try again," the Chief said, spearing a forkful of eggs. "It's just morning, is all. I hate the morning."

Fay took a deep breath. "These people are so clean," she said, "that you won't even find parking tickets on them. They pay their taxes, they work for a living. They're regular folks. The only way they'll do something criminal—"

"Something *else* criminal," the Chief corrected.

"Right, something else criminal, is if you push them into it. If you corner them, they'll fight you. If you let them alone, they'll do the right thing."

"If that's who they are," the Chief said, "then I don't understand why they did this in the first place."

"It's something personal," Fay said. "That's all I know." And she looked across the room to watch the woman in the beige pantsuit pay her bill and leave.

As the Chief waved to the waitress for more coffee, the announcer on the radio interrupted the program to say there was a special news bulletin about the twenty-seven missing children. Fay, Arnie, and the Chief froze in place.

"One of the children abducted from the state fair is now recovering in Duncan Memorial Hospital from an attack of asthma, which police say caused his captors to release him."

"Hot damn," Arnie said. "That's my girl," and he slung his arm around Fay and gave her a good squeeze.

"City detectives," the newscaster continued, "acting on a tip from the local psychic who has been retained to help in the investigation, alerted all the hospitals to watch for the child. Bobbie Jenkins, the receptionist at St. Vincent's, where the child was brought for help, said she didn't know he was one of the missing youngsters. She just knew he was sick. She said she would have done the same thing even if he hadn't been famous."

Fay looked up at Arnie. "He's all right?" she asked, not quite believing it.

"I'm the Chief of Police," the Chief grumbled from across the table. "Will somebody tell me why I have to hear this news on the radio in a coffee shop?"

"Your radio's in your car, that's all," Arnie said.

The Chief turned to Fay. "That's good work, lady," he said. "Real fine."

"But is Timmy really all right?" she asked. "Or do they just not want the kidnappers to know he died?"

"He must be all right," the Chief said. "I'm the only one who could make a strategy decision like that." He paused. "Or I was when I left the house."

Just then, one of the Chief's assistants rushed in the door and over to the table.

"They've got him!" the man said. "They've got another kid!"

"Yeah," the Chief said. "We know."

Then the man told them that Timmy's parents hadn't arrived yet, so the detectives hadn't been allowed to talk to the child. But the brown Ford described by the receptionist at St. Vincent's had been found abandoned about three miles from the hospital, with its license plates removed.

"They're no dummies, these people," the Chief said, taking the man's radio and patching into headquarters. "Give me Sergeant Barnes," he said to the dispatcher.

"Somebody in this city knows who drives a car like that," he said to Arnie. "We'll put it in the paper tonight. Offer a reward to anyone who can lead us to the owner. Not a big reward though. We don't want all the crazies in town calling. Just enough to be worth the trouble. Fifty bucks, something like that."

The sergeant came on the line.

"O.K.," the Chief said. "Send somebody back out to talk to that receptionist. Show her pictures of old Fords. See if she can pick out what year it was. Then get DMV to run a list of the registrations for brown Fords in that year. If these people think we can't find them just because they took off the license plates, they're crazy. We're the fucking government here."

The Chief signed off in much better spirits. The call had made him feel like the Chief again.

"There it is," Fay said quietly, pointing at the eighteen-wheeler just pulling into the huge parking lot. "There's the truck. Right over there."

Arnie and the Chief jumped up, but the radio in the Chief's hand stopped them before they could take off. "Attention all units," the dispatcher said. "A message has just been received that any interference with the truck now parked at the Indian Point Shopping Center will result in the deaths of the kidnapped children."

"We were sitting right here!" the Chief screamed.

"Are the kids in the truck, Fay?" Arnie asked.

"No," she said.

The three men bolted away from the table, ran out the door and across the asphalt. Fay sat back down and watched as the truck stopped on the far side of the lot. Even from here she could see that the oranges on the side had been painted out and replaced with a huge red cross. She kept her eye on the driver's door, in case he got out and tried to run away. Later she realized she should have been watching the people passing behind the truck, watching for someone new to join the crowd walking to their cars.

As a stream of police cars entered the shopping center and surrounded the truck, Fay ate the last bite of her French toast and motioned to the waitress for a glass of water.

*   *   *

BY THE TIME Arnie and the Chief reached the truck, other officers had climbed up to the cab, found it empty and locked, and tried the back doors, which were also locked. The Chief talked with the officer in charge, and Arnie inspected the tires. But they both knew there was nothing more for them to do here, and so they started back for the coffee shop. The Chief hadn't finished his breakfast, he said.

"Fay said they would do this," Arnie said.

"Too bad she didn't know it in time for us to grab the driver," the Chief said.

"So," Arnie said, "I think we have to wait, like she said. Wait for them to tell us what they want."

"Wait for them to think it up, is what we're doing," the Chief said. "Bunch of goddamn . . ."

"Right," Arnie said.

"What's the matter with her anyway?" the Chief asked. "I thought you said she wanted to do this."

"She's all right," Arnie said. "Any news on that boat I asked you about?"

"If that *Mia Querida* is the one," the Chief said, "she's still out there sitting in the harbor."

"Are you sure?" Arnie asked.

"What do you mean, am I sure? The harbormaster saw it. He was looking right at it while I was talking to him." The Chief paused as a teenage girl in a pair of shorts took his breath away. "Said she was a real beauty too."

"Who owns it?" Arnie asked.

"It's registered in California. Orange County. But they took delivery here. Taking it back to California through the canal. New boat. The guy is one of these stock market whizzos. Banker too, maybe. South America. I forget."

"And they're not leaving until tonight?"

"Right," the Chief said. "They had a helluva party last night, though. Lots of champagne. Limousines up the wazoo at the pier."

"So Fay's right about that part anyway," Arnie said.

"What is this about, drugs?" the Chief asked.

Arnie shook his head. "Fay is convinced her daughter sailed off on that boat last night. Thinks the kid isn't coming back."

"Nope," the Chief said. "The harbormaster said there

wasn't one private boat left the harbor last night from midnight on. Not a one."

"O.K.," Arnie said. "Thanks." He lit a cigarette.

"Kids are a bitch," the Chief said. "Nothing but trouble."

"I guess," Arnie said.

"I don't have to see mine much anymore, though."

"Why not?" Arnie asked.

"Why do you think?" the Chief said calmly. "They hate
my guts."

Arnie could see the coffee-shop window now, but Fay
was no longer sitting at their table. Normally he wouldn't
have worried about it. He would've just assumed she was in
the ladies' room. But somehow, this morning, he wasn't so
sure. Maybe she'd called the coast guard, found out on her
own about that boat in the harbor, and called a cab to go
there and look for Lizzie. Suddenly Arnie was afraid that if he
let Fay out of his sight just once today, he might never see
her again.

That wasn't the kind of thought he was comfortable with.
Arnie wasn't a worrier, and he certainly couldn't spend this
whole day worrying about Lizzie, and neither could Fay. She
had to understand. If she didn't, then she didn't understand
much about him, did she.

Would she ever love him the way she loved Lizzie?
Would she be this distracted and jumpy if *he* were missing?
Probably not. But Lizzie wasn't missing, or at least she wasn't
missing the way Fay thought she was. Maybe Lizzie did go to
that party on the boat, but she was bound to be home asleep
by now, unless she went straight to dance class. Maybe that's
where she was.

Arnie did care about Lizzie. She was as close as he
would ever come to having a daughter. But she wasn't his.
He didn't have to put her first. He couldn't. If anybody came
first, it was Fay. But since Lizzie was first with Fay, didn't
that mean Lizzie should be first with him? No. How could it?
Then what did it mean? Was Fay first, or work? Fay. Defi-
nitely. But not today. Tomorrow she would be first again, or
the next day, or whenever they found these children.

But what if it took a year? What if Fay went off to find
Lizzie without him? She would do it, he knew. If Lizzie were
his daughter, he'd do the same thing. He'd drop this case in a
minute and go find her, Chief or no Chief. What did work

matter when your child was in trouble? What did work matter anyway?

Anybody could do what he did. If he wanted proof of that, all he had to do was quit. They'd replace him the next day, and nobody would know the difference. But if he quit this case and helped Fay find Lizzie, they'd fire him. He didn't want to be fired. What if he got to Wyoming and needed a job?

Well, sure, there were things that paid better than police work, but nothing he knew as well. No. He had to stay on this thing till all those kids were safe in their beds, Lizzie or no Lizzie. No Lizzie. Oh boy. No Lizzie. No Fay. No job. No. Arnie couldn't start worrying about this. No sir.

FAY COULD SEE Arnie and the Chief walking back toward the coffee shop, but that wasn't the conversation she heard.

Paul and his father were standing on the top deck of the big boat. The breakfast had been cleared, and the boat was moving much faster. The day, the trip, and the father-son conference were all well under way. They leaned against the railing as two stewards removed the breakfast table and set up an exercise bicycle in its place.

"She's a beautiful girl," Paul's father said.

"Lizzie?" Paul said.

"Yes, Lizzie," his father said. "Do you have another beautiful girl on board?"

"She's sweet." Paul was admiring his deepening tan.

"She looks like a dancer."

"Maybe she is," Paul said. "I didn't ask."

"Where did you meet her?"

"Her mother's a gypsy," Paul said, accepting a bottle of suntan oil from one of the stewards. "I had my fortune told. The girl came home while I was there."

"A gypsy?"

"The woman is a nightmare," Paul said.

"Does your mother know that? A gypsy?"

"No," Paul said.

Paul's father walked over to the exercise bicycle and used it to steady himself as he did a few knee bends and stretches. "Will she be any trouble?"

"She adores me," Paul said. "She does whatever I say."

"No," his father said, "I mean the mother."

"What trouble?" Paul said. "Has there ever been any trouble? I'm very sweet about it. When we get to California, I'll say thanks, that's all. Then I say good-bye."

"Yes." His father mounted the bicycle and began to pedal, slowly at first. "That's all one can say, really."

"What she tells her mother is her business. If she were afraid of the old frump, she wouldn't have come. Besides," Paul added, "when's a girl like that ever going to get a trip like this in her life?"

"Oh, now you're the Good Samaritan." His father grinned, and started pumping harder.

"Why not?" Paul said. "It doesn't cost *me* anything. Why should she have to work hard and be miserable her whole life?"

"Because that's who she is."

"Well, a little fun first won't hurt her." Paul poured some oil into his palm and rubbed it into his shoulders. "What was I supposed to do all this time? Sit up top and look for whales?"

His father slipped his forefinger into the pulse meter on the handlebars and smiled as the digital readout flashed a figure not much above his normal resting rate. "Would Lizzie be here if she knew about Alyson?" his father asked.

"Maybe," Paul said. "And maybe she'd try to take me away from her."

"When they fight over you, son, you lose them both."

"Well it's not like they're the last two, Dad."

His father had to laugh. "No, you're certainly right there." He set the timer for twenty minutes and turned the odometer back to zero.

"Alyson will never know," Paul said. "She can't meet the boat in California because she's in Tibet."

"Missing you desperately," his father joked.

"That's what she says."

"Oh, son." The trim gray-haired man sighed.

"What?" Paul grinned as Lizzie came up from below, saw that they were talking, and went to the aft deck for some sun.

"Not a thing," his father said, as the boy walked away. "Enjoy."

Paul left his father and walked down the steps to where

Lizzie was spreading the thick white beach towel across the slatted wooden chaise. He watched as the sun played in her hair, envying its absorption in the lustrous mass.

When she saw him, she smiled, inviting him to watch as she removed her cover-up to reveal the white string bikini his mother had so thoughtfully provided in the guest room.

He walked across the deck as she lay back on the double lounger, then sat down beside her and stroked the long smooth arm she offered him.

"Why did you come with me?" he asked.

"I wanted to," she said easily.

"And you want to stay?" he asked. "What about your mother?"

"I don't want to talk about Mother," Lizzie said. "She'll hear me."

Paul's instincts for human weakness were infallible. "She'll hear you?"

"All my life," Lizzie said, "all my whole life, she's known everything I thought, everything I did, told me every dumb thing I was going to do right before I did it."

Paul had to laugh. "Made it a little hard to breathe, huh?"

"Took all the fun out of it, yeah," Lizzie said. "This" —she opened her arms to the sea air—"is the first morning of my life, of a life that's not hers to spy on."

"Spy on?" said Paul, putting on his sunglasses, coaxing the rest of it out of her without seeming to be interested.

"She may know where I am," Lizzie said, "what I'm doing, even what I'm saying right now, but she can't tell me she knows it, and she can't stop me. I don't want to know what's going to happen. Whatever happens, happens. I'll just . . . wait and see," she grinned.

"Dad would like to meet her," Paul lied.

Lizzie laughed. "No, no. She doesn't like to meet people. She just likes to stay in her little apartment. She doesn't even have friends she talks to. And she can't leave the city because of her clients."

"Not even to come to California to see you?" Paul asked, fully aware of the implications of what Lizzie was saying.

"I don't think so," Lizzie said.

"Even if you invited her? Paid her way?"

"No. She wouldn't—you know, she wouldn't know anybody."

"How did you escape?" he asked. "Why aren't you like her?"

Fay thought about the piano lessons, the dancing lessons, the children's theater, the book clubs, the arts camps, summer school, the honors program, the school trips, and the money that had bought it all.

"I was quiet about it," Lizzie said. "But I've been gone a long time now. She just thought, I don't know, she just thought I was somebody else."

Fay's heart was breaking. She had waited so long to hear Lizzie talk, really talk. And this, this was what she was saying.

"So who are you?" Paul reached for the portable tape deck.

"Do you like me?" Lizzie flirted.

"Wild about you." He opened the box of tapes under the chair.

"Then it doesn't matter, does it?" Lizzie put on her sunglasses.

He squeezed her arm. "Not in the slightest, babe. Not in the slightest."

Fay's eyes filled with tears; the coffee shop blurred around her. The waitress asked her something, but she couldn't make it out. If there hadn't been an empty plate smeared with congealing maple syrup in front of her, she would have put her head right down on the table and sobbed.

Maybe the waitress asked if she was through with the plate. If so, then Fay had understood too late. A lot of things. Understood a lot of things too late.

10:00 A.M.

 WHEN ARNIE OPENED THE DOOR OF THE COFFEE shop, Fay was standing at the pay phone.

"I'm calling Gail," she said, dialing the number.

"Good idea," he said, and leaned over to kiss the top of her head. "I've got some good news for you when you're finished."

"Anything over there?" she asked, nodding in the direction of the orange truck.

"Not a thing." He sat down on the edge of the big concrete planter near the window.

"Marvin?" Fay said, disappointed that he had answered. "It's me, Fay. Is Gail there?"

"Yeah," Marvin said, sounding lonely. "She's in the kitchen talking with Lizzie."

"Lizzie!" Fay shrieked. "What's Lizzie doing there?" Arnie jumped up and came over to stand with Fay.

"Looking for you, I think," Marvin said. "Want to talk to her?"

"Are you sure it's Lizzie?"

"What's the matter with everybody today?" Marvin said. "Of course it's Lizzie. She's been here about an hour, and I'm real glad she came, too. I just didn't know what to say to Gail after that phone call."

Fay heard a click on the line.

"Wait a minute," Marvin said. "Let me get this other call."

Fay turned to Arnie. "Marvin says Lizzie's sitting in Gail's kitchen!"

"That's what I was going to tell you," he said. "They had a party, but the boat didn't leave yet."

Marvin came on the line again. "Fay, it's the kidnappers," he said.

Arnie was close enough to hear what Marvin said. He grabbed the phone.

"Marvin! Don't hang up!" Arnie said quickly. "Did the men come to put the tap on your phone?"

"Yeah," Marvin said. "About a half hour ago."

Arnie was dialing headquarters on the other phone. "I just want to patch in so Fay can hear them, O.K.? So go get Gail, but give me a minute."

"O.K.," Marvin said. "Good luck, I guess."

"Right." Arnie was talking to the operator on the other line. He raised his eyebrows to Fay, as if to ask if she were ready. And she nodded back, as if she really felt like doing this.

Arnie handed her the phone and the Chief reached in Arnie's pocket for a cigarette. He knew it wouldn't taste good, but he wanted it anyway. He knew he shouldn't have quit smoking. But what can you do? You're the head of the force. You're supposed to be fit. You have to set an example.

Then Fay heard Gail's voice. "Hello?"

"Mrs. Wilkins?" the other voice asked.

"This is Gail Wilkins. Who is this?"

"You know who this is," the kidnapper said. "We have Beth here."

"Can I talk to her?"

"No," the voice said. "Come to the Indian Point Shopping Center at one o'clock this afternoon and meet the other mothers in front of the big white truck in the parking lot. On your way there, stop by the bowling alley at First and Cedar and pick up the package with your name on it, but don't open it. When all the mothers are together, you can open the packages and that is how you will know what to do next. Good luck, Mrs. Wilkins, and God bless you."

"I want to talk to Beth."

"Mrs. Wilkins," the voice said, "if the police interfere by

picking up your package, Beth will not be returned to you. Is that clear?"

"I understand," Gail said, and the phone went dead.

Fay motioned to Arnie that the call was over. He took the receiver.

"Gail, it's me, Arnie. Are you all right?"

"No, Arnie," she said. "I'm not all right at all."

"I'll let you talk to Fay in just a minute, but I want you to do exactly what they said to do."

A recorded voice interrupted Arnie, announcing that if he desired to continue his conversation, it would be necessary for him to deposit another five cents, which would buy him an additional three minutes. Arnie swore under his breath and jammed a nickel into the slot.

"Gail," he continued. "We're not going to do anything to scare these people. Don't you worry about that. We're at the shopping center right now. And we'll be here when you get here. We'll do exactly what they say. So you be brave and we'll get this all straightened out in no time. All right?"

"I'm fine," she said softly, but she wasn't really talking anymore, she was just saying words she remembered from somewhere.

"Here's Fay." He handed the phone to Fay. He didn't for a minute believe it was going to be as easy as he'd made it sound.

"Gail," Fay said quietly, "you did just fine."

"Are they going to give her back?" Gail cried.

"They're not killers, Gail. They're not. You do your part and they'll do theirs. I promise."

Suddenly Gail attacked her. "How can you promise me that?" she screamed. "You don't know any more than I do!"

"They don't want to hurt the children, Gail," Fay said. "They're just using them to make some kind of point."

Gail was screeching. "Well, you just tell Arnie and his gang to stay the hell away from that truck!"

"Gail, the only reason the police are going to be there is to make sure nothing goes wrong."

Gail was frantic. "I'm coming out there right now." Fay heard her call out to Marvin to go start the car.

"There's nothing to see, Gail," Fay said. "The truck is just sitting there. Nothing's going to happen till twelve-thirty at the earliest."

Gail didn't answer. Fay waited. Arnie gestured, wanting to know what was going on. Fay motioned back that she didn't know.

"Gail?" Fay said, finally.

"What?" Gail screamed.

Fay knew she had to be very careful, but she had to ask. "Gail, can I talk to Lizzie?"

"She left," Gail grumbled. "She said she'd see you later."

"When later?" Fay asked. "Where?"

Gail completely lost control. "I don't know when! I don't care where!"

Fay tried as hard as she could to remain calm. "Gail, please. I've worked all night trying to find Beth, and I'm going to keep working until I do find her, but I have to know about Lizzie. Please."

Something in Fay's voice reached Gail, touched her. "She went to a big party on a boat last night. She's madly in love, and they're going out again tonight."

"Thank you," Fay said.

"I'm sorry," Gail said, trying to sound like herself.

"Don't be sorry," Fay said. "That just means I still have time to stop her."

"Oh, Fay," Gail said, weak from fear, weary with frustration, "let her go."

"Are you letting Beth go?" Fay asked, then knew instantly she shouldn't have said it.

"Of all the goddamn nerve!" Gail screamed, and slammed the phone down in Fay's ear.

Fay was numb, paralyzed by the pain she had caused, and the pain she felt. Gently, Arnie took the receiver out of her hand.

"I can't believe I said that," she said.

"It's O.K.," he said, leading her back into the coffee shop. "We don't have to be perfect today." He sat her down. "We'll be perfect tomorrow."

"What's the matter with me?" she asked.

"You were scared," he said. "But Lizzie's home now. She's come back."

"No," she said. "It just means I've been seeing the future instead of the past. I'm losing her, Arnie."

"You just sit here and rest a little. I'll go see what the Chief wants us to do." He grasped her shoulder and gave it a hang-in-there squeeze. "And if the waitress comes by, order me a Coke float, huh?"

As he walked away, she envied his assured, easy progress through the world. She had no idea how it must feel to be a man like Arnie. Wherever this basic comfort came from, Fay knew she'd never have it.

WHEN THE WOMAN in the beige pantsuit came back into the coffee shop, Fay looked up. Why was she back here? Had she forgotten something? There was a young man with her now, a brittle-looking cowboy wearing black jeans, hiking boots, and a blue shirt buttoned all the way up. Even the collar button. If this woman were involved in the kidnapping, this man could certainly have driven the truck, Fay thought.

But there was something else about the woman. Where had Fay seen her before? Somewhere, she knew it. In the neighborhood? For a reading? Where was it? Was she that stern typist at the driver's license bureau? Or a Christmas bell-ringer for the Salvation Army?

No, no. Fay had it now. It was Edith Masters, the receptionist at Lizzie's dentist! That bloodless, efficient Mrs. Masters, who had no patience with the children's patter and no sympathy for their fears. Edith Masters. With the daughter. Oh boy. Now Fay remembered the whole thing.

She'd met the daughter just briefly one day in the office. But Mrs. Masters must have told the girl that Fay was a fortune teller, because about six months later, Colleen—or Coreen, which was it?—Colleen, right, Colleen, showed up at Fay's parlor. She said she was pregnant and wanted Fay to read the cards for the baby to see if she should have an abortion.

Fay was startled, but tried not to show it. "Abortions are illegal," Fay had said.

"A girl at school gave me the name of the place," Colleen said.

"Has *she* had an abortion at this place?" Fay asked.

"I don't know." Colleen paused. "I've got the money, if that's what you're worried about."

"It's not safe." Fay was genuinely alarmed for the girl, who couldn't be more than seventeen. "Those places are dirty, Colleen, anything could happen. No, child." Fay reached over to squeeze her hand. "You don't need me to read your cards. You need to go tell your mother about this, and see what she thinks."

The girl shook her head. The excitement of coming to a fortune teller had worn off now. She sat forward in the chair, her head drooping, her arms bracing her body, her hands clasping the edges of the seat for support. "I can't tell my mother," she said. "I already know what she thinks."

"I've known your mother a long time," Fay said. "I don't know her well, I'll admit, but she seems like a good woman. Let her help you."

"I've got the money for the reading," Colleen said. "I just want a reading. I didn't come here to talk." And then, afraid she had offended Fay, she looked up and tried to smile.

"Fine," Fay said, but she didn't mean it. She didn't like to expose her cards to such wild fear. She didn't even like to sit in front of it herself. Nevertheless, this little girl needed somebody, and Fate, or whatever you call it, had appointed Fay. So there she sat.

Fay asked Colleen to shuffle the cards, and then cut them in three piles to her left. "How far along are you?" Fay asked.

"Two months," the girl said.

"Have you been to a doctor?"

Colleen didn't answer.

Fay collected the cards and dealt the first seven onto the table. "Well," Fay said, smiling, looking at the Three of Cups, "at least it wasn't a rape."

"No," Colleen said, and managed a smile.

Fay pointed to the Emperor. "*That* we already know," she said.

"What?" the girl asked.

"The law is *not* on your side," Fay said.

"No," the girl said.

"You don't want the child at all?" Fay asked, pausing at the next card.

"I want to grow up," the girl said, and tears appeared at the edges of her eyes.

Fay looked out the window while Colleen wiped her eyes. She was angry suddenly, thinking about the laws that are supposed to protect teenagers. They can't drive till they're

sixteen, vote till they're eighteen, or drink till they're twenty-
one. But we'll let a girl have a baby anytime she gets pregnant. In fact, we'll force her to have that baby.

We make those other laws to protect us, Fay realized,
not them, to protect us from their driving, us from their
drinking, us from their ignorance. But their mistakes? No,
no. Their mistakes are *their* problem. Their mistakes, *they*
have to *pay* for.

"I think it should be against the law for girls like you to
have babies," Fay said.

Colleen nodded, but remained silent.

Fay looked at the next card, the Ten of Swords. Total
defeat. Oh, terrific, Fay thought. Just terrific. That was the
best possible outcome of the situation? The client's goal? Fay
went on to the Seven of Wands, the past.

"It looks like you've been up against it for quite a while
already," Fay said.

"It's not so bad," Colleen said. "Mother's getting better.
She'll be back to work in another three months or so."

"What happened to her?" Fay asked.

"Just some surgery," the girl said. "She had insurance
and everything, so the money wasn't a problem, but I had to
do all the house stuff—you know, feeding everybody, getting
the clothes clean, all that."

"And keeping your grades up," Fay guessed, as she
turned over the Eight of Coins for the more recent past. Then
she saw the Seven of Swords. Some scheme was in the works,
all right.

"You're doing the wrong thing," Colleen said. "You're
reading for me. I asked you to read for the baby."

"I can't read for the baby," Fay said, "because the baby
can't shuffle the cards. It's a very old rule."

"Then I want my money back," the girl said, straightening up in the chair.

Fay thought a minute. The one thing she did not want to
do was turn this girl out into the street. "That's fair," she
said. "I should have told you about the shuffling business in
advance. So I won't charge you. But I'd like to finish the
reading, if you don't mind."

"It's free?" the girl asked.

"Absolutely," Fay said.

"O.K., then," the girl said. "But I have to be home at three-thirty." It was then just one o'clock.

Fay studied the last four cards. The King of Cups, probably the abortionist; the Moon, so his place was filthy after all; the Empress, so this girl was more worried about her mother than she was about herself; and finally, the Star, so at least there was hope. Well, what good was that? Hope was cheap.

"What should I do?" the girl asked.

"I don't know," Fay said. "Can you make tuna fish?"

"You mean right now?" Colleen asked.

"You haven't eaten yet, have you?"

"No," the girl said.

Fay stood up. "I always eat. It makes me feel better. Do you like tuna fish?"

"I like it," Colleen said, following Fay into the kitchen. "But I don't like eggs in it."

"Me either," Fay said. "If we wanted eggs, we'd make egg salad, right?"

"Right," the girl said. She opened the refrigerator, reached for the mayonnaise, and an embarrassed grin flickered across her face. "I'm starving," she said.

"Another good reason to eat," Fay said.

"I know," the girl said. "But I don't want to . . . show, you know."

"What will you do if you don't have the abortion? If this man says he won't do it, or your mother finds out and locks you up somewhere?"

"I don't know," she said. "Run away, I guess. Get a room. Get a job."

"Do you have family you can go to?"

"Not without Mother finding out."

"Can you marry this boy?"

"It wasn't his fault."

"He was *there*, though."

Colleen was silent a moment. "I don't want to," she said. "That really would be the end of me."

Fay couldn't help noticing, as the girl put the slices of bread into the toaster, that her fine blond hair needed washing. And the limp gray T-shirt probably looked better on the older brother who had worn it out.

"I know I have to have the abortion," the girl said. "I'm just scared, that's all."

"I'd be scared too," Fay said.

"What I thought," Colleen said, as she washed the lettuce, "was maybe you could tell me who the baby was. And then, if it was going to be the president someday, or Beethoven, then I'd think about it some more."

"What do you want to drink?" Fay asked. "I have Cokes and milk and water."

"A Coke," the girl said, as the toast popped up.

"You fix the glasses, then, and I'll make the sandwiches," Fay said.

They worked now in silent comfort. Fay was not thinking about what to say. She just wanted the tuna not to squeeze out of the other end of the sandwich when Colleen took her first bite. There was a trick to that, and Fay was proud to know it.

Colleen carried the plates out the back door to the tiny garden behind the apartment. Then she came inside for the glasses and picked two paper napkins out of the plastic pumpkin Fay kept them in.

"This is nice out here," Colleen said, as Fay followed her out and they sat down in the rusty iron chairs. Fay knew the rust wouldn't ruin anything either of them had on, and though the air was heavy and still, there was at least more of it outside. She took a bite of her sandwich.

"Somebody special," Fay said, more to herself than Colleen. "What if the baby is somebody special?"

"Yeah," Colleen said. "Somebody there's only one of in the world. Somebody born to do something."

Fay reached for her glass. "Colleen," she said, "there are a lot more people born to do something than ever grow up to do it."

Fay wished she'd made iced tea. Or lemonade. Lemonade would've been perfect.

"It's not enough to be born Beethoven," Fay continued. "For all you know, you might have been a Beethoven yourself."

"No," Colleen said, shaking her head with absolute certainty. "We couldn't have afforded the lessons."

"That's what I mean," Fay said. "A lot of special people are born. People who could straighten out this mess we've made in the world. Healers. Singers. Horn players. Good people. Real gems. Magicians. Inventors. Storytellers. People who know about money, people who can fix anything, people who can make things that won't break."

"So where are they?" Colleen asked.

"We just can't raise them," Fay said, "or don't know how to, or don't recognize them soon enough, so they get away from us. We lose them. You see them later on the streets, though, hundreds of them, all the time. And you wonder why they look so empty. It's not surprising, really."

"I'd try to raise it right," Colleen said.

"I know you would," Fay said. "And if you have the baby, I'll help you. You can bring him over here every week and play every phonograph record I've got."

Colleen took the last bite of her sandwich and stared at the paving stones. She wished Fay wouldn't watch her chew. Her mother had told her she chewed her food like nobody she ever saw.

"I'll help you in any way I can," Fay said. "But I won't tell you you've got a Beethoven in there because, with you so young, and things so tough, I just don't think he'd make it."

Colleen nodded.

Fay went on. "And I don't want you to have the baby and then blame him later if he cost you so much and didn't turn out to be Beethoven after all."

"But I want him to be special."

"When you're ready to have a baby," Fay said, "you'll take any kind you can get. You won't care about special. In fact, you'll get down on your knees every night for nine months and pray to God he's normal. That would be blessing enough."

Colleen drank the last of her Coke. "I'm not ready, then."

"No," Fay said. "You're too young."

Colleen brushed something away from her face, like a mosquito she wished were there. "It makes me feel bad," she said.

"I know," Fay said.

"Is it a sin?" the girl asked, her voice breaking. "Is abortion a sin?"

Fay took a deep breath. "Maybe," she said, as the first drop of rain plinked on the table between them. "But it's not the only one."

There was no more talk. They carried the dishes inside.

Fay's mind was racing, flipping through the rest of what might be said. What comfort could she give the girl? And what else was worth giving? Nothing. She had done all she could do.

She gave Colleen an umbrella, handed her a banana to eat on the way home, kissed her good-bye, closed the door, and wept.

But the next time Fay took Lizzie to the dentist, there was a new receptionist. The dentist told her Mrs. Masters had resigned due to a death in her family.

"It wasn't Colleen, was it?" Fay asked, terrified to hear the answer.

"I don't know," the dentist said. "She didn't say, and I didn't ask."

Fay was furious. "You mean there was a death in that lady's family and you didn't even ask who it was?"

"No," the dentist said. "Sorry." And he turned to Lizzie, certain that the Novocain had taken effect by now.

Fay got up from her seat at the end of the room, pushed back the tray in front of Lizzie, pulled her up out of the big gray dental chair, and never saw the man again. She didn't try to explain it to Lizzie, but she did apologize to her all afternoon. She held her, rocked her, and didn't let go of her hand until they both fell asleep that night on the rug in the living room, with every last one of Lizzie's stuffed rabbits tucked in tight around them.

STANDING BY THE pay phones, the Chief and Arnie had worked out a pretty fair plan for controlling the scene at the truck. The mothers would meet at the Burger King lot across the street. Policewomen would escort them to the truck. The shopping center would remain open, but the Chief would tape a personal message for TV and radio asking the public to stay away. That way, they hoped they could limit the crowd to hoodlums, of course, and bookish types who didn't watch TV during the day, and a few hundred normal people whose car radios had been stolen by the hoodlums.

"I'll be downtown," the Chief said, as he left. "If you get anything new from the spirit world"—he nodded in Fay's direction—"let me know."

"Will do," Arnie said, and placed one more call, arranging for a detective to watch Fay's apartment and alert him the minute Lizzie showed up. Then he went back into the coffee shop and sat down with Fay.

"They never put enough ice cream in these things," he said, picking up his Coke float. "You're supposed to fill up a glass with ice cream, then pour the Coke in a little at a time."

"That's the way you do it." She laughed.

"Sure it is," he said. "That's the way I like it."

She smiled. "*They* do it *this* way because the ice cream is supposed to float, Arnie. Coke float."

He took a big sip through the straw and caught her up on everything they'd learned. Little Timmy Willis had no idea where he'd been. It sounded like he'd been asleep the whole time.

The kidnappers had called all the mothers from pay phones in supermarkets. But nobody in any of the supermarkets remembered seeing anyone use the phones. Anyone special, that is. People used the phone all day, they said. That's what they were there for.

The Mayor's wife had gotten a call too, so there wasn't any point in keeping their boys a secret anymore. She'd be at the truck with everybody else.

Arnie looked up from his float and noticed the woman in the beige pantsuit. "There's that lady again."

"Yes, I know," Fay said. "She came back in just after you left. Her name is Edith Masters. She used to be the receptionist at Lizzie's dentist. I'd like to go say hello to her before we leave."

"Fine with me," Arnie said, standing up. "I'll meet you outside."

He took the check to the cashier while Fay made her way over to the table by the window.

"Hello, Mrs. Masters, it's . . ."

"Of course I remember you, Fay," Mrs. Masters said, blotting her mouth with a napkin. "How are you?"

"I'm fine," Fay said. She was shocked to see how old Mrs. Masters looked up close. The lines in her face were so deep, they looked like scars.

"How's Lizzie?" Mrs. Masters asked.

"She's fine. She's all grown up," Fay said. "How's Colleen?"

"She's in California," Mrs. Masters said.

Fay tried not to show her relief. "What's she doing there?"

Mrs. Masters retied the bow at the neck of her blouse. "She's working."

Fay was not good at casual conversation, but she had to keep trying. "I hear it's pretty in California. What does she do there?"

Mrs. Masters nodded at the black-jeaned cowboy. "Fay, I'd like you to meet a new member of our church."

Fay shook his hand. "Pleased to meet you," she said, noticing his hammer thumb. "What church is that?"

"He's just moved to town," Mrs. Masters said.

Fay tried not to stare at his hands. She'd never seen a thumb hug a forefinger so close. It wasn't a good sign. But she saw the bitterness in his face, too. This was a vengeful, spiteful man.

"Where are you from?" Fay asked him. "Someplace south, I guess, with that tan you have."

"Fay is a fortune teller," Mrs. Masters said. "She even helps the police from time to time."

The young man swept his hands off the table quickly and clasped them together in his lap. But he didn't say a word. That was peculiar, Fay thought. Almost everybody says something when they hear you're a fortune teller.

"I didn't get your name," she said.

"It was nice seeing you again, Fay," Mrs. Masters said quickly.

"Yes," Fay said, backing away, "you too. Tell Colleen hello for me the next time you talk to her."

"I'll do that," Mrs. Masters said. "Good-bye, Fay."

Fay walked quickly up to meet Arnie. Were they or weren't they? Should she tell Arnie? Tell him what? That Colleen was working in California?

"How is she?" Arnie asked.

"She's fine," Fay said.

Arnie held the door open for her and they walked down the steps into the parking lot. When they passed the window of the coffee shop, he looked up and caught Mrs. Masters staring at him.

"Is she screwing that boy?"

"If she is," Fay said, "she's not paying him enough."

"I have to go to the radio truck," Arnie said. "Want to come?"

"No," she said. "I want to talk to Lizzie."

"There's a man in front of your house waiting for her," he said. "As soon as she shows up, I'll take you there."

"No matter what else is happening?"

"Scout's honor."

"All right, then," she said. "I'll come." Then she thought a minute. "Can you find out if somebody's dead?"

"If they died in the state, we can know it in two minutes."

"Her name is Colleen Masters," Fay said.

"No problem," he said, writing it down. "Colleen Masters."

11:00 A.M.

THE PARKING LOT WAS BEGINNING TO LOOK LIKE the practice ground for police training maneuvers. The truck, roped off and guarded, sat at the far end like a time bomb. Shoppers who stopped to look at it were waved away by the officers, but the police themselves gathered in small groups to stare, to study the truck as though it were a tactical assault problem at the police academy.

"So," Arnie said, as they approached the police command center, "what do you think about Wyoming?"

Fay had said she would tell him tomorrow. Was this tomorrow? "Wyoming?" she asked.

"We can do whatever you want about furniture," he said. "Take it all or leave it all. Makes no difference to me."

"I don't know," she said. "I like your bed."

"I like that big armchair at your house," he said. "And your porch things—you know, that wrought-iron table and chairs. They'd be good in Wyoming." Then he pointed to the benches set up by the first-aid station. "Are you going to be O.K. out here?"

"You go on." Fay wiped her forehead on her sleeve. "I'm happy to sit for a while." Then she walked to the first-aid station and asked for a glass of ginger ale. Where was Lizzie? Dance class? Shopping for deck shoes?

Fay knew she couldn't get the answer by demanding it

like this. She should just relax, think about something else. Like what? Like where were the other twenty-four children? No.

What if Lizzie didn't want Fay to find her? Could she disappear? No. Lizzie wouldn't do that. She never minded Fay knowing where she was. Or did she? Fay tried to remember another time Lizzie had disappeared, tried to remember what she actually knew about her daughter, tried to decide how much of it was true.

Oh, sure, Lizzie disappeared all the time as a little girl, but all kids did that. Lizzie would ask if she could go get a Popsicle, and an hour later, between clients, Fay would charge up the street and find her in the girly-show ticket booth, where old Charlie would have her counting out quarters and putting them in little paper rolls. That didn't mean anything, did it?

Well, that particular time it did, but they worked it out, they talked about it. Lizzie liked the girly-show girls. She said they smiled at her when they came to work, even the one with the pink hair. She asked if she could see them dance sometime.

"Absolutely not," Fay said, taking Lizzie's hand. "It's dirty."

"What's dirty?" Lizzie asked, waving good-bye to Charlie.

"They dance around naked," Fay said. "Don't make me drag you down the street, O.K.?"

"Why is that dirty?" Lizzie asked.

"Because men come to see the girls dance," Fay said, unlocking the door, "and men shouldn't see women naked unless they're married to them."

"Why not?" Lizzie leaned up against the front of their building, pretending that the door wasn't open and her mother wasn't standing there holding it for her.

"Because your body is just for you and your husband," Fay said. "Now come into this house, please."

"It's not a house," Lizzie said defiantly.

"We call it a house."

"I don't." Lizzie was more determined than ever, digging into the sidewalk with her heels.

"All right," Fay said, closing the door. "What do *you* call it?"

"It's a rattrap," Lizzie said.

"*Who* said that?" Fay asked, trying to keep her voice low so people walking past them on the sidewalk wouldn't hear. "Did one of those girls say we lived in a rattrap?"

Lizzie tugged on her hair and didn't answer, concentrating instead on the stoplight turning from green to red at the corner.

"Elizabeth . . ." Fay grabbed her arm.

"Arnie sees you naked," Lizzie said, "and he's not your husband. Your husband is my daddy."

"Your daddy's not my husband anymore, Lizzie, you know that," Fay said. "We got a divorce. And I'm sorry he doesn't come to see you, but that's just who he is, and that's why we got the divorce in the first place."

Lizzie looked down at her feet. "That's not what you told me before," she said. "You said . . ."

"I know what I said before," Fay sighed. "I said he didn't want to help take care of Granny, but it's the same reason."

Lizzie kicked at the patch of grass trying to take root between the concrete squares under her feet. "I bet Daddy doesn't live in a rattrap now," she said proudly.

Fay knelt down beside her. "Lizzie," she said, "I know you miss your daddy, but we do *not* live in a rattrap. Our house is the cleanest house on the block."

Lizzie started to object. "It's not a—"

"I know it's not a house," Fay said. "But I wish it were a house, so I pretend, all right?"

Fay's knees were shaking from trying to stay on her knees, from trying not to touch the sidewalk, from trying to stay on the little girl's level.

"All right?" Fay asked again.

"O.K.," Lizzie mumbled. "It's a house."

"Good," Fay said. Then she grasped Lizzie's chin and turned her face around so she could see her eyes. "Now, I want to know how many times you've been in that girly show. If I can't trust you to go where you say you're going, I can't let you go, Lizzie."

"You're hurting me," Lizzie cried, jerking her head away.

Fay knew she'd said the wrong thing. She ran back over the conversation. Girls. Dirty. Naked. Arnie. Daddy. There it was. Arnie saw Fay naked and Lizzie had seen it. Oh boy.

"Lizzie," Fay asked, "are you mad that Arnie comes to see me?"

"It's dirty," Lizzie said.

"It's not dirty," Fay said, as calmly as she could.

"He's not my daddy," the girl said simply.

Fay took a deep breath. "What did you see, Lizzie? Did you see us in the bed together?"

But Lizzie couldn't answer that. Her head hung limp now. She was ashamed, she had done something bad, but she didn't know what it was, or what was bad about it. Fay pulled Lizzie to her and hugged her tight.

"Oh, Lizzie," Fay said, stroking her hair, and patting her back as she would a baby, "Arnie loves me, and I love him, and we sometimes sleep in the bed together because it makes us have good dreams. The reason we're not married is I love you more, and I never want anybody to come between us."

She picked up the little girl's hand and kissed it. "Lizzie," she said, "when I tell you a place is dirty, I mean that it's not safe."

Lizzie's knees gave way and she slipped down the door and sat on the sidewalk.

Fay stretched her legs out beside the girl, but kept talking. "Arnie spends the night with us to make sure we're safe. He loves us. Both of us." She paused. "O.K.?"

Please God, Fay thought, let it be O.K.

Lizzie was crying. "I'm sorry," she whispered.

"I know you are," Fay said. "I'm sorry too."

Fay stood up, clasped Lizzie's hand tightly in hers, and opened the door.

"Miss Morgan?" a voice behind them said.

"Yes?" Fay turned.

"I'm Brenda Cross," the dull-eyed matron said. "I have an appointment at five o'clock."

Fay felt Lizzie's hand squeeze even tighter. "We've had a little problem this afternoon," Fay said to the woman, nodding down at Lizzie. "Would you mind if we made it another time? I know I have Monday at five free."

"Please," the woman begged, "I'm getting married tomorrow. I have to know now."

Fay looked at the woman's rounded shoulders and puffy gray cheeks, and sensed immediately that the marriage was being made out of nothing but fear.

Fay shook her head. "If you really loved him," she said, "you wouldn't have been able to wait—what is it, eleven years?—to marry him."

"Yes," the woman nodded, startled by the accuracy of Fay's count. "Eleven years tomorrow."

"Go spend a week with your mother," Fay said, reaching for the doorknob.

"She's sick," the woman said.

"I know that," Fay said. "Make your peace with her before she dies." Fay opened the door. "And then," she said, "there's somebody else at home who's eager to see you. Stewart somebody."

The woman brightened instantly. "Stewart Day?"

"Go," Fay said. "Your boyfriend knows it's not right either. You've both just given up on the world, that's why you've been together. But that's no reason to get married."

The woman leaned over suddenly and kissed Fay on the cheek. "Thank you," she said. "How much do I owe you?"

"Nothing," Fay said. "Not a thing."

The woman wanted to say good-bye, but was too embarrassed, so she made a peculiar waving gesture with one hand and simply backed away.

Fay smiled, turned, walked in the door, drew the drapes, and flipped over the sign that said CLOSED. Lizzie scampered off to see what was in the refrigerator, and Fay sank down deep in her old rust velvet armchair and missed Arnie desperately. She wanted nothing more than for him to walk back in from the kitchen with Lizzie, the two of them holding hands and eating cold fried chicken.

Maybe she should have married Arnie years ago. Given Lizzie a real daddy. Given Arnie a real place in her life. Made a real home. Was that what Lizzie had been asking for that day? For more than just a mother? And how would Fay ever know?

"Good news or bad?" Arnie asked.

Fay jumped. She had no idea how long he'd been standing behind the bench where she was sitting. "Bad," she said.

He walked around to sit beside her. "That girl you asked me to check on, that Colleen Masters? She's dead. Fifteen years ago. She was seventeen. The death certificate said massive internal bleeding, cause unknown."

Fay nodded. "Did you ask them what . . ."

"Abortion," Arnie said. "The coroner said the guy before him didn't like the word, so he always put 'cause unknown.' "

Fay looked away.

"Is Colleen her daughter?" Arnie asked. "The woman in the coffee shop?"

"Yes," Fay said. "What's the good news?"

"Lizzie's on her way out here to have lunch with us!" He grinned. "Our man picked her up at your house ten minutes ago."

"Here?" she asked.

"Why not?" he asked. "We have to stay here anyway. I thought you'd be happy to see her."

"I am," Fay said. "It's just that I know I'm going to say the wrong thing."

"Are you sure?" he asked.

"Absolutely," she said, smoothing out her skirt.

"Well"—he put his arm around her, gave her a comforting squeeze—"whatever you think's best."

She had to laugh.

"They say the food at the bowling alley is pretty good."

"Fine," she said.

"We can go on over there if you want," he patted her arm. "Unless you have something I should tell the team."

"You mean like where the other kids are?" she asked.

"Yeah," he said.

"No," she said.

"O.K., then." He pulled her up. "Let's go."

THE MAYOR SAT at his desk. His fears that the kidnappers would use his children against him politically were turning out to be unfounded. His new fear was that his *wife* was going to use his children against him politically.

In the ten-o'clock staff meeting, Vi had said she wasn't going to the truck, wasn't going to give in to the kidnappers' demands. She said if nobody else was brave enough, she was. She would go on national television, stand up to the kidnappers, and defend abortion to the whole country.

He knew it was exactly the opportunity she had been waiting for. The real reason she'd go on national television was to become a star. He wondered how long he had felt this way. He was afraid it was a long time. He tried to think of somebody else he might love. Secretaries, salesgirls, old girl friends, neighbors, anybody. But no names came immediately to mind.

When the Mayor heard Vi knock on his door, he was studying the photograph of his two boys, his wife, and his big Irish Setter, who had died in March.

"Yes?" he called, and slipped his personal address book back into the drawer.

"See that we're not disturbed," Vi said to his secretary as she opened the door.

"Good morning, sweetheart," he said, standing up as she entered.

"Sit, sit," she smiled.

And he wished for an instant that he was that dead red dog in the picture.

"I guess it's time for us to have a little chat," she said, taking the chair the secretary used for dictation.

"How are you feeling?" he asked. "Did you get any breakfast?"

"Juice is all I need in the morning, Peter," she said.

He wondered if that was something new, a diet, maybe, or if she'd stopped eating breakfast sometime ago and he just hadn't noticed. He was sure he remembered her eating breakfast sometime. When was that?

"I think there's something you ought to know," she said, crossing her legs at the ankles, then tucking them neatly behind the leg of the chair.

"All right." He knew he had to convince her to go to the shopping center. But he could let her talk first.

She cleared her throat. "I had an abortion when I was in high school."

"I see," he said, and put the top back on his pen.

"And then I helped some other girls get them from the same man. I imagine he's dead now, but they're not."

"I don't understand what you're getting at, Vi."

"They could be part of this, dear," she said.

"Vi," he said wearily, "if you helped those girls then, why should they want to hurt you now?"

"I don't know. Maybe they wish they had those babies back."

"Do *you*?" he asked.

"No, I don't," she said. "But I'm not like a lot of other people."

The Mayor stood up, walked to the window, opened the blinds, and looked down at the street. He envied the shoppers with their packages, the lawyers with their briefcases, and the mailmen with their heavy pouches. He wished *he* had something to carry down the street. He wished he could say where he was going.

"I just wanted you to know," she said, "that if the press ask me about it, I won't deny it. I'm not ashamed of it."

"The press won't know to ask about it unless you tell them," he said. "I think you're safe."

She sighed. "I am not interested in being safe," she said.

"No, I can see that," he said. "You're proud of it, aren't you."

"I was right to help those girls."

"It was against the law."

"The law was wrong. Everybody can see that now," she said.

"Who was the father?"

"Just a boy."

"Did he have a name?" he asked, turning back to the window.

"Yes, darling, he had a name," she said, "but that isn't really the point, is it?"

"Do you not remember his name, or do you just not want to tell me?" He was surprised by his own anger.

"What are you asking, Peter?"

"Did you tell the boy about it, or did you just have the abortion and then tell him later?"

"Peter, darling, I fail to see what this has to do with—"

"You didn't tell him at all, did you?"

"No," she said, "I didn't, but—"

"It wasn't his business, was it. Like my boys aren't my business now, are they."

She grabbed the arms of the chair. "And just what does that mean?" she hissed.

"The other mothers—"

"You want me to be like the other mothers."

"The other mothers want their children back. The other mothers are scared."

"You want me to be scared."

"I want you to go to the truck."

"This is no time to be scared," she said. "What do you think they're going to do? Kill the children? No. They'd be crazy to kill the children. Look what they did already. They turned one in, right?"

"Right," he mumbled.

"And that's exactly what they'll do with the rest of them as soon as they've made their point."

"What point?"

"That abortion is wrong. But we can't let them say that. We have to stop them right now."

He lashed out at her. "Can't you think about anything else!" He was nearly choking on his rage. "Not *once* have you talked about Kevin and Kerry! Do you remember *their* names?"

She took a deep breath. "You think I don't care about the boys, is that it?"

"Yes. That's exactly it."

"You're wrong," she said.

"All right, then. Prove it."

"I have to prove to you that I love my boys?"

"You have to pick up your package and go to the truck because your package may have some important piece of this puzzle in it, and my boys are missing and I want them back."

Her voice was clear, but as cold as he'd ever heard it. "I am their mother," she said. "But that is not all I am. I refuse to stand here and grieve for your entertainment."

And now he realized the difference between them. "All I am," he said, "*all* I am is their father."

She shook her head. She hoped he wasn't going into one of his "worthless me" moods.

He walked back to his desk, sat down, and straightened a pile of papers. "You will go to the truck?" he asked, as officially as he could.

"I will go to the truck," she answered, "because that's where the press is expecting me."

"Then I will see you there." He buzzed his secretary. "Mrs. Foley, I have some letters for you, please."

Vi reached across the desk, snatched up the photo of the two boys, turned and prepared to smile at Mrs. Foley, who was just opening the door.

"Don't you look lovely this morning," Vi said to the secretary.

* * *

FAY AND ARNIE found a table near the front of the bowling-alley snack bar, and waited there for Lizzie and the other detective to arrive.

"Are you hungry?" she asked, putting on fresh lipstick.

"No," he said. "But who knows when we'll eat again?"

She looked better. The lipstick actually made a difference.

"So . . ." he started, genuinely sorry he'd had to leave her sitting on that bench outside. "How are you?"

"Arnie," she blurted, "did you ever want to have children?"

He drained his water glass. "With you, sure," he said.

"Why didn't you say so?" she asked.

"I don't know." He set the glass down on the table and motioned for a refill. "I figured you were happy with Lizzie."

"I was."

"I don't mind it," he said, picking up the menu.

"Not having children?" she asked.

"Yeah," he said. "I wouldn't have seen them very much," he said.

"You could still have them," she said. "With somebody younger than me, of course, but . . ."

"No thanks," he said.

"Arnie," she said, annoyed at his seeming indifference to his own needs, "if you wanted to have children, you should have said something. And if you want them now, you should go do it."

He dipped his handkerchief in her glass of water and mopped his forehead with it. "I don't think about it, Fay," he said. "There are plenty of kids in the world, and I'm happy, O.K.?"

He turned and checked the front door for Lizzie and the detective. "It's all right that I don't have kids," he said. "I'll do that next time."

"What next time?" she asked.

"Next time around," he said, "next life. You know. Don't you think there's a next time?"

"I don't know," she said, quite surprised but trying not to show it. "I didn't know you ever thought about it."

He smiled. "There has to be, don't you think? How can people feel as strongly as they do about certain other people here, unless they knew them before? I mean, one life is barely long enough to learn people's names, much less love them or hate them."

Fay didn't quite know how to respond. "So you think there's another life, huh?" she said.

He shrugged. "I'm not sure I believe it, exactly. But it's a real good explanation for something I'd be real confused about otherwise."

"Like what?" she asked, marveling at how one new piece of information could rearrange everything else she knew about him.

"Well, look," he said. "Detectives don't fall in love with psychics. Detectives don't believe in all that shit."

She flinched.

He continued. "But I'm a detective, and I love you. So I must have known you before."

"Arnie Campbell!" she laughed. She couldn't hold it back any longer. "I don't believe this is coming out of your mouth!"

"Well, it is." He grinned. "You ought to be real grateful too. Think how many lives you've had to live to hear me say it. The first time around, I was probably some sheriff's henchman. I probably burned you at the stake."

And then they both laughed, and Fay was about to ask him what he thought happened the second time, when the front door opened and Lizzie walked in.

ARNIE FELT FAY freeze. He grabbed her hand. "Just remember," he said to her, "Lizzie is proud of you. She's probably been listening to the radio. All they can talk about is you."

He stood up to wave to Lizzie, but she had already seen them and was on the run.

"It's fabulous," Lizzie said, hugging Fay, then kissing her on the cheek. "You found three kids!"

Fay steadied herself, using the back of the chair. "Thanks, love," she said.

"No," Lizzie said, sitting down. "Everybody's talking about you. The radio, the TV, everybody!"

Fay looked at Arnie. This was sounding a bit rehearsed. "It was both of us," Fay said. "It wasn't just me."

"Hi, doll," Arnie said to Lizzie, genuinely glad to see somebody smiling today.

Lizzie patted his stomach affectionately. "Hi, Arnie."

The other detective sat down, and Lizzie introduced him. "This is the famous Fay," she said gaily.

"Proud to meet you, ma'am," he said, extending his hand to Fay. "Jake Hawley."

"Thanks for finding my girl," Fay said.

Jake spoke with a dry Western accent, and had the lean, muscular build of a ranch hand. His hair was too long for the regular force, but then so was Arnie's.

"Texas?" Fay asked.

"Yes, ma'am. Abilene."

"It's just great, Mom," Lizzie said.

"It's not so great if the rest of them are dead," Fay said.

"Mom." Lizzie paled. "They can't be dead."

"Well, let's hope not." Fay opened the menu.

Lizzie had expected Fay and Arnie to be more excited. She looked at Arnie, then back to her mother, who'd put on her glasses to read the menu, then decided Arnie was a better bet for an answer.

"So," she said, "you guys been up all night?"

Arnie winked at her. "You're not supposed to tell us old people we look bad," he whispered. "It hurts our feelings."

"No!" she said. "You look terrific! I didn't mean that!" She tried to calm down.

"Well, for people who've been up all night, I guess we do," Arnie said. He patted Fay on the arm. "What are you going to have?" he asked her, looking around for the waitress.

"I just had breakfast," Fay said, taking off her glasses. "I'll have cottage cheese."

"Have some soup," Lizzie said. "Soup is good for stress."

"I don't want any soup," Fay said. "I want to know where you were all night."

Lizzie shook her head. "I was on a boat," she said, with a sly look at Arnie. "On the biggest boat you ever saw!"

"All night?" Fay asked.

"I'm having the tuna melt," Arnie said. "Jake?"

"I always order chicken out," Jake said, "but I'm going to my dad's house for dinner, and he always has chicken, so sure. Tuna's good."

"Whose boat was it?" Fay asked.

Lizzie reached for a menu. "Mother," she said, "you don't even *know* these people. You can't hate them already."

"I don't hate them," Fay lied. "I just want to know who they are."

"You already know who they are. You're the one who told me he had a boat, remember?" Lizzie leaned over to Jake. "Mother knows everything already, see. She just asks so we can fight. The guy is gorgeous."

"He's lazy," Fay said.

Lizzie opened the menu. "What difference does it make if he's lazy? He's rich."

"It makes a big difference," Fay said. "Everything is too easy for him. Including you."

Lizzie looked at Jake again. "Is my mother calling me a whore?"

Jake laughed. "I don't think so," he said. "Not yet, anyway."

Something about Jake's quiet eyes and easy self-assurance made Lizzie feel better. "Will you let me know when she does?" Lizzie said.

"You bet," he said.

"So tell me what you did with him, then," Fay demanded.

Arnie interrupted again. "Is there any trick to getting waited on here?" he asked.

"Mother," Lizzie said, trying to speak calmly, "we just went to a party on a boat, O.K.?"

"What kind of a party?" Fay asked.

That did it. "A party," Lizzie grumped. "You know. Fun? You remember fun, don't you?"

"So all he does is go to parties, is that right?"

Lizzie made no effort to cover her exasperation now. "It was a party, Mother. You don't ask that at a party."

"He would've lied about it anyway," Fay said.

Lizzie didn't answer, as the sudden appearance of the waitress startled them all.

"What do *you* want?" the waitress said, as if they had knocked on her door for a handout.

Lizzie pointed to Fay. "We'll both have cottage cheese and a Tab and she likes lots of crackers, so bring the whole basket, and they'll have the tuna melt."

"And a Coke," Arnie finished.

"Beer for me," Jake said. "I'm done for the day."

The waitress wrote down the orders and a busboy re-filled their water glasses.

"I'll let you drink your beer," Arnie said to Jake, "but you're not off duty."

"Oh, I know," he drawled. "I just don't like to alarm the subject."

Lizzie caught on. "Am I the subject?"

"Yes, ma'am," he said. "As far as I know, I'm on your tail till midnight."

She laughed. "Are those your official orders? On my tail?"

He winked at Arnie and lit a cigarette.

But Lizzie wouldn't quit. "I thought you had to go to your dad's for dinner," she said. "Do I have to go to your dad's for dinner?"

He looked at her, shrugged his shoulders as if her long legs and loose blouse didn't matter at all. "I made that up," he said.

"Lizzie," Fay asked, "did Paul want to know what you do?"

"I don't do anything," Lizzie said. "I take dance class."

"You're studying," Fay said.

"Not very hard," Lizzie said.

"Well, how *can* you be studying if you spend the whole night on boats?"

"Boat, Mother," Lizzie said. "Boat."

"I don't pay all that tuition for you to go to a party on a boat."

"You need some sleep, Mother," Lizzie said. "You're making a scene."

"I'm worried about you," Fay said.

"So what else is new?" Lizzie grumbled.

Arnie was relieved when the manager appeared with their lunch. He'd seen this fight before. But then, when he looked down at his food, he felt like he'd seen that before, too. Maybe it was Fay, being with her all day like this. It changed the way you looked at things.

"I just want to know," Fay said, "what you're doing with this boy."

With her free hand, Lizzie pinched Jake's arm. "With *this* boy?"

"Let's eat, huh?" Arnie begged.

"With Paul," Fay said.

"We're going to the boat again tonight, if that's what you mean." Lizzie attacked her cottage cheese.

"You are not," Fay said. "I absolutely forbid it."

"Mother," Lizzie said, "it's just another party. Except it's a better band, Paul says. I survived last night, didn't I?"

"It's not like last night," Fay said. "This time the boat is sailing, and once it goes, you're on it for good."

Lizzie tried to understand. "It's not me that's lost, Mother, it's all those little kids. I'm just fine."

Fay started to interrupt, but Arnie wouldn't let her. "Eat your lunch, Fay," he said.

Lizzie tried again. "We're going to a party, Mother, that's all. A party. The boat's not going anywhere. I'm not going anywhere. Except to the party." Lizzie looked at her watch, wadded up her napkin, and reached for her purse. "I've got to go," she said, nudging Jake to let her out of the booth. "I've got class in twenty minutes."

Fay stretched across the table and grabbed Lizzie's arm. "I said no," she said.

Lizzie looked at Arnie, Arnie looked at Jake.

"You're with her every minute, right?" he asked. "She takes a shower, you take a shower?"

Jake said that was right and Arnie gently pried Fay's fingers away from Lizzie's arm.

"Let her go, Fay," Arnie said quietly.

"I'm all right, Mom," Lizzie said. "I've got my class, I've got my cop . . ." She turned to Jake. "You can even take the class if you want to," Lizzie said. "Anybody can take a class."

"Now that's something I'd like to see." Arnie laughed.

"Lizzie—" Fay was still trying to stop her.

"It's all right, Fay," Arnie said. "She's just going to class." He looked at Lizzie. "Right, kid?"

"Right, Dad," Lizzie said, leaning over to kiss the top of his head. She stroked his face. "You got a good shave this morning."

"Thanks," he said. "I try."

"O.K.," Lizzie said carefully. "See you later."

"When, later?" Fay asked.

"I don't know, Mother. Just later, O.K.?"

"I want to know when," Fay said.

"Please, Mother," Lizzie said. "I just want to have a good time."

Fay took a deep breath. "And I just want you to be there when I wake up."

"I'll be there," Lizzie said. "I'll be there." She blew Fay a kiss. " 'Bye."

Arnie watched Lizzie and Jake leave, looked around for the waitress for a cup of coffee, then wondered why, if the waitress didn't feel like doing anything today, she didn't just stay home where nobody would bother her.

"I said the wrong thing," Fay said.

"It wasn't so bad," Arnie said. "You just acted like her mother. She's used to that."

"What would you have done?"

"All Lizzie wanted to do was trade stories. She's not going anywhere, Fay. She wouldn't leave while this case is going on. No way."

Fay knew better, but she didn't say anything. She was mad and hurt, and she wouldn't admit to being jealous, but she was. "Who is this Jake person?" she demanded.

Arnie sighed. "Oh, you know," he said, "he's just another one of those convicted rapists we hire from time to time."

"That's not funny."

"It is to me," Arnie said.

Fay gestured angrily toward the other customers in the snack bar. "Stand up and tell everybody, then," she snapped. "See if they think it's funny."

"Fay, Fay," he said.

"What?"

"Eat your cottage cheese."

Fay knew she was behaving badly, but she didn't know how to stop it. "I don't like cottage cheese," she said. "I never liked cottage cheese."

"Eat some crackers, then," Arnie said. "You like crackers, I know. You have to eat, Fay. So you'll feel better. So you'll act better—" he paused—"so I don't strangle you before we find those kids."

He reached for the basket of crackers, pushed it toward her, unwrapped a packet of butter, and picked up his knife. "Want me to fix one for you?"

Fay looked at him and shook her head. "I'm sorry."

"It's all right," he said.

She coated a cracker in butter and took a bite.

Arnie knew not to talk about Lizzie, but he wasn't sure if he could talk about the missing kids either. He wondered if he could bring up Wyoming again. The longer this day got, the better Wyoming looked to him. Maybe they could rent a little farm out there and buy a horse. Lizzie would come visit if they had a horse. Fay would like riding, too, he knew it. He was sure he'd remember how. It had a lot to do with how you talked to the horse; he remembered that much, anyway.

Fay was into her fourth packet of crackers now.

"If Lizzie makes one move toward that boat," she said, "packing, buying a bathing suit, anything, I want her stopped."

"Will do." Arnie stood up. "Are you ready?"

The waitress saw Fay stuffing the rest of the crackers into her purse and came over with the check.

"Don't go away," Arnie said to her, "I think I have it right here." He counted out sixteen dollars and twenty-eight cents, the exact amount of the bill, and put it in her hand.

"What about a tip?" the waitress snarled.

"O.K.," Arnie mused. "I'd say you probably ought to quit before they fire you."

The waitress turned abruptly and left.

"What do you want to do now?" Arnie asked Fay.

"See Gail," she said. "Find Beth."

"Good," Arnie said. "Good."

12:00 P.M.

FOR THE LAST HOUR GAIL HAD FOUGHT OFF HER fear and anger by writing sick sympathy cards, cards she already knew she couldn't sell. Who wants to buy a card that says

I'M SO SORRY,
(turn the page)
BUT WHAT DID YOU EXPECT?

Or

FATE
(turn the page)
DOESN'T GIVE A SHIT

She did like

JUST WHEN YOU THINK IT CAN'T GET ANY WORSE,
(turn the page)
YOU DISCOVER IT WAS ALL YOUR FAULT

But her favorite was

THE DARKEST HOUR
(turn the page)
IS JUST BEFORE THE END

169

Then, her fear winning out after all, she wrote what she knew would happen if her daughter died. She wrote the reason people would send cards instead of visiting:

I WOULD HAVE CALLED OR COME BY TO SEE YOU
(turn the page)
BUT I DIDN'T WANT TO

Her career was finished. She threw the notebook into the trash and poured herself a glass of water.

Marvin was still in the bedroom, sitting on the side of the bed reading *Sports Illustrated*. It was an old issue; Frank Shorter was on the cover. Marvin didn't know why he'd saved it. It had been years since Shorter was winning marathons. But every week, despite the arrival of a new issue, Frank had stayed on the top of the pile. Somehow just sitting there with the elegant, articulate, Ivy League runner made Marvin feel in control.

Marvin did not have, that he was aware of, any special skills, or even any particular personal traits. His childhood had not been especially tortured, and his high school career was largely undistinguished. He had graduated from State College with a degree in sociology and married an average-height, brown-haired woman. For twelve years they'd slept in a regular double bed and lived within their means.

Marvin had spent some forty years following his dad's advice to "show up and be friendly." Today was no exception. He couldn't imagine anyone wanting his daughter, Beth—a plain-looking child whose parents didn't have much money; he thought this kidnapping business simply had to be a mistake. When the kidnappers realized they had the wrong girl, they would give her back. All he had to do until then was encourage the police and cheer up his wife.

He checked his watch. It was time to go pick up the package the kidnappers had left for Gail at the bowling alley. Then they had to meet the other parents at the Burger King across from the Indian Point Shopping Center.

"Are you ready?" he said to Gail, as she appeared at the door of their bedroom.

Gail had been ready for the last three hours, but she didn't tell him that. She didn't say what a stupid question she thought it was, or how angry she was that her husband was so cheery. All that could wait. Maybe it wouldn't have to be said at all. Gail's mother was meeting them at the shopping center. Maybe Gail could just grab Beth's hand as she came down out of that truck, take her to her mother's car, and never see Marvin again.

"I'm ready," Gail said finally, and turned around and walked back down the hall.

"Let's go then," Marvin said to the empty doorway.

They drove to the bowling alley in silence. Gail picked up the package—a small white envelope—and they started for the shopping center.

"What is it?" Marvin asked.

"Just a slip of paper," Gail said, holding the envelope up to the light.

"Could be the combination to a lock," he said, pulling the car out into the traffic.

"You haven't even looked at it!" she snapped.

"I know," he said. "But that's how they lock those big trucks. With chains and a combination lock on the back door."

Gail bit her lip. Marvin didn't know anything about big trucks. He'd just followed them down the highway, followed them for a hundred miles because he didn't have the guts to pass them.

As they neared the center, traffic slowed to a crawl. Gail cursed and turned on the radio. They heard the Chief of Police tell people to stay away from the shopping center, and they heard the traffic control helicopter say that cars were backed up bumper to bumper for three miles on all routes leading there.

"How far away are we?" Gail asked, as Marvin pulled onto the shoulder and passed ten cars. Then he came to a bridge over the expressway and had to flag the car behind him to be let back onto the road.

"About a mile, I think," he said, shifting into neutral as the traffic came to a dead stop.

"I'll have to walk," she said, opening the door. "It's the only way I'll make it on time. We should have left earlier."

She put the envelope into her purse and stepped out of the car.

"Gail?" he called after her.

"What?" she said, closing the door.

"I love you."

Gail bent down to look in the window. "Good-bye, Marvin," she said.

AS GAIL WALKED along the highway, people stuck in the traffic jam rolled down their windows and asked if she could see anything up ahead, asked her if she wanted a lift, asked her if she was, by any chance, one of those poor mothers.

She said the road looked like a parking lot, that's why she was walking. She said she just got out of her own car so why should she get in theirs, and she said no, she wasn't one of those poor mothers, she was just trying to get to the Burger King for lunch.

The scene was worse than she could have ever imagined. The Burger King looked like a fort under siege. The parking lot was jammed. Gail could see two remote camera crews, at least eight police cars, a couple of ambulances, and a whole flock of motorcycle cops.

Finally she saw Fay and Arnie across the lot and screamed at them. Fay waved, and Gail ran toward them, dodging policemen who told her to slow down and cars that honked at her to get out of the way.

Fay and Gail got in the backseat of Arnie's car.

"Did you get your package?" Fay asked.

Gail showed her the envelope. "Marvin thinks it's the combination to the lock on the back door of the truck."

"Could be," Fay said, feeling the slip of paper inside it. "How's Marvin holding up?"

"Please," Gail said. "Let's not talk about Marvin."

Fay patted her on the knee. If there was some state just before shock, Gail was in it.

"I'm sorry I asked you about Lizzie this morning," Fay said, "but all night long I'd been seeing her going away on this big boat. I just didn't think about how it would sound to you."

"It's O.K.," Gail said. "I didn't mean to scream at you. I was just so upset. Marvin was . . . I don't know, I guess he was trying to make me feel better, telling little jokes and straightening up the living room, but why isn't he mad at them, or something?"

Fay reached over for her hand. "Honey, Marvin is every bit as scared as you are. I promise."

Gail put the envelope back in her purse. "Lizzie and I had a nice visit," she said. She zipped her purse closed, then open again. It was hard for her to just sit here like this, but she knew it wouldn't be any better outside.

"Is Beth in the truck?" Gail asked.

"No," Fay said.

"Did somebody look?" Gail asked.

"No," Fay said. "The police are doing exactly what the kidnappers said to do, leaving the truck alone till the mothers get here."

"Then how do you know the kids aren't in there?" Gail asked, her eyes watering suddenly.

"We would have heard them," Fay said.

"Not if they were tied up and gagged."

"They're not there, Gail. The most we can hope for in the truck are the instructions for finding them."

"That's not enough," Gail said. "I want Beth back right now."

The Mayor knocked on Fay's window.

"Who's that?" Gail asked.

"The Mayor," Fay said. "Let's get out and see if they need you."

Gail followed Fay, numb and blind.

"This is Gail Wilkins," Fay said to the Mayor as they stood together, the car between them and the crowd. "Her daughter, Beth, is one of the missing children."

Fay turned to Gail. "And this is Peter Ewing. His boys, Kevin and Kerry, are missing too."

"The newspaper didn't say anything about your boys," Gail said.

"I know." The Mayor extended his hand to shake hers. "I thought, if the kidnappers . . . never mind. It was stupid, what I thought."

"How old are they?" she asked, noticing his palms were clammy and cold.

"Three and five," he said. "Yours?"

"Five," Gail said.

"Are you a hiker?" he asked, referring to her shorts, but basically trying to keep talking.

"Yes," Gail said, looking back at the crowd. "You?"

"I'm sorry," he said. "What a dumb thing to say. I'm going crazy."

"I'm hating everybody I know," she said. She shook her head and tried to laugh.

Fay saw her chance and took it. "I have to find Arnie," she said. "Can you two keep each other together here?"

They said sure, and when Fay left, they walked around to sit on the back bumper of the car.

"Shouldn't you be . . . somewhere?" Gail asked.

"I'd just be in the way," he said. "My wife is talking to the press, and my staff is handling the rest of it. Where I should be . . ." He couldn't finish.

"Go on," she said, knowing that as long as he kept talking, she wouldn't have to.

"I'd like to be at my desk making kidnapping punishable by death in this city," he said. "Or making everybody stand outside their houses while I went door to door and found our kids. Or appointing somebody else mayor so if I ever get my boys back we can go camping or something until they're grown up."

Gail was quiet a minute. "You're abolutely right," she said. "We're the ones who ought to be kidnapping our kids. Take them away where the world can't mess them up."

"What do you do?" he asked.

"I write greeting cards," Gail said, "and think about where I'd rather be."

"Is it any place in particular?"

"Someplace cool and high," she said, staring at the hideous commercial landscape and the clogged highway that ran through it.

"Sounds like the mountains," he said, then looked at her and added impulsively, "or drugs, I guess."

"Or both," she said.

"God, are we depressed."

"Are we going to get them back?" she asked.

"I don't know," he said. "They keep telling us we are."

"Right," she said. "Do you believe it?"

He loosened his tie. "I have to. I just have to."

"Yeah," she said. "We can do that, I guess."

"I have to have another chance with them," he said. "I've . . . missed too much of their lives already."

She nodded, knowing exactly what he meant. "Beth is

the only thing in my life that makes any sense," she said. "I'd do it all different except for her."

"So," he said, grasping her hand, "we've got to find them. If we don't . . ."

She squeezed his hand. "We'll find them," she said quietly. "We will."

They stood up, and she shielded her eyes with her hand so she could look directly up at him.

"Thanks," she said.

"Yeah." He put his arm around her and patted her shoulder. "You too."

"O.K.," she said.

"I'll be here all day." He glanced behind him at the women beginning to gather under the MOTHERS sign.

"Yeah," she said. "Me too."

"So I'll see you later," he said.

"O.K.," she said. "What do we do now?"

"Whatever they say," he said, and walked off toward his press aide, who had promised the *Today* show woman an interview with him.

Gail scanned the crowd briefly for Marvin, didn't see him, smoothed her shorts, and walked over to join the other mothers in front of the cameras.

"WHAT WAS THAT all about?" Arnie asked. He had been watching the Mayor talk to Gail.

"They have to talk to somebody," Fay said. "They're doing what we're doing. Trying to get through this."

"Did they know each before?" he asked, thinking the conversation looked more than polite.

Fay saw what he meant. They looked better together than she'd seen either one of them look all day. Of course, she also knew that both marriages were in trouble, but that wasn't so unusual anymore.

Fay's favorite thought about marriage came from a Russian psychic she'd heard speak at a dusty old library in an Italian neighborhood. The woman had said that when married people went to sleep, their souls, free of the captivity of their bodies, flew off to spend the night with their spiritual mates. They never had to decide what to do next, they just did it. And they didn't relate the events of their days, they just played. They'd take long walks and whistle, they'd tilt their heads back and drink the dew as it fell, or sometimes just dance till daybreak to the blue strains of the moon.

Occasionally, the woman said, people did recognize these soul mates in their waking life, and if that happened, then sooner or later, not usually in this life, but sometimes, they would find a way to be together, though that was often quite costly. But, she said, even if soul mates married, the life they'd spend together in the kitchen would bear very little resemblance to the deep satisfaction their spirits would enjoy without them at night.

Fay remembered the looks exchanged by some of the couples in the room. One person would squeeze the other's hand as if to say, "We're one of the lucky ones, we've found each other." And the other person would return the squeeze, but turn back quickly to face the podium and sigh, wondering how long it would be until the next life got here.

In the Tarot pack, on the card called the Lovers, there is a picture of a young man standing between two women, trying to make a choice. Depending on the pack you are using and the interpretation you've been taught, the choice is either between virtue and vice, between celibacy and the carnal life, or between the beautiful maiden and the loyal mother. The odd thing is that in nearly every deck there is a little Cupid over the boy's head about to let fly with an arrow and, presumably, make the boy's choice for him.

When this card appeared in a prominent position, Fay usually told people they were torn between two loves—work and life, for example—and that the choice had to be made. That wasn't so much an interpretation of the cards as it was a common fact of everyday life. It was so common that Fay could, if she felt like it, call people at random from the phone book and tell them that. In a reading, however, her clients generally responded quickly to this insight, and told her their version of this ancient dilemma.

Fay liked it when someone recognized that one of their loves was, in a sense, sacred, and the other profane. Profane loves weren't so bad. They were certainly distracting, moderately entertaining, and relatively inexpensive to maintain. For most people, profane loves were just fine, and whole industries had developed to help people find them. But the choice to honor a sacred love was always a costly one, and

Fay could help a client determine if they were willing to pay the price. A sacred love, she insisted, could cost your whole life and then leave you anyway in the end.

Occasionally, Fay talked to artists, or people who wanted to be artists, who felt, for their talent, something they called a sacred love. All too often, it turned out that they simply adored the idea of being famous—which, of course, had very little to do with art, and was just about the most profane kind of love going.

Real artists, Fay knew, had no choice. Real lovers had no choice. That's what Cupid was doing in the picture, making the choice for these people. Fay figured if you could make the choice yourself, you should. But if there didn't seem to be a choice, well then, that was your answer, but you'd still have to pay for it.

The thing about love was that feeling it *for* someone, *for* something, feeling it in the first place, was the gift. It filled you with energy and purpose, and the more of it you gave away, the more of it there seemed to be. To love one person was to like everybody a little better, and to love some one thing was to begin to understand the rest. Usually, love made you generous and brave, but even if it made you obsessive and grasping, it at least pumped you up, pointed you toward the path, and sent you charging into the world believing that you and the world were somehow related for a change.

Receiving love, however, was a totally separate matter. To *be* loved was to know you didn't really deserve it, to worry about losing it, to try to keep doing whatever it was that made someone love you in the first place, and to feel somehow responsible for it although you knew it really wasn't yours. Yes, receiving love was quite complicated, and very difficult to do with much grace. Better to feel it. Better to be the one who loves. Better to love something that can't love you back. Better to serve.

As far as Fay knew, God was the only one bighearted and gracious enough to allow Himself to be loved completely. And how did He do it? Like a good soldier, by staying in the fields of Heaven, sending the occasional homesick telegram but never actually applying for leave.

The people who loved Him had it made, Fay thought. The martyrs, the saints, even just ordinary believers had it pretty good. They got to love as much as they wanted to and

God never said, Stop, that's enough, I can't take it anymore, love the dog, why don't you, I need a break.

"Why don't the police just open the packages?" Fay asked Arnie.

"They checked for bombs," he said. "But the Chief is still taking your advice, going along with the kidnappers."

Fay nodded, and wished she'd brought a hat. The sun was really brutal now.

Arnie wanted something to happen. He wouldn't have minded if, say, a bomb went off. Then at least he could tell somebody what to do. He'd already told the Chief he should clear all these extra people out of here, but when the Chief pointed out that with the highway blocked it would take an airlift to get rid of them, Arnie gave up. This wasn't his show and he knew it. The Chief had told him his job was to protect Fay, and that even if he saw somebody breaking the law, he wasn't to interfere unless Fay was threatened.

"Are they in the crowd somewhere?" he asked her. "The kidnappers?"

"I don't know," she said. "It feels bad here, but I don't know how it could feel good. It's just all this fear."

"I want to know where all these tacky people came from," he said. "I've never seen so many fat—"

She had to stop him. "Arnie, just calm down. These people are worried for the mothers. That's why they came. They thought there might be something they could do."

"There's not a damn thing anybody can do," he said. "All I wanted to know was why they're all so fat."

"They're not fat," she said. "They're just hot and their clothes are wrinkled, that's all; they just *look* fat."

"You could never love a fat man, could you, Fay?"

"No, Arnie." She smiled. "I don't think I could."

He was silent a moment. He seemed to be a little better. "How many minutes now?" he asked.

"Four, Arnie. Four," she said.

VI HAD ENJOYED her interview with the woman from the *Today* show, although she was disappointed to find that she was so short. Once she thought about it, though, Vi realized that height, like depth, just didn't matter on TV.

Vi had begun by stating that this incident was a direct

attempt to destroy the women's movement. Then she went on to say that the women's movement was the obvious target for all kinds of hostilities now, remarking that it wouldn't be long before the growing epidemic of AIDS was blamed on the women's movement. The reasoning would go something like: If women were who they used to be, then men wouldn't be turning gay in droves and heading for the bathhouses instead of taking a shower at home, where somebody who loved them disinfected the stall once a week.

The *Today* woman asked Vi if she wasn't putting words into the mouth of the enemy. Vi said gays weren't the enemy, the world was just in a mess now. And, since there were only two new things in the last twenty years, Moslem fundamentalism and the women's movement, one of them had to have caused all this trouble. Probably women.

"Everything is our fault," Vi said. "Restaurant prices are higher because women don't cook like they used to. Clothing prices are higher because women have to have clothes to work in. More men are unemployed because women are taking their jobs. City services are less dependable because there aren't enough housewives left to call up and bitch about things. Products are shoddier because women aren't mechanical, divorce rates are going up because women aren't making happy homes, and kids don't read anymore because their mothers don't teach them how to."

"Are you going to lead the mothers' group?" the woman asked.

"Yes, I am," Vi said, and excused herself. She had done quite well, she thought. And she knew she looked good. She had dressed for the cameras—a high-necked blue silk blouse, and a straight flower-printed skirt.

Most of the other mothers were wearing whatever they had on when the call came: work clothes, jeans or khaki pants, and old shirts. Dolores Garcia came straight from the studio, so she still had on her leotards, but she had borrowed a dance skirt and put it on as she drove out. Betsy Griffith had an arbitration that morning, so she was wearing her gray suit and red paisley bow tie.

As they waited for someone to take charge, the mothers talked uncomfortably with one another, exchanging accounts of how their children had disappeared and what the kidnappers had said on the phone. They were scared and angry.

They wanted to storm the truck. They wanted to sue the fairgrounds. They wanted to kill the kidnappers for putting them through this. None of them wanted to be here, and none of them had any choice.

Fay was standing with Arnie just behind the mothers. The *Today* woman came up, introduced herself, and asked if, by any chance, they knew who the local psychic was who was working on the case. Arnie lit a cigarette, and Fay said she'd heard about it, but she, herself, was only here because one of the mothers was a good friend.

When the reporter left, he took her hand. "You can't dodge the reporters forever, you know."

"It's not that I mind talking," she said, glad to have his hand in hers. "It's just that I don't have anything to say right now."

"What do you think of the group?" he asked, looking at the mothers.

"They're scared," she said. "That's going to be a problem."

"Scared they won't be able to do what the kidnappers want?" he asked.

"No," she said. "Scared of each other. Each one of them thinks she'd do better by herself." She paused. "It's . . . it's a problem women have."

"Do *you* have this problem?" he asked.

"Oh yes," she said. "I know it's wrong, but it's another one of those real old things."

Vi began to address the group. "We have," she said, "one minute to cross the street. The police will clear the path and protect us as we go. All we have to do is ignore the crowd and walk calmly. When we arrive at the truck, a policeman will ask each of you for the names of people you want admitted to a kind of family circle over there. We will work inside the barricades next to the truck, but your husbands or mothers or friends will at least be a little closer than the rest of the city."

Vi stretched out her hand, and the police path opened up. Several of the women gasped. Nobody had quite believed they could rearrange such a large crowd so quickly.

"And now," Vi concluded, "God bless us. And everybody else . . . get out of our way."

Vi walked to the path the police had made and the mothers formed a line behind her. Fay and Arnie followed at the end of the line, in a group that included the Chief, the Mayor, two emergency medical men, and the owner of the shopping center.

Their passage was a silent one. Once they reached the other side of the street, however, once Vi stepped into the shopping center parking lot and the newly positioned cameras switched their lights back on, everybody started to talk again. What will they make us do? Who are they? How long will it take? What do they want? Where are our children? And who the hell are all these other people?

"LIZZIE THINKS I spied on her," Fay said to Arnie as they made their way to the truck.

He wasn't listening. He was surveying the security setup along the route. "What?" he asked.

"All Lizzie wants is to get away where I can't know what she's doing."

"You can't help it if you know things," he managed, wondering what the big hook and ladder was doing here.

"I'm not prying," Fay said. "I want her to have her own life. I always have."

He saw the four officers on the roof of the shopping center, saw their rifles and telescopic sights. "You just want her to tell you things," he said.

"She doesn't have to tell me everything," Fay said. "It's just that it was so nice to share it."

"When she was little, you mean?"

"Remember how she'd run in the door all full of what the teacher said, or what her girlfriend said, or how she saw a daddy longlegs crawling up a stop sign?"

"I remember," he said. The coroner was here too, he noticed. "But she doesn't have the same kind of things to tell you now, Fay."

"Yes she does," Fay said. "I don't know anything about her dance classes, I don't know where she buys her shoes. Or she has a new dance bag, only it doesn't look new, so she must have found it or traded it with somebody, but who was it?"

"Here." He pointed to a row of bleachers set up for the police. "We'll sit here."

"Why won't she tell me?" she asked.

"Want anything?" he asked. "Coffee, soda, anything?"

"I want to know why Lizzie won't tell me things."

"It's not that she won't, Fay," he said. "It's just that she doesn't."

"All right," she said. "Why doesn't she tell me things?"

"She's busy,' he said. "She's doing them. She doesn't have time to tell you about them."

"How much time would it take?" Fay protested.

"To know everything you want to know?"

She wound her watch.

"To know everything you want to know," he said, "you'd have to be *her*. That's why she won't tell you. She doesn't want *you* to be her. *She's* her. She's just trying to keep it that way."

Fay scooted across the bleacher seat and forced herself to look at the mothers standing around the table in front of the truck. Where were these children? Where was Lizzie?

1:00 P.M.

THE MOTHERS STOOD AROUND THE LONG TABLE set up in front of the truck. Vi had asked the Chief for folding chairs, but nobody felt like sitting. This wasn't a committee meeting.

Behind the mothers, three bleacher sections held the police, the press, and the fathers and families of the kidnapped children. Camera crews were positioned to the right of the bleachers, and emergency vehicles to the left. Behind the bleachers there were portable toilets, a first-aid station, and a barricade of police cars and fire trucks. The whole encampment was then ringed by firemen standing shoulder to shoulder.

The firemen were the Chief's idea. Something about firemen made people feel better. Even the Chief. Actually, when he was a little boy, he'd wanted to be a fireman, but when he grew up somehow he knew he wasn't nice enough.

Fay looked more closely at the mothers. "Something's wrong," she said to Arnie. "I mean, somebody's wrong. One of these mothers is not a mother."

"The one in the pink sweatshirt," Arnie said. "Undercover. The real mother's in Spain."

Fay saw immediately that the policewoman was trying too hard to be calm, to seem normal. The other mothers were agitated, eager to get started.

183

Arnie wiped the sweat from his forehead. "The father's here, though." He pointed to the man. "Merriweather."

Vi set her package down on the table in front of her, and the other mothers followed. "I think we should open them one at a time," Vi said.

The mothers grumbled among themselves. What did Vi think this was, a baby shower? The point was to get it done, wasn't it?

Gail held up her envelope. "Mine has the combination to the lock on the truck," she said.

The mothers shouted almost in unison, "Open it!"

And Gail tore the end off the envelope and fished out the tiny strip of paper. "Nine right," she said. "Twenty-one left, three right."

Nobody moved. What if the truck blew up when they opened it?

"It won't blow up," Fay said to Arnie.

"I know," he said. "The bomb squad checked it."

"But the kids aren't there either," she said. "There's a letter in one of their packages. That's what we have to find."

But at the table, the mothers were ripping their packages open with no regard to what might be in them, or what order might make the contents understandable.

"There's the key to a padlock," Arnie said.

"And a slide projector." Fay was standing up to get a better view of the table. "And slides," she added, as the mother who got the projector opened a box of slides and held one of them up to the light, then sank back into the chair behind her, clearly sickened by what she saw.

"It's an abortion," the mother said to the woman next to her.

But before she could get the slide back in the box, a woman at the far end of the table screamed. "It's our babies!" she cried, and flipped through the stack of photos to find her own boy asleep on a kitchen table, his head leaning up against a toaster.

The mothers left their places and swarmed around the photos, desperate to see their children. Were they really sleeping? How could they know they weren't dead?

"They're not dead," Fay said to Arnie.

"Till we find them, they might as well be," he said. And now he could see some of the other things the mothers had unwrapped. Megaphones, felt-tip markers, poster board and wooden stakes, a ream of white paper, two dozen ballpoint pens, flashlights, a cassette tape player, twenty-seven pairs of white baby shoes, and nine jars like you'd see in a laboratory, containing little white things floating in liquid.

Gail looked up to find Fay in the bleachers and held up the photo of Beth.

Arnie grabbed Fay's arm to keep her from running to her friend. "It won't help," he said. "They have to finish."

But Fay knew what Gail was thinking. It was time for Beth's nap. Had they fed her any lunch? Any breakfast? Was she tied to the bed? Did they let her go to the bathroom? Give her any water? Were they watching her at all?

The woman next to Gail held her photo in her teeth while she finished unwrapping her package. A clock. Gail sat down, took the clock from the woman, and shook her head. A harmless wind-up kitchen clock with a bright yellow face and a sunflower in the middle of the dial. The kind of clock you hear ticking when you don't know what to say to the person across the table.

Arnie was mad. "This is the most cruel, goddamn mean thing I've ever seen. How can these women . . ."

"Oh my God," Fay interrupted.

At the far end of the table, a mother in a wheelchair had just lifted the top off a black plastic garbage can, pulled out a sack of little arms and legs.

Fay's hand flew to her mouth. "Oh no," she whispered. "Please God, no."

But the woman next to her pulled one of the little arms up to the edge of the bag so she could see it better. "It's dolls," she said, checking another one just to make sure. "It's not babies."

But the woman in the wheelchair was crying anyway.

"They can't go on like this," Fay said.

"Anti-abortion," a mother called to the group, pulling pamphlets out of her envelope.

"Class photos," said the woman who had checked on the doll arms. "Only every fourth head is cut out."

The woman in the wheelchair had stopped crying. "What does that mean, one out of four?" she asked, looking numbly at the class photos.

"It's abortion," the other woman said. "I read it somewhere. That's the number now. One in four conceptions ends in abortion."

"One out of four?" the woman in the wheelchair said blankly.

"That's what the number's *always* been," the nurse on the other side said. "These people are sick."

Most of the mothers were sitting down now. There were only two packages left to open.

"That one's going to take all of them to unwrap it," Fay said, pointing to the box, which was easily the size of a coffin.

But a Chinese mother started pulling white sheets out of the duffel bag she had been given, and a letter fell on the ground.

"There it is," Fay said.

Three mothers dived for it.

"Wait!" Vi called. "Don't—"

But nobody was about to damage this letter. They weren't sure they wanted to hear what it said, but they weren't going to fight over it, either.

The Chinese woman walked around the table and handed it to Vi.

"Good," Fay said. "They should wait till they know what's in that big one."

The outside of the big box was secured with metal tape, and the box itself was double-wrapped in heavy brown paper. The edges were taped all the way around, and each item inside was enclosed in bubble-pack reinforced with masking tape, then surrounded by those Styrofoam amoebas that fly all over everywhere and three months later you're still finding them down between the sofa cushions.

It took three women ten minutes to get it all undone. They spread the items on the table: one life-size inflatable woman, and a full set of surgical equipment necessary for an abortion—the stirrups, the dilators, the curettes, the works.

Nobody said a thing. They were finished. A bitter depression settled around them. This was not what they'd expected. Maybe they'd thought they would each receive directions for finding their children. Or maybe they thought they would simply break into the truck and their kids would come running out, hungry and tired but alive. But no. They saw now that this was not the end of the anguish. This was just barely the beginning.

They had been mad before, but now they felt the ragged anger of outrage, the hostile anger of despair. And none of them could move.

Vi was still standing. "I'll read the letter now," she said, looking around the table.

"Kill them," somebody whispered. "Kill them all."

The Mayor came up to sit with Fay and Arnie.

"I don't understand," he said. "I just don't—"

"Just sit," Fay said, patting the bleachers. "Just sit down. It's not much longer now."

" 'Good afternoon,' " Vi read from the letter. " 'Your children are safe. But you will not see them again until you have collected forty thousand signatures and addresses on a petition demanding that abortion once again be outlawed in the United States.' "

"Can't do that," Arnie whispered. "It's blackmail."

"Abortion?" the Mayor said. "What's abortion got to do with my boys?"

Vi continued. " 'You will set up an exhibit in the truck. When people have toured the exhibit, they can then sign the petition.' "

"It's ridiculous," Arnie said. "They could get that many signatures just passing the thing around the parking lot."

"Would you sign it?" Fay asked.

"Sure," he said. "If I thought that's all it took to get those kids back, I'd be first on the list."

Vi was still reading from the letter. " 'You will keep a vigil around the clock, carrying signs you will make, until you have the required number of signatures. Do not be tempted to cheat. We are watching from very close range, even, perhaps, from inside your group. You will turn the signatures over to the Mayor's wife, who will take them to Washington and put them in the hands of the Chief Justice of the Supreme Court of the United States. Then, and only then, will your children be returned.' "

"Would she do that?" Fay asked the Mayor. "Take the petition to Washington?"

"I don't know what she'd do," he said. "Maybe."

Vi cleared her throat, grasping the letter firmly in her hand. " 'There is only one right position on this issue,' " she read. " 'Abortion is murder, murder is wrong. If you are energetic and passionate as you talk to people about it, that will weigh heavily in our decision as to the fate of your children.' "

Vi had spoken very distinctly. No planes had flown over while she was reading. Fay and Arnie and everyone else in the bleachers had heard every word of the letter.

"Goddamn them," Arnie said to Fay, as Vi folded up the piece of paper.

"What do we do?" the Mayor asked.

"It's up to the mothers," Fay said. "They have to decide whether to go along or not."

"What choice do they have?" the Mayor asked.

But the fight had already started at the mothers' table. Vi, determined to stay in charge, asked the Chief if he didn't need to go over the contents of the packages for clues. What she meant was that the mothers would listen to him if he said to take a break. And maybe during the break she could decide what they should do.

"If I could have your attention," the Chief said to the mothers.

They kept talking.

"We have no intention of letting you go through with this preposterous plan," he said.

They heard him, but they didn't believe him. They weren't even sure it was any of his business.

"We need to search this material"—he gestured toward the table—"for clues."

They went back to talking.

"If you will eat your lunch now," he said, a little louder, "that will make it easier for us."

"I brought mine," one mother said. "Let's go on."

"What is there to talk about?" another mother said. "We have to do what they say or we won't get our children back."

Four mothers stood up and headed for the lunch table. There was going to be an argument, that was clear. And the argument was going to take more energy than the work the kidnappers were demanding.

They didn't need the Chief to tell them to eat. They were all mothers. Mothers know when to eat.

The Mayor stood up. He'd been watching Gail for the last ten minutes. He had to go to her. He stepped down out of the bleachers and headed over to her. She needed him.

*   *   *

"WOULD YOU REALLY sign the kidnappers' petition?" Fay asked Arnie, as the police garrison around them broke up to go to work.

Arnie threw his cigarette on the ground, stubbed it out with his shoe, shook his head slowly from side to side, then took out his handkerchief and wiped the sweat off the back of his neck. It might have looked, to someone who didn't know him, as if he was thinking about it. Fay knew better.

She asked again. She had to know. But she tried to ask in her normal tone of voice. "What *do* you think about abortion, Arnie?"

He looked up and watched the mothers walking away from the table. For some reason, he couldn't look directly at Fay.

"It doesn't matter what I think about abortion," he said. "It doesn't matter what any man thinks about abortion. It doesn't happen to us."

"Of course it happens to *you*," she said.

"No." He shook his head again. "It happens real close to us, but not directly to us, like it does to women."

"If somebody aborts our child," he went on, "we might be mad it's gone or glad it's gone, but we didn't feel it go. But if she *had* the baby, we wouldn't know what that was like either, because we wouldn't be there all day with it. So we shouldn't be making this decision. This is for women to decide."

He stopped for breath. "I think it's wrong. But I don't want to be asked what I think. It doesn't matter what I think."

"Do you think the fetus has a soul?" she asked.

"It has something," he said. "Maybe not a soul, exactly. But maybe the threat of a soul."

"And that's what you want to save?" Fay asked.

He thought for a moment. "No," Arnie said. "That's what makes me sad to kill it. I'm a Catholic. Remember?"

"I remember," she said.

"I like being a Catholic," he explained. "I mean, I like being something besides a cop, so I'm a Catholic. But I don't believe much of it anymore. Maybe abortion is the only way I can still call myself a Catholic. It's something to hold on to, anyway."

"Do you believe in contraception?" she asked.

"Sure I do," he said. "Same way I believe in locking the front door at night."

"So it's all right to stop babies from coming into the womb, but not all right to stop them from coming into the world?"

"I guess so," he said. "I don't know."

She looked up at him. "Don't I have the right to defend myself if somebody breaks into my house?"

"You don't have the right to kill him except in self-defense," he said. "And babies aren't trying to hurt you." He stood up. "Let's go see the Chief."

"No," Fay said, pulling him back down beside her. "Please. One more minute."

"All right," he said, almost angrily. "Yes, if somebody breaks into your house, I'd say shoot him. You don't have the right to do it, but you do it just the same. But I don't like it. And I don't like abortion either. And you can talk at me all day if you want to. I still won't like it."

"I'm not trying to convert you," she said. "I'm just trying to understand what you feel."

"I don't want people to hurt each other," he said. "That's why I became a policeman in the first place. But the first thing you learn being a cop is you can't stop them."

"Arnie—" she began.

But Arnie wasn't through. "I don't want the women hurt, you understand. I just don't want the babies hurt."

"The only way to keep women safe is keep abortion legal."

"You're right," he said. "I know that. All right, then. I just want them to be sorry."

"I think they are sorry," Fay said.

Arnie shook his head. "They just want it over with," he said.

Fay was beginning to suspect Arnie was talking from experience. She spoke softly. "Maybe they do," she said. "But they're still sorry."

He turned away.

Did she dare ask him about it? Why had he kept it a secret all these years? Was he still ashamed of it? Still sad about it?

She asked as carefully as she could. "Weren't you sorry? Wasn't she sorry?"

"Yes." He nodded. "We were the sorriest two people I ever knew."

"Well," she said, "that's how sorry they all are."

Arnie wound his watch distractedly, looked up and saw that the mothers had all left the table, and the Chief was motioning for him. "All right, then," he said. "I guess I can't sign the petition, can I?"

"We can sign it to get the children back."

"No," he said. "That wouldn't be right. We can find those children, you and me."

Fay wondered if she would ever hear this abortion story of Arnie's, wondered how many other people had one to tell, people she thought she knew.

Arnie couldn't ignore the Chief any longer. "Let's go," he said, standing up. "Here, give me your hand." He helped her down from the bleachers.

Fay saw through the crowd that Gail was talking to the Mayor at the lunch table, while Vi gave yet another interview. She hoped Gail would be careful with the Mayor, hoped she wouldn't get confused about what was happening, hoped she could forgive herself if she did.

When Fay and Arnie arrived at the mothers' table, the Chief was ready for Arnie, wished he'd been with him the whole time, in fact. "Well," he snapped, "got any good ideas?"

"I think you should send the mothers home," Arnie said, leafing through one of the anti-abortion pamphlets.

"They wouldn't go," the Chief said.

"Yeah," Arnie said, picking up a set of dilators and trying to suppress his revulsion. "I guess you should've picked up the packages yourself and never let this thing get started in the first place."

"How could I do that?" the Chief asked.

"I'd like to see the pictures of the children," Fay said. "Where they're sleeping, I mean."

The Chief glanced over at the mothers at the lunch table, noticed that they were no longer chatting among themselves, but instead were now totally absorbed in the sandwiches he knew to be completely tasteless.

"Let's let the gals finish their lunches, huh. When they come back to the table, I'll gather up the pictures for you."

Fay nodded.

"It's going to be a goddamn circus out here," the Chief said, irritated at Arnie's seeming lack of interest. "This thing could go on for weeks."

"I think you'll be through before dark," Arnie said.

"I don't see how." The Chief bit off the end of his cigar. "The people have to walk through the truck before they can sign the petition, right? Now how many people can walk through a truck in an hour? Maybe a hundred, and that's with nobody stopping to read anything. Forty thousand people at one hundred an hour is four hundred hours. That's"—he paused to do the math—"sixteen days, Arnie."

"If you want to get names," Arnie said, "just set up twenty tables and let the people who are already against it go ahead and sign. I mean, nobody's going to change their mind about this just because they get a few new facts. Abortion isn't about facts."

"But the letter said—" the Chief began.

"Yeah, I know what the letter said." Arnie slid the full-color abortion close-ups out of the envelope. "What are they going to do, send a team of kidnappers over here to validate the signatures?" He threw down the pictures in disgust. "It's all just a show, Chief, just a damn show for the damn TV. Just get it over with so the rest of us can go to work."

"Doing what?" the Chief asked.

Arnie didn't answer. He was examining one of the pickled embryos floating in its jelly jar.

"What is it you want to do?" the Chief repeated, as calmly as he could.

Arnie shoved the jar back down in the box. "I have to stay with Fay. But somebody needs to talk to the pro-life groups around here," Arnie said. "See if they know who could have done this, see what they have to say about it."

"Good," the Chief said, relieved that Arnie had started thinking again. "Good idea."

"I want to talk to Gail," Fay said to Arnie, "before they start up again."

But the Chief wasn't finished with her. "Do you think there's a kidnapper in the group?" he asked. "One of the mothers?"

"Has to be," Arnie said. "Probably the lady who got the slide projector."

Fay gasped. Of course. That's exactly who it was.

"What makes you think that?" the Chief growled. Then he looked over at the lunch table and saw that Lynn Waldo, who had gotten the slide projector, was also the only one who'd brought her lunch.

"They don't want it broken, that's why," Arnie said. "So they gave it to somebody they knew could run it."

"Anybody can run a slide projector," the Chief said.

"No," Fay interrupted. "I can't. A lot of people can't. I think Arnie's right."

"So what good does that do us?" the Chief asked. "We can't arrest her for anything."

"No," Arnie said, checking his watch. "But you can go to her house and see if her kid's there."

Fay saw it instantly. "She's at her grandmother's," she said.

"Right," Arnie said, taking Fay's arm. "Send somebody to see the grandmother."

Grandmother, Fay thought. Grandmother. She turned around to look back at the coffee shop.

"What is it?" the Chief asked, sensing her alarm.

"I don't know," she said. "It might be nothing."

"What?"

"Do you remember that woman in the coffee shop this morning, the one I said could be one of them?"

"Beige pantsuit?" the Chief said. "Gray hair?"

Fay nodded. "Her name is Edith Masters. And if she's still in there watching all this, then I think you should keep an eye on her."

"We can take her in is what we can do," the Chief said, his spirits lifting at the thought of it.

"No," Fay said. She didn't know what to tell him. "Just don't let her get away."

Arnie pointed toward the mothers. "Gail is looking for you," he said to Fay.

"I'm ready," she said.

The Chief watched them go, envied their hold on each other, wished he weren't married, and wondered why the hell he hadn't gone on vacation last week.

Fay took Arnie's hand as they walked. "Maybe we should have gone to the grandmother's," she said.

"No," he said. "I know you want to get out of here, but I

want you to be the first one inside that truck when we open it. And we can't do that till the mothers leave."

"Are you sure they'll go?" she asked.

"If they've got any guts they will," he said.

Fay looked up at Arnie. Whatever his story was, the pain had never gone away. However long ago it was, he felt as bad today as he did the day it happened. She had never seen this look on his face before. There was no other word for it. Lonely. Arnie was lonely.

ONE OF THE firemen had pulled Gail away from the other mothers and was giving her what looked like bad news.

"I hope it's not Marvin," Fay said to Arnie.

But it was.

Gail turned to Fay, her eyes crazed, her hands out of control. "Marvin climbed the goddamn Indian," she blurted, pointing high off in the distance, clear to the other end of the shopping center. "My daughter is gone and my husband is sitting on the goddamn Indian."

Fay looked where Gail pointed. It couldn't be. That little speck on the giant Red Man's bicep was Marvin?

"But how did he get there?" Fay asked, her arm wrapped tight around Gail's shoulder.

"He was halfway up before anybody spotted him," the fireman said. "Latched on to the loincloth and scooted up easy after that. Then the crowd closed in, I guess." The fireman chewed on a toothpick. "If it was a kid, we'd go after him right now. But the Chief said wait. He's safe enough. Somebody's likely to get hurt if we try to move the ladder truck through this crowd." He paused and looked at Gail. "Unless you want us to, ma'am. We'll go get him right now if you say so."

"No," Gail said weakly. "Whenever you think's best." She looked up at Arnie. "Why did he do this?"

"Got the best seat in the house," Arnie said.

The fireman shook his head. "We don't think so," he said to Arnie. "We figure, the way that big arm is crooked at the elbow, him sitting on the arm where he is, we don't think he can see a thing."

Arnie swallowed his laugh, not altogether successfully.

Gail blew her nose. "It's all right," she said. "Go ahead. Laugh." She sniffed. "At least I know where he is."

"I'm afraid there's more, ma'am," the fireman said.

Gail looked at Fay. "Do I want to know this?"

"It's your car," the fireman said.

"It's his car," Gail said.

"Well," the fireman said, "it's our car now, ma'am."

Gail nodded.

The fireman explained. "It seems he paid this lady ten dollars to park it in her yard. Only he didn't want to park too far up in the yard, so he eased it right up against the hydrant. We had to impound it." He took the toothpick out of his mouth. "You understand."

"Can I go now?" Gail asked.

"How did you find out it was his car?" Arnie asked.

The fireman turned around to look at the Indian, easing his hat back on his head. "Just a guess," he said.

Fay took Gail's arm and walked her back toward the lunch table. "I'm so sorry," Fay said.

"I just don't understand how I got to here," Gail said. "All my life I did just what I was supposed to do. I went to church, I was sweet to my mother . . ."

"You didn't do anything," Fay said. "This is not your fault."

"I married Marvin," Gail said. "Was that it? I mean I knew he wasn't the right man, but the wedding was all planned and everything by the time I knew . . ."

"Marvin didn't do anything either," Fay said. "He climbed the Indian because it's real hard to think straight when there's something this awful going on."

They stopped a moment. Fay couldn't go any further with Gail. Most of the other mothers were back at the table now. The mood over there looked pretty grim.

Gail grasped Fay's hand. "Peter says we shouldn't do it," she said. "Make the signs and all. Get the signatures."

"Yes," Fay said. "I saw you talking to him."

"But I'll do anything to get Beth back. I don't care how crazy it is."

"But the problem is"—another mother had come up beside them and interrupted—"even if we do exactly what they say, we still don't know if they'll give our children back."

"What does Arnie think?" Gail asked Fay. "What do *you* think?"

"I don't know," Fay said. "I wish I did." She looked around for Arnie. "And it might work, they might give them back if you do what they said." She squeezed Gail's hand. "But what I really think is—"

"I have to go," Gail faltered, pointing to the table. "They want me."

"I'll be right here," Fay said.

"It's O.K., if you have to go. If it's Lizzie or something . . . I'm all right."

"I'm going to try to find Beth," Fay said. "But I can't promise I'll be able to. I just don't know where to start."

"I'm O.K.," Gail said again. They embraced and Gail walked blindly toward the table.

Fay did not want to sit back down and listen to the discussion. She wanted to know where Lizzie was. If she left on the boat with Paul tonight, what would happen? Would the boat sink? Would Lizzie become addicted to some terrible drug? Would she die in childbirth or get bitten by a scorpion and be paralyzed for life? Would he sell her into white slavery in Brazil? Would an anaconda drop down out of the trees and squeeze the breath out of her? What?

"WHAT'S GOING ON?" Arnie asked, coming up behind Fay.

"I can't stay out in this sun anymore," she said. "Is there some other place where we can—"

"Listen to the mothers?"

She nodded.

"Sure," he said, looking around. "The radio truck, the Chief's car, the undercover van, the coroner's wagon . . ."

"And when are we going to hear from Lizzie? Isn't that Jake person supposed to call you?"

He led her toward the undercover van. "She's fine, Fay," he said. "He'll be with her all day."

"I've been with her all her life," Fay said, "and she's gotten away from *me*."

"Not yet, Fay," he said, opening the back door of the brown UPS delivery truck. "Not yet."

"Is this yours?" she asked, grasping the handrail and stepping up into the van.

But one look inside the truck answered her question. The walls were lined with television monitors. Arnie nodded to two detectives who were wearing earphones and sitting in front of sophisticated-looking consoles.

"Lizzie's at dance class," Arnie said. "Jake called in about ten minutes ago. He's sitting on a bench outside the door, watching. Got her in plain sight. He'll call us when it's over."

But Fay didn't hear him. She was startled by the sudden darkness of the truck, the slight moist chill in the air, the eerie green computer glow, the steady hum of the machinery, the total tomblike silence. She sat down on the folding chair Arnie opened for her, and saw Lizzie for herself.

Wearing champagne lace and long spun-honey strands of antique pearls. Walking up the aisle. Alone.

A mission. A big one. An old one. San Diego maybe.

Carrying a single orchid. Someone whispered as she passed. The orchid was flown in this morning. Blessed by the archbishop of Portugal, they said.

A single stream of sunlight came through the big window, lighting her way. A blessing.

Her hair was loose, but brushed back from the rare topaz drops that fell from her ears. Villa-Lobos from somewhere behind her. Ahead, a sandalwood altar with its alabaster votaries and burnished gold tapers.

Paul extended his hand and they knelt close together as an angel child sang a Brazilian love song.

Fay turned back to find herself in the crowd, but her pew was empty. Her whole side of the church was empty, in fact.

Fay blinked back the tears, and Lizzie was dancing with Paul's father at the reception. Laughing about the half-empty church.

"I liked it." Lizzie smiled. "I had so much room over there."

She was as light as Fay had ever seen her.

Paul's father was all silver, black and white, elegant and at ease in the center of things. "You will at least allow me to send pictures to your mother," he said.

They swept across the sparkling floor. "She doesn't look at pictures," Lizzie said. Her voice dropped to an amused whisper. "It's something about the spirits, I think."

"But it's her own daughter's wedding," he protested gently.

Lizzie laughed again. "She has a thing about weddings, too."

"She doesn't believe in them?" he asked.

"Something about the church," she said, a glint in her eye for him. "An old gypsy thing."

"What a wicked girl you are," he teased. "What a dream." And they spun off the floor together and the guests applauded.

"What did I do?" Fay asked. "Did I say something? Why didn't she invite me?"

"Shh," Arnie said, patting her arm. "We can't talk in here. They're almost ready to go out there."

"Lizzie isn't going to invite me to her wedding," she whispered.

He handed her a pair of earphones. "It's just another five minutes now," he said. "Vi is collecting the pictures for you."

She knew what he was asking: *When are you going to start seeing something other than Lizzie? Don't you care what happens to these children? Aren't you even going to try?*

2:00 P.M.

 THE CHIEF HAD DECIDED TO TAKE THE COFFEE-shop assignment himself. He wanted to arrest somebody, anybody, and Edith Masters was the only name he had. He was actually thrilled to see that she was still there, sitting in the booth next to the window.

He sat down at the table directly across from her and asked if he could borrow her ashtray. She said he certainly could, and even seemed relieved that the disgusting thing was out of her sight. When he thanked her, she smiled, revealing a mouthful of perfect little teeth, like rows of young white corn.

"What's going on out there?" he asked her, hoping to pass as a businessman.

Her smile vanished instantly. "I should think you'd know that by now," she said crisply. "You've been in charge all morning, haven't you?"

"Just because I'm there doesn't mean I'm in charge." He laughed, and ordered the fried chicken platter and coffee. "You probably know more than I do."

"One of the mothers is a friend of mine," she explained, not looking at him. "I just wanted to be nearby in case she needed me."

"Well, how about that?" he said. "Which one?" He dumped two packets of artificial sweetener in his coffee.

"Lynn Waldo," she said.

"She got a slide projector," the Chief said.

199

"Did she? I couldn't see that from here."

"In her package, I mean," the Chief said.

"Yes, I know about the packages." Mrs. Masters' voice was steady. "Lynn called me right after the kidnappers called her."

She was nervous. He liked that. "Do you always come here for breakfast?" he asked.

"No," she said, adjusting her watchband. "I don't."

"But you *were* here this morning?"

"Yes, I was," she said, looking up at him now. "A young man at our church, a new member, needed someone to talk to."

She was a pretty cool customer, this lady. It was possible that she was telling the truth, but the Chief didn't think so.

The waitress brought his food and he asked for a glass of iced tea, then turned back to Mrs. Masters. "So what church is it?" he asked. "Does Mrs. Waldo go to the same church?" He took a bite of coleslaw. "What do you believe at this church?"

"We believe in God," she said.

"Yes, I thought you might." He laughed. "What else?"

"Are you a religious man?" she asked.

"I don't know," he said. "Maybe."

"Do you believe in the life hereafter?"

"Well, I'd sure like to," he said, motioning to the waitress. "But how can I believe in it till I know what it is?" He asked the waitress for some vinegar.

She reminded the waitress about her check and then asked him, "Are you lonely?"

"Sure," he said. "Isn't everybody?"

"No," she said. "There's your answer."

"What answer?" he asked.

"Whether you're religious or not."

"You mean if I'm lonely, then I must not be religious?" He tore the chicken leg away from the thigh.

"Jesus came so we wouldn't be lonely," she said.

"But then He left again," the Chief said. "Doesn't that make us more lonely?"

"He didn't go so far away," she said. " 'Where two or three are gathered together in my name, there am I in the midst of them.' "

The Chief hadn't done battle with a real Christian for a

long time. Looking across the table at the brittle matron, he remembered now that it wasn't worth it.

"What's it all about?" she asked, as he buttered his roll. "Do they know that yet?"

"Abortion."

"I see."

"The kidnappers want the mothers to conduct a vote," he lied, "like a referendum, I guess. Set up tables and let people sign their names, pro or con."

She coughed and covered her mouth. "A referendum?"

"Yeah," he said. "Crazy, huh?" He splashed the vinegar on his fried chicken.

"But didn't they—" She stopped herself and looked out the window.

Good, the Chief thought. She went for it. I've got her.

She cleared her throat. "How did they know about this . . . referendum?" she asked.

"There was a letter," he said. "One of the girls got a letter of instructions. It said the government needed to know what the people thought, all the people, give everybody a chance to have their say. As soon as the mothers finish the voting, they get their kids back."

"I see," said Mrs. Masters, and reached for her purse.

He saw the waitress coming with the check and knew it was time to push. "But we're not going to let them do it. We're sending them all home."

"But what about the children?" she asked.

He lowered his voice. "We have to assume the children are dead," he said. "We found two of them dead already."

She reached for her water glass.

"The newspeople don't know it yet, though," he said. "We didn't want to scare the rest of the mothers."

"No." Mrs. Masters turned slightly more gray. "That wouldn't be right."

He watched as she took her wallet out of her purse. She was scared, all right.

The Chief wondered what was in that purse. A list of phone numbers? There had to be some paper somewhere in this scheme. You didn't plan a thing this big without writing something down. The waitress put Mrs. Masters' check on the table.

"I guess they're lucky there's no more death penalty," the Chief said.

"Who's lucky?" she asked.

"The kidnappers," he said. "Just life in prison."

"What makes you think you'll find the kidnappers?" she asked.

"Even planning a kidnapping is a life sentence in this state, you know. You might not have touched a single one of those children, just planned it, it doesn't matter, off you go, 'bye-bye."

"Excuse me," she said. "I have to make a phone call."

"There's a pay phone in the hall."

"Yes, I know."

The Chief took a swig of tea and congratulated himself for keeping the tap on the line out there.

"I'll watch your purse," he offered.

"Thank you," she said, reaching for her jacket and looping her purse over her shoulder, "but I won't be coming back. I've enjoyed talking with you."

"Yeah, same here," he said. "If you think of anything, anything at all that might be helpful, just come right up to the front over there. I'll leave your name with the officer. Tell them I said to let you in. It's Masters, right? Edith Masters? Where do you live, Edith?"

"Excuse me," she said, and marched off.

The Chief waited until she rounded the corner and then pulled out his radio, identified her for the officer he'd left standing outside the coffee shop, and told him to follow Mrs. Masters wherever she went.

"Watch her purse," he said. "I want that purse. And I want to know where she goes if she leaves the parking lot, and who she talks to if she doesn't."

Then he realized he'd better get back to the mothers, took one last bite of his mashed potatoes, put a ten-dollar bill down for the waitress, and left.

FAY, INSIDE THE UPS truck, had trouble hearing over the earphones, but from what she could gather there were three groups around the table: mothers who wanted to do what the kidnappers said, mothers who thought it was blackmail and wouldn't give in, and mothers who couldn't decide.

The lawyer mother had just suggested a compromise. Turn it into a vote, she said. Ask people to come up and sign for or against, like a referendum. Someone else objected instantly, saying the kidnappers wouldn't be very happy if the vote turned out for abortion to stay legal.

But the very mention of the word abortion produced a new argument, or rather, the old argument about abortion. It was murder, some said. And somebody had to stop it. But if you take away our right to an abortion, others said, what's next? Our right to own property? Our right to work?

Then somebody said abortion was a sin. And very quickly somebody else said she didn't believe in sin, she only believed in bad luck, but she didn't believe you should have to send your bad luck to college.

When the hubbub over that died down, a weary voice spoke with conviction. "It doesn't matter how we feel about abortion. This is an act of terrorism, pure and simple, and we can't give in. The president himself wouldn't give in to this kind of threat, and he hates abortion."

"He doesn't just hate abortion," someone else said, "he hates women. And he's doing everything he can to keep women poor. First he's going to force them to have all these babies, then he's going to cut their welfare so they can't feed them."

So then they fought about the president. "He's cutting the welfare," one said, "because he wants people to get jobs instead of mooching off the rest of us."

But two other mothers had tried to get jobs lately and they wondered what jobs the first woman was talking about.

Vi tried to stop them, saying they weren't here to talk about the president.

But they wouldn't listen. "One old man cannot dictate to all the women in the country what they should do with their lives," somebody said.

"Yes he can," another mother said. "That's why we elected him."

And then there was a chorus of "I didn't elect him" from around the table.

So Vi was firmer this time. "The president is not the subject here," she said. "We are. Our children are gone. Now, please, these people have told us what we must do to get our children back."

And there was silence.

Sitting in the undercover truck, Fay looked over at Arnie and shook her head. "This could go on all day," she said.

But then one of the undecided mothers offered a new solution. "It seems to me," she said, "that the people who want to make signs should make them, and the people who don't want to can just sit."

And that made somebody else lose control completely. "They'll kill our children!" she screamed.

Then Fay recognized Gail's voice. "Nobody would kill twenty-seven children," she said. "I don't care how crazy they are."

Arnie reached over and squeezed Fay's hand. "That's our girl," he said. "Good for her."

Gail went on. "I mean, O.K. What do we know about these people? One thing. They're against abortion."

The mothers seemed to be listening to her.

"They think abortion is killing children and they want to stop it."

Fay nodded in agreement.

"Now if they're really against killing children," Gail said, "do you really think they'd kill our children to stop people from killing children? No. They wouldn't. Our children are safe."

And the silence was with them again. Gail had offered them the opportunity to feel better, but could they really accept it?

The Chinese mother interrupted their thinking. "What would happen," she asked quietly, "if we all just walked away from the table and went home?"

Arnie nodded his approval.

"Kidnapping is a crime," she said. "The police should solve this crime and we should all just go home."

"Right," Arnie whispered. "Right."

"But it would look like we didn't care about our children," somebody said.

Gail spoke up again. She liked the Chinese woman's idea. "Yes," she said. "When they see that it hasn't worked, they'll have to give the kids back. These aren't rich people who did this. They can't afford to feed another kid forever. And they can't actually want another child in their house, can they? A child that isn't theirs? A child who's crying and saying she wants to go home all the time? No," she said, "they can't."

"God, that's brave," Fay said quietly.

But then a strident voice announced that she was staying, was doing exactly what the kidnappers told them to do, and a number of others, Fay couldn't count how many, said they were, too.

"That's seven," Vi said, apparently counting the hands held up around the table. "And how many refuse to go along with the kidnappers?"

There was quiet while she counted.

"Seven," she said. "A tie."

"How many didn't vote?" Fay asked Arnie.

"Six," he said, adjusting his earphones.

"And the rest of you?" Vi asked.

There was a different kind of tension now. Opinions were no longer the issue. Issues were no longer the issue. Their children's lives might be on the line here, and they all felt it.

The undercover policewoman spoke first, saying she wasn't really one of them, so she didn't feel entitled to a vote. Then Barbara Chambers said that since Fay had found her two girls, she didn't feel she should vote either.

"All right," Vi said, going on to the next woman. "Diane?"

It was a voice Fay hadn't heard before. A hesitating, frightened one. Thin and weak. "I want Robert back," she said, "and I'll do anything to get him back. But I just had an abortion last month, and if I hadn't gotten it, well, we just couldn't afford . . ." she faltered. "I'm sorry. I just don't know what to say. We have four children as it is."

Silence.

"Oh boy," Fay said to Arnie. "Here we go."

"I had one too," another voice said softly. "But that's what turned me against it. They told me the baby would be sick, that's why I did it. And then they checked the"—she paused—"they checked the scrapings, and they were right, she was sick. But then it didn't make sense anymore. She was my baby, sick or not. A lot of people have sick children and they do just fine."

Something was happening at the table.

Fay knew exactly what it was, and so did Gail, who spoke next.

"Maybe we better find out how many of us have had abortions," she said.

Fay could feel the women looking across the table at one

another, then glancing back at their husbands and families behind them.

"I have," someone said, finally, "in college."

"I have," Vi said, "in high school."

"And me," said another. "When my husband left me. And I can vote now. I don't want to make the signs for these people. I want to go home."

And around the table they went, accounting for sixteen abortions among the twenty mothers. Some of them had had more than one. And there were as many reasons as there were abortions. These weren't teenagers who had resorted to abortion because they didn't think about contraception. These were devoted mothers who had all felt, at some moment, that they had no choice, that their other children, or their marriages, or even just their futures came first.

As Fay listened, she felt them becoming a whole group again, a sadder, older group. A random group of women telling the sad, old truth.

A return to the days of illegal abortions would affect every woman at this table.

Vi sighed. "So what do we do?" she asked.

"Can we please just go home?" the tiny-voiced Diane said.

Vi asked for another show of hands. And this time all but two of the mothers voted to go home; to leave their packages on the table for somebody else to clean up, and go home.

The group agreed that if those two women wanted to make signs with the materials the kidnappers had sent, that was all right, but the official answer of the group would be NO.

Vi said she would go on television and explain their position, and explain that the two remaining mothers were just two individuals doing what any two individuals are free to do in this country—speaking their minds.

"Good," Arnie said, taking off his earphones, "good."

"I guess so," Fay said, exhausted from listening. "I guess they didn't really have a choice."

But she felt their loss, knew their confusion, and wondered what they would do all afternoon, alone in their houses.

By the time Fay and Arnie got back outside, the Chief had collected the pictures of the missing children, and assured the mothers that every lead was being followed. Then he gave them a special number to call, and asked that no one leave the city without telling him where they could be reached.

Then, just as everyone thought they were finished, the Chief made another announcement. "And now, Mrs. Waldo," he said, smiling at the woman who had gotten the slide projector, "I have the great joy of telling you we have just found little Karen."

Lynn Waldo practically jumped out of her chair and into the arms of the detective who was standing behind her to make sure she didn't get away.

"If you'll go with Officer Corbin, he'll take you to her," the Chief said.

The group applauded and Lynn started to cry as she was escorted to a squad car.

Fay grabbed Arnie's arm. "Where was the little girl?"

"Just where you said she would be," he said. "At her grandmother's." They stepped back a little so he could explain the rest of what he knew. "But it's real strange. Everybody—the grandmother, the neighbors—says the kid just got there. They say she was dropped off in the grandmother's front yard ten minutes before the police got there."

"How old was she?" Fay asked. "Was she old enough to know her grandmother's address? To tell the kidnappers, I mean?"

"I don't remember," he said.

She thought a moment. "Could anybody else have been listening to what went on around the table?"

"What do you mean?"

"Well, if they heard it," Fay said, starting toward Gail, "then they could be about to return the kids of the anti-abortion mothers."

Arnie rushed over to the Chief to tell him what Fay thought. If she was right, then those mothers who had originally voted to go along with the demands should be told to get home fast and stay there.

VI WAS GIVING another interview, so the Mayor found Gail as she walked away from the table.

"You did the right thing," he said, wanting to put his arm around her but well aware that everyone would see it if he did.

"I guess," she said. "I feel so weak. I feel like I need to sit down. But I've *been* sitting for the last forty-five minutes."

"You need for this to be over. Maybe"—he paused—"maybe your husband should take you home so you could rest."

She sat down on the hard bleacher seat behind her. "Do you see the man sitting on the big Indian?" she asked, staring down at her feet.

He shaded his eyes with his hand and looked across the parking lot. "Is that a man?"

"It's my husband," she said.

He sat down beside her.

"You're supposed to be laughing," she said.

"No," he said, and took a deep breath. "My wife is telling the press that if the kidnappers give the children back, she'll travel all around the country speaking out against abortion."

Gail looked up. She wasn't sure she'd heard him correctly. "Against abortion?" she asked. "I thought she was for it."

"She was," he said. He rubbed his knee. "She says she changed her mind." He loosened his tie. "I think it has something to do with the size of this crowd out here."

Gail wanted to respond, but had no idea how to.

"I tried to tell her they wouldn't do that," Peter said, "that it wouldn't work. But she didn't agree."

"Maybe," Gail offered, "she's just so worried about your boys that she doesn't know what she's doing." She stopped. "Like Marvin."

"Maybe," he said, and thought a moment. "And if I asked you to have a drink with me later, or take a walk, or offered to take you home when you're ready, would that be because I didn't know what I was doing either?"

"No," she answered quietly. "You'd just be trying to help me feel better."

"I'd like to do that," he said, "if I could."

Gail looked up and caught Fay watching them.

"If it would help you," Gail said, "if it would make you feel better"—she patted his knee and stood up—"then, yes. The answer is yes. I'll have a drink with you, or take a walk, or let you take me home when I'm ready, or whatever you say."

He stood up too, but tried not to seem too eager. "So where should we meet?"

"I'll be here," she said, squinting up into the sun at him. "You come get me when you're ready."

But when Gail looked back into the crowd to find Fay, to ask her if this was a mistake, if she was already in enough pain today and shouldn't make it worse, Fay was gone.

Gone on purpose. Fay had seen Arnie looking for her, too. She just wasn't ready to be found yet.

FAY WANDERED UP to the sidewalk, and paused in front of the poster in a tea-and-sandwich shop window, a poster of a quaintly dressed Englishwoman holding a cup of tea in each hand.

Anybody else would have seen a two-for-the-price-of-one offer. Fay saw the Temperance card.

The Tarot's vision of Temperance is a willowy blond angel in flowing white robes mixing the liquids contained in two vases by pouring back and forth between them.

In general, Tarot readers took this card to be a warning: Let your passion cool, they said, dilute your rage with reason, control your desires. Remember that the past is all mixed up in the present, they said. Wait and see.

But Fay had trouble with that interpretation. Sure, she appreciated the virtues the card represented—patience, tolerance, and humility—but she also thought the modern world was too cool already. People didn't need Fay to tell them to take it easy. Everybody told them that.

Relax, the world said, don't let it get you, don't say anything you'll be sorry for later. Calm down, people said, think before you speak. Think before you act, too. Be fair. Play it safe, don't dwell on it. Don't blame them and don't blame yourself. These things are nobody's fault. Breathe deeply. Sit down. Good. None of this is going to matter in a thousand years, anyway, so don't worry about it.

Yes, that's what the world said to people these days, with the result that nobody ever bothered to do anything anymore. Nobody stopped you from talking, so nobody said anything. And nothing was forbidden, so nothing ever really happened.

It was all just O.K. now, whoever you were, whatever you did. Even if you chopped up your neighbors and put them out in the alley in plastic garbage bags, it would only mean you were crazy, and we certainly wouldn't punish you for that.

When the Temperance card came up in a reading, Fay ignored it. Why should she tell people to be careful? She already knew they would be. That was what was the matter with them.

Fay thought there were too few fires for us to go around stamping them out. There was precious little passion today, or rather, what passed for passion today was too precious and too little. No, Fay wasn't about to go tell Gail she was making a mistake talking to Peter. But she couldn't tell her to have an affair with him, could she? What she had to do was stay out of it for a while.

Maybe if she got busy and found their children, they would have a chance to cling together out of something other than terror.

"O.K.," ARNIE SAID, coming up behind Fay on the sidewalk. "All done. Now what?"

He had startled her. She turned around, her eyes open once again to the scene in front of her: the table, the mothers, the police, the truck. "I'll look at the pictures of the kids, I guess," she said.

"He's ready when you are." Arnie pointed to the Chief.

But as soon as Arnie took her hand, Fay realized the other reason she had avoided talking to the Mayor and Gail.

"Arnie," she gasped. "The Mayor's boys are in trouble."

He whirled around, convinced he was seeing them behind him. "Where?" he asked.

"It's a quarry." She shook her head. "Some big rocky place."

Arnie's mind raced. There was a gravel company down by the river. And Rock Creek Swimming Club was in an old quarry. And how about Cliffside Park?

"They're climbing on these rocks?" he asked, hurrying her back inside the police barricade.

"These are little boys, Arnie." She was running to keep up with him. "They don't know *what* they're doing."

He grabbed a remote radio from the first officer he saw, and rattled off the details.

"Red shorts," Fay said, "white shirts. Both blond, both thin. By themselves."

"Goddamn," Arnie said, as they neared the table, and quickly told the Chief about it.

"It's not their fault," Fay said, walking carefully toward the stack of pictures on the table.

"Whose fault?" the Chief snapped. "What does fault have to do with it?"

"The kidnappers," she said, sitting down at the now-empty table. "It could happen to anybody." She spread the pictures out in front of her. "Kids go off and get in trouble, that's all."

Arnie and the Chief backed away. Fay had forgotten the Mayor's boys as quickly as she had remembered them. All she could see now were those pictures. She planted her elbows on the table and clasped her hands in front of her.

Arnie had never seen her do this before. Was she praying? They were both worried. What if she failed? What if the pictures didn't help? What if all of the children were in trouble like the Mayor's boys? How could they possibly find them in time?

Fay grabbed the edges of her chair and scooted closer to the table. She closed her eyes again, and wiped the shopping center from her mind. Then, in the blackness, she let her eyes fall on the pictures. Gently, they were drawn to one picture in particular. In the middle row, to the left of center. A little girl, she thought. She opened her eyes and picked up the photograph. Yes, a little girl. Kimberly Chen, lying on a yellow-flowered sofa, covered with a khaki army surplus blanket.

Get up, Kimberly, Fay thought, take me through the house. I'll follow you wherever you go.

The child's eyes opened slowly and she brought one tiny fist up to her mouth and chewed on her knuckles. Fay smiled. That's good, baby, but let's take a walk, why don't we. Like over to the telephone maybe, or past some piece of mail so I can see the address?

The little girl raised her head and saw a truck on the floor, a carved wooden one with a long string, and a stuffed toy right beside it. Daffy Duck? Is that Daffy Duck? Fay didn't know they still made Daffy Duck.

Kimberly pulled her knees up under her like an inch-worm, then pulled herself into a sitting position, using the arm of the sofa for balance. Now, Fay thought, hop down, go see the duck.

The child scooted off the edge of the sofa and down onto the blanket, then crawled across a brown braided rug past the duck to the truck. And not the truck itself, but the string. Smart girl, Fay thought. Now pull the truck to you. Or how about racing the truck out the front door so I can read the number on the house.

Kimberly held the truck in her lap and looked up. Directly in front of her was a rocking chair with orange foam-rubber cushions on the seat and back. Fay looked around, and saw what she needed: a basket of magazines on the floor between the end table and the chair. But Kimberly didn't care about magazines.

Well, then, Kimberly, Fay thought, let's roll the truck the other way. Good. Now Fay could see the other side of the sofa, where there was a round orange ottoman, vinyl; another chair, brown, like a recliner; and a small bag, a flight bag or a gym bag maybe, on the floor beside the ottoman.

Kimberly jumped. Somebody was coming. She scrambled across the rug toward the recliner, looking for a place to hide. Get behind the bag, Fay coached.

The door opened, and a very tall woman with straight brown hair walked in. She scooped Kimberly up in her arms and went out of the room.

But Fay was still down behind the gym bag. Could she get into it without Kimberly to help her? She could try, she guessed. No, wait. There was a plastic thing on the front, like a see-through tag for an address. Fay moved her eyes carefully—up to the zipper, around over the top of the bag, down the front. There. There it was. A name. An address. O.K., Fay thought, calm down. Real easy now. Just read it.

She got the numbers first. "Two, two, eight," she said out loud, then called out the letters one at a time. "H . . . U . . . M . . . M . . . I—Hummingbird Drive."

"Arnie!" Fay screamed, jumping up out of her chair and into Gail's arms.

"I've got it," Gail said, waving a piece of paper. "I wrote it all down. But what on earth were you—"

Fay collapsed back into her chair, sweat springing out on her forehead and temples, then pouring down her face.

Arnie got there fast. "Are you all right?" he asked.

Fay was shaking.

Gail held her tight, stunned by what she had just witnessed. "I've never seen anything like that in my life," she said to Arnie. "I mean, I came over here and said hello to her and she didn't even hear me. She was just staring at that picture and talking to herself like she actually went right into the picture."

"Please," Fay whispered, pointing to Gail's piece of paper. "That's where Kimberly is."

Arnie grabbed the piece of paper and headed for the radio truck.

Gail still couldn't believe it. "228 Hummingbird Drive? How did you do that?"

But Fay couldn't answer.

Gail felt for her pulse, but it was very faint, her hands cold and clammy. She rubbed Fay's right hand between her palms, trying to get the circulation back.

"I'm O.K.," Fay nodded, her arms falling limp into her lap.

"Let's not do any more of that, huh?" Gail said gently.

"Any more of what?" Fay asked, still not completely conscious.

"Whatever you call it," Gail said. "That trance stuff. There has to be some other way." She felt Fay's forehead, which was now blazing hot, and motioned for one of the officers to bring her some water.

But as Gail continued to hold her hand, the tears began streaming down Fay's face.

"Fay," Gail said, "come on. You're scaring the shit out of me."

"Is she all right?" Arnie asked, coming back up behind them.

"I'm all right," Fay said, drinking the water the officer had brought her. She looked at the two of them staring at her so intensely, laughed, and choked on her water.

And then Arnie couldn't wait any longer to tell her. "There's more news, Fay," he said carefully.

Fay sat up straighter and Gail tensed behind her.

Then he realized he'd scared them. "No," he said. "Good news!" He crooked his elbow and tightened his fist in the traditional gesture of victory. "We got two more kids!"

"Where were they?" Fay asked.

Gail tightened her grip on Fay's shoulders.

The Chief came over to congratulate Fay. "Jennifer Bell and Alice Hart," he crowed. "And you were right on the money. The kids were dropped off in their own front yards.

And both of their mothers had voted to go along with the kidnappers."

Behind Fay, Gail was ashen. "But how did the kidnappers know how we voted?" she cried.

"We don't know," the Chief said, "unless one of these reporters is a lip-reader. Or somebody could be patched into our radio truck somehow."

Gail sank into the chair beside Fay, burying her head in her hands.

"Gail," Fay said quickly, turning around to comfort her, "you did the right thing. You can't feel bad about it, you just have to—"

"I can feel as bad as I want," Gail said, and stood up, her anger rising with her.

And now it seemed to Gail that this was all Fay's fault. "I believed you!" she screamed at her friend. "You said she would be all right!"

She stopped for a breath, and realized it was her own fault. "What was I thinking about? I don't care about abortion! How could I have sat there and—"

"Gail, Gail," Arnie said firmly. "Fay is right. It won't help to get mad now. We need you to stay real cool here." He grabbed her arm, forcing her to listen. "And it doesn't matter if we find Beth first, or we find her last. We're going to find her."

Gail tried to pull away from Arnie but he held her firmly. She couldn't listen. She couldn't. How could she have risked her child's life for some— She couldn't finish the sentence, even in her thoughts.

"Gail," Arnie said. "I promise you."

Gail looked away. All there was to see, though, were the walls of humans surrounding her. So she looked up. And no, that's not all there was to see. There was also Marvin.

3:00 P.M.

ALL IN ALL, MARVIN HAD ENJOYED HIMSELF ON
the Indian. He had studied the air-conditioning
system on the roof of the shopping center,
and figured out the synchronization of the
traffic lights for a mile in every direction.

He couldn't see Gail in the crowd gathered below him,
but he had seen things break up over at the truck, so he
assumed it was all over. Maybe Gail was even home with
Beth by now, in which case he wanted to get down and be
with them. But getting down by himself was not really possible, a fact he had known for some two hours.

On their way across the parking lot, the Chief put his
arm around Gail. "Poor Marvin," he said, with as much
compassion as he could muster. "Has he ever done anything
like this before?"

"Not this exact thing," Gail answered, letting his arm
rest where it was.

The Chief wondered why she was so calm. "Are you mad
at him?"

"Not anymore," Gail said. "What would be the point?"

"We'll have to take him downtown, you know," the
Chief explained, "procedures and everything; after we get
him off the Indian, I mean."

"What will you do with him?" she asked.

"Have him talk to the psychiatrist, I guess."

215

"And then he can go home?"

"No. Then we charge him with something and let him out on bail." He felt sorry for her. "What else can we do?" he said. "We can't have people climbing the fucking Indian all the time."

"It's just so ugly," she said. "I wouldn't even want to touch it, much less climb it."

"We ought to put a fence around it," he said.

"Electrified," she said. "Barbed wire on the top. Like a reservation."

The Chief laughed. He liked this woman. She didn't think much of her husband, but at least she wasn't bitching about him. He wondered if she'd like to come to work at the department.

"I'll go get him myself if you want," he said. "Some of these firemen could be pretty hard on him, pulling a stunt like this."

"I thought firemen were sweet," she said.

"That's what everybody thinks," he said. "Makes it tough being a cop."

"I'll stay here," she said, as they approached the ladder truck.

"You do that," he said. He winked at her. "You stay cool, now."

"Thanks," she said.

"Come on up!" Marvin yelled, as the Chief grabbed hold of the ladder. "Plenty of room!" he called. Marvin was feeling better all the time. As the Chief took his first step, Marvin sang out gaily, "Don't fall!"

"Thanks, Marvin," the Chief mumbled to himself, his hands beginning to sweat.

Marvin saw that the Chief was not used to climbing ladders. He was looking down, for one thing, concentrating on his feet instead of his hands. And every time he took a step, he stopped and waited for the ladder to stop swaying before he took another step. Marvin knew that wasn't the way to do it.

"Don't fight it," Marvin coached. "Just let the momentum carry you. Don't think about where you've been, think about where you're going. Look up! Look up!"

The Chief's shirt was soaked through, and his street shoes were slipping badly on the treads. But people were watching him. He couldn't stop or go back without embarrassing the whole department. He was, however, beginning to remember the other reasons why he hadn't become a fireman.

The top of the ladder was resting on the Indian's clavicle. Marvin decided it was time to turn around so he could face the Chief. He grabbed the Indian's mouth and pulled one foot up under him. "Here I go!" he shouted.

"No!" the Chief screamed. And there were shrieks of terror from the ground below. "Sit down," the Chief shouted. "I'm coming, I'm coming."

"I know," Marvin said pleasantly, now that the Chief was within talking distance. "I'm just turning around so I can see you."

The Chief didn't believe him. "I said *sit down*, Marvin."

When Marvin sat down, the crowd cheered.

"Well," the Chief said casually, as if they had just met on the sidewalk, "how are you doing, Marvin?"

"Pretty good," Marvin said. "Thanks."

"Your wife is down there, you know," the Chief said.

"She's the best wife in the world." Marvin spotted Gail and waved.

The Chief looked at the crowd below and a wave of nausea came over him. "How do you think this makes her feel, Marvin?"

"Wait till she sees the parking place I found!"

The Chief shook his head. "You know we set up a place over there at the truck for all you fathers."

"No," Marvin said. "I didn't. I never got that far, I guess."

The Chief grinned. "You just saw the Indian and knew he was for you, right?"

"There were just so many people everywhere else," Marvin began. "But I'm ready to come down now. I'm thirsty, for one thing."

"In a minute, Marvin, in a minute." The Chief pulled his handkerchief out of his pocket and dried his palms.

Marvin thought he should keep the conversation going. "You can see pretty good up here, don't you think? Kind of like a fire tower."

"I can't see a goddamn thing, Marvin," the Chief said, "except your feet and his neck."

"Don't lean back!" Marvin yelled, as the Chief tried to put his handkerchief back in his pocket.

"Listen, Marvin," the Chief said, clutching the ladder and waiting for it to stop shaking, "I want to know why you did this. I mean, your wife says you're not crazy."

"She's sweet," Marvin said. "I told you she was sweet."

"Yes she is, Marvin. And you're not a kid either, so you didn't do this just for fun; and you're not malicious, are you, Marvin?"

"No, sir," Marvin declared.

"So you didn't do it to cause trouble. So why did you do it? I mean, I'm a policeman, Marvin."

"Yeah, I figured you were."

"And policemen need to know why people do things. People do all kinds of things, Marvin. You wouldn't believe the things people do."

"Oh yes I would too," Marvin said. "I read the paper every day."

"Well, if we're ever going to get people to quit doing these things," the Chief said, "we have to know why they did them."

"Right," Marvin said. "I'll go along with that."

"So?"

"So *what*?" Marvin asked.

The Chief sighed. "So why did you do this?"

Marvin thought he saw something in the Indian's mouth.

"Don't play with the Indian, Marvin."

"There's something in his mouth."

"I asked you a question."

"I'm sorry." Marvin was feeling around the Indian's molars. "Ask me again."

The Chief tried a confidential whisper. "I asked you why you did this."

"I've got it!" Marvin wrenched his wrist back out through the Indian's lips.

"I'm happy for you, Marvin," the Chief said. "Answer my question, please."

"I don't know," Marvin said. "If it wasn't for the view, then it doesn't make much sense."

"No, it doesn't." The Chief was sorry he'd ever started this discussion. "I'm going down now, Marvin."

"Wait a minute!" Marvin said. "Don't you want to know what this is?"

"No, Marvin," the Chief said, one knee shaking wildly. "I don't."

"Didn't you come up here to get me?" Marvin asked.

"No, Marvin, I didn't," the Chief said.

"I could get down by myself now that the ladder's here."

"Yes, Marvin, I know," the Chief said. "Why don't you do that?"

"Hey, look!" Marvin shouted at him, holding the hard little ball out so the Chief could see it. "It's bubble gum!"

"That's great," the Chief said wearily. "That's just great, Marvin. So you're not even the first one up there."

"The sculptor put it here," Marvin explained. "It's a joke, see?"

"No, Marvin," the Chief said, stopping his descent for the last time. "It's not a joke. My coming up here was a joke. This whole day is a joke. But I tried, O.K.? I wanted to try. I wanted to give you a chance. I wanted to prove to myself that I still cared. But you know what? I don't."

He paused. Marvin was listening.

"I'll tell you why you climbed up here, Marvin, in case you're interested," the Chief grumped. "And I knew it from the ground."

"O.K.," Marvin said.

The Chief couldn't help saying it. "It's because you're one stupid fuck, Marvin." And with that he went down the ladder.

Marvin just didn't understand a man like this. Where was his spirit of adventure, his sense of fun, his joy in doing something just for the sake of doing it? And what about the wad of gum? Wasn't he the slightest bit intrigued by that? It made Marvin sad to think about a man giving up on his life that way.

Marvin put the gum in his pants pocket and reached for the top of the ladder. When he was three steps from the bottom, the crowd began to applaud. He saw the photographers waiting on the ground, smiled and waved as the flash-bulbs popped. He hadn't prepared anything to say to the reporters, but he guessed he'd just show them the gum and the conversation would go from there.

As his foot hit the bottom step, someone grabbed his

jacket roughly and snapped a pair of handcuffs around his wrists.

"What do you think you're doing?" Marvin asked.

The officer had to laugh. "You're going to jail, Tonto."

"What for?" Marvin asked, incredulous.

"Let's go," the man said, and grinned at one of the firemen. "We'll let the nice doctor tell you later."

Another officer pushed Marvin off from behind, and when he landed, he recognized Gail's shoes four inches from his face on the ground in front of him. He didn't want to stand up, but he did.

"Are you all right, Marvin?" she asked.

"I'm sorry, sweetheart," he said, leaning over to kiss her. "I was just trying to see everything."

"I know you were, Marvin," she said.

"I just didn't think about all of this," he said. "I just knew we were in trouble and I had to do something."

"I know, Marvin," she repeated, as the policeman pulled him away. "I'll see you later."

"Yeah," he said, hoping to reassure her. "This shouldn't take too long. Can you get home all right?"

Gail gestured toward the truck. "I'll be fine," she said. "The Mayor offered me a ride."

"O.K., then," he said, as the officer pushed him into the car. He stuck his head back out the window. "How's Beth?" he asked.

Gail took the Chief's arm. "She's gone, Marvin," she said.

"Still?" he asked, as the policeman reached across him and rolled up the windows.

Gail didn't answer, but she did manage to wave.

Marvin couldn't wave back because his hands were cuffed behind him. So he just nodded.

He looked nervous, Gail thought. And hungry. She was glad they were keeping him overnight. Maybe they could help him.

DOWN AT POLICE headquarters, Lynn Waldo, the mother who got the slide projector in her package, the mother whose daughter was the first one returned by the kidnappers, was being questioned by Bud Heller and Benjie Davis, the two detectives who had gone through the church with Arnie earlier in the morning.

Benjie Davis had begun by asking Mrs. Waldo what kind of bloody Nazi crusade this was anyway.

Then Heller tried to comfort Mrs. Waldo. "You have to understand," he said. "Davis is Jewish."

Mrs. Waldo didn't understand.

"Jews never forget," he said.

Mrs. Waldo asked when she could see her little girl.

"Not till you tell us where you've got the rest of the kids," Davis snarled.

"I don't know what you're talking about," Lynn Waldo said.

"We're talking about those other mothers' children," Davis barked. "Yours was at your mother's the whole time."

"No she wasn't," Lynn pleaded. "She was gone."

"Tell us who's in this with you," Davis said, "and we'll let you see your girl."

"Please," Lynn begged. "Is she all right?"

Heller patted her hand. "She's all right. All we want to do is find the rest of the children before anything happens to them."

Davis jumped back in. "If you go to prison for this, you'll lose your little girl for good, you know."

"You can't send me to prison," Lynn said, reaching for a Kleenex. "I haven't done anything. I don't know anything."

"Oh, you know all right," Davis said. "We saw that church this morning. Is that where the group meets?"

"What group?" Lynn asked, near tears. "What church?"

"The group who planned this kidnapping," Davis said. "The one that meets at your church."

"I go to church," Lynn said, "but the only group that meets there is the Ladies' Bible Class."

"Is the Ladies' Bible Class against abortion?"

"We've talked about abortion," she said. "It's the sixth commandment. Thou shalt not kill."

Davis spat his gum into the wastebasket. "If one of these children dies, that will be killing, Mrs. Waldo."

"Please," she said, "I don't know why you're asking me these questions."

Heller thought it was time for his approach. "Mrs. Waldo," he said softly, "we're just as confused as you are about this.

Why would the kidnappers return your child and keep all the rest of them?"

"You didn't say they returned her," she said. "I thought that fortune teller found her!"

"No," Heller said. "The kidnappers brought her back. Or that's what your little girl says, anyway. Now the only reason we can think of, why the kidnappers would bring her back, is that you're one of them."

Suddenly Mrs. Waldo was scared. "Is she sick?" she asked. "Is that why they brought her back?"

Heller continued in his helpful tone. "Maybe this group thinks you're on their side because you belong to some other group. Have you ever gone to an anti-abortion meeting?"

Mrs. Waldo was silent.

"Answer him," Davis snapped.

"Please," Heller said to Davis. "Shut up."

Lynn Waldo did have something to say, but she began quietly, looking down at her Kleenex. "When I had my abortion, there was a lady outside the clinic handing out pamphlets. It was the same pamphlet that was in one of the packages this morning, the red one with the big knife on the cover."

"That's good," Heller said. "Go on."

"That's all there is," she said.

"The hell it is," Davis said.

She turned back to Heller. "I felt real bad about the abortion," she said.

Heller handed her another Kleenex. "Of course you did."

"And I couldn't tell anybody about it. I didn't even tell my husband."

"So," Heller said calmly, "you called the phone number on the pamphlet and somebody talked to you and they made you feel better."

The tears ran down her face. "Yes," she said. "They told me that everybody feels bad."

"So," Heller said, "when you got to feeling better, you called them back, is that right? To thank them?"

"Please," she said, "I didn't have anything to do with this kidnapping."

"Come on, honey," Davis said. "We don't have all day."

Mrs. Waldo looked at Davis. She didn't want to tell him

anything. Heller told Davis he could handle it from here and Davis stormed out of the room.

"I'm sorry he's so rough," Heller said. "I don't think he likes women much."

Mrs. Waldo blew her nose.

"I don't think he likes anybody much," Heller said. "His family left him a coupla months back." He smiled.

Mrs. Waldo knew she had to tell the rest of the story, but she appreciated the detective's patience.

"When I called back," she said, "I asked the lady what I could do to help."

"What was this lady's name?" he asked.

"Edith Masters," Lynn said.

He wrote it down. He'd heard the name on the police radio. Edith Masters was the woman Arnie's fortune teller had seen in the coffee shop.

"And what did Mrs. Masters say?" he asked.

"She said they had this special phone system. That the phone number on the pamphlet rang at her house during the day, and at this other lady's phone at night. Then she said if they could send the calls to my phone one morning a week, then she wouldn't always have to go to the grocery store at night."

"How long ago was this?" Heller asked.

"Three years."

"Are you still doing it?"

"Yes," Mrs. Waldo replied. "Every Tuesday morning. But all I do is talk to the people who call up crying."

"And how often do you talk to Mrs. Masters?" he asked.

"She calls once a month to see how I'm doing."

"And how often do you call her?"

"I don't," Mrs. Waldo said. "She's told me about some meetings, but I can't go to them because Karen isn't in school yet."

"So your only contact with this Mrs. Masters is when she calls you?"

"Yes. I know there are other women answering the phone now. But I don't know any of them."

"And you just listen when people call?"

"Yes. Or sometimes, if they want more information, I take their names and when Mrs. Masters calls me, I give the names to her and she sends them things, but I don't know what things."

Heller stood up. He believed her. And he believed that this was everything she knew. "All right, Mrs. Waldo," he said, "you can go. Your mother is waiting with Karen just down the hall."

"You're not going to put me in jail?" she asked.

"Can you think of any reason why I should?" he asked.

"No," she said, managing a smile.

"All right, then," he said. "But I might be calling you again if I can't find this Mrs. Masters."

"That's fine," she said. "I'll help all I can."

"I know you will," he said. "Oh, what's the number, the antiabortion phone number you answer on Tuesday mornings?"

"It's 456-LIFE," she said. "456-5433."

Heller wrote down the number, opened the door, and escorted Mrs. Waldo down the hall to meet her mother and little girl.

FAY SAT AT the table in the parking lot, poring over the other pictures. But she knew it was no use. The only reason she'd been able to find Kimberly was that there was, apparently, some very old spiritual bond between them. Fay did believe in that. But the other kids—no, she had never known them.

She looked up from the pictures to the truck. It was a closed, forbidding mass. A time bomb. A tomb. A road-worn brute, a silent, stolid, scheming crate. The answer, she knew, was inside it. But that was the one place she didn't want to go.

Maybe the kidnappers would return all the rest of the children. Maybe the police would find them. Maybe she wouldn't have to see what was inside the truck. Or see it in person, anyway. She'd already seen a good bit of it, just sitting out here trying to ignore it.

There was a sign written in blood on the back wall. But she couldn't read what it said yet. And a gray T-shirt. Why, she wondered, of all the things in the truck, would she be so certain there was a limp gray T-shirt in a cardboard box? And what did it mean?

Nobody had asked her to go into the truck yet, but Arnie was coming toward her now. That could be exactly what he was going to say. She wasn't ready. She hadn't even been able to stand up since she found Kimberly. How could she do it? This truck scared her. Whatever was in there was awful.

"More good news!" Arnie said, sitting down beside her. "Six more kids!" He read from the list. "Juan Garcia, Robert Vick, Matthew and Michael Wilson, Vicki Layne, and Scott Lewis."

"So how many do we have now, altogether?" she asked, blinking hard to bring her eyes into focus.

"Twelve," he said. "Timmy from the hospital this morning, then Shelley and Susan from the house by the church, and nine from the mothers who voted to cooperate."

Fay cleared her throat. "Where's Gail?" she asked, looking around. "Does she know this yet?"

"No," he said. "But there's something I want you to hear." He pulled out a tiny tape recorder and set it down in front of her.

"What is it?"

"From the radio," he said. "They called in."

"The kidnappers?"

"Play it," he said. "I thought you might want to listen more than once, so I had them make a tape for you."

"I don't think I even want to listen the first time."

But he'd already punched the PLAY button. He hated to push her like this, but it was almost four o'clock.

". . . fear for their safety," the voice said. A male voice. Gruff. Commanding. "They are safer where they are than in homes where their mothers do not understand the value of human life. We will not be mocked. The other fifteen children will not be returned. They will remain, like all the victims of abortion in this country, missing for all time. There will be no further communication."

Then there was a click, and silence.

Fay shifted in her chair and stared back up at the truck.

"Well, look," Arnie said. "I just thought it might help. You know, trigger something."

Fay shook her head.

"O.K.," he said. "Now the other thing"—he paused—"is that Lynn Waldo, that woman who got the slide projector—"

"I remember," Fay said, gathering the pictures of the children up into a pile.

"Lynn Waldo named Edith Masters."

"Named her as what?" Fay asked, squaring the edges of the pictures against the table.

"Said Edith hands out pamphlets at an abortion clinic, and runs a counseling service on the phone."

"That doesn't necessarily mean she's involved in this, Arnie," Fay said.

"O.K.," he said, "but the Chief had her tailed when she left the coffee shop, and she made a phone call."

"To whom?"

"To another phone booth. Somebody she called 'dear one.' "

"And what did she say?" Fay asked, putting the photographs into her purse.

" 'Dear one, don't forget to feed the chickens,' " he said.

"What does that mean?" Fay asked.

"Beats me," Arnie said. "But it was about two-thirty when she made the call."

"So?"

"Well . . ." He hesitated. "Everybody *I* know feeds their chickens in the morning."

Fay nodded.

"But she never left the shopping center. Been here all day. They're bringing her over here right now."

Fay jumped. "I can't see her, Arnie. I can't."

"You don't have to," he said. "I'm going to talk to her."

"Have we heard from Lizzie?" she asked.

"They went shopping," he said. "Jake took her shopping."

"For what?"

"Jesus Christ, Fay!" Arnie snapped, and stood up. "What do I have to do to get you to work on this? I put a man on Lizzie all day. Do you want me to put her in jail? Is that what it takes? We've got fifteen kids to find, and no sign of them, anywhere!"

She swallowed hard. Swallowed the hard words she had ready. She stroked her throat. "I need a glass of something," she said. "Tea, or something." She pushed her chair back from the table. "And I have to get out of this . . ."

"I'm sorry," he said, reaching for her arm. "I'm really sorry. It's just . . ."

"No," she said. "You're right. You talk to Edith, and I'll go have a glass of tea." She pointed to the tea shop where he had found her before. "I'll be right over there. And when I've had my tea, I'll go inside the truck." She paused. "O.K.?"

"I won't be long," he said.

"And I won't run out on you."

"Good," he said. "The further we get with this, the more I know we can't do it without you."

"Yeah, yeah." She smiled.

"EYEWASH," FAY SAID to herself as she made her way to the tea shop. "It's not me that's not working, it's my eyes. It's being out in this sun all day."

She thought about going back to the first-aid station the police had set up, but decided not to. She wanted to sit someplace cool and try to forget about Lizzie.

The tiny bells on the door tinkled shyly as she opened it. "One," she said to the hostess.

"We have a lovely garden, if you'd care to sit there," the hostess soothed.

"No thank you," Fay said. "Just a quiet table will be fine."

The woman led Fay to her most quiet table, and smoothed the lace tea cloth as she left, and Fay sighed deeply. Her mother would have loved this little place.

Fay wrapped her arms around herself and remembered. She had asked her mother one night, "Was there a day when you first felt old? Were you standing there in the kitchen eating a dinner you wouldn't force on your own worst enemy, and did you realize that's exactly who you were, exactly what you were doing?"

But her mother didn't remember.

Fay had followed her into the bedroom, sorry she'd asked. "It's easier to forget, I guess."

"Oh no, child," her mother said. "It's damned hard to forget, but you'd better learn how. Unless you want to feel old for the rest of your life."

"You don't really mean *forget*, do you?" Fay asked. "Don't you mean find some other way to think about it?"

"No," her mother said, stepping out of her house slippers, "there isn't any other way to think about it. You just forget."

"Forget what?" Fay asked.

"I don't know, dear," her mother said, getting into bed. "What are we talking about?"

Fay pulled the quilt up over her. "Does it matter?"

"No," her mother said, "I don't think it does. But then" —she turned out the light—"I forget."

Now, reading the tea-shop menu, Fay couldn't remember what had made her feel so old that day. So at least she *was* forgetting. But she still felt old. Maybe she wasn't forgetting the right things.

She ordered a scone and a glass of iced chamomile, then closed her eyes. Lizzie was in the shower, a big shower, marble walls, gold fixtures, soap that smelled like apples. The day was hot, the air a heavy yellow out the bathroom window, a canyon in the distance, brown and blistered from a searing summer sun. California. It had to be California.

Lizzie tilted her head back and let the stream of water soak her hair. She grabbed the sponge and soaped it foamy then ran it down her now-huge belly.

Fay was ecstatic. Lizzie was having a baby! And pretty soon, too. Maybe a little Leo. Oh yes, if anybody could handle a Leo it was Lizzie. What fun that would be. Let her blow and fume, let her get her way, let her run the show. Oh, a little Leo!

Lizzie lifted her hands high above her head and stretched. Bless her heart, Fay thought, seeing the untanned bikini line under the baby, Lizzie's gone swimming the whole time, happy to be pregnant, happy to have everybody know.

Lizzie stopped. Water running down her legs. She'd heard about her water breaking, read about her water breaking, but would she know what it was when it happened? Yes. This was it. The baby was coming.

Lizzie whirled around to turn off the water, then stood holding the handles. "Mother!" she screamed.

"I'm here, I'm here," Fay said. "Call me. I'll come get you. I'll stay with you. I'll talk with you, you'll grab my hand, I'll . . ."

Lizzie wiped her eyes, stepped out of the shower, and reached for the towel. She checked between her legs. It *is* water. Good. It's just water. It's not blood.

Not yet, Fay thought. "Call me."

Lizzie stepped into her house slippers, wrapped herself

in the oversize terrycloth robe, then steadied herself a moment, grasping the sink.

"Call me," Fay said. "Call your mother."

Lizzie walked into the bedroom, picked up the phone and dialed—Fay counted—seven numbers.

O.K., Fay thought. Call the doctor first. Then call *me.*

The doctor told her he would meet her at the hospital. He asked her if Paul was still out of town, then told her to call a cab.

"I'll be all right," she said, "I'm not a baby." She laughed and patted her stomach. "The baby is the baby." She told the doctor good-bye.

"Now," Fay said, "one more call."

Lizzie dialed again and told someone named Lucy to see if she could find Paul and tell him the baby was coming.

Sure, Fay thought, that's all right too. But now Mother, O.K.?

Lizzie held the receiver in her hand. "Mother, Mother, Mother," she whispered.

Fay smiled.

But Lizzie didn't dial again. She held the receiver, held it with both hands, pressed it between her breasts, then slid it down to rest on the mound made by the soon-to-be-born child.

"Lizzie, what are you doing?" Fay asked.

But she knew what Lizzie was doing. Lizzie was not calling her. But why wasn't she calling her? Fay would be there as fast as she could. Would stay as long as Lizzie needed her. Why didn't she call?

Lizzie pulled on a pair of sweat pants and a big shirt, Paul's probably, slipped on her sandals, grabbed her purse, then stopped to pick up the already-packed leather satchel waiting beside the door.

Outside, Lizzie put the top down on her convertible, turned on the radio, and backed out the drive.

Fay reached out and held the glass of iced tea between her hands to steady herself. The baby was a girl. Her name was Katie. And she was coming fast.

Lizzie drove through the canyon and down onto the flats—speeding, Fay thought, but who wouldn't? Then she made a sharp turn onto a tree-lined residential street.

A huge red moving van was sitting out in front of a

house. The movers, eating lunch on the tailgate of the truck, waved. One man whistled. Lizzie waved back, patted her huge stomach, and sailed past them, honking her horn.

As Fay reached for her butter knife, the baby was born; taking her first bite, the name was given. Taking a sip of tea, Lizzie's room was filled with orchids and Paul was on his way.

Lizzie would have to call sometime, wouldn't she? Or would she have someone else call for her? And someone else take care of her. And someone else bathe the baby while Lizzie napped.

Lizzie would have to let Fay see Katie, wouldn't she? Send a present? See Katie wear the present? Wouldn't she?

Fay covered her pounding heart with her hand, then looked up quickly, as the little bells rang again, and the tea-shop door opened. No one could have known she was here. But Fay had a visitor, just the same.

4:00 P.M.

 INSIDE THE POLICE BARRICADE EDITH MASTERS was sitting with the woman officer assigned to guard her. Arnie was ready to talk to her, but he wanted her to wait a minute, wanted her to worry a little.

"Don't you want to sit in on this?" he asked the Chief.

"I want the prune in jail," the Chief said.

"Do my best," Arnie said, lighting a cigarette, studying Mrs. Masters from the back.

Edith was making no effort to talk to the officer. And she wasn't watching the traffic police clear the parking lot, or the TV people pack up their cameras. She wasn't smoking, of course, or rummaging through her purse, or fiddling with her hair. She was simply sitting perfectly still. She didn't seem worried at all.

"Does Fay think they're serious?" the Chief asked Arnie. "They won't give the other kids back? They won't make any other demands?"

"She said that's what women do," Arnie said. "She said the way they win is to quit."

"They can't just quit," the Chief said. "They're terrorists. How are they going to win if they don't keep playing?"

"Fay says it's not a game." Arnie stood up. "O.K.," he said. "Let's see what old Edith has to say for herself."

"I just don't get it," the Chief said, turning to walk away. "I don't know what we're doing here."

"Go back downtown then," Arnie said.

"Can't," the Chief said. "I want to know what's in the truck."

"You and me, pal," Arnie said, dropping his cigarette and stubbing it out with his shoe. "There's a bowling alley down at the end there. Maybe that would straighten it out for you."

The Chief shook his head. "I can't bowl for shit."

"That's too bad," Arnie said. "Be just the thing."

Arnie signaled to the officer that he would talk to Mrs. Masters now. The officer nodded, stood up, picked her cigarettes up off the table, and walked away. But Mrs. Masters took no notice of the officer's departure.

As he started toward her, Arnie was annoyed by the lone gray curl lying limp along her neck. He didn't want to do this. He had no idea how he would begin the interview. He wished he weren't a policeman so he could honor his first impulse, which was to grab her purse and run.

"Good afternoon, Mrs. Masters," he said, laughing at himself, "I'm Detective Campbell."

"Something has amused you?" Mrs. Masters drew herself up in the chair.

"Don't know what it is," he said, still chuckling. "I almost stole your purse."

"Actually," she said, lifting the purse into her lap and folding her arms around it, "my purse *has* been stolen a number of times."

That made him laugh out loud. He reached quickly in his pocket for his pen and notebook, hoping that would restore his concentration. "And you always find it, or somebody turns it in?"

He wet the point of the pen in his mouth. "I mean, if they keep stealing this same little purse of yours, that means you keep getting it back so it's there for them to steal again. Right?"

He looked up, composed and detached, saw her squinting eyes, and burst out laughing all over again.

"I'm very sorry," he said, desperate to get control of himself. "But I've been up all night, and all this confusion today and everything, I guess I'm cracking up."

"That's quite all right," she said primly, "you take your time."

She placed the poor purse square in front of her on the table, and studied it. She held it at the top, with both hands as if it were trying to get away. She turned it to the side, tried the clasp, then snapped it shut. She examined the seams, moistened one finger and rubbed off a spot of something yellow on the lizard vinyl trim. Finally, she looked up at Arnie. "I just can't imagine what it is about this purse."

"Well," he said, reaching for it, "let's have a look."

"Am I under arrest?" she asked, pulling the purse toward her.

"We can do it that way if you want," he said. "But I think you'll find it much more pleasant to let me look at the purse here rather than at headquarters."

"I haven't done anything you could arrest me for," she said.

"Suspicion," he said. "That's all we need."

"Suspicion of what?"

"Planning this whole thing," he said. "Getting your group organized, finding the driver who stole the truck, kidnapping the children, contacting the mothers by phone, buying the stuff for the packages, then delivering the packages so the mothers could pick them up."

"That's absurd."

"You did a helluva job," he said, smiling. "With planning like that, you could've pulled a pretty nice robbery, Mrs. Masters. Why didn't you? A Brinks truck, maybe? The Federal Reserve Bank? That kind of money would have bought a lot of TV time for your cause. Done a helluva lot more good than this stunt."

"Yes," she said, smiling. "I see what you mean. But you have the wrong person."

"No, I don't think so," he said.

"I wish I could help you," she said, "but I don't know anything about this. I'm only here because one of the mothers is a friend of mine."

"Lynn Waldo," Arnie said.

"Yes," she said.

"From your church."

"Yes."

"What church?" he asked. "Where is it located?"

But she didn't answer.

He looked up. "Mrs. Masters?"

"My religious persuasion is my personal affair," she said.

Arnie was getting annoyed. "I can look up the damn address in the phone book," he said. "Who's your preacher at this church?"

She looked away.

"All right," he said. "Tell me about this telephone tree, your group of anti-abortion mothers who answer the phone."

She opened her purse and took out a roll of Necco wafers. Arnie couldn't remember the last time he'd seen that candy, but he did remember he liked the brown ones best. He was never sure what the brown flavor was exactly, chocolate maybe, or root beer, he just knew he liked it. If she offered him one, he'd take it, he knew. But she didn't.

He resumed his questions. "Mrs. Waldo told us all about this telephone tree, Mrs. Masters. We know that you recruit these women, that this phone number is listed in your name, and the bill is paid from your checking account."

She unwrapped the wafers, picked through the stack to find a pink one. "Counseling is not against the law," she said, slipping the candy into her mouth.

"Who is 'dear one'?" he asked.

She bit the wafer in two.

"You called someone named 'dear one,' Mrs. Masters. Is 'dear one' your husband?"

She chewed the wafer properly and swallowed it.

"What does 'feed the chickens' mean?" he asked.

She rolled the tube of candy back and forth in her hands like cookie dough.

"Who is Mitchell Masters?" he asked.

"My husband," she said, opening the Necco package again.

"And what does he do?"

"He's disabled," she said. "He's retired." She selected three more pink ones and put them all in her mouth at once.

"What did he do when he worked?" Arnie asked. "Did he sell surgical supplies, maybe?"

She crossed her legs.

"You have a daughter named Colleen, is that right?"

"Colleen is no longer with us."

"Did she die having an abortion?"

"Colleen is in California."

"No," Arnie said. "I'm afraid not. Of course, we're not absolutely positive it's your Colleen who died, but somebody named Colleen Masters with a mother and father named Edith and Mitchell, who live at your address, died of internal bleeding at General Hospital fifteen years ago this week."

Mrs. Masters closed her eyes.

"We checked the property tax rolls, Mrs. Masters. The house has not changed ownership in twenty years. So if I could see your driver's license to verify your address, please."

She opened her eyes. "Absolutely not," she said.

"You refuse to let me see your driver's license?"

"I do," she said.

He closed his notebook. "Mrs. Masters, you are under arrest," he said. "You have the right to remain silent. Anything you say can and will be used against you in a court of law." He motioned for the officer standing to one side of the table. "You have the right to be represented by counsel. If you cannot afford a lawyer, the court will appoint one for you."

"You are wasting your time," she said.

"If I am wasting my time," he said, standing up, "at least I have the comfort of knowing I am also wasting yours."

The officer came up behind her and took her arm.

"Put the cuffs on," Arnie told him. "And get me a warrant to search the house."

She offered him the purse. "You can search my purse, my house, my car, everything I have, Detective. But you will not find one shred of evidence that links me to this crime." She flinched as the officer snapped the handcuffs around her wrists.

"Help me, Mrs. Masters," Arnie said. "If Colleen died from an illegal abortion, shouldn't you want to protect other girls by keeping abortion legal and safe?"

She didn't answer.

"Is it your husband who planned this thing?"

She didn't answer.

Arnie nodded to the officer. "Take her downtown. And when you get her prints, check them against the ones we found in the church this morning."

Arnie watched her go. He knew he could be making a mistake, taking her in. If she stayed loose, she might do something that would lead to the others. But he was beginning to think there weren't any others. He was beginning to think this whole thing could be the work of two little people. It was, he thought, the American way.

THE MAYOR AND Vi didn't know yet that Fay thought their boys were in trouble. The Chief had decided not to frighten them until there was something real to be afraid of.

They stood together on the sidewalk, at Vi's request, having what felt to Peter like a meeting.

"Are you listening to me?" she asked, smiling at the people passing by.

"I don't think so," he said, also smiling at the people passing by. "Are you saying anything?"

She signed an autograph. "I said I want to borrow one of your speech writers to help me prepare a statement against abortion."

"I can't do that," he said, shaking someone's hand. "They're on the city payroll."

"I have to do this. It's the only way I know to get our boys back."

"I don't think that's why you're doing it at all."

"I've helped *you*," she said. "I've campaigned for you, posed for pictures with you, given little dinners for you . . ."

"I heard what you told that reporter, Vi. And I *don't* think women's real work is re-creating the lost world of the American family. I *don't* think the women's movement sold American women to industry as cheap labor. And I *don't* think legal abortion is why mothers don't have time for the PTA."

She shook her head. "The PTA was just an example, Peter. What I meant was that women are too tired from working to take care of their children."

"You've reversed yourself completely!" he said. "You've betrayed everything you ever stood for."

"Who was that woman you were talking to?" she asked. "During my interview."

"You know very well who she was," he said. "Gail Wilkins, one of the mothers."

"And what were you talking about?"

He smiled. "Why her husband climbed the Indian."

"And what else?"

"What else is none of your business, Vi," he said.

"So you admit it?"

"Admit what?"

"That you were talking to her about something else."

"Yes," he said. "Terrible, isn't it."

She tugged at the tail of his jacket. "All I was doing in that interview was admitting I'd been wrong about abortion."

"No," he said. "You just looked at the crowd and said what they wanted to hear."

"Peter," she said. "Think how many people there are who have no one to speak for them on this."

"Oh yes," he said, "and a lot of people secretly thought lynching was a good idea, too. How do you feel about that?"

She turned away. "It's not the same thing, and you know it."

He ran his hand through his hair. "The real reason I'm not giving you one of my speech writers," he said, "is that none of them is really good enough to handle your problem."

"Your attitude right now is the only problem I can see," she sighed.

"Oh no," he said. "It's slightly bigger than that." He scratched his head. "If you're going to become the chief defender of the American family, how are you going to explain our divorce?"

"We're not getting a divorce."

"Oh yes we are," he said. "And it can be messy and public or quick and quiet. Whatever you want."

"A divorce will destroy your career."

"Yes," he said, "if people like you get in power, I imagine it will. You're not very forgiving, as a group. Anybody that fucks up, pays."

"Don't use that language with me," she snorted.

"Vi," he said, "it is my fondest desire not to use any language at all with you. But I have to say just one more thing. The boys are mine. As soon as I get back to my office, I'm suing you for divorce and custody of the boys."

"On what grounds?" she demanded.

"You forget," he said. "This is a no-fault state. But maybe you can get rid of that too when you get elected."

She pulled a small mirror from her purse and checked her lipstick. "Peter," she said, in her most soothing voice, "a more active life for me does not mean there will be less of our life together. The more involved I am, the better I'll understand the pressures you've been under all these years."

He motioned for one of his aides to come get him. "I'm not happy, Vi," he said. "It's as simple as that."

"Of course you're not," she said. "But now that I'm in politics myself, you'll have a real ally instead of just a wife."

"No, Vi," he said, as the aide approached. "To be allies, you have to be on the same side."

Vi extended her hand to the aide. "Hello, Rudy," she said. "I want to send a letter to all the mothers. Can you get their addresses for me?"

"Sure," Rudy said, assuming Vi had the Mayor's approval here.

"I need Rudy myself," the Mayor said, clapping his arm around the aide's shoulder and standing his ground.

Vi took a step backward. "I'll just go downtown, then."

"Fine," he said.

"I have my car."

"Good," he said. "If I hear anything about our boys, I'll call you."

And the Mayor stood with Rudy and watched as Vi strode off toward the black-and-white police cruiser that was waiting for her.

As she drove away, he sent Rudy for some coffee and spotted Gail, sitting by herself at the mothers' table.

THE SIGN ON the door of the tea shop said CLOSED, but Arnie knocked anyway. Maybe they knew where Fay had gone.

But there was no answer.

Then he tried the door and found it open. "Fay?" he called, seeing the pleasant-looking hostess reading a mystery novel at a table by the wall.

"Would you be Detective Campbell?" the hostess inquired.

"I'm looking for Fay Morgan," he said. "Sexy black-haired lady, about this tall?"

The hostess blushed at his description. "She's in the garden," she fluttered. "She said if you came, I should ask if you'd be so kind as to wait in here."

As Arnie walked toward the back window, the hostess stood up. "Could I bring you a cup of tea?"

"No thanks," Arnie said. "Unless you've got a beer."

Arnie took her silence to mean no, and pulled the curtains away from the window.

And sure enough, there was Fay, sitting quietly, studying two acorns she held in the palm of her hand. But she was not alone. Perched like a snowy egret on the edge of a wrought-iron table was an old lady Arnie had never seen before.

He couldn't believe it. Who was this woman? Fay seemed to know her all right, so why hadn't he ever met this bird? And where did she come from, a tree? Yes, he thought, this lady might very well have come from a tree—the only tree in this acre of concrete, the knotty oak planted in the middle of the tea-shop patio.

Arnie had never seen Fay sit so still, or listen so intently. But what in God's name were they talking about?

He couldn't interrupt them, he knew that, but could he stand here and spy on them? He wasn't spying, he was waiting for them to finish. He did have to go to the bathroom, though. But what if he missed something? What if this old girl left while he was gone, and Fay never mentioned it again?

What if it had something to do with the case? He had informers, didn't he? So why couldn't Fay? But who knew more than Fay?

He really did have to go to the bathroom. But now something was really happening out there. Fay was shaking her head. "No, no," she was saying. But the old woman was insisting, "Yes, yes," and tapping a bony finger on the table, pressing her point.

Fay looked away. She didn't even want to discuss it anymore. The old woman pulled herself fully erect, grabbed Fay's shoulder, and demanded her attention. This was the whole shooting match, right here.

Fay looked up at her, mad and hurt, and started to bolt from the chair. But the old bat blocked her. Fay sat back and crossed her arms over her chest. Then the woman backed up, propped her hands up on her hips, and nobody said anything.

Then, just as Arnie thought it was all over and he better go out there and try to make peace, the old woman spoke.

Fay's fists clenched even tighter, so the old woman bent
toward her and spoke again.

And this time, Fay softened. She uncrossed her arms
and lifted one hand out straight toward the woman, uncurling
her fingers, and offering up the two acorns.

Arnie couldn't believe they were fighting over two acorns.
But then, he wondered, where had they even gotten the
acorns? It wasn't time for acorns yet.

The old woman reached carefully into the center of Fay's
palm and picked up one of the acorns. She rolled it between
her thumb and forefinger. Then, with Fay watching, the old
woman brought the acorn to her lips, kissed it sweetly, then
put it in her pocket and patted it. Nice and safe, she seemed
to be saying.

And that made Fay start crying! Made her look at her
lonely little acorn and cry. What the hell was this?

And then the old lady lost her balance, and grasped the
edge of the table to steady herself.

Fay was still crying, but could see that the woman was
falling, and sprang up to help her into the chair on the other
side of the table.

Then Fay laughed a little, apparently at something the
old woman said, bent down and kissed the crest of her head,
and the woman laughed too, a little.

Good, he thought, straightening up. Now I can go to the
bathroom. And when he returned, the door to the garden
was open.

"Arnie," Fay said to him as he came out, "I'd like you to
meet my godmother, Katherine. Katherine Swift."

"It's a pleasure," Arnie said, extending his hand and
trying not to crush hers as he pressed it. "Where's Fay been
keeping you all this time?"

"Oh no," she said in her silvery voice, "I don't like to
bother her."

"Katherine," Fay protested, "I can never find you! I call
your house all the time but you're never there."

"I'm always there," the old woman said calmly, "but if
you're just calling me to make me feel better"—she smiled—"I
don't answer it. I go rest." She paused. "Resting always
makes me feel better."

Fay shook her head.

"How do you know it's Fay?" Arnie asked.

Godmother Katherine squinted. "How do *you* know it's Fay?" she asked. "She looks like Fay, doesn't she? She sounds like Fay." She folded her hands in her lap. "So it must be Fay!"

As a triumphant grin frisked across her face, Arnie knew he was way out of his league. He looked at his watch. "Fay," he said, "if you want to go in the truck, you have to do it soon because . . ."

"Yes," Fay said. "I'm ready." She pushed her chair under the table. "Godmother Katherine, can we get someone to take you home?"

"No," the old woman said. "I'll just rest here awhile, I think."

Fay rubbed her hands down her skirt. "Well, then . . ." she said.

As Godmother Katherine rose from her chair, her arms swept open and Fay rushed, released, into the infinite compassion of the embrace. "Please, Fay," the old woman whispered, "please, please be careful."

Arnie didn't know how long they held each other. Maybe it was only a minute, but he knew he had no business watching. He backed up toward the door.

This was a love he knew nothing about. This was an ancient, unbreakable bond. But not just between Fay and her godmother. This went all the way back to the edge of time, he thought, to the first two women who stood up, walked out of their caves, saw each other, and hugged.

Somehow, he thought, that same embrace had been passed down to these two. And while it was fully theirs to hold for the moment of their lives, he knew they wouldn't keep it, couldn't keep it, but had to pass it on.

Then he realized what they had been talking about, and he felt a little dim for not knowing it sooner, and then a little blessed for getting it at all. Fay and Godmother Katherine had been talking about Lizzie.

"AN AMAZING WOMAN," Arnie said, once they were back inside the tea shop.

"Who, me?"

"Yes, you." He laughed. He knew she didn't want to talk about it, but he couldn't just pretend it didn't happen.

"How long were you standing there watching us?" Fay asked.

"I don't know. Ten minutes," he said, nodding to the hostess, who was setting out trays of tea sandwiches. "You don't have to tell me what you were talking about," he said. "Just tell me how she found you."

"She always knows where I am," Fay said.

Arnie nodded. "Does Godmother Katherine read cards?"

"No," Fay said. "She just came today because she knew I needed her."

"She looks like one of your cards," he said. "The lady, what's her name?"

"The High Priestess," Fay said. "Yes. She does."

"Will she be all right by herself?" he asked, opening the tea-shop door.

But Fay wasn't quite ready to face the scene out there. "She's been by herself her whole life." She looked back toward the garden. "She told me to tell you I had a gun in the house."

"What house?" Arnie asked. "What gun?"

"My house," Fay said, stepping out onto the sidewalk. "It was Mother's."

He followed her quickly, taking her arm as they neared the curb. "What did your mother need a gun for?"

She looked across at the truck. "Snakes," she said.

"Snakes?" Arnie hooted, holding his arm up to stop a car crossing in front of them.

Fay nodded. "Yes, snakes. You know, for winter in the country, when they crawl into the house to get warm."

Arnie had to laugh. "It's damn tough to hit a snake with a gun," he said. "You're better off with an ax."

"Yes, I know," Fay said. "I think Dad used an ax."

"Where is this gun of yours, Fay?" Arnie asked, as he waved to the Chief.

"In the hall closet."

"Are there any bullets for it?"

"I don't have any extras," she said. "But it's loaded, if that's what you mean."

"Jesus, Fay," he said. "You've got a loaded gun in your house?"

"What's the matter with that?" she asked. "I'm the only one who knows about it."

Arnie moved a piece of the barricade so they could slip through. "Did Godmother Katherine have any ideas about the kids?" he asked.

"No," Fay said. "She thinks it's awful."

THE HIGH PRIESTESS, the card Arnie thought looked like God-mother Katherine, is the most powerful card in the Tarot deck. The High Priestess does not, however, derive her power from religion or law or earthly force or womanly charm. She doesn't, in fact, *do* anything. She simply knows all the mysteries by name and understands how they work.

The High Priestess represents what so many people are afraid of—that there might be uncontrollable currents which influence their lives, secrets which sway their decisions.

One reason people go to psychics is to cozy up to these mysteries, to hear about them so they can feel in control again. Control, however, is simply not to be had where mystery is concerned. You cannot know a mystery, you can only know it's there.

Did Fay know what the secret system was? Did Fay know how things worked? Yes and no. She did know some of the patterns, but she had no idea why they were necessary. She did see some of the connections, but didn't know why they were so inevitable. She knew that separation was one of the evils, but she didn't understand why closeness was so difficult.

When Fay was a girl, and first learning the cards, she figured the High Priestess probably looked like Carole Lombard and slunk around heaven wearing a silver slip, listening to old Sinatra tunes. But as Fay got older she realized that if there were a heaven, and if the High Priestess were there, she would just wear a pink chenille bathrobe and make tea and toast when folks were feeling blue.

To Fay, the High Priestess was the sense it would all make when she finally understood. In the darkness, this wise old woman grasped Fay's hand and found her a safe place to sit.

The High Priestess kept things from getting lost. The loose ends that people left dangling, she gathered up and held until they were ready to pick them up again. When things fell apart, she kept the pieces in one place until you were ready to put them back together. If you swore never to speak to your brother again, she'd stay in touch with him, keep him thinking about you, until you realized you needed him back.

And as for power, Fay's High Priestess didn't make things happen to you, she simply moved you toward things that were going to happen, then stood by to see if you got it. Most of the time, of course, you wouldn't get it. What she did then was calmly arrange another opportunity.

Fay knew the High Priestess was at work on her today; she could feel it. And she knew it had something to do with Lizzie, but what was it? These visions Fay was having, Lizzie getting married, Lizzie having a baby, Lizzie not talking to Fay, what did they mean?

Maybe the High Priestess was warning Fay that this was her last chance to hold on to her daughter. Maybe Fay was supposed to do something different this time. But how could she? All she'd ever done was try to keep the girl from getting hurt.

This was exactly the same thing. Paul was *not* the right man for Lizzie. His family just barely tolerated her. They probably laughed at her behind her back. They didn't appreciate who she was.

Lizzie would starve there, would turn into someone as materialistic and shallow as they were. She would forget everything Fay had taught her, might even forget Fay altogether. If Lizzie went away with Paul, she would turn into someone else, someone Fay didn't know. She had to be stopped.

Godmother Katherine meant well, but she was wrong.

5:00 P.M.

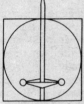

GAIL AND THE MAYOR WERE WAITING FOR FAY AT the mothers' table with the Chief. They were all glad to see her coming now. The Chief wanted her to make this whole thing disappear.

Gail and Peter had been talking about their children. He said he didn't think either of his boys would go into politics, that Kevin liked science and Kerry wanted to be a baseball player. Gail said her little Beth liked applesauce and wanted to be a cat. Peter said he had always wanted a big family. Gail said she came from a big family, and it was nice except in the morning.

Then Gail asked the Chief if the city would send them a bill for rescuing Marvin.

"You already paid," the Chief said. "Taxes."

Gail forced herself to laugh. "I think Marvin cheats on our taxes," she said.

Now the Mayor laughed. "Well, we'll just have to keep him in jail, then."

"Marvin would like jail," Gail said. "He doesn't care what he eats, and he always wanted to learn to fix radios."

They were real uncomfortable here. Gail stood up and walked over to meet Fay. Another detective rushed up to the Chief with a message, and Arnie came over to the Mayor, who had been left sitting by himself.

"Is she going to go in the truck now?" the Mayor asked.

"That's what she says," Arnie said.

"What does she think is in there?" the Mayor asked, as he watched Gail talking to Fay.

But before Arnie could answer, the Chief came back with the news.

Fay saw the look on his face and grabbed Gail's arm. "It's Peter's boys," she said. And they rushed up to the table in time to hear the end of it.

"Shit," the Chief said, "I didn't even think about the weather. An electrical storm with the two of them on that cliff . . ."

Arnie was mad. "Why can't somebody just climb out and—"

"It's like a natural bridge," the Chief said, as the Mayor waved for his driver. "And the only way to get to it is the same way the boys did, crawling through this tiny passage."

"Why can't the boys crawl back out?" the Mayor asked.

"From where they are," the Chief said, "they can't see the opening anymore. What we need is somebody small, real small, to go after them. Somebody small enough to sit on the ledge with them and convince them they can crawl back."

"And what's on the other side of the ledge?" Gail asked.

"Air," the Chief said. "Almost a straight drop, hundreds of feet, and pretty serious rocks at the bottom."

Fay knew what Gail was thinking.

"Am I small enough?" Gail asked.

"No, Gail," the Mayor said. "There has to be something they haven't thought of yet. I don't want you to—"

"At least let me come with you," Gail said, as the Mayor's car pulled up in front of them.

"No," he said. "You should be at your house in case the kidnappers drop Beth off there."

Gail grabbed his arm. "Mother's there," she said. "Mother's waiting for Beth. Please." She lowered her voice. "I can't just sit at home and wait."

"Go on," Fay said to Peter. "Take her with you."

And that was all the encouragement Peter needed to sweep her into the car.

"Be careful." Fay waved to Gail through the window, and then they were gone.

As they walked to the truck, the Chief had some other news for Fay. They had found Kimberly Chen sound asleep at 228 Hummingbird Drive. But by the time the detectives arrived, the woman Fay had seen was gone.

"Somebody is listening to everything we do," Arnie said.

"Who owns that house?" Fay asked.

"Vernon Lockhart," the Chief said. "Out of town. Nice people, the neighbors say. Haven't caused a minute's worth of trouble in the five years they've been living there."

"Maybe the neighbors are lying," Arnie said.

"Maybe," the Chief said. "We're checking on the car."

"Was Kimberly all right?" Fay asked.

"Looks all right," the Chief said. "They're doing a blood test on her now, for tranquilizers, that kind of thing. I mean, if I had to deliver twenty-seven kids in the middle of the night, I'd sure put them to sleep first."

Fay was glad they'd had something to talk about on the way to the truck, but she froze as another detective handed the Chief the keys.

"You ready?" the Chief asked.

She didn't trust herself to answer, so she simply nodded. She hadn't been this close to it all day.

"Want me to come with you?" Arnie asked.

"Yes," she whispered, and squeezed his hand. "Thank you."

The Chief climbed up to the step tread and put the key in the padlock. It worked easily and he pitched the padlock to the leader of the lab team, then spun the cylinder on the combination lock.

Fay was trying to remember the contents of the packages now. "Did anybody play that cassette tape?"

"Yeah," Arnie said. "It's real cute. One voice says 'Can I see my baby?' Then another voice says 'No.'"

"That's all?" she asked, trying to keep her knees from shaking.

"That's all," Arnie said. "For forty-five minutes, over and over."

The Chief unwrapped the chains and dropped them to the ground. "Everybody ready?" He jumped down. "Fay?" he asked.

She shook her head. "Arnie's going in first."

Arnie stepped up to the truck, grabbed hold, and pulled himself up to the step tread. Then he grasped the door handles. "Stand back," he said. With one massive effort, he jerked the doors open, then pulled them apart. A wave of darkness washed over him.

He stood there stunned by the chill inside the truck. He'd expected it to be hot, an oven. "Somebody got a flashlight?"

"What about prints?" a lab man asked the Chief.

"I'm not touching anything," Arnie said, as another lab man handed the flashlight up to him. "Come on, Fay," he said, "get up here."

She backed up quickly. "No, Arnie," she said, "I'll go through it once you've . . ."

"It's O.K.," he said, catching the Chief's eye. "Help the little lady up, huh?"

And before she could resist, the Chief put both hands around Fay's waist and hoisted her up into the bed of the truck.

"Just relax," the Chief said. "It's just an ordinary truck. Nothing's going to hurt you."

But Fay knew better.

Arnie flashed the light around the inside of the truck and found, just as Fay had feared, a sign taped to the back wall. The letters, easily four feet high, were red. Blood, the lab would say later, type O positive.

Arnie read it aloud. "MISSING CHILDREN."

She shook her head. "There's more," she whispered. "Little words." She couldn't move.

He walked forward and saw them himself. "Oh boy." He shook his head. "Oh boy oh boy." Then he read the whole message to Fay, pointing out the words with his flashlight. "WE . . . ARE . . . MISSING . . . OUR . . . CHILDREN."

She nodded and swallowed.

"What does it mean?" he asked.

"It means what it says, Arnie," she said, and closed her eyes.

The Chief yelled up to them. "What have you got?"

"A sign," she said. "Come see." She wanted more company in here.

Once the Chief was inside, Arnie lit up the words one more time. "WE . . . ARE . . . MISSING . . . OUR . . . CHILDREN."

The Chief nodded, just as Fay had, then stood there, sad for a moment, unable to speak.

Behind him, someone called that they had portable lights, if they needed them. Grateful for something to do, the Chief turned and reached down for them.

"Some sign, huh?" he muttered to Fay.

It was clearly a plea for comfort.

"Yes," she said. "Me too. I miss mine too."

"I wasn't home enough," he said.

She smiled wearily. "Terrific," she said. "I was home all the time."

Arnie walked forward and took the lights from the Chief.

"See anything else back there?" the Chief asked him.

"Pictures," Arnie said.

"What pictures?" Fay asked.

"Girls," Arnie said. "Under the sign." And he placed the lights down the middle of the truck. "There." He flipped the switches and looked around.

The lamps did not fully illuminate the inside of the truck, but created pools of light separated first by dim and then by dark places.

"Let's each take a side," Arnie said, "and call out what we find, just to get a sense of it, and then we'll call in the team. Fay, you take the pictures."

The Chief began: "Folding chairs, a lectern, a portable microphone system, and three electric fans."

Arnie continued with the inventory. There were posters rolled up in cardboard tubes, and a folding cork screen.

"This box is all books," the Chief said, holding one of them up to the light. "This is some kind of source book for people wanting to adopt children. And a camera."

Fay spoke for the first time. "How fast can we get the film developed?"

"Twenty minutes," the Chief said; he walked to the door and handed the camera to the lab team.

"What have you got, Fay?" Arnie asked.

"Boxes," she said, stooping down under the row of pictures. "Is it O.K. if I open one?"

"Just one," the Chief said.

Carefully, she lifted the lid of the small cardboard box, reached inside and picked up a ragged scrap of faded pink fabric. As she rubbed it between her fingers, her eyes welled with tears.

"What's that?" he asked.

Fay cleared her throat. "It's all that's left of her favorite blanket," she said, "you know, the one she wouldn't go to sleep without, the one she dragged around the house all the time, the one she'd put up to her face and smell when she was scared."

"Whose blanket?" he said. "Colleen's?"

"I don't know," Fay said. "Her." And she pointed to the picture above the box.

Fay counted the pictures. "Arnie," she asked, "how many tables were there in that church this morning?"

"I don't know," he said.

"One for each of these girls?"

"Maybe," he said. "The report would have it. Want me to find out?"

"I have to get out of here," she said, turning around to face the open back door of the truck.

"Oh no you don't," he said.

"I have to find Lizzie."

"She's with Jake at a place called Sound Effects," he said. "Having a drink."

"It's a tomb in here, Arnie. I have to go!"

He grabbed her arm and held her fast. "No, Fay."

She turned around angrily, twisting her arm to get free of him. "Arnie, I've got to make sure Lizzie doesn't . . ."

"No," he said firmly. "No. You've got to do what only you can do. You've got to tell us who these people are and where they're keeping the rest of the children."

She was really mad now. She looked away from him.

"While my own child disappears."

"We'll shut the doors," he said, "and turn out the lights and leave you in here for a while."

"No," she said.

"It's what you came here to do. You can't just walk out of here as though you were any other woman on earth and not—"

"Arnie," she begged, "you *know* what I'll see."

He had never seen her this afraid. "No, love, I don't. That's just the point."

He let go of her arm and she turned to face the side wall.

"Fay," he said, speaking more softly this time, "as soon as we find these children, we can spend the rest of the night with Lizzie. We can kidnap her ourselves if that will make you feel better, put her in the car and drive all night, all the way to Wyoming if you want to."

She stared at the wall. "They were all here," she said finally. "The children were all in this truck."

"That's good," he said. "That's a good start."

She turned back to face him, her face drawn and pale. "But we already knew that, Arnie."

He reached for her hand. "Just try," he said. "That's all I'm asking you to do."

"And where will you be?" she asked.

"Right outside the door," he said. "I'll sit on that little step and knock every now and then if you want me to."

"No," she said. "Don't knock. Just stay there."

He rubbed her shoulder.

Tears filled her eyes again. "And what if I can't do it?" she asked.

"Then you can't, that's all. Then I'll take you to Lizzie while I go to the Masters house."

"No," she said. "I want to go to the Masters house with you."

"How long do you need?" he asked.

"Ten minutes," she whispered. "Open the door in ten minutes."

"And if you want to come out before then, just knock and I'll open the door."

Her hand started to tremble.

He wanted to help her somehow. "I wish there were something I could—"

"Just go," she said, squeezing herself as though she were cold. "Just go on. Let's get it over with."

Arnie took a step backward and gave her a thumbs-up sign.

When she turned away, he walked quickly to the big doors, stepped out, and closed them behind him.

THE HEAVY DOORS clanged shut, and the sound ricocheted around the walls of the truck. Fay flipped the switch on the light next to her, then walked to the other one, took a deep breath, and turned it off. Then she simply stood quietly and waited as the history of this truck, pressed back against the walls by the light, sensed its freedom and crept toward her in the darkness.

First there came the whispers, the soft sobbing, the furtive shuffling of little sneakers. Then the sound of sandals and a pair of flip-flops.

A baseball cap fell to the floor. A hand reached down to get it, brushing past knees, shorts, and shirttails. Little overalls and spotted T-shirts sagged in the shadows. Two hands clasped tight. Somebody sat down. Kerry leaned back against the wall. Kevin curled up beside him. Beth sucked her thumb. All the children were breathing at once, but slower now, softer now, as sleep settled over them like a down comforter.

"Before this," Fay whispered, "before you were here, you were outside, at the fair." Beth listened. "Tell me who brought you here. Tell me why you came with them."

A clown; she saw floppy clown shoes, green like pickles. Pickles. Of course they would follow a clown. They might even ask, Can I go see the clown? And the clown had brought them here for the magic show.

"But we can't start the magic show till everybody gets here," the clown said, "so why don't you have some lemonade. Cowboy Bob will give you some lemonade, and after the lemonade and the magic show, he'll let you ride his pony."

But after the lemonade they were all asleep. Cowboy Bob and Pickles the Clown drove the truck out the main gate to a farmhouse in the country, a dirt road, a big black dog.

They unloaded the kids, all asleep. Put them in the barn. Kevin. Kerry. She didn't see Beth, but she had to be there. Dark. Mirrors, Bathtubs. Beth? Where's Beth?

Look closely, Fay.

It's Edith Masters.

And the young man in the coffee shop this morning.

The other one's in a wheelchair. An older man in a wheelchair. Small legs, big chest, sleeves rolled up, arms like a boxer. Stubble on his face, wire glasses, and a hearing aid. Gray stubble on his head, an army blanket over his legs.

Where is this barn? she asked. And Beth? Where did you take Beth?

But all she saw was the church. The church with the Tarot's Hanged Man in the yard. Inside the church, husbands and wives were standing in back of the tables, their boxes in front of them. Pictures in their hands. Pieces of blankets. Baby clothes and rattles in the boxes.

Were those the pictures on the wall of the truck? Yes. Were those the boxes on the floor below? Yes.

"Lay it down," the man in the wheelchair was telling them. "Lay it down and let her go."

Let who go? The girl in the picture?

Fay struggled to put it together. The Tarot card. Edith. The pictures. The boxes. The man in the wheelchair.

Had Colleen Masters bought a deck of Tarot cards after she had come to see Fay? Did Edith find them? Did Edith say they were evil? And then did Colleen die? Yes.

Fay whirled around, opened her eyes, and raced toward the sliver of light between the massive metal doors.

"Arnie!" she screamed. "Arnie, are you out there?"

She heard him jump up, felt his hands grab the handles.

"I'm here," he shouted back. "Are you all right?"

"I'm all right," she managed, "I just wanted to make sure you were there." His voice steadied her.

"Are you ready to come out?"

She knew she couldn't. Colleen had to be there, had to be one of those children on the back wall. Her toys had to be in one of those boxes. If Colleen were there, that would be real proof. They could force Edith to tell them where she took the children.

"No," she said to Arnie. "I need another two minutes."

"All you have to do is knock, love," he said.

"Thanks." She stood up straight and took a step, then a second.

"Find Colleen," she said to herself. "Find Colleen."

Fay stopped at the back of the truck and stared into the wall of pictures, but it was too dark to see any more than the outlines of their white frames. She turned around to get a flashlight, and then stopped. Suddenly, she understood.

Edith wouldn't put anything in this truck that could lead to her. If a group like that had met at the church, she'd just used the idea of it, not the actual pictures and boxes. She'd cut these pictures out of magazines. She'd collected these boxes at the Goodwill. These girls did exist, all right, and these girls all died having abortions, but these weren't their real pictures. Fay was finished. Edith had won.

She sighed and sat down in the darkness. What was she

going to tell Arnie? That Edith was insane? That a cowboy and a man in a wheelchair helped her? What good would that do?

She nudged one of the boxes with her foot. She knew exactly which box it was, the one with the little scrap of blanket in it. She knelt down in the darkness, lifted the lid, reached for the piece of blanket, raised it to her face and inhaled, deep and long.

A new smell. Sharper, younger. This little girl had dark curls and long, thin legs. Like a colt she was, with bright black eyes. And she never could hold still, but now her mother was trying to brush her hair. "Katie!" her mother said, and the little girl squealed in laughter, and Fay shivered in recognition. It was Lizzie's laugh. It was Lizzie's little girl.

"Hold still!" Lizzie said. "I have to brush your hair before Grandma comes. You *know* how Grandma likes your hair to look nice."

"I like it like it is," the girl said.

Fay liked it the way it was, too. Her hand, still clutching the blanket, dropped to her side as she watched them play this ancient, squirming game.

"It has to hurt," Lizzie said, "or it won't do any good."

Fay smiled. She didn't believe that anymore, but she remembered saying it often enough.

"But it won't stay combed," the little girl protested.

"It would if you would behave yourself," Lizzie nagged.

Fay shook her head.

The little one tried again. "Grandma says the next time I go over there by myself she's going to cut it all off anyway."

Fay stood up. She wasn't the Grandma they were talking about, was she? No. But they were saying Grandma like there was only one. Didn't they have some way to tell the grandmothers apart? How could there be only one Grandma? Fay didn't know. But she did know the little girl had Paul's blazing devil-black eyes.

Fay wrapped the little piece of blanket between her fingers and turned around slowly. Once again she was alone in the truck. The odor of spoiling oranges engulfed her. She gagged.

"Arnie!" she screamed, as the metal walls seemed to close in on her.

"Arnie!" she screamed again, racing for the doors and pounding to be let out.

He jumped up from his seat on the tread. "O.K., O.K."

"Arnie! Hurry!"

"I'm right here, hon," he said through the door, "but back up a little, O.K.? I don't want you falling out when I open the doors."

Fay stepped back, shaking with terror, and stuffed the scrap of blanket into her pocket.

Arnie jerked the doors open and she fell into his arms.

"It's all right, love," he said. "Everything's all right now."

"It's Edith and a man in a wheelchair," she whispered into his shoulder. "They did it to get back at me, to punish me for what I did, for what I told Colleen that day."

"Fay, Fay," he said. He didn't hear most of this, and didn't understand what little he heard. He carried her down the steps and walked her toward an empty chair. "You need some air, love," he comforted. "You're all right."

"Do we need the medics?" the Chief asked, then turned around and barked at one of his aides for some water.

Arnie smoothed her hair, talking quietly. "Now then," he said. "Isn't that better. Isn't that better to have some air?"

She nodded and reached for his hand.

The lab team stormed the truck now, with their gloves and bags and labels. Fay knew the Chief was eager to hear her report, but she didn't know if she could talk at all, much less remember what she had seen.

Arnie motioned to the Chief to back off a little, then waved him in when Fay cleared her throat and sat up a little straighter in the chair.

"Just tell us if there's something we should do, Fay," Arnie said.

She looked up at the Chief. "It's Edith," she said, "and a man in a wheelchair."

"Her husband, Mitch, is in a wheelchair," Arnie said. "She just told me."

"Mitch Masters," the Chief said, drawing a piece of paper from his pocket. "Purple Heart, Korea."

"I thought we sent somebody to their house," Arnie said.

"He's not home," the Chief said. "Our guy just left there. The nurse said he went to the fair."

"He has wire-rimmed glasses and gray stubble on his head," Fay said. "Sixty maybe."

"Great," the Chief said, and headed for the radio truck.

Arnie didn't like the wildness in Fay's eyes.

"This *does* have to do with me," Fay said, when the Chief was out of range. "Edith and Mitch think *I'm* responsible for what happened to Colleen. That's why they put the Tarot card in front of the church."

"But Colleen has been dead a long time now," he said. "Surely they don't think you could bring her back."

"No," she said, "but . . ."

"They did all this to get back at *you*?"

"I know," she said. "I know how it sounds, but that's what I saw."

"Did Edith drive the truck away from the fairgrounds?"

"No," she said. "That man we saw her with this morning in the coffee shop, that Cowboy Bob, he did. He drove it to a farmhouse. A farmhouse with mirrors and bathtubs in the barn."

Arnie shook his head. "Was there any proof in the truck"—he paused—"any proof that it was Edith?"

"No," she said. "Nothing a judge would believe."

"It's O.K.," he said. "We'll get her."

She didn't answer.

"Don't be scared of them," he said. "They can't hurt you. We'll find Mitch at the fairgrounds, get him to tell us where Cowboy Bob is, and lock them all away."

"Beth wasn't there," Fay said. "They took Beth someplace else."

"We'll find her," Arnie said.

The Chief returned from the truck. "O.K.," he said. "They're looking for him. There's a wheelchair race at six, some veterans' thing. He's signed up for it." The Chief was looking better. "I think we've got these bastards."

"Well," Arnie said, "we still don't have anything to prove it."

"We'll get it," the Chief said. "We've got a million people on this thing. Do you want to be there when they find him?"

"I want to go *somewhere*," Fay said, beginning to recover. "This is longer than I ever spent in a shopping center in my life."

"Yeah." The Chief nodded. "I don't know how my wife does it."

"She has things to carry," Fay said. "That helps."

Arnie offered his arm and she stood up.

"I'll be downtown if you need me," the Chief said, checking his watch. "And sooner or later, I guess I'll have to go home."

"Yes," Fay said, looking at him, "I think you should."

Her tone alarmed him. "Is something the matter?"

"No," she said, realizing she'd scared him. "They like you, that's all. More than you think."

He decided not to ask her how she knew that. He was afraid she was right.

"I NEED A cup of coffee," Arnie said, as they started for his car.

"Not that coffee shop again, please," Fay said.

"I know," he said. "I'll get it at the fair." He took her arm. "Do you want anything?"

She stopped. "I want you to believe what I said. About this whole thing happening because of me."

He lit a cigarette. "If they wanted to get back at you, hon," he said, "they could just hire somebody to kill you."

She nodded, oddly undisturbed by the idea.

He went on. "To dream up this drill, all these mothers, twenty-seven children, and a tractor-trailer truck, would be positively demented."

She didn't answer.

Arnie got in his side of the car and started the engine.

"Does it hurt to get shot?" she asked.

"It's no fun." He laughed. "Why?"

"Because maybe when this doesn't work, they'll just give up and kill me," she said.

"I won't let him kill you, Fay."

Somehow, they both knew they were talking about the man in the wheelchair.

"Don't even think about it," he said.

"Wouldn't you think about it," she asked, "if somebody were planning to kill you?"

"Nobody's planning to kill you," he said. "We're just talking about all of this."

He pulled out of the shopping center, picked up his radio, and told the operator to find Jake and Lizzie and have them come to the information booth in the west wing of the fairgrounds.

"Because if he did," Fay said, as though they hadn't stopped talking, "then that would explain why Lizzie doesn't call me."

"Lizzie calls you all the time."

She started slowly, fearing that he wasn't going to believe this either. "No," she said, "when I was in the truck I saw Lizzie, years and years from now. She has a little girl."

A proud smile spread over Arnie's face. "Did she get the family hair?" he asked.

Fay nodded, but couldn't quite manage a smile. "Yes. She did. But she has Paul's features."

He sighed. "Come on, Fay, don't you think you're overdoing it here?"

"Lizzie was brushing her hair. For Grandma," she said. "But this Grandma wasn't me. This little girl only has one Grandma, otherwise they'd use some other name to say which Grandma they were talking about."

"O.K." Arnie was trying not to comment.

"So," Fay asked, "if he kills me, maybe that's why there's only one Grandma. Maybe that's why Lizzie doesn't call me when Katie is born."

"Fay, for Christ's sake."

"It's what I saw, Arnie."

"Fay," he said, "can you just let the future take care of itself? Can you stop trying to . . ."

"You said you didn't want me to think about Mitchell Masters killing me, so this is what I'm thinking about instead."

He threw the cigarette out the window. "Isn't there anything, *anything* else you can think about, Fay?"

"You want my full attention," she said. "Is that right, Officer?"

"Yes," he said. "I do."

She thought a minute. "And would you give me your full attention in return?"

"Sure," he said. "I always do."

"You do not."

"O.K.," he said. "I don't."

"So what would we do with our full attention?" she asked.

"For how long?" he asked.

"For forever," she said. "Isn't that what we're talking about? You quit the force and I give up the future?"

"I don't know what we'd do, Fay," he said. "Maybe we could rent boats."

She had to laugh. "I'm sorry?"

"Rent boats," he explained. "Have a little boat rental shop. Live on the lake and rent boats."

"For what?" she asked.

He was no longer able to conceal his frustration. "For fun, Fay."

"That's what Lizzie says," she said. "That I don't know what fun is."

"I didn't say that, Fay."

"You're both right," she said. "I don't."

"You could," he said.

"I'd like to learn it," she said. "Really I would. I don't know how I missed it."

"Tell you what," he said, reaching over for her hand. "As soon as Mitchell Masters doesn't kill you and Lizzie doesn't run off with Paul, we'll work on it. We'll have some fun."

Neither one of them knew what to say next, so they didn't mind when the radio operator broke in with a report from the fairgrounds. Mitch Masters hadn't shown up for the wheelchair race.

The information hit Arnie like a jolt of electricity. He turned on the flashing red lights, pulled up on the median of the six-lane expressway, made a terrifying U-turn, and floored it.

"Where are we going?" she screamed over the siren, bracing herself against the door.

"We're goddamn fools, all of us," he shouted back. He got on the radio again and ordered the operator to find Jake and Lizzie and redirect them to the Masters house. But Jake was to call Arnie before he went in.

"Arnie! What are you doing?" Fay screamed, as he sped down the exit ramp with his left tires on the shoulder.

"We've done this all wrong," he said. "We've just been following you around waiting for you to do our work for us.

This is a crime. And that's exactly how we're going to proceed from now on. If it gets too bad for you"—he swerved around three cars and sailed through the red light—"close your eyes."

There wasn't anything for her to do now but hold on. However jarring the ride was, it was good to have him back in control again.

And she was glad they weren't going to the fairgrounds. If Mitch Masters were planning to kill her, that had seemed like an ideal spot for it.

LET THE FUTURE take care of itself, Arnie had said. Rather like "mind your own business," Fay thought. Like the future wasn't your business. But then, people said all kinds of strange things about the future.

They'd meet your new boyfriend and say, "That's got no future, honey." But what they'd mean was, you'd spend a lot of years, or it would seem like a lot of years, and after all that screaming and screwing and watching TV and going over to his mother's for dinner, you'd find yourself alone, right back where you started.

But you weren't really back where you started. You were older, and you *knew* you were older. No, the more life seemed to go in circles, the more inexorable was its forward march.

Some people thought about it another way. They stood still while the future came to them, like weather. "Someday" —that was like one of those weird storms off the coast of Peru. "In the not-too-distant future"—that was like a hailstorm over in the next county. "The immediate future"—*that* was "Put on your boots."

Fay thought the future was never too distant, but as close as your next breath. You exhale the past, she thought, and inhale the future. And the present? Well, Fay wasn't sure there was a present.

No present? Of course there's a present, people said to her. My old job is the past, the job I have now is the present, and the job I'll have next is the future. Simple.

Yes, she'd say, but the first time you were passed over for a promotion, or the first day you didn't want to come back after lunch, that was when the future started. A long time ago. And the end of the past? Well, as far as Fay knew, nobody ever outlived it.

They were, the past and the future, two powerful parallel rivers, Fay thought, flowing side by side in opposite directions, each carving out its own side of the same great valley. If you *had* to have a present, maybe you could draw a line across the two rivers and say, "There. Where the past and the future meet, that's the present." But you wouldn't want to try to walk that line. You couldn't even see it for more than a second. How could you think you could live there?

Fay's advice was to let the past carry you, let the future come, and try to keep your head up. But the currents are tricky, she'd caution. They can trap you against the shore, send you back downstream, pitch you over the falls, or dump you into the white water with no warning at all. The only real comfort, she'd say, is that we're all in the water. It's not just you.

Sometimes people would ask if they could influence the future. Could they change what would happen later by what they did now?

"Can you survive the white water if you choose the route?" she'd ask.

They wouldn't answer.

"Right," she'd say. "It depends." She'd smile. "Which route are we talking about?" She'd take their hand. "And who else is in this boat?"

Fay wasn't sure that made people feel any better about the future, but it was all she knew to say.

6:00 P.M.

BY THE TIME THE MAYOR AND GAIL ARRIVED AT
the quarry, ominous yellow-gray clouds had
choked off the entire sky, and funnel swirls of
loose gravel spun out wildly from the mouth
of the ravine and swept across the road. They parked behind
the last ambulance and headed up the hill.

A paramedic jumped out of the ambulance and pointed
the boys out to them, huddled together on the distant ledge.
"Kerry's baseball cap just blew off," he said.

Gail strained to see the blue dot in the distance that was
Kevin, and hoped Kerry didn't look over the edge to see
where his cap went.

One of the firemen called to the boys through a mega-
phone. "Don't move," the voice said. "Stay right where you
are."

The boys called back, but the wind carried their words
off in the wrong direction, bounced them around the walls of
the quarry, then dumped them in the pile of boulders below.

"I can't stand it," the Mayor said, "I can't stand it." He
grabbed Gail's hand.

"We'll figure it out," she said. "It's going to be all right."

They were close enough now to see that a rock-climbing
team had descended into the quarry and was trying to approach the boys from below. Then they both heard the shot
and ran toward the edge of the path in horror.

"Jesus Christ!" Peter said, as he saw the net drop down over the boys and flatten them on the rock, "I thought it was the kidnappers."

"But what do they do now?" Gail asked.

"I guess they pull the ends together," he said, "and use it like a slide or something."

But then they both realized that the net hadn't gone far enough over the boys, that there wasn't enough hanging down on the other side to gather up.

"Goddamnit to hell," Peter said, his eyes filling with tears.

"It's O.K.," she said. "At least the net will hold them there for a while."

And they both turned and ran the rest of the way up the hill.

"That was our last good idea," the firemen said. "The only thing to do now is call the chopper."

The Mayor shook his head, handed Gail the binoculars, and turned away from the sight of his frightened boys bagged on the ledge like mad mountain lions.

She lifted the glasses to her eyes, found the boys, who were lying facedown now, and watched as Kevin scooted closer to Kerry and put his arm around him. To get back, they'd have to go up over the ledge, then back across an eight-inch natural bridge, then drop down about two feet into an open chamber in a section of honeycombed limestone. That tunnel, she guessed, opened again somewhere on the top of the cliff.

"Peter," she said, "If I can get through that channel, would that help?"

"No, Gail," he answered, taking her hand, "I don't want you to . . ."

The fireman interrupted him, speaking to Gail. "It could be real slippery in there, miss," he said. "Are you afraid of snakes?"

She smiled. "Do you have a snakebite kit?"

"No," the Mayor said. "Call the chopper."

"Peter," Gail said, "I can't do a damn thing for my Beth. Let me do something. Please."

"It's worth a try, sir," the fireman said. "The smallest man we've got weighs twice as much as she does."

Gail trusted this fireman. "Let's get going," she said, not looking back for fear of losing her nerve.

"If you bring my boys back . . ." the Mayor said, understanding at last.

Gail rubbed her palms together, building up her courage. "You'll do whatever I want, right?"

The fireman motioned to one of his men, then turned back to her. "I'll do whatever you want, too," he said. "The entrance is up there."

As they started up the hill, Gail grabbed small trees to pull herself forward. "I want to eat dinner at the firehouse," she said. "With all the men sitting around polishing their boots and the cook feeding the leftovers to the dog."

The fireman reached back to help her up over a moss-covered boulder. "I'm sorry, ma'am," he said, "but the dog doesn't get the leftovers. He gets his dinner right after the blessing, right out of the pot like everybody else."

At the entrance to the cave, the fireman strapped her into a harness and handed her two additional harnesses for the boys. He explained that the rigging to the harnesses would be anchored to one of the trucks, but that didn't mean you couldn't get hurt if you fell. He gave her a flashlight and a miner's hat with a light on the top. He said he figured she would lose the hat in the tunnel, but it still seemed like a good idea to have it along.

The Mayor reminded her that Kevin was the big one, Kerry the little one, and hugged her. "Please be careful," he said. "I don't want anything to—"

"Me neither," she said, kissing him on the cheek. "We'll be fine."

"We found their jackets right here," the fireman said, pointing out the hole, which was roughly two feet in diameter. "We shined a light in as far as we could," he said. "We think it opens up a little once you get past this first part."

"Let's hope so," Gail said, stooping down to look, then stretching out on the ground.

"The man at the geologic survey says he doesn't think there's a big drop-off or anything," the fireman said, "but he couldn't be absolutely sure the cave on his map was this exact cave."

"Thanks," she said.

The fireman knelt beside her and attached something

else to her harness. "This is a light cord," he said. "Before you leave the cave, just unhook it. Then when you get back the little lights will lead you right here."

"Like bread crumbs," she said.

"Better," he said.

Finally, there wasn't anything else to do. "O.K.," Gail said, grabbing the inside of the opening. "Here we go."

GAIL CRAWLED INTO the opening on her side, then found it was easier to slither on her stomach, snakelike, using her hands to pull herself along. The ground was getting wetter, the smell danker, the air blacker, and she was sure she heard scurrying sounds ahead of her. Little claws scratching the walls. Maybe the Mayor's boys didn't want to crawl back because of something they had found in here, something she hadn't come across yet.

"Go on," she barked at the whatever-it-was. "Get out of here. You don't want to see me and I don't want to see you, so beat it!"

It occurred to her that babies must feel something like this as they are on their way to being born. But if there were some fascinating insight to be gained from this comparison, she didn't know what it was. Maybe she was just desperate to find something to think about other than how bad she was going to look if she ever got out of here.

The passage opened up a little, and there was a sharp new smell that made her nose tingle, a cold green smell, like the inside of an old tin can. Gail stopped to readjust the miner's cap, allowed herself to look ahead, and was immediately sorry.

He wasn't a big snake. Or she. Not fat anyway, and not a constrictor. But a snake is a snake. If the snake knew Gail had arrived, though, he wasn't letting on. Was there, she wondered, the slightest chance that he was dead? Or was he simply playing dead? And would she be able to tell the difference fast enough?

Well, she couldn't turn back because of a snake. The only way she could turn back would be if she couldn't get through some curve in this passage. Even then, she wouldn't actually be able to turn around but would have to back out feet first. That alone was reason enough to continue.

So why was the snake just lying there in the path with his head around the corner? Her eyes burned from the smell. She wanted to hold her nose, but realized the smell was on her hands now too, under her fingernails, beginning to penetrate her skin.

It would be so much easier if the snake were dead, if he had done what every good snake should do. Crawled into a hole and died.

She batted the snake's tail with the flashlight. Nothing. Then she smacked him again just because nobody was watching. Good. Dead. She nudged him over into the ooze and slipped by him to the corner, which was such a sharp bend that she had to turn over on her side to get through.

She could see some light from the outside now, and could see that the snake's head wasn't on this end of him at all. Where the hell was the snake's head? And why did she care?

If the boys came through here without a light, they probably missed the snake, she thought. Good thing. Maybe they crawled right over it. And now, for the first time, Gail wondered what had made the boys come this far into the dark in the first place. She could understand two kids starting into a tunnel like this just out of curiosity, but what kept them going in the pitch black of the middle section? Something about who was waiting for them if they went back, she guessed.

She could make it the rest of the way on her knees. The fresh air felt good and she even indulged herself in a cough, now that she wouldn't risk bumping the miner's helmet and losing her light.

She crawled out of the tunnel and brushed off her hair, hoping to dislodge any loose spiders she'd picked up. Then she stared, still on her knees, at the narrow rock bridge that led to the ledge.

"Shit, shit, shit," she said out loud, her stomach knotting at the prospect of crossing four feet of air on eight inches of rock. She leaned back against the mouth of the tunnel and decided to scoot across sitting down. "Kevin!" she yelled, "can you hear me?"

A terrified scream came back immediately. "Mom!"

This wasn't the time to explain who she was. "I'm right here!" she screamed, moving onto the bridge. "I'm coming to get you!" She inched forward, holding the bridge with both hands in front of her. "Just stay where you are!"

She leaned over to hug the bridge. That felt better. She moved another inch and heard a burst of applause from somewhere in back and to the left.

"Shit," she said again, out loud. "They're watching. The firemen, Peter, everybody. They've got their goddamn binoculars too, don't they?" She reminded herself to watch her language when she got to the boys, scrambled up onto the ledge, tripped, and fell flat on her face.

As she rested there, she knew exactly why the boys didn't want to go back the way they came. She didn't want to go back, either. Except that was the only way to collect from the Mayor for this mission. And see Beth again, if Beth was there, if she got to see Beth again. She stopped herself. She couldn't think about Beth. Not now. Beth would be all right. Somebody would save her little Beth the way she was saving Kevin and Kerry.

"Mom?" Kevin called to her.

She rose to her knees again and crawled over the curve of the ledge to them.

"My name is Gail," she said, patting Kerry's head through the net. "I was the only one little enough to get through that tunnel."

"Did you see a snake?" Kevin asked her.

"I sure did," she said. "I didn't see his head, though."

"Show her," Kevin said, nudging Kerry.

"Be careful," Gail said, judging the ledge to be around the size of a pool table. "We don't have a lot of room up here."

Kerry reached into his pocket and pulled out the beady little beginning of the long black tail. "It's mine," he whined.

"It's yours, it's yours," Kevin said wearily, then turned to Gail. "He thinks it's a big deal."

"What are you going to do with it?" Gail asked the smaller boy, wondering why the snake's eyes didn't pop out onto the ledge.

"Put it in my room," Kerry said.

"The thing to do," Gail said, unhooking the extra harnesses, "is pick up his tail on our way back, and then get a taxidermist to stuff him."

"No!" Kerry cried. "I want to keep him!"

Gail strapped him into the harness. "He'll keep better if a taxidermist puts him back together," she said. She reached past Kerry and slipped the other harness over the older boy's head.

"I want to keep him under the bed," Kerry said.

"I know what you mean," Gail said. "When I was a girl, there were snakes under my bed all the time."

"Big snakes?" Kerry asked. He wanted to hear all about it.

"Now, look," Gail said, "what we've got to do is go right back the way we came."

Kerry's voice dropped to a whisper. "We can't go back. The rat will get us."

"If we go back right now and get the snake," she said, "then the rat can't eat it."

"But then the rat will starve to death," Kevin said, remembering what his teacher had said about Nature's Way.

Gail shook her head. "The rat is gone," she said. "I just came through there, and he was gone."

That was exactly what they wanted to hear. She smiled to see them relax, then checked the harnesses and retied Kerry's shoes. "O.K.," she said. "Who wants to go first?"

"Me," Kevin said, suddenly sounding very brave. "But you better hold on to Kerry because he forgets things."

"If anybody falls, the harnesses will catch us," Gail said, hoping it was true.

"I want to wear your hat," Kerry said.

"All right," Gail said, "but I can't put it on you out here. As soon as we get in the cave . . ."

Kevin was tired of Kerry getting all the attention. "Well, what are we waiting for?" he asked.

"I'm ready when you are," Gail said, grateful for his help.

Kevin crawled over Kerry and past Gail, lifted the edge of the net, and crept across the ledge to the bridge.

"Wait for us, Kevin," she called, but she was too late, he was already over, knowing, instinctively, that the trick was to keep going.

She wrapped one arm around Kerry and they crawled up the ledge together.

"I have to pee," he said.

"A cave is a great place to pee," she said. "Everybody pees in caves."

"They do?" He grinned.

"Sure they do," she said. "That's what the smell is in there."

"It didn't smell like pee to me," he said.

"New pee doesn't smell the same as old pee," she explained. "Old pee smells like caves."

When that satisfied him, she asked about the snake. They didn't see the big rat kill it, he said, but they heard this grindy sound and a flip-floppy thing, and then a scratchy sound and then something ran away. And then he put his hand down right on the snake's head, only he didn't know it was a snake's head until they got out of the tunnel. Gail said she thought it all worked out just about perfect, and blew Kevin a kiss across the bridge.

She sat Kerry down in front of her, their legs on either side of the bridge, then decided it was too dangerous to push him across like that. She turned him around to face her, and wrapped his arms around her neck, his legs around her waist.

"What you have to do now," she whispered in his ear, "is pretend you're asleep. You're the Baby Bear and I'm the Mama Bear, and I'm taking you back to the cave so you can sleep for the winter."

He liked that idea a lot, went completely limp, and started making sleepy bear-cub sounds into her shoulder. Beth liked bears, too. They played bears all winter. Sometimes in the morning they ate their oatmeal out of great big bowls and said they were The Three Bears.

She had to stop worrying about Beth. Think about this little boy, she said to herself. You're not out of this yet. Please, she asked, please let me think about what I have to do here.

And suddenly the sweetness of his tiny embrace took her breath away. His skin smelled so new, his round little belly nestled just under her breasts, his bottom in her lap. This was different from Beth, this was what it was like to have a little boy, this hot little hug, this little penis nuzzling her navel.

She inched across the bridge. Halfway. Boys and their mothers, she thought. Two more feet. Men and their mothers. She grinned. Boy oh boy. With six inches left to go, she pushed him into the opening to the tunnel and leapt in behind him.

"Can I pee now?" he asked.

"Be my guest," she said, wiping her hands on her shorts and pulling the harness ropes in after her. Instantly, a fierce stabbing pain shot through her head. They could have died out there. All of them.

She told the boys to go on ahead now, sneezed violently four times, and tried to push her hair out of her eyes with her forearm. By the time she got to the corner where the snake had been, Kevin was already outside waving it around for his father and telling him about the taxi driver who was going to stuff it.

Gail was close to the opening of the cave, close enough to crawl on out. But for some reason she wasn't quite ready to leave yet. She reached behind her and reeled in the light cord, gathering it into a neat little bundle the way she would a string of Christmas tree lights.

The Mayor's head appeared at the opening. "Gail?" he called. "Are you all right?"

"I'm fine," she said. "Here's the flashlight." She handed it out to him. "Now the lights."

He took the lights, then stretched out on the ground so he could see her face. "I wish I could get in there with you," he said quietly.

"Yeah, I know," she said, looking back the way she'd come. "It's nice in here."

"Can I see you tonight?" he asked. "Can I meet you someplace or come over and thank you?"

"I'll be at home," she said softly, wiping her eyes on her shirt.

"Where's home?"

"248 Sixth. Third floor."

"Good," he said, reaching in for her. "Give me your hand."

"I'm a mess," she said, grasping his wrist and pulling herself toward the opening.

"You're fine," he said.

"I don't think I'll ever get clean," she said. "I smell like snakes. Don't touch me, you'll ruin your shirt."

"Gail, please . . ." he said, hauling her up into the light. He lifted her up off the ground and held her tight, while the firemen clapped and cheered. His skin smelled just like Kerry's, she thought. Cleaner, yes, and more tired, but it was the same dear male smell.

"Please," she said, her nose buried in his neck, "don't let me fall in love with you."

"It's not a problem," he said, setting her down gently. "I like the idea."

Then the boys ran over to hug her. She kneeled down, folded them up in her arms, squeezed them as tight as she could, and wished with all her heart that Beth were here too.

IN THEIR CAR, Arnie and Fay heard the report. And if they hadn't had any proof before that Fay was right, they had it now.

At the fair, Kevin had seen the clown with the green shoes give Kerry something to smell, then pick him up. So Kevin followed them to the truck. The clown said they were going to see a magic show with the other kids, but once they got inside, Cowboy Bob wouldn't let them out. He gave them some lemonade and cookies, and the next morning they woke up in this old farmhouse.

Kevin knew he should call home, but there wasn't any telephone. There was just this growly dog chained to the fence. So they took off, looking for another house with a phone, but Cowboy Bob came after them in the pickup truck. He chased them up to the quarry and they hid in that little cave. Once they were in there, they kept crawling because he said he was coming back to get them with that growly dog.

The truck was blue and rusty. Cowboy Bob was skinny with a blue shirt and tight black jeans. The farmhouse was white and there were a lot of bathtubs out back in the barn, toilets and doors and things, like the insides of a lot of houses all taken apart. Kevin thought there was a swing on the porch, and Kerry said there was a redbird on the mailbox, but Kevin said Kerry was just making that up so he'd have something to remember.

"Good," Arnie said. "That's just what I was waiting for."

Fay didn't ask Arnie what he meant. But she did wonder where they were going that took so long to get there.

She tried to relax.

"Close your eyes if you want to," Arnie said. "We're still about fifteen minutes away."

Fay knew if she closed her eyes she'd see Lizzie again, and she didn't want to keep seeing Lizzie in the future. She wanted to see Lizzie in their house, now, asleep, safe for the night, with Paul gone from their lives.

She wanted to ask Arnie where Lizzie was, but she already knew what the answer would be. With Jake, he'd say. On their way to the Masterses' house.

"This wind is really whipping up," Arnie said. "Can you feel it?"

She looked out the window and saw the edge of a huge gray thunderhead rolling in from the west. The air had been heavy all day. A good storm might break this heat.

She smiled. Lizzie would like a storm, too. Lizzie had liked storms even as a little girl. Awakened by a deafening thunderclap in the night, Fay would rush around the apartment closing windows, only to find Lizzie standing at her bedroom window, clutching the sill with her tiny hands, squealing happily and hopping up and down as the rain pelted her face and the curtains whipped her ears.

"Did they say it was going to rain?" Fay asked Arnie, trying not to think about Lizzie.

"Not that I heard," he said. "But what do they know?"

"Right," she said, and looked out the side window again, closing her eyes and wishing desperately she'd closed them when Arnie had first told her to. What did *anybody* know? Could you really say when something was worth your time? Really be sure that someone loved you? Really know what they would do, or not do? No. So how were you supposed to decide anything? Were you just supposed to believe? Were you just supposed to look at those other Tarot cards, like Marriage and the Sun and the World, and believe it would all work out?

AT HEADQUARTERS, THE Chief called the Mayor and congratulated him.

"I'm so relieved," the Mayor said. "So grateful. I don't know what I'd have done if . . ."

"That Gail seemed like a good little woman to me," the Chief said. "Just the kind of thing she'd do, save your boys."

"Yes," the Mayor said. "She insisted. I was afraid for her, but she just . . ."

"You ought to take her out to dinner," the Chief said. "Someplace with dancing. Good oysters, you know."

"I'll find some way to thank her," the Mayor said, "but until her Beth is back, I don't think—"

"Harbor Lights is nice," the Chief said. "There's a table by the window with the best view you ever saw."

The Mayor was eager to get off the phone. "I'll remember that," he said.

"Look," the Chief said. "If you want to go, use my name." He paused a moment. "Hell," he said, "use my account. I'd like to do something for the two of you."

"Thanks, Chief," the Mayor said, then called out to his aides who had just arrived at the house.

"O.K., then, I'll let you go," the Chief said. "Tell Gail I said congratulations."

"Right."

"Tell her anytime she wants a job, all she has to do is call."

"I'll do that, Chief. Good-bye."

The Chief didn't want to hang up. "Right, right," he said, hearing the click of the Mayor's phone.

He said good-bye to the dead air, then sat still for a moment. He didn't want to go to the jail to see Edith Masters, but he didn't want to go home either. And if he kept sitting at his desk, people would just keep asking what he was doing there. So there wasn't any choice, really.

"Mrs. Masters?" he said, approaching her cell. "I'd like to speak with you a moment."

"Not without my lawyer," she said.

"It isn't about the case," he said, and motioned to the guard to unlock the door. "There's a little conference room just down the hall."

"I'd rather stay here," she said.

He sighed. "Mrs. Masters, I've been on my feet all day. I have to sit down."

"Come in, then," she said. "There's a seat right over there." She pointed to the toilet.

"Lock it," he said to the guard as he walked in.

She rubbed her palms together as if she were trying to

warm them up. Or, he thought, as if she were getting ready
to eat him.

"What is it you want to talk to me about?" she asked.

But he didn't know, of course. "I grew up in the church,"
he said, hoping that would make her more comfortable.

"So did I," she said, leaning back against the bars.

"I don't go to church now, though," he said.

"No," she said. "You think you don't need it. You think
you can do it by yourself."

"Do what by myself?"

"Direct your own life," she said. "Comfort yourself, forgive yourself—"

"And I can't?" he asked.

"For a while you can," she said.

He got up, walked to the bars, and banged on them.
"Let's have some coffee," he called to the guard.

"None for me, thank you," she said.

"You were drinking it this morning," he said. "I saw
you."

"Decaf," she said.

"So you like the taste anyway." He wondered why he'd
said that.

"Actually," she said, "I can't taste anything anymore. It's
a medicine I take. It kills my taste buds. I can't even tell hot
or cold."

"Can you tell if it's a liquid?" he asked, reaching through
the bars as the guard handed him a mug.

"I can *see* that it's a liquid," she said.

The Chief was beginning to wonder if this was better
than going home. Maybe, he thought, if I stay here long
enough, I'll actually *want* to go home.

"Now," he said, "you said I couldn't forgive myself.
Forgive myself for what?"

"For your bad thoughts."

"I don't have bad thoughts," he said. "I just don't know
what I'm doing here."

"You're protecting society."

He took a sip of coffee. "Can't be done," he said. "Society is just people. To protect society we'd have to give
everybody a bodyguard."

"No," she said. "That wouldn't help. It's their thoughts
that are the problem."

"Oh yes," he remembered. "Bad thoughts."

"All of us"—she paused—"have bad thoughts. Without the love of God, we are all criminals."

"I don't have bad thoughts," he said. "What bad thoughts do I have?"

She clasped her hands together, then pointed her two index fingers at him and smiled. "You wish your wife would die," she said.

He turned around quickly to face the bars. It was exactly what he did wish.

"That's a fairly common one," she said. "Lots of people wish that."

"I've thought about a divorce," he said, "but I'm just too old to go through it all, then make a fool of myself over some young—"

"But if your wife were to die," she said, "if the Lord were to take her—"

"Yes," he said. "That would be different. Then I'd have to do something, you know, to go on living."

She nodded. "And the children would understand, of course."

"Everybody would understand," he said.

"And instead of laughing at you over this young woman, they'd be happy you'd found somebody."

The Chief looked into his cup. This might be the most peculiar conversation he'd ever had.

"So, Edith," he asked, "what do I do? May I call you Edith?"

"Ask the Lord how you're supposed to carry this load," she said. "He never gives us a burden but what He gives us the strength to carry it."

"Has He helped you that way?" the Chief asked.

"Not just me," she said. "Anybody who asks."

"So why don't we all feel better?" he asked. "Why isn't the world a happier place?"

She thought for a moment. "What is your name?" she asked finally.

"Chester," he said.

"Chester, the world is a happier place than you think."

"Sitting in jail you can say that?"

"Only my body is here."

"And the rest of you is . . ." He stopped. "What *is* the rest of you, Edith?"

"My spirit."

"Where is your spirit, Edith?"

"With my husband, of course."

"Has he been down to see you?"

"Oh no."

"Why not?"

Edith rubbed her palms again. "It's hard for him to get around," she said. "I know he misses me."

He finished his coffee and set the mug on the floor. "I think you're just a swell woman, Edith." He smiled. "What the hell are you doing in jail?"

"You put me here."

"All you have to do is give us some reason for letting you out and you can go."

She folded her hands in her lap. "I can wait," she said.

"Edith," he said, "nobody likes to spend the night in the jail."

"It's comfortable enough."

"Do you have a picture of your husband?" he asked.

"You have my purse, Chester."

"Oh, that's right," he said.

"What did you really want, coming to see me?" she asked. "Did you want to talk about my husband?"

"No," he said. "I just didn't want to go home."

"There seem to be plenty of empty beds here," she said.

He leaned toward her. "You know what, Edith?" he said confidentially. "I think you got yourself arrested on purpose."

"Why would I do that?" she asked.

"Because you didn't want to go home," he said.

"Why wouldn't I want to go home?" she asked.

"I don't know," he said. "But you must want to be here, or else you'd have called your lawyer. And I know you didn't call your lawyer because if you did, you'd be out of here."

"Is that so?" she asked.

"Yes it is," he said. "We don't have anything on you."

"No?" she asked.

"But I know you made a phone call, Edith. Who did you call?"

"Isn't the line bugged?"

"No," he said. "Can't do it. Freedom of speech, or something. Freedom of something."

"They didn't tell me I could call my lawyer," she said.

"I see," he said.

"I called the weather."

"Right," he said. "Who's the weather?"

She sighed. "The weather number—you know, they tell you what the weather's going to be tomorrow."

He banged on the bars for the guard. "And what did they say?"

"Hot," she said. "Hot and humid."

"Like today."

"Like today exactly," she said, as the guard appeared. "I appreciate you coming."

"My pleasure."

"Do you feel any better?" she asked.

The guard unlocked the door. "I do," he said. "I actually do."

"Good," she said. "I'll see you tomorrow."

The Chief walked straight down the hall, up the stairs, through the lobby, and out the front door before he allowed himself to think about anything. Then, standing on the inlaid marble seal of the city, he knew exactly what to do. There was a bar right across the street with a big-screen TV. If he hurried, he could catch the beginning of the local news. He had to be on it, right? With all those reporters, and all the film they'd shot today at the shopping center, he had to be there somewhere.

It was a great idea. He didn't have to think about his life; he could just go watch it on TV.

7:00 P.M.

"I THOUGHT WE WERE GOING TO EDITH'S HOUSE,"
Fay said, as Arnie turned off the main highway and onto a narrow country road.

"He wouldn't go home," Arnie said. "He
knows we're looking for him."

"Mitch?" Fay asked.

"Cowboy Bob. We just passed the quarry, so the farmhouse has to be—"

He slammed on the brakes, pulled a hard left turn, and
bumped off the road onto a gravel path.

"Right here," he said. "See the redbird on the mailbox?"

"No, I didn't."

"Right back there," he said, as his front left tire sank in a
crater in the road.

She turned back to look as Arnie gunned the engine and
the car shot up out of the hole, slamming them back, then
forward as the rear tire chunked into the same depression.

"Arnie," she pleaded, bracing herself against the dashboard, "he's dangerous, this young guy. If he's out here, you
know he's—"

"He's trying to get rid of the rest of the kids," Arnie said.
"Taking them to other hiding places."

"Does anybody know where you are?" she asked.

He grinned. "I'm with you," he said.

The Mayor's boys had not mentioned the low overhang-

278

ing trees, or the bullet-riddled No Trespassing sign, or the barbed-wire fence that ran along Arnie's side of the road.

She reached for the radio. "Call headquarters, Arnie. Tell them what you're doing. Where we are."

He didn't move.

She picked up the handset. "If you don't, I will."

They rounded the last bend and the house came into view. He stopped and looked at the radio in her hand.

"I'm just trying to speed things up a little," he said, taking it from her.

"You don't have a warrant," she said.

"I'm counting on an invitation," he said. "There's the barn."

She forced herself to look at the house. The roof was a wreck and one gutter hung down across the front door. There was a washing machine on the porch, and a hay wagon full of trash half buried in the front yard.

They heard the door slam and a fierce-looking Doberman tore around the side of the house.

"Roll up your window," he said to her as he unlocked his door, then smacked it open into the dog's chest.

"Arnie, no!" she cried, reaching for him, but she was too late. The dog rebounded quickly from the blow and charged into Arnie at full speed.

She watched in horror as he tore the dog's mouth away from his shoulder. Arnie's yells and the dog's barks rose together in a vicious crescendo. Fay tried to understand what Arnie was saying to the dog, but it sounded more like cheerleading than combat.

Then Arnie bolted up from the ground, cuffed the dog sharply on the head, and the beast backed off. "There now," Arnie said, daring him to move, "all you needed was a little exercise, huh, boy?"

Arnie knocked on the window, and the dog came around to his side as if on command. "You stay here, Fay," Arnie said, winded but flushed with victory. "I'm going in."

She cracked the window. "Arnie, please, don't—"

The dog bit down on Arnie's hand, eager for more. "I think he's in there," he said. "You just stay put."

She was frozen with fear for him.

He wiped his mouth on his shirt. "Look, Fay," he said, "if I got by the dog, the man's a snap."

There was a bright red stain on the back of his shirt and his right sleeve was ripped to the shoulder. She tried to remember if he'd had a tetanus shot lately.

Fay reached for the radio, lifted the handset out of its cradle, and pushed the button. "This is Fay Morgan," she said. "Is anybody there?"

"Go ahead, Fay," the operator responded.

"I'm with Arnie Campbell." She stopped. "He's gone into this farmhouse." She looked out the window. "Can you send somebody out here?"

"What is your location, please?" the operator asked.

"It's that road where the quarry is," Fay said.

"What quarry, please?"

"The one where they found the Mayor's boys."

Arnie disappeared around the side of the house.

"Which direction from the quarry?" the operator asked.

"Further out," Fay said. "There's a mailbox at the road with a redbird painted on it."

"How far out, please?"

"I don't know," Fay said. "But the driveway turns off to the left."

"Just a moment, please," the operator said.

"No! Wait!" Fay said. "I just got you!"

Now the operator sounded like a recording. "Keep the channel open, please."

Fay let the handset fall into her lap and stared up at the farmhouse.

"Mother?" Lizzie's voice came over the radio.

Fay grabbed it. "Lizzie! Where are you?"

"Where do you *think* I am?" Lizzie said. "I'm outside this dumb little house you sent us to. Locked up in Jake's car!"

"At Edith Masters' house?" Fay asked, staring into the handset, wondering how this happened.

"I guess," Lizzie said. "Where are you?"

"I'm nowhere, Lizzie," Fay said. "I'm staring at a farmhouse waiting for Arnie to get blown up."

"What *is* all this, anyway?" Lizzie asked.

The operator interrupted them. "Mrs. Morgan, officers are on the way. Stay with your vehicle, please."

"O.K., O.K.," Fay answered.

"What's going on?" Lizzie asked again.

"There were three people who kidnapped the kids, Lizzie. One of them is in jail. One of them lives at the house where you are, and one of them lives out here."

"Terrific," Lizzie said, and Fay could hear her lean back against the seat and sigh.

And then Fay heard the shot.

SHE JUMPED OUT of the car and ran halfway up to the house before it occurred to her that that might not be the best thing to do. The front window shattered and a second shot stung the ground just to her left, causing her to trip and fall against a rusted wheelbarrow.

Two more shots blasted the old pickup truck beside the house, and as Fay watched, the back left tire began to deflate.

When the next barrage of gunfire sent the front door flying into the yard, she tucked her purse under her arm and sprinted for better cover under the old hay wagon, about five feet ahead.

Then Cowboy Bob, the young man who had been with Edith Masters in the coffee shop, backed out of the hole where the door used to be, shooting up the front of the house with a submachine gun.

He stopped suddenly, listened for a moment, then broke into a run toward Arnie's car; he got in, revved the engine, and backed out of the driveway.

She waited as long as she could, then started for the house. She wondered where the dog was. After the smoke cleared, wasn't a dog supposed to start barking? Should she go around to the back? Peek in the windows? She tried to remember what people did in the movies. When the shooting was all over, could you just walk in the front door?

"Arnie!" she screamed.

"In here!" he called back, somewhat muffled, from somewhere on the left side of the house.

She ran toward the sound of his voice, into what, owing to the presence of a squatty old refrigerator, would have to be called a kitchen.

"Jesus Christ," she gasped.

"I'm all right," he said.

But he was covered with debris, pinned to the floor by a massive oak table and a dead dog.

"What happened in here?" she said.

"The dog got the worst of it," he said from the floor.

"I like him better this way," she said, studying the placement of the table.

"I don't think there's anybody else around," Arnie said, "but all the same, let's get me out of this, huh?"

She stooped down to peer at him. "Are you hit?"

"Winged," he said. "Can you lift the table?"

"The dog's the problem," she said, standing back up.

"Oh, for God's sake, Fay . . ."

"O.K., O.K.," she said.

She held her breath, grabbed the dog's leg and slung the beast across the room, where he thwacked up against the refrigerator, then slid to the floor.

Arnie winced at the sound. "I liked that old dog," he said.

She wedged her knee under the end of the table, got hold of one corner, and lifted it up.

"That dog saved my life," Arnie said.

"And me?" Fay wheezed from the effort.

"Thanks," Arnie said, scooting up to sitting.

She saw his arm clearly now. "How bad is it?" she asked.

"It's nothing," he lied. "Come here."

As she helped him up, Arnie looked over her head and out the back window. Someone was in the barn.

Fay slipped out of his arms. "I talked to Lizzie," she said. "They're at the Masters house."

"Is Masters there?" Arnie asked.

"She didn't say. Jake was still inside the house."

"Must not be, then." He tucked his gun into his belt. "Somebody ought to bury that dog."

"I called headquarters," she said. "They're sending some cars."

"Good," Arnie said. "They can do it." He stepped over the rest of the trash and started for the hallway.

Fay wanted to tell him how scared she'd been, how scared she still was, how the sight of his blood on his shirt bothered her in a way she couldn't quite explain. But he was still on duty.

They made their way through the rest of the Cowboy's heap of a house, through the living room, furnished only with orange crates and beer bottles, and into the bedroom, which was completely empty except for a sleeping bag laid out against the far wall.

"Travels light, this guy," Arnie said. And then he opened the closet. "Holy shit."

"What?" Fay asked, from across the room.

"Two flannel shirts and a pair of black jeans," he said.

"So?" Fay asked.

"And four shotguns and a case of ammunition for them, two deer rifles, a telescopic sight, a hatchet, a skinning knife, a machete, a chain saw, a pair of binoculars . . ."

"I told you he was dangerous," Fay said.

Arnie stooped down to check. "And an empty box of Milk-Bones," he said.

"Does this prove he's in on it?" Fay asked.

Arnie walked to the bedroom window and looked at the barn. Something just moved past the open half door at the far end.

"I don't know," he said, walking into the bathroom.

She started to follow him.

"Stay away from the window, Fay," he said. "There's somebody in the barn."

She froze.

"It's O.K.," he said, motioning for her to crawl under the window. "I just wanted you to know. If he were coming after us, he'd be here by now."

But Fay couldn't move.

He had never seen her so scared. "I think we're all right," he said, then smiled. "All we have to do is stay inside and wait for the police."

Fay didn't know what they should do, but just waiting didn't sound right, didn't sound like Arnie.

"We have to wait," he said, "because I'm out of bullets." He turned back to examine a small photograph taped to the mirror of the medicine cabinet.

"Right," she said, and forced herself to sneak under the window on her knees.

"So who do you think this is?" Arnie asked. "His girl-friend? His wife?"

Fay joined him at the mirror and stared at the wallet-sized high school yearbook photo. "It's Colleen," she said. "It's Edith's daughter, Colleen."

"It looks like Beth," he said. "Like Beth will look in ten

years." He studied the photograph. "Same pale skin, same watery blue eyes." He held it up to the light. "Is this a pink barrette in her hair?"

Fay walked out of the bathroom and leaned against the bedroom wall. She was shaking. Was that why Beth wasn't with the other children? Had Mitch seen Beth, seen the resemblance to Colleen and changed the plan?

She walked on into the living room and stared at the orange crates. "Where did the Cowboy sit?" she asked. "How can you live without chairs?"

Arnie looked around the room. "Chairs," he said. "Chairs!" he shouted, and ran for the front door. "Come on!"

"Arnie!" she screamed. "What are you doing?"

But he was gone.

When she caught up, he was at the back corner of the house, watching that half-open barn door.

"You're right," he whispered. "You have to have chairs. I don't care how weird you are, you can't live without chairs. So he did something with all his chairs."

"Maybe he burned them."

"Or maybe he tied somebody up in them." He leaned over to kiss her. "Like kids, Fay. That's who's in the barn!"

Fay wasn't so sure. "I thought we were waiting for the police."

"You wait if you want to," he said. He dropped her hand and bolted across the scrubby yard, dodging the tin cans and broken tools that lay in his path as he ran.

Angry and afraid, Fay fell back against the house and waited for the shooting to begin again.

"Fay!" Arnie called to her from the barn.

"Oh, thank God," she breathed, and ran toward the open door.

But she didn't get four steps forward before a tiny, terrified face peeked around the side of the barn door. She stopped again. The child waved. She recognized him instantly. He was the only black child in the group.

"You must be Mondo," she said, trying not to scare him by running or screaming.

He grinned.

"Your mama is sure going to be glad to see you," she said, kneeling down in front of him.

"I was tie to a chair," Mondo said, squeezing her tight. "And then a man come."

"He's a policeman," Fay said, standing up. There was blood on Mondo's shirt, but she decided it was Arnie's.

Inside the barn, she saw the rows and stacks of bathtubs and sinks that the Mayor's boys had described.

"Here they come," Mondo said, pointing to another doorway on the right wall of the main room. Fay turned quickly and recognized two more of the missing children, Tinker and Sandy Talbott, fair-haired five-year-old twins. They still looked scared.

She pointed to their feet. "Somebody needs their shoes tied," she said, still holding Mondo's hand.

"Mommy ties them," Tinker said, "but she isn't here."

"How about if I do it now," she said, moving toward them carefully, "and then when you get home Mommy can do it again."

The twins nodded, and met her halfway, starting to tell the same story about being tied up.

"Arnie," she called, "are you all right?"

"Doing fine," he called back. "Just keep them all together."

As Fay finished tying the fourth shoe, a truly stately six-year-old came up behind the twins.

"And who are you?" Fay grinned.

"John Merriweather," the boy reported. "I'm the oldest. Are we on TV?"

"You're all over the place," she said. "You're big stars."

"My mother is in Spain," he said. "Are we on TV in Spain?"

Fay stood up. "John, can you watch these little ones while I go help Arnie?"

But the twins clutched at her skirt and held on tight. "O.K.," she said, smoothing their hair. "I'll just stay right here then."

"There's more," John Merriweather informed her. "There's nine of us."

"Nine!" Fay said, and tried to remember if that was all the rest of the missing children.

"There used to be more, but the Cowboy took them away," John said.

"How did you get here?" Fay asked.

"We woke up here," John said.

"Was it the Cowboy who tied you up?"

They all nodded.

"Did you see anybody else?"

They all shook their heads.

"What's your name?" John asked her.

"I'm Fay," she said. "Let's go help Arnie." But none of them would move. Not even the cerebral John Merriweather wanted to go back into that room.

"Who's Arnie?" the twins asked.

John sighed. "He's the man who untied us. He killed the Cowboy and then he came to get us."

"No," Fay said, "he didn't kill the Cowboy, he just chased him"—but she couldn't finish, because Noah and Seth Clark bounded through the door like little linebackers. "Two more!" she said, beginning to believe this now.

"Where *is* this?" Seth asked her, little hands on little hips, ready to go. But before she could answer, he ran to one of the bathtubs and jumped in. "Full steam ahead!" he shouted, as Mandy Jones appeared in the doorway.

"Be careful," Fay called to him, reaching out to Mandy.

"I don't think you should let him play over there," John said. "There could be bombs."

"Enemy approaching!" Seth shouted, grabbing the side of the bathtub. "Fire torpedoes!"

"Oh, I don't think there would be any bombs," Fay said to John.

"I saw a rat," Mandy said.

"A mouse." John didn't move an inch.

Noah was sitting in a sink now, high above his brother's bathtub. "Turret gunner ready!" he shouted.

"If those people didn't want us to get out," John said to Fay, "they should've buried us."

"Noah," Fay said, "please don't . . ."

John went on. "Buried us in little coffins with little breathing holes so we didn't die right away."

And then Arnie walked through the doorway with a child in each hand. "This is Todd Griffith," he said, "and this is Bonnie Boyter."

They looked up at him, waiting.

"And I told them I would tell you"—he smiled—"that the reason they don't have the same last name is because they don't have the same daddy."

Fay counted the children. "Nine," she said. "Nine of you."

John Merriweather nodded. "I told you that a while ago," he said.

Then they all heard the sirens come screaming up the drive.

"Don't run!" Fay shouted after Seth as he took off for the door.

"Let him run," Arnie said. "The kid's been tied up all morning."

And with that, all the children except John Merriweather flew across the barn floor, whooping and screeching as they decided that the last one to reach the police cars would be a rotten egg.

Arnie laughed and put his arm around John. "It was a rotten egg when *I* was in school," he said to Fay. "You'd think there'd be some new rotten thing by now."

"They don't even know what a rotten egg looks like," John said, relieved to be with the adults where he belonged.

"John," Arnie said carefully, "was there a little blond girl tied up with you? A little girl that looked like this?" And Arnie pulled Colleen's photo, the one he'd found in the bathroom, out of his back pocket.

The boy took the picture and looked carefully at it. "No," he said.

"Was she with you in the truck?" Arnie asked. "At the fairgrounds? Before you had the lemonade and went to sleep?"

"I don't know," John said, handing the picture back to Arnie. "There were too many of us then."

Arnie put the photo back in his pocket. "O.K.," he said. "Thanks."

"Haven't you found her yet?" John asked.

"No," Arnie said, glancing at Fay. "We don't know where to look."

THE POLICE ARRIVED at the farmhouse prepared for a hostage action. And while they weren't exactly disappointed to find the captives already free, the lack of a real situation did leave a lot of them standing around with nothing to do.

While the medics tended to Arnie's injuries, Fay walked

back to the barn. Since they couldn't disturb the evidence, it was the only place to sit down.

She stepped around the bathtubs, counted the mantels, found a box of doorknobs, and looked at herself in maybe fifty mirrors stacked against the wall. It was oddly disturbing to see so many useful things lying around useless on the floor. But then Fay was feeling that way herself, like a sink that had been disconnected from the pipes that filled it.

Arnie had known to come here, known this was where the Cowboy would be. Arnie had known there was somebody in the barn. Arnie had found these children, she hadn't.

But nine wasn't enough and Fay knew it. Two boys and Beth were still missing. Gail's little girl, Beth. Why couldn't Fay see where they had taken her?

But Fay knew the answer to that. She didn't see where they took Beth because all she could think about inside that truck was Lizzie.

She walked into the room where the children had been tied up. Seeing the chairs, the ropes, the blindfolds, she understood. The Cowboy had not planned to take care of them, feed them, make sure they were safe. No. His plan was to leave. His plan was to let them die.

Fay sat down. Beth was in trouble. Those other two boys were in trouble. The kidnappers were no longer worried about keeping them alive. All they could think of now was getting away.

She heard a baby crying.

Not in the barn. Where? She closed her eyes. Where are you, Beth? Beth in the yellow overalls. Beth with the pink barrettes.

But the voice Fay heard was too old for Beth. Katie. It was Lizzie's little girl, Katie. And Lizzie, deep in a sleep of exhaustion, was trying to wake up, pushing herself out of the chair beside the hospital bed.

Katie is so hot, fiery hot and wet all over. Lizzie runs across the room, pushes the door open, and steps out into the bluish light in the corridor. She staggers down the hall and collapses at the nurses' station. "Please come," she says, "my little girl . . ."

The nurses respond quickly, leaving Lizzie slumped on the counter, and rush silently down the hallway. Lizzie can't

move. Her eyes close, her knees give way, her hands lose
their grip on the counter, and she faints to the floor.

Orderlies rush by her on the way to the child's room.
Why doesn't somebody pick her up?

Slowly she regains consciousness. A cool cloth on her
forehead. She's lying in a bed now. "Katie," she whispers.

"She's all right," a voice says. A pleasant voice, a practiced calm. "You're the one who needs some attention."

Lizzie reaches up weakly, slides the cloth back on her
forehead, and opens her eyes. A young doctor.

"Where is your husband?" the doctor asks.

Lizzie tries to sit up. "Colombia," she says.

The doctor continues. "His parents, then? A friend?"

Lizzie shakes her head.

"Don't you have somebody who can come help you?
What about your mother?"

"No," Lizzie says. Her head falls back on the pillow.
Asleep. The doctor checks her pulse, takes off her shoes,
pulls a blanket up over her, and walks out of the room.

Fay didn't hear Arnie come into the barn.

"There you are," he said, walking over to her. "What are
you doing in here?"

But Fay couldn't answer.

"Fay?" he said. "We can go now if you want."

Still no response.

"The kids are all taken care of," he said.

She bent over double in the chair. "Arnie, Arnie," she
whispered finally, reaching up for his hand. "Something's
happening to me."

"Something's happening to me too," he said, straightening up. "I'm getting hungry. I want a real dinner, with, like,
salad and drinks. How's that sound?"

"I don't understand," she said. "I keep seeing these . . .
I don't know what they are. I don't know what I'm seeing.
They're not the right thing. They're not what I want to see."

Arnie didn't know what to say to that, so he put his arm
around her and helped her stand up. "How about seeing me
home?" he asked.

She nodded. This wasn't the time to tell him. "Are the
kids all right?" she managed.

"They're fine," he said. "The Chief is going to present

them to their parents on TV. They asked me if you could be there, but I said you had a date."

"Good," she said. "Thank you."

"Now," he said, "I'm serious about this nice dinner. We'll go to my house and I'll change, and then we'll go to your house and you'll change . . ."

He waved to the group of officers smoking on the farmhouse steps, then pointed her toward the black-and-white cruiser he'd have to drive till the highway patrol found his car.

As he opened the door, she seemed so frail, so small, he began, for the first time today, to worry that she might not pull out of this, whatever it was.

He started the engine. "What are you seeing, Fay?" he asked. "Lizzie again, or something about the kids?"

She sighed, as if it were an old story, one she'd heard before. "Katie was in the hospital," she said. "The doctor asked Lizzie if her mother could come help her, and Lizzie said, 'No.' "

Arnie wished he were better at this. The best he could tell, Fay was trying to determine what could explain a series of events that hadn't happened yet.

"Maybe," he said, as he pulled the car up into the yard and turned around toward the driveway, "maybe Lizzie just lives too far away for you to come on such short notice."

"Arnie"—she turned to him in desperation—"I'm seeing a world where I don't exist!"

"Fay," he said, "I promise you. Mitch Masters isn't thinking about killing you. Not anymore he isn't." He looked over at her. "We're after him now and he knows it." He hoped this was working. "All he's thinking about is getting away with this, throwing us off the trail. You're all right. You're safe."

But he wasn't sure she was listening.

"O.K.?" he asked, raising his voice.

"O.K.," she said quietly.

"That's better," he said, hoping it was. "Now, what kind of food would you like?"

"Tell me what else is going on," she said, "with the police, I mean."

Arnie was encouraged. At least she remembered what was at stake here. "Masters is still loose," he said. "But Jake found a picture of him with that Cowboy at the house. And two people who took packages for the mothers recognized the Cowboy as the one who left them. And it looks like Edith bought the stuff from the stationery store—you know, the pens and paper they gave the mothers."

He paused for breath. "And we found the lab where they got the jars of fetuses and the dead frogs. Edith worked there a couple of months ago, some Kelly Girl temporary thing." He grinned. "And there's a whole passel of fingerprints inside the truck."

"His or hers?" Fay asked.

"Hers," he said.

"I'd like to talk to Edith, I think," Fay said.

"Sure," he said, "but we better do it tonight. Masters has to be thinking of leaving town. And I have a hunch he has the last three kids with him."

"Tonight, then," she said.

Fay was sounding better, he thought, but he knew she needed a break, so he lit a cigarette and turned on the AM radio. Maybe if she heard what a hero she was, she'd feel better. He needed her to feel better. He needed her help here.

AS THEY PULLED out onto the highway and headed back toward town, a single star was rising in the mauve-streaked sky. Yes, Fay thought, the Star. Think about the Star, the Tarot card the Star. The quacks all said it meant hope. Maybe it did.

Hope the other kids could be found, hope Edith started to talk, hope Mitch made a mistake, hope the highway patrol caught the Cowboy in Arnie's car, hope Lizzie wouldn't leave, and yes, hope that the world where Fay didn't exist would wait till she was ready to go.

But since Fay didn't tell her clients the Star meant hope, how could she say it to herself?

The picture on the card is a naked woman kneeling by a stream emptying one jar onto the ground and the other jar into the stream. A single star presides in the night sky.

When the card came up in a reading, Fay would counsel a period of quietness. She would tell the client it was time to return the books he had borrowed. She would remind him that all the gifts we receive must ultimately be given away again, and anything we have learned here must be taught to someone else, lest the lesson leave the earth with us.

But right this minute, as Fay thought about the picture, she wondered if it didn't just mean that sooner or later everything would be empty.

Then she remembered Mrs. Peace.

"Are those our dreams?" the fourth-grade teacher had asked her. "Is that an angel pouring our dreams into our heads at night?"

Fay smiled, knowing that if she just kept quiet, the teacher would keep talking.

"How can I know what my dreams mean if I don't remember them?" Mrs. Peace asked.

Fay remained still.

"What are dreams, anyway?" the teacher asked. "Are they the same as hopes?"

"No," Fay said. "Hopes are what your waking mind can imagine. Like prayers. Like bridges you can cross to a better place. And however wild these hopes may be, they are still basically thinkable things. But dreams," she went on, "dreams are the unthinkable, the unsayable. Dreams are . . . I don't know, illustrations from the book your soul is writing about you."

Mrs. Peace flinched at the word "soul."

"I'm sorry," Fay said, "but you do have a soul. If you didn't, it wouldn't make you so uneasy to hear about it."

Mrs. Peace tried to relax. "So my soul is only active when I'm asleep?"

"No," Fay said. "During the day, our souls gather their . . . impressions of us, how our lives feel. And sometimes we even sense these impressions ourselves. Sometimes, right in the middle of a sentence I'll suddenly realize I'm saying it to the wrong person."

"Yes," Mrs. Peace said. "That happens to me, too."

Fay took a deep breath. "Our spirits collect these impressions, keep them together, like wisps of smoke in a bag. Then, when we're asleep, our brains open up these bags of smoke"—Fay smiled—"and take a look."

Mrs. Peace was quiet now.

"So dreams," Fay went on, "are our poor old brains trying to say, sometimes in words but mainly in pictures, what the smoke is. Or was. And sometimes dreams don't make any sense because the brain can't or won't understand. But other times they're so real that you wake up screaming. Or smiling, or turning to the person in bed with you and . . ."

Mrs. Peace stood up, angry now. "What good is gathering up this smoke if I can't understand it?"

Fay spoke as gently as she could. "Your dreams can't tell you what to do," she said. "That's not their purpose."

Mrs. Peace looked away. "Then what good are they? What is the point of trying to remember them?"

Fay was weary now, and well aware that she was talking to the wrong person.

"There is no *point* in trying to remember your dreams," Fay said. "There is only the unspeakable joy of eavesdropping on your spirit, catching tiny glimpses of its independent life, resting for a moment in its wisdom, puzzling, laughing sometimes, over what it's up to, what it makes of you."

"Forty dollars?" Mrs. Peace asked, opening her wallet.

"That's right," Fay said. "Cash if you have it."

After Mrs. Peace left, Fay considered taking the Star out of the deck altogether. She couldn't do that, of course, but she did vow never to discuss the card this way again. People wanted control of their dreams like they wanted control of their lives. And what they didn't want was anybody knowing more about their life than they did, even if it was their own spirit who knew.

Fay hadn't understood Mrs. Peace's anger that day. But she understood it now. Fay wanted control of her dreams today, wanted her spirit to think better of her, wanted to know what she was so guilty of that her daughter didn't want her around. Wanted her dreams to turn out differently. Wanted different dreams.

Arnie had seen the star now too, and thought maybe Fay was ready to talk again. "Did you ever meet Mitch Masters?" he asked.

"No," she said. "I thought he was dead. Or they were divorced or something. Edith never talked about him. Neither did Colleen."

"Could you tell anything about him, when you saw him in the truck?"

"Just what he looked like," Fay said. "Why?"

"We checked on his Purple Heart," he said. "The guy's a

fucking hero, a real one. Decorated to death. If we charge him with something and we're wrong, it'll look real bad."

"Am I sure it's him?" she asked. "Is that what you want to know?"

"Yes," he said. "I don't want to get fired over this." He laughed. "Take all the fun out of quitting."

"I'm sure," she said.

He didn't respond.

"It's the one thing I know for sure," she said.

"O.K., then. Here we go."

And he turned off the expressway and headed for Fay's house.

8:00 P.M.

SEVEN PEOPLE HAD CALLED GAIL TO TELL HER the children found at the farmhouse were going to be given back to their parents on TV. She had just turned the television on when she heard the Mayor buzz downstairs.

She checked her hair in the mirror, then walked to the intercom and buzzed him in without answering. She wondered if he was wearing a suit—or rather, if her peach blouse and silk balloon pants looked all right.

"They found some more kids," Gail said, as Peter arrived at her door.

"Yes," he said, noticing the television. "Are you sure you want to watch?"

"No," she said. "But I can't just . . ." She turned and walked back to the sofa, sat down, and clasped her knees to her chest. "I'm not talking very well anymore," she said, patting the cushion next to her.

On the screen, the Chief of Police looked wrinkled but proud. In the audience, the reporters and photographers outnumbered the mothers and fathers three to one. But it was easy to spot the mothers and fathers. They were the ones who didn't seem to be doing anything.

"It is my great pleasure," the Chief said, "to announce to the city and to these worried parents that nine more missing children have been found."

Peter wanted to hold her hand. "You're real brave to be . . ."

"Where was the farmhouse?" she said.

"Near the quarry," he said. "Fay and Arnie found them."

"And they didn't see anything of Beth?" she asked. "A shoe or a sock or—" She couldn't finish. "Come on, come on," she said to the TV. "We want to see the kids."

The Chief turned to the officer guarding the door and nodded. "As I call the children's names," he said, "would the parents please come forward to receive them."

The Mayor had told them not to make such an event of this, but he didn't want to tell her how cruel he thought it was.

The Chief looked at his piece of paper, then leaned over the microphone. "Mandy Jones," he said proudly.

The cameras had some difficulty locating Mandy's mother, and missed the actual moment when she heard the name. When they did catch up with her, the announcer said this was Linda Graves, Mandy's mother, but the man leading her through the crowd was unidentified.

Gail stared hard at the screen as Mandy ran into her mother's arms. "They should've had the parents up front," she said. "It's mean to make them wade through all those people."

"Mondo Washington," the Chief announced, and Mondo's mother, Monica, squealed and ran forward. Her mother, standing beside Monica, said "Praise Jesus," and followed her daughter to the front of the room.

"We've found the kids, all right," Peter said, "but now the dads are missing."

"Todd Griffith and Bonnie Boyter," the Chief called out. And the Mayor was pleased at first, and then puzzled to see not just one but two daddies escorting Betsy Griffith toward the front.

Gail stared at the reunited parents and children standing inside a circle of police officers. "Can't they just go home now?" she asked.

"Not till they're all together," he said.

"It's a show," she said. "It's all a damn show, isn't it." She stood up and walked to the window.

As Anne Clark walked toward her boys, the announcer informed the audience that Dr. Rowland Clark had been called to the hospital to perform emergency surgery, but the hospital had installed a television set in the operating room so he wouldn't have to miss the occasion.

"I liked her," Gail said, pulling back the curtains and looking down at the street.

"I've met her before too," Peter said. "I think she's in Historic Homes or something." He wished the Chief would hurry up with the last two.

"And finally," the Chief said, "last but not least, Miss Tinker and Master Sandy Talbott."

An enormous cheer rose up from the crowd, and Gail turned around to look. Sissy and David Talbott, husband and wife, mother and father, walked up to their twins, knelt down, and embraced one child each.

The Mayor knew instantly why the Chief had saved them for last. There on the floor, in a circle of light, was the all-American family that all of America wanted desperately to believe still existed.

The tears poured down Gail's face.

The Mayor stood up, walked over to her. "She's all right," he said, pulling her into his arms, his shoulder muffling her sobs. "I know Beth is safe. All the rest of them have been all right, haven't they?"

Gail was shaking badly.

He stroked her hair. "Every single one," he said.

"But why wasn't she with the others?" Gail sobbed. "What have they done with her?"

"They just hid her somewhere else." Peter tried to sound convinced.

Gail pulled away from him and walked across the room for a Kleenex. "I want to believe that, Peter, I really do." She blew her nose.

He came up behind her, put his hands on her shoulders, and spoke as quietly as he could and still be heard over the commercial on the television.

"You have to believe it," he said. "You have to."

She reached for another Kleenex.

He knew he had to keep talking. "We're real good at thinking up all the terrible things that could happen," he said.

"They *do* happen," she said.

"Yes," he said. "They do. But the truth is, terrible things

don't happen very often." He paused. "Think how long you've been driving a car, right? And in all that time, have you ever had a real front-page accident?"

She shook her head.

"I didn't think so. Or sick. Sure people get sick, but we only need one hospital bed for every ten thousand people or something, so not *that* many people get sick."

"Everybody dies," Gail said, hoping he had an answer.

"Not every day," he said. "Not every day."

Gail turned around quickly and clung to him.

"Beth is just fine," he said. "She's hungry and tired and scared, but she's just fine. Everybody in the city is looking as hard as they can."

"I'm not!" she cried. "I'm not doing anything. My baby is gone and I'm watching television! Tell me what *I* can do. Can I walk the streets? Can I knock on doors? I'll do anything!"

"You can believe she's all right," he said. "And you can hold yourself together for just a little longer. Can you do that?"

"Can you stay with me?" she asked.

"I'll stay with you as long as you like," he said. "And if you're hungry . . ."

"Peter, we can't go have *dinner*!" she said.

"We'll have it delivered if you want," he said, "but you have to eat. I've told the police chief that you're with me, so he knows how to find you. And believe me"—he smiled—"he finds me real fast."

"What if they call me to come get Marvin?" she asked.

"I checked on Marvin, too," he said. "He can't go before the judge till ten o'clock tomorrow morning."

"Did you talk to him?"

"No," Peter said. "They said he was asleep." He shook his head. "Hard to believe, I know; jails are usually pretty noisy at eight o'clock, but—"

"No," Gail said soberly. "Marvin is a good sleeper."

He was pleased to see her standing a little straighter. "So let's have some supper."

"O.K.," she said.

"Out or in. Up to you."

"Out," she said. "I sent Mother home." She paused. "And now I don't want to be here either." She wiped her eyes. "Are these pants too silly?"

He thought she had more guts than anybody he ever saw. "They're not silly at all," he said. "They look good."

As he walked over to turn off the television, he hoped Gail hadn't heard the announcer say what was coming on next.

"Ladies and gentlemen," the announcer said, "Mrs. Vi Ewing."

Peter switched off the set.

"Don't you want to hear what she says?" Gail asked.

"No," he said, "I don't."

Gail turned the television back on.

"All right," he said. "We'll watch her. But let's not sit back down."

Gail smiled for the first time since he had arrived, and they stood in front of the television and listened.

Vi was wearing a white suit with a lavender flower at the neck of her blouse.

"I have come here tonight," she said, "to plead for the return of the three children who are still missing. Their names are Beth Wilkins, Joshua Beckstein, and Richard Isaac."

"She ought to show their pictures," Gail said.

Vi looked directly into the camera and addressed herself to the kidnappers. "I know what you were doing," she said. "You were trying to warn us."

"Oh boy," Peter said. "Here she goes."

Vi seemed quite composed. "You were trying to warn us that thousands of American children are being taken from us every day, legally murdered by abortionists in every state of the Union."

"Show us Beth's picture," Gail said.

"I see now," Vi said, "that you are right! And I will lead your fight all the way to Washington."

Peter shook his head.

Vi raised her right hand. "We will replace the addled graybeards on the Supreme Court with men of spirit, spiritual leaders, leading citizens who live by Our Heavenly Father's holy commandment, Thou shalt not kill."

She turned to face the other camera. "In return for the lives of these three children, I pledge myself, my energy, my money, my very life itself, to the elimination of legal abortion in this country."

Vi folded her hands on the desk in front of her. "Abortion is a sin against God, a sin against the future of this country, and a sin against ourselves. Only when we reclaim our proud religious heritage can we believe in ourselves again. Only when we stop this massacre of innocents can we stand and say, 'One nation under God.' Only then can we return to the prosperous and blessed America of our childhoods."

Vi put her hand down on a Bible. "I, Vi Ewing, give you my solemn oath. The age of abortion is over."

Vi's face was replaced by the station's logo, and the announcer said that the preceding message had been paid for by People Against Murder.

Then Beth's picture flashed on the screen, and Gail dropped to her knees.

Peter knelt with her and held her tight as the announcer said Beth was five years old, had dark blond, straight hair which, when she was last seen, was held back with a pink barrette.

Then came a picture of Joshua Beckstein, who wore thick brown-rimmed glasses and cowboy boots, and finally Richard Isaac, who had braces on his teeth and Superman on his T-shirt.

As the hotline phone number flashed on the screen, Gail stood up. "Let's go," she said.

He looked away. "I feel as bad as I have ever felt in my life," he said. "Absolutely powerless."

She took his hand and they walked to the door. She looked up at him. "I haven't had a date in a long time." She forced a smile. "Is this how they go now?"

He had to laugh. "It's just this first part that's hard," he said. "After this, all we have to do is eat."

"Are you hungry?" she asked.

He laughed again. "No," he said. "You?"

"No," she smiled, heading down the stairs. "I think we're in for a rough time, you and me."

AS ARNIE STOPPED for the light, a block from Fay's house, they both saw the glossy old Rolls-Royce parked directly in front of Fay's building.

"It's Paul!" Fay shrieked. "Run the light!" And she beat on the dashboard as if she were honking the horn.

"Lizzie's getting out of the car," Arnie said. "What's the problem?"

"Go, Arnie," Fay screamed.

But a wrecker was coming through the intersection in front of them, and by the time it passed, the Rolls was pulling away from the curb.

"Arnie!" Fay shouted, as though he couldn't hear her. "You have to catch him! You have to tell him he can't take her!"

"He didn't take her," he said. "Lizzie's standing right there on the sidewalk."

The light turned green, and Arnie proceeded through the intersection even more slowly than normal.

Fay was furious. "You're letting him get away!"

Arnie answered firmly. "I can't go after him, Fay. All the guy did was leave me a parking space."

"Do you want Lizzie to go off with him?" she demanded.

"I want you to settle down before you talk to her."

Lizzie had seen them now, and was walking up the sidewalk to meet them.

"Here she comes." Arnie pointed. "Now straighten up."

She bristled at his tone.

"If you looked at me the way you're looking at her," he said, "I'd run away from you, too."

Lizzie waved now, then laughed while Arnie intentionally parked badly, then pulled the car up to try it again.

Fay was still fuming.

"I'm buying you some time here," Arnie said to her. "Are you using it?"

Lizzie could see the blood on Arnie's shirt and pointed to it, asking her mother, in gestures, what happened.

Fay made a gun shape with her hand, at which point Lizzie's hands flew to her mouth in fear.

"See?" Arnie said. "She's worried about you."

"She's worried about *you*," Fay said.

He stopped the car abruptly. "She's worried about *us*," he said. "Look at me."

Fay turned to him in a rage.

"Did you see Jake leaning up against the building?" he asked.

She started to turn around.

He pulled her head back to face him. "No, you didn't.

Well, he's been there all the time. But if Lizzie wanted to escape, she could have, easily enough. She could've driven right off with Paul. But she didn't. Did she?"

"You're treating me like a child," she said.

"Yes," he said.

She dropped her head, then shook it, finally getting the message. "You're right," she said. "You're absolutely right. I'm sorry."

"It's O.K.," he said, settled the car perfectly into the space, and unlocked her door.

"Mother!" Lizzie squealed, as Fay got out. "You found nine more!"

"Yes," Fay said. "But not Beth. We still didn't find Beth."

"And what happened to Arnie?" Lizzie could see the bandaged arm clearly now.

"Somebody shot him," Fay answered and waved to Jake.

Lizzie met Arnie as he came around the car. "Are you all right?" she asked, wanting to touch the wound.

"It's O.K.," he said, amused by her concern. "Happens all the time."

"It does not," she said.

"No?" He kissed the top of her head.

"What's the matter with Mother?" Lizzie asked.

"She saved my life," he said. "It's hard work."

Now Jake came up to join them. "You folks have a nice afternoon?"

Lizzie put her arm around her mother. "Did you really save Arnie's life?"

"No, no," Fay said. "Somebody would have found him sooner or later."

"But what if they hadn't?"

"Well," Fay said, getting out her keys, "if they hadn't, then I saved his life. How was dance class?"

And as Lizzie told her it was too crowded today, but the new teacher was terrific, Fay fished her keys out of her purse, opened the door, and they walked in.

Arnie turned back to Jake. "What's the story on the Cowboy?"

"He ditched your car real fast," Jake said, lighting a cigarette.

"He's the one we won't find," Arnie said, as they followed the women into the apartment. "This guy could live under a rock the rest of his life. A real goon." Arnie's arm was beginning to throb.

Fay put her purse on the table and turned back to Arnie. "Do I have time for a shower?" she asked.

"A quick one," he answered. "And see if you've got an old shirt of mine anywhere around here. Save us a whole lot of time if we don't have to go over to my house."

"Have you had dinner?" Lizzie asked.

"No," Arnie said, "and we're starved. Want to come with us?"

"Sure," she said, not knowing whether to follow her mother into the bedroom or stay out here with the boys.

Fay squeezed Lizzie's hand. "Stay out here," she said. "We'll talk later."

Lizzie smiled. "Thanks, Mom."

"You're welcome, Lizzie," Fay said and left the room.

"So nobody saw Masters at the fairgrounds?" Arnie asked.

"Not yet," Jake said. "But I thought you'd want to see this." He handed Arnie a promotional flier he'd found on Masters' desk, and a receipt for a basketball trophy.

Fay walked back in the room wearing her bathrobe and holding up a faded old blue workshirt. "Is this yours?" she asked Arnie.

Lizzie jumped up in protest. "Arnie gave that to *me*, Mother!"

"Do you mind, Lizzie?" Arnie asked, stuffing the flier in his pocket and taking the shirt from Fay. "I'll give it back, I promise."

"Give me ten mintues," Fay said to Arnie.

"Great, hon," he said, then turned to Jake. "Help me put this thing on, huh? My arm's getting a little lazy from this hole in it."

"We've got an APB on Masters' van," Jake said, "and every tollbooth leading out of the state's got a picture of him on the wall."

"He wouldn't drive his own van," Arnie said, as he undid the buttons and slipped his torn shirt down over the bandage on his left arm.

Lizzie hadn't seen Arnie's bare chest for a long time. She stared shamelessly, admiring its various scrapes and scars and scattered gray hairs.

"Let's take the bad arm first," Jake said.

Arnie gave a slight gasp as the shirt sleeve passed over the bandage. "Does anybody else know about the ballgame?" he asked Jake.

"The guys at the fairgrounds have to know," he said. "It's on the marquee."

"Yeah," Arnie said, pulling the flier out of his pocket. "But Masters Invitational Handicapped Basketball . . ."

"Yeah," Jake said. "Could just mean skill level. Doesn't have to mean the guy it's named for."

Arnie lowered his voice. "But this *is* his signature on the trophy receipt?"

"I'm no expert," Jake said. "But it sure looks like the rest of his signatures to me."

"Good work," Arnie said. "So how's he getting around till it's time to present this trophy?"

"You don't think he'll really show up there, do you?" Jake asked.

"He's a hero," Arnie said. "And the one thing heroes always do is show up."

"He wouldn't have the missing kids with him, would he?"

"No," Arnie said. "But I think he stashed the little girl somewhere."

"Well," Jake said, "he can't drive anything other than a handicapped vehicle, so . . . he borrowed one?"

"Something with a sign on it," Arnie said.

"A hospital, maybe, Disabled Vets," Jake said.

"Jesus Christ!" Arnie said. "We've got to stop every van on the road," Arnie said, and flew out the door to his car.

Fay stepped to the door of the living room. "Lizzie?" she called.

Lizzie stood up, putting her magazine down on the table. "Arnie and Jake went outside," she said. "They didn't feel right, talking with me listening. Want me to go get them?"

"No," Fay said quietly. "I need you to help me." She motioned for Lizzie to follow her.

"Sure," Lizzie said, happy to have something to do.

Fay picked a light jacket from her closet.

"You look better," Lizzie said.

"Thanks," Fay said, putting on the jacket. "I feel better."

Lizzie walked over to Fay's dresser and opened one of the drawers. "You need a scarf or something," she said, selecting a green one with coral stripes. "I mean if you're having a big-deal dinner, the least you can do is deck out a little."

"I don't want to have dinner with Arnie," Fay said, tying the scarf around her neck. "I want to go down to the jail and talk to Edith Masters before she goes to sleep."

"Edith Masters at the dentist?"

Fay was startled. "Do you remember her?"

"Sure I do. She was mean," Lizzie said, sitting on the bed. "What do you want me to do? Have supper with Arnie?"

"I want you to come with me to see Edith. I think if you're there, she'll . . ."

"She won't remember me, Mother."

"Her daughter died, Lizzie, having an abortion."

"I'm sorry," Lizzie said. "Did I ever meet *her*?"

"No," Fay said, "it's just that Colleen's death is connected to this kidnapping thing somehow. Edith is in on it, that much we know."

"Sure," Lizzie said.

But Fay wanted her to understand. "I guess I thought if I took you with me . . ."

Lizzie stood up. "Sure, Mom."

Fay didn't believe it was this easy. "What?"

"Do I look all right?" Lizzie tucked in her shirt.

Fay smiled. "You look fine."

Lizzie grinned. "So how do we ditch the boys?"

"We'll just tell them," Fay said, and turned out the bedroom light behind her.

"Fay!" Arnie called, coming in the front door. "It's time to go."

"I'm not hungry, Arnie. I want to—"

"Of course you're hungry," he said. "What are you talking about?"

"O.K., I'm hungry, but I want to go eat with Edith. They have food at the jail, don't they?"

"I'll take you to the jail after dinner. I thought we decided this already."

She looked at Jake, whose smile told her all she needed to know. "Arnie," she said, "I know there's something you want to do without me, so why don't you just go do it?"

"Because I don't want you running around loose, that's why," Arnie said.

She shook her head. "Lizzie will come with me. As soon as we're finished, we'll come back here and wait for you. Now, how do I get in the jail?"

"Front door," he said. "I'll call ahead to the desk." He paused. "Are you sure about this?"

Lizzie thought it was all pretty funny. These two were dying to get away from each other.

"I'm sure," Fay said, as Arnie stepped onto the sidewalk.

Arnie gave her a light kiss, told her to be careful, and practically ran to his car.

Fay watched as they drove away, then, as Lizzie waited on the sidewalk, went back in the living room and picked up her deck of Tarot cards. She remembered the spread she had dealt for Colleen that day. Maybe she could show it to Edith, prove she was innocent. Or maybe Edith would convince her she was indeed guilty, and Fay could simply destroy the cards and quit.

"WHY DIDN'T YOU ever marry Arnie?" Lizzie asked, as they walked down the dark street to the parking lot where Fay kept her old Buick.

"Because I didn't have to," Fay said. "It never came up."

"Are you kidding?" Lizzie asked. "In all this time?"

"Believe it or not," Fay said.

"Not," Lizzie said, then turned to her mother and grinned. "Do I get married?"

Quickly, Fay unzipped her purse and started what she hoped was a convincing search for her keys. "I don't know," she managed. "What do you think?"

"I think you *do* know," Lizzie teased.

"Well," Fay said, as casually as she could, "you probably do get married. Most people get married sometime or other."

But Lizzie was serious. "Why don't you want to tell me?" she asked.

"Because I don't know," Fay lied.

But Lizzie knew she was lying. "What else haven't you told me, Mother?"

"What do you mean, hon?" Fay asked, unlocking her door and flipping the switch to unlock Lizzie's side of the car.

"I mean," Lizzie said as she got in, "what else do you know that I need to know . . . that you haven't told me?"

Fay started the engine. "That you *need* to know? Like what?"

"Mother," Lizzie said, exasperated at Fay's evasion, "I can't tell you what it is I don't know"—she buckled her seat belt—"because I don't know it."

"Like what it is to be a mother?" Fay asked, driving out of the lot. "Like how you think they'll feel about you? Like what you'll get back for all that work?"

"Is it work?"

"It wears you out like work," Fay said. "And it takes all your time like work. So you can't help but feel you ought to get paid for it like work, or get something to show for it, anyway."

"And you don't?"

"No, you don't. Not like you think."

"I haven't thought about it," Lizzie said.

But Fay knew better. "You feel a little foolish doing all that work," she said, "so you say to yourself, 'I'm doing all this because they're mine.' My children. My husband. Whatever. And that keeps you working. But after a while, you begin to believe it."

"Is that so bad?"

"Well," Fay said, "just about the time you believe they're yours, they leave you." Fay paused. "And you feel betrayed, you feel lied to. Like they made you a promise and they didn't keep it."

Lizzie was silent.

"But the truth is, they never made you any such promise. You only dreamed up this promise business so you wouldn't feel foolish. But in the end you feel foolish anyway, so it didn't work. It only . . . got the job done."

Lizzie had understood. "Are you sorry you did all that for me?" she asked quietly.

"No," Fay said, staring straight ahead. "No."

"But if I stayed with you forever," Lizzie questioned, "wouldn't you feel like I was a little weird, like I never grew up?"

Fay couldn't look at her. "No," she said, "I wouldn't. I'd think . . . I'd just think you loved me, that's all."

"But I do love you," Lizzie protested.

"All right," Fay confessed. "I'd think you loved me best."

Lizzie turned away and stared out the window, twisting a lock of hair between her fingers.

"Are you sorry you asked?" Fay asked after a while.

"Oh no," Lizzie answered softly.

Fay laughed. "Are you sorry I answered you?"

"No, Mother," Lizzie said, trying to reassure her.

"Then what? Are you sorry it's the truth?"

"No," Lizzie said, "I'm not sorry about anything. I don't think it *is* the truth." She paused. "I don't believe you."

Fay thought about that for a minute. "No," she said finally, "I wouldn't have believed it either."

And in the silence that settled around them, Fay understood that Lizzie was the one irreplaceable love of her life. That it was a love affair, only there wouldn't be, couldn't be, other lovers to comfort her when Lizzie left. Lizzie loved her as a daughter loves a mother. But, Fay realized, that was never going to be enough.

Lizzie picked up the deck of Tarot cards lying on the seat between them. "Edith isn't a client of yours, is she?"

"No," Fay said. "But her daughter came to see me when she was pregnant."

"And you told her to have an abortion?"

Fay shook her head. "She wanted to know if the baby was going to be Beethoven."

Lizzie laughed. "Because she'd have it, if it were Beethoven?"

"Something like that," Fay said. "I told her it probably wasn't Beethoven. Or that she wasn't old enough to raise it to be Beethoven." Fay felt uneasy, suddenly. "She was just a kid, Lizzie. Younger than you."

"So you told her to have the abortion."

"No. I didn't say that."

"You might as well have, Mother."

Fay hesitated. "Yes, I guess so. I'm sure that's what Edith thinks, anyway."

Lizzie fiddled with the old blue scarf wrapped around the cards. "You did the right thing, Mom," she said. "Can I look at these?"

"Lizzie," Fay said, thinking the girl didn't understand. "Colleen died."

"I know," Lizzie said, thinking her mother didn't remember telling her. "But you couldn't help that, could you? Can I look at your cards?"

Fay was having trouble keeping up. "Sure," she said. But she had to know more. "Lizzie, is this really all that simple for you?"

"Huh?"

Fay spoke slowly. "Is abortion all that simple for you?"

"Yeah," Lizzie said brightly, flipping through the deck. "It's like anything else. Either you get pregnant on purpose, or it's an accident. If it's on purpose, you break out the champagne. If it's an accident, you try to fix it."

Fay was quiet a moment. "Is that what your friends think too? Is it only us old people who have trouble with this?"

"I guess so," Lizzie said. "You make everything a lot harder than it has to be."

"You don't think life is sacred?" Fay was testing.

"No, I don't," Lizzie said. "I mean, it's nice, but it's not sacred. What is this card?" She held it up.

But Fay didn't want to talk about cards. "Lizzie," she asked, "what *is* sacred to you?"

Lizzie didn't have to think very long. "Time," she said.

Fay turned down the street where the church was, just to see if the Tarot card was still standing in the front yard.

"Is this the way to the jail?" Lizzie asked, convinced that her mother was lost.

"I just wanted to see this church again," Fay said, slowing down in front of it. "We think this is where—"

"I know this church," Lizzie said, rolling down her window. "This is where that women's health thing is."

Fay stopped the car. "What women's health thing?"

"I've never been to it," Lizzie said, getting her hairbrush out of her purse, "but I've heard people talk about it. I thought it was closed, though." She ran the brush through her hair. "Yeah, I remember, they had some trouble or something, some weirdo kept putting acid in their water, stealing things, you know?"

"What did they do at this place? Was it a clinic? Did they do abortions here?"

"Mom," Lizzie groaned, "it's just an information thing, feel good about your body, don't be ashamed of it, you know, do pelvics on each other, look at your vagina in a mirror, that kind of thing. It's no big deal."

"Well," Fay said, pulling out to the street again, "you may not think it's a big deal, but a lot of people would."

"They're just scared of it," Lizzie said.

"They think it's bad," Fay said. "Wrong."

"O.K.," Lizzie said. "It makes them sick, women touching themselves, women knowing that stuff. But that's *their* problem."

Fay was astounded at Lizzie's ease with all of this. "Lizzie," she said, "if these people are in Congress making the laws you have to live by, it's not just *their* problem. They will make it *your* problem."

"What are they going to do?" Lizzie asked. "Tell me I can't have an abortion if I want one?"

"Maybe," Fay said.

"If I want an abortion," Lizzie said, trying to end this conversation, "I'm going to have an abortion, whether it's against the law or not."

Fay was dumbfounded. "And that's all there is to it?"

"Yes." Lizzie turned on the radio. "That's all there is to it."

9:00 P.M.

THE WAY ARNIE HAD IT FIGURED, MITCH MASTERS really thought he was going to get away with this. Edith would get nailed for the kidnapping, and the Cowboy, if anybody ever found him, would go to jail as an accomplice. What Mitch would do then was walk off with Beth and start over somewhere, take his new little girl and disappear.

As he and Jake approached the main entrance to the fairgrounds, Arnie waved to the guard, drove through the pass gate, then circled the horse barns and parked behind the west wing, where a huge HANDICAPPED OLYMPICS sign hung over the ramp leading to the back door.

"Once we're inside," Arnie said, "you don't know me." He looked out across the acres of vans and handicapped vehicles. Beth could be locked inside any one of them. But Arnie didn't think so, and they certainly couldn't search them all. Their only hope was getting Masters to lead them to the girl.

"Masters could be monitoring the band," Arnie said. "So don't report in, huh?"

"Got it," Jake said.

As they approached the entrance to the exhibition wing, two clowns passed them headed for the portable toilet, sharing a joint.

"What's security do out here anyway?" Jake asked, inhaling the secondhand marijuana cloud.

"They deal the stuff," Arnie said. "They confiscate it from the farmers, and sell it on the midway."

Arnie was unprepared for the size of the crowd inside. He waited while a teacher passed in front of him leading a covey of children on crutches toward the candy stand, then made his way toward the bleachers that surrounded the basketball court.

He stepped aside to make room for the orderlies transporting an overwrought paraplegic out of the arena for some air, then caught sight of the scoreboard. Eight minutes left in the last quarter, fifty-two to fifty in the finals of wheelchair basketball.

He scanned the courtside officials, then the players, then the benches and coaches, but Masters wasn't there. Just his name on the banner hanging over the court: MASTERS INVITATIONAL TOURNAMENT.

There was time to make a quick tour of the huge hall. He stopped for a moment to watch six blind children race a hundred yards holding on to ribbons dividing the lanes, then passed a seated tug-of-war, noted the pile of discarded crutches, braces, and other therapeutic devices beside the contestants, and then spotted the real heavyweights, the real brutes, grunting and swearing at each other in the arm-wrestling competition.

Yeah, these were the big guys, Vietnam vets, motorcycle accidents, fullbacks off the field for good. Their wheelchairs were rolled up to sturdy tables, which had a center line marked on them in masking tape.

Arnie noticed a sign over a registration table. HANDICAPPED CHAMPIONS TAKE ON THE CROWD, it read, and he saw several normal guys signing up on pieces of paper below. He got in line, just to get a look at the list of champions, and when it was his turn, there it was. Just the name he was looking for.

MITCH MASTERS. He had a sheet of paper all to himself. And there was a special condition typed in under his name. $100 FEE, it said, DOUBLE OR NOTHING. Then, in smaller type, PROCEEDS TO GO TO THE MASTERS INVITATIONAL TOURNAMENT. So far, nobody had signed up to wrestle him.

Arnie reached for the cheap ballpoint chained to the table, and signed his name. "Will you take a check?" he asked the young one armed black man sitting behind the table.

"You got your I.D.?" the man said.

"Sure do," Arnie said. "Do you want the check now or after the contest?"

"Up to you," the man said, then laughed. "But you gonna have to write it, man. I been sittin' here for ten years, and he's never lost a one."

"I'll wait," Arnie said, realizing his driver's license identified him as a policeman.

"Starts at ten o'clock sharp," the man said.

"I'll be here," Arnie said, and moved away to make room for the next man.

"You got a light?" a familiar voice said from behind him.

"Sure," Arnie said, turning around to face Jake.

"Catch the game?" Jake asked, in his best all-purpose male-conversation-with-a-stranger style.

"The real action's right here," Arnie said. "Guy named Mitch Masters, supposed to be some kind of undefeated hoo-doo, arm-wrestling Arnie Campbell at ten o'clock."

"Thanks," Jake said, indicating the cigarette, and disappeared into the crowd.

Arnie made his way back to the arena. He didn't know what kind of man would present a trophy in handicapped basketball, then drive a kidnapped girl across the state line, but he knew he was about to find out.

INSIDE THE RECEPTION area of the jail, Fay and Lizzie surrendered their handbags and filled out the visitors' forms. Fay hadn't said anything about Paul, about the boat, about Lizzie leaving for good. She was proud of that.

"What if Edith won't talk with me sitting there?" Lizzie asked.

"If I think she's uncomfortable with you," Fay said, "I'll just ask you to call Arnie and tell him we'll be late."

"But we don't know where he is," Lizzie said, confused.

"He's at the fairgrounds," Fay said, "but I don't really want you to call him. Just come back down to the lobby and wait for me."

"How do you know Arnie's at the fairgrounds?" Lizzie asked, as the matron motioned for her to walk through the metal detector. "Did he tell you?"

"No," Fay said, following her through the machine and

holding her hand out to be stamped by the guard. "It's just radar."

Lizzie thought a moment. "If he were out with some other woman, would you know that?"

"Not only would I know he was with her," Fay said, "I'd know what she had on, *if* anything."

The guard led them to the elevator.

"Is that how you know where I am?" Lizzie asked. "Radar?"

"Yes," Fay said.

She grasped Lizzie's hand as the gray elevator walls closed in around her. A terrible thought flew into her mind and lodged in a dark corner. When the doors opened again, would a psychotic killer be standing there with a machine gun?

"Can't you turn the radar off?" Lizzie asked.

"No," Fay said. "I can't."

Fay held her breath as the elevator stopped and the guard opened the door. But instead of a psychotic killer, she saw a dead white wall flooded with fluorescent light, and then, as she stepped out onto the floor, more white walls and, beneath them, organized groups of defiant blue furniture.

The guard ushered them to a carpeted lounge area, off which, on either side, ran two long hallways of cells. There was a second tier of cells above each hallway, and ten, maybe twelve guards stationed at a central vertical command post. Out of sight, above and to the left, Fay heard male inmates playing pool. And in the lounge just across the way, women inmates dressed in neon-bright orange cotton jumpsuits were watching reruns of *Mary Tyler Moore*.

When Edith came through the door, Fay stood up and started to walk toward her. But a shrill whistle pierced the air, and a harsh voice over the loudspeaker ordered her not to move.

Lizzie reached out for Fay's hand and pulled her back to the built-in upholstered seat. Then the guard explained that they would have twenty minutes and that smoking was allowed so long as nobody dropped ashes on the carpet.

"Hello, Edith," Fay said, extending her hand. "This is my daughter, Lizzie."

"Yes," Edith said, her orange jumpsuit hanging on her much as it had on the hanger. "I remember. How nice of you to come see me." She said it as though she were in a convalescent home.

"Are they treating you all right?" Fay asked.

"I don't know what you mean," Edith said, dusting some invisible speck off the sofa before she sat down.

"Are they feeding you? Is anybody bothering you?" Fay asked.

"I'm fine," Edith said, folding her hands in her lap. "How old are you now, Lizzie?"

"I remember you from the dentist," Lizzie said sweetly. "I remember Colleen, too. What is she doing now?"

Fay gave Lizzie a silencing look.

But Edith didn't flinch. "Colleen is in California teaching school."

Lizzie looked delighted. "Oh yeah?"

"American history," Edith said proudly. "Tenth grade."

"Edith—" Fay tried to begin.

But Lizzie interrupted. "I thought Colleen died," she said. "I thought she had an abortion and died. That's what I heard anyway. I wanted to tell you I was sorry."

Fay was horror-stricken.

Edith was cool as could be. "Where did you hear that?" she asked.

"At school," Lizzie said.

Edith smiled. "You couldn't have heard that at school, dear," she said. "Colleen was much older than you are."

"Oh I know," Lizzie said calmly. "But the teachers still talk about it. In health class they tell us about the clinics they have now. They say girls like Colleen Masters don't have to die anymore."

Edith was a little more tentative this time. "I didn't know you went to the same school," she said, fiddling with one of the zippers on her jumpsuit.

"Well, you never asked, did you?" Lizzie said, her voice cold, her childlike hurt surfacing. "You never asked anything about me. You never even saw me, did you? I was just one more mouth, wasn't I?" Lizzie stood up. "No, I wasn't even a mouth to you. Teeth. I was four-year-old teeth."

"Lizzie," Fay said, "please." Then she turned to Edith. "I'm sorry, Edith, this is not what I—"

"California?" Lizzie blurted. "Who are you trying to kid?" She grabbed her purse. "First you force your daughter to go to some butcher in the middle of the night, and then you don't even have the guts to admit it was your fault."

Edith didn't answer.

"I'll wait for you downstairs, Mother," Lizzie said and walked off.

"Edith," Fay said quickly, "I had no idea she was going to—"

Edith cleared her throat. "Why are you here, Fay?"

Fay realized that Lizzie had destroyed all possibility of a gentle entry into this conversation.

"I'm here because of Beth," Fay said.

"Beth who?" Edith asked.

"Beth Wilkins," Fay said. "We've found all but three of the missing children. Two boys, and my neighbor's little girl, Beth."

Edith's face was a complete blank. "Yes," she said, "I saw that on TV. But that doesn't tell me why you're here."

"I'm here," Fay said, "because I think you know where Mitch is keeping that little girl."

"My husband Mitch?" Edith asked.

Fay wished desperately that Lizzie were still here. Her approach had worked a lot better than this one was.

"Oh my God!" Fay stood up.

"What's the matter?" Edith asked calmly.

But Fay couldn't tell her. Lizzie was gone again. Escaped, just like that. Gotten Fay all settled in with Edith and then vanished. She was probably calling Paul right now from the phone in the lobby. Why hadn't Fay seen what she was doing? How could she fall for a trick like that?

O.K. Maybe it wasn't a trick. Maybe Lizzie was sitting in the lobby right now, looking through a magazine. But it sure felt like a trick. And from what Fay could remember, there weren't any magazines in the lobby. And Lizzie never could just sit. She was gone.

"FAY?" EDITH ASKED, looking up at her, "Are you all right?"

Fay turned around, and started over. She couldn't afford to be patient now.

"I know that Colleen died," Fay said. "We found the death certificate."

Edith swallowed. "You're right," she said. "She did. She died."

Fay continued. "And I'm real sorry about that. I am. But that's no excuse for killing these last three children. Now I want to know where they are."

"I don't know anything about this," Edith said.

Fay sat down. "Edith. You have to help me."

Edith was quite stern. "You are the last person I would help, now or anytime," she said. "It was you who told Colleen to have that abortion."

"I did not tell Colleen to have the abortion," Fay said. "I just told her that she was as important as the baby was."

"Exactly," Edith said coldly, standing up. "I have nothing more to say to you."

But Fay grabbed her hand and pulled her back down. "Edith," she said, "your fingerprints are all over the inside of that truck at the fairgrounds. That Cowboy Bob, whatever his name is, we know he delivered the packages for the mothers, and we found nine of the children tied up at his house."

Edith blinked. She hadn't known they were tied up.

Fay noticed, and pressed harder. "We know you bought the stationery, and—"

Suddenly Fay saw it clearly. "That clown suit you wore when you kidnapped the kids, we found it in a box marked HALLOWEEN in that closet under the stairs in your basement."

Edith looked away. That's where it was, all right.

Fay tried to keep her voice down. "You're going to spend twenty years in jail for this, Edith, and I *know* it's not your fault! I know it was Mitch who was behind it. But we have to stop him now before he leaves the state with Beth and gets rid of you for good."

Edith looked down at her hands. "Gets rid of me, Fay? No, I don't think so."

"Well, I do," Fay said, convinced she was right. "Beth's hair is exactly the same color Colleen's was, and her face—she has that same transparent skin and freckles. She even has freckles like Colleen."

"Is that so?" Edith asked.

But Fay went on. "Now whatever point there was at the beginning of this, fighting abortion, whatever it was, Mitch has forgotten all about that now. Your husband has found himself a new little daughter and he's planning to keep her!"

Edith closed her eyes.

"Edith!" Fay whispered. "It won't work! Even if you go to jail for him, even if they convict you and electrocute you, he still won't love you, Edith!"

"My husband does love me, thank you," Edith said, crossing her legs.

"No, Edith," Fay said, "he doesn't. Oh, maybe when he couldn't take care of himself, when he was first learning to do without his legs, maybe he appreciated you then. But he doesn't need a nurse anymore. He doesn't want to be dependent now. And he hates you for reminding him he *ever* was."

Edith was quite pale. She rubbed her sweating palms against the cotton legs of her jumpsuit. "In the nursing literature," she said, "his anger would be interpreted as a healthy sign."

"O.K., then," Fay said. "You've done your duty. You've healed him. But your assignment is over, Edith."

Fay reached in her pocket, pulled out a Kleenex, and blew her nose.

"It's so dry in here," Edith said.

Fay was tired, and couldn't hide it any longer. "I don't want to guess about this, Edith," she said. "Why don't you just tell me?"

"Tell you what?" Edith asked.

Fay gasped as the truth hit her. It was perfectly obvious. She would have gotten it sooner if she hadn't been so tired.

"It was *you* who gave Colleen the money!" Fay said. "That's why you're willing to go to jail. You think that's what you deserve for giving your daughter the money for the abortion, the money that killed her."

Edith's head snapped around, her jaw clenched, her eyes burning with hatred. Fay was right.

"Edith, Edith," Fay pleaded. "What else could you have done? She was a child."

Tears stung Edith's eyes now, but she made a valiant effort to bat them away.

"You didn't kill her," Fay insisted. "The abortionist, the hack she had to go to because it wasn't legal, he killed her."

Edith pressed her index fingers into the corners of her eyes, hoping to hold off the flood.

Fay spoke very softly. "What you did, Edith, was what mothers have done for all of history, or what they have had to do until now. You sacrificed your child because it was the law. A law that made her mistake a crime."

Edith's head bobbed sadly.

Fay couldn't say anything else. If Edith didn't want to be forgiven, there wasn't a thing Fay could do.

A full minute passed in silence between them, and then Edith began very slowly.

"Colleen," she whispered, "was not my daughter."

Fay was dumbfounded. "Whose daughter was she?"

"Mitch and . . . I don't know her name," Edith said. "I've called her Candy all these years"—her eyes watered—"just so I'd have something to say, but it could have been a nicer name, I guess. When I met him, in the Veterans Hospital, he didn't say anything about having a girlfriend. But a few years later, after we were married, he came home one day with this baby."

"Did Colleen ever know?" Fay asked.

"No," Edith said. "I said I'd raise her as my own as long as we never talked about it again, as long as Colleen never saw her real mother."

Fay handed her another Kleenex.

"I have always imagined," Edith stared at the blank wall behind Fay, "that her real mother was very," Edith searched for the right word, "lively, I guess; a different sort of woman from me."

"So when you found out Colleen was pregnant," Fay said, "just like her mother before her—"

"I didn't know what to do," Edith said. "I don't, as you know, believe in abortion. But I didn't want the baby. We didn't have anything then. I was the only one working. I thought I couldn't feed the baby."

"You can always feed a baby, Edith," Fay said.

Edith looked down. "All right." She clasped her hands together. "Yes." She twisted her plain wedding band. "I was ashamed of her."

"And?" Fay knew that wasn't all.

"And," Edith said, giving up, "I didn't want another one of this Candy woman's children to raise, another person Mitch would love more than me."

"Where did you get the money?"

"I took five hundred dollars from the dentist and mailed it to her."

"And the dentist fired you?"

"He could never prove it was me. He just fired everybody who worked for him then."

"So where did Colleen think the money came from?"

"You." Edith swallowed. "I guess."

"And where did Mitch think the money came from?"

"You," Edith said. "I told him Colleen had been to see you, and he drew the . . . natural conclusion."

"So," Fay said. "I was right. He really *did* want to kill me."

"Yes," Edith said. "For almost fifteen years now."

"And you have kept him from it?"

"You're sitting here, aren't you?" Edith said, her face drained of all emotion.

Fay spoke simply. "Thank you," she said.

"I'm not proud of it," Edith said.

"How did you . . ." Fay wasn't sure what to ask.

"Distract him?" Edith asked. "I convinced him that abortion was the enemy, not you. I found the names of doctors who performed abortions, and he turned them in. Then, after it was legal, he robbed the centers, stole their equipment, things like that."

"You could've reported him, Edith, anytime."

"No," she said. "I couldn't. I didn't want that." She dabbed at her eyes. "I needed him."

Fay understood that.

Edith went on. "But when the bombings started, when people in Florida and New York started bombing abortion clinics . . ."

Fay nodded. "He knew he had to do something more—"

"Manly," Edith said. "Yes." She cleared her throat. "That's important to him."

"And suddenly, you were afraid he might—"

"Yes," Edith said again. "I was afraid he would kill somebody. So I told him to think of something else."

"So the kidnapping—"

"Yes." Edith winced. "It was his idea."

"Who is the Cowboy?" Fay asked.

"Somebody Mitch met at the V.A. hospital. That's all I know." Edith paused. "The children he tied up, are they all right?"

Fay nodded. "Edith, who were the people at the church? The parents of the other girls."

"What other girls?" Edith asked, genuinely surprised.

"The group that met at the church," Fay said.

"They don't have anything to do with this," Edith said.

"No?" Fay asked.

"How do you even know about them?" Edith asked.

"Just tell me," Fay said.

"That was actually a good thing Mitch did," she said. "Counseling, I guess you'd call it. He just got those parents together to . . . tell their stories. He just let them grieve over their girls."

The guard came to tell them their twenty minutes was up.

"I have five minutes I didn't use with my last visitor," Edith said. "Go check the report."

"This is the goddamn jail, lady," he said, reaching for her.

"Yes," she said, crossing her arms. "And unless you start checking things like reports, you will continue to be the lowest-paid person in this jail."

"Five minutes," he growled and walked away.

Edith was calmer now. "I don't know where that little girl is," she said. "Or the boys. All I was supposed to do was watch what happened at the shopping center. Mitch and Bob were hiding the children."

"If we got you out of here," Fay asked, "could you find out where Beth and the two boys are?"

"I don't think so," Edith said. "I think Mitch was already . . . beginning not to trust me."

"Edith," she ventured. "This plan had to cost a couple of thousand dollars. Where did Mitch get the money?"

"I don't know his name," Edith said. "He's a foreigner, a banker. Brazil, I think."

"All right," Fay said.

The guard returned and Edith stood up, willingly this time.

"I'll do what I can to help you," Fay said, standing up too. "I'll tell them you talked to me."

"Just find that little girl," Edith said.

Edith extended her hand, and Fay shook it, then stood there while Edith was escorted back to her cell.

Fay walked to the guard station and waited silently for the elevator with the guard who had brought her up. Finally, as the door opened and he turned the key to the control panel, she had to ask.

"Did you take my daughter downstairs?"

"I sure did," he grinned, "but I thought you were sisters!"

"No," Fay said.

"Could've fooled me," he flirted. "She said she'd see you at home."

When the door opened on the empty lobby, she turned to the guard. "Take it easy on my friend up there," she said. "She doesn't really belong here."

"Yeah," he said. "That's what they all say."

And Fay pushed open the wide glass door and stepped out into the night.

BY THE TIME Fay reached her car, it had started to rain. She felt desperately alone. Edith was, she realized, the Hermit. Number nine in the Tarot deck. And whatever Fay may have thought about the card before, she knew now it was a warning.

The picture is a bearded, robed recluse, who leans on his shepherd's crook for support and holds up a lantern to light his solitary path. But he is not searching for his sheep in the darkness. He is just alone, sentenced to life in exile for some unpardonable crime. But it is the Hermit himself who has pronounced this sentence.

Edith had done exactly that: decided she was unfit for life with other people, walked into the empty cell, and locked the door behind her.

And the more Fay thought about it, the more Hermits she knew. Some of them even admitted it. They said they'd rather be alone, or couldn't handle the demands that other people made on them, or could only live or work where it was quiet. And some of these people actually did move to remote areas. But most of them just went so far inside themselves that they weren't reachable by ordinary human means, like physical contact or conversation.

They were polite, as a rule, but they never talked to you for very long about anything. Occasionally they did hold odd or unusually strong opinions, or exhibit quirky behavior, but they didn't ever try to convince you their opinion was right, or invite you to enjoy their eccentricity.

In social situations, they would always expect to pay the check but would never expect to enjoy themselves. They took their exercise like everything else, as a punishment for getting older. And although they did have sex, it was primarily because refusing to might provoke a conversation about it.

The main way you could tell you were dealing with one of these exiles was you somehow felt you didn't have much room to move around. The wrong word, the wrong gesture, the suggestion of some silly entertainment, or the sharing of a personal story would elicit an only slightly disguised sneer from them. You would be terribly embarrassed and walk away. Unless, of course, they pretended not to hear any of it and walked away first.

It didn't bother these people if their children didn't call them. In fact, as they saw it, the children weren't really theirs. In having them, the Hermits had merely acquiesced to the desires of their mates. They didn't ignore their children, though. Far from it. They watched, hawk-eyed, for the first indication that the child was as flawed as they were. When they spotted the aberrant behavior, they punished it immediately. And kept punishing it until it became an established part of the child's personality.

These isolates were, finally, despite their skills and intelligence, spectators. They watched the world through the tiny window in their cell. They were, in fact, comfortable in there. They knew the routine, they recognized the guards' voices, and had found ways to pass the time. Why should they venture out? They would no doubt commit the same crime again, have to come back inside again. What was the point? They might not even get as nice a cell next time.

That was what Edith had done, all right, locked herself up. And that's what the Hermit was about: deadly self-seclusion. What was deadly about it was that people actually became proud of their solitude, like it meant they didn't need anybody else, like need was another crime they might commit if they were free.

LIZZIE WAS NOT home when Fay got there, and the only message on the machine was from Gail, telling Fay she was going out to dinner with the Mayor and would be back by ten o'clock probably and to please call when Fay saw the lights go on.

Fay knew that Arnie wouldn't be back for a while; she didn't want to read or watch TV, but she was afraid if she just sat in the dark she'd fall asleep, and she couldn't do that. This night was not over yet.

She walked to the window and saw four angular young men leaning against a car parked in the shadows. They had seen her come in, she was sure of it. But who were they? Were they just waiting while their friend went inside to get his raincoat? Or was this the robbery she had seen in the cards last night?

Or were these boys the ones who would kill her? Was this why Lizzie wouldn't call?

She edged over to the side of the window and pulled the drapes. She bolted the door and tried to remember the last time she had actually been scared to be in the house by herself. Then she called the police station at the corner, told the man taking Arnie's place that she was here by herself and there were suspicious characters on the street. Finally, she opened the hall closet and fished her mother's pistol out of the sack of knitted scarves where it had lain buried all these years. She cleaned it, checked to see that it was loaded and the safety was on, then stuffed it behind the needlepoint pillow in her big chair.

That done, she went to the kitchen, got one of Lizzie's yogurts out of the refrigerator, turned on the radio, and heard the last part of an announcement that an additional ten-thousand-dollar reward had been offered by a Brazilian businessman for anyone who located the remaining three missing children.

10:00 P.M.

WHEN ARNIE GOT BACK TO THE BASKETBALL COURT, the second overtime was just beginning. Those three minutes were the most violent he'd ever seen in a sporting event. And the victory celebration was even more dangerous than the game had been. Coaches and trainers who had useful legs were well advised to keep them off the court, away from the cracking wheels and reeling chairs of the "helpless" cripples.

As the floor was being cleared for the presentation of the trophy, the announcer informed the fans that the Mayor, who had been scheduled to present the trophies, was unable to attend, but that substituting for him would be his wife, Vi Ewing.

When the crowd settled down, Vi appeared in her fifth outfit of the day, this one a flouncy yellow suit with a polka-dot blouse. She praised the spirit of the youngsters she had seen competing in the hall, then introduced the chairman of the fairgrounds board, who presented the trophy to the winning coach.

Then the lights dimmed and the band played the Marine hymn. "The Most Valuable Player Award," Vi said, "will be presented by the man whose heroic labors on behalf of the disabled have earned him a citation from the surgeon general, as well as the love and the gratitude of thousands of determined victims of accidents and disease." She paused as the searchlight found him. "Ladies and gentlemen, a four-star general in the war against physical limitations—Mitchell Masters!"

325

Arnie stretched to get a look. Entering the arena wearing his Marine Corps dress whites and brandishing his riding crop like a sword, Masters raised one arm high over his head in a bold salute that brought the crowd to its feet in deafening applause. With his taut muscular neck, broad tanned forehead, his bulging shoulders and massive chest, he was a startling if not downright stirring sight wedged in a wheelchair.

As for his lower body, well, the chair *was* his lower body. This was not a man in a wheelchair. This was man on wheels, a man-machine, a satyr with steel rims instead of hooves.

Arnie made his way to the floor as Masters took possession of the crowd. His voice was deep, his manner deliberate and demanding, as he told the life story of the young man he was about to name.

Arnie wondered if Vi, smiling down at Masters, her hands clasped in classic rapture, had any idea who this man was, or what else he had done today. It was almost funny. Just two hours ago she had made that desperate public appeal to the kidnapper, and now here he was right beside her.

Jake came up behind Arnie. "So that's the famous Mitch Masters," he said casually, one bystander to another.

"Yeah, he's quite a guy," Arnie said back.

"You hear about his partner?" Jake asked, picking his teeth.

"What partner?" Arnie asked, his eyes straight ahead.

"A cowboy," Jake said.

"No, I didn't," Arnie said, determined not to react. "What about him?"

"Blown to bits in a garage downtown," Jake said.

"He killed himself?" Arnie asked.

"No," Jake said, "a bomb. The parking attendant's just sitting there and he hears this *boom*, you know? Goes down to look and finds this Cowboy"—Jake's arms flew out—"all over the place."

"Jesus Christ," Arnie said.

"Yeah," Jake said. "Only whole piece left was his hat." Jake threw his cigarette down on the floor. "See you later," he said, and left.

At the center of the court, Masters gave the Most Valuable Player his trophy, and sat by the boy's side as the band played the national anthem. Then, as the crowd applauded, he invited the young man to be his coach at the arm-wrestling matches.

The kid, whose name was Dwight, said he better not, because his mother had planned a party for the team at home. Masters said he better go on then, because mothers were worse than Marines. The boy laughed, thanked him anyway, and followed as Masters led a great crippled parade off the court.

Arnie arrived at the sign-up table just in time to see Masters approach, chomping a cigar and entertaining the troops as he rolled along.

"You my latest victim?" Masters boomed as he saw Arnie.

"It's a long list, I know," Arnie said.

The followers laughed and Masters' cold gray eyes took stock of Arnie.

"You ever do this before, son?"

"Not lately," Arnie said.

"Too bad," Masters said, cracking his knuckles. "I was hoping for some exercise."

"I'll do my best," Arnie said.

"I hope that's enough, soldier," Masters snorted.

The crowd was growing around them. Arnie shifted in his chair, and wiped his hands on his pants while Rodney explained the rules.

Elbows here, shoulders like so, one foul and you're out. Best two out of three, no disputing the umpire, and the winner takes all and gives it to the tournament.

"Got that?" Rodney asked.

"Got it," Arnie said, massaging his shoulder.

"Left arm or right?" Masters asked. "Challenger's choice."

"Right," Arnie said.

"What's the matter with your left?" Masters smirked, taking off his watch.

"Hunting accident," Arnie said, scooting closer to the table.

"Oh yeah?" Masters said, taking his cigar out of his mouth and laying it on the white line directly under where their hands would lock. "What do you hunt?"

"Somebody was hunting me," Arnie said.

Masters liked that idea. "What do you do, son?"

"I'm a cop," Arnie said, just to protect himself in case Vi showed up.

"You're too old for a cop," Masters said, digging his elbow into the table.

"You *get* old being a cop," Arnie said, stretching his fingers wide apart. "If you're lucky, that is."

Masters snarled. "Come on, Dick, get your elbow up here."

"The name's Arnie," he said, planting his elbow, and grabbing Mitch's hand.

"All right!" Masters said, squeezing Arnie's hand and nodding to Rodney to give the signal. "Let's find out what we've got for cops these days."

"*Go!*" Rodney shouted.

Standing at the back of the crowd, Jake heard the cheering begin. But after a full minute their hands were still straight up, and both men were straining hard to keep it that way. Arnie's forearm was a half-inch longer than Mitch's, but the general's was at least two inches broader. And Arnie was at least ten years younger than the man, maybe fifteen. But Masters was mean.

"So what brings you out with the cripples, Arnie?" Masters used his free hand to reach for his cigar and take a puff.

"I tried to get in the tractor pull," Arnie coughed, "but they were sold out."

Masters grinned and stuck the stogie back in his mouth. "Just had the night off, huh?"

"Yeah," Arnie said, wiping away a drop of sweat from his temple. "I've been on that kidnap drill all day. I had to do something."

Masters' elbow slipped slightly on the table. Arnie took advantage of it, snapped his wrist, and drove Masters' arm down about two inches. But Masters gave a fierce grunt and held.

Keeping the pressure up, Arnie went on talking. "Yeah," he said, "been standing in the sun all day out at that shopping center guarding a goddamn truck."

Masters looked up at Rodney, winked, and whipped Arnie's arm back to upright. The crowd cheered.

"So," Masters said, scratching his head calmly, "you gonna catch those people?"

Arnie's biceps had begun to quiver. "Already got one in jail," he managed. He took a breath and shoved Masters' arm back to where it had been, and then down another inch toward the table.

"The other one"—Arnie paused—"just blew himself up in a parking lot downtown."

"Oh yeah?" Masters said, looking down at his watch.

"Yeah," Arnie said. "They don't know his name yet, though. Calling him the Cowboy on the radio."

Two vets in fatigues started chanting in support of Masters, but he nodded to them that there was nothing to worry about.

"So that's who did it?" Masters asked, digging his nails into Arnie's hand.

"They think there's one more." Arnie leaned forward in his chair, hoping to get better leverage. He only needed four more inches and he'd have him.

"Watch it," Rodney said, pointing to Arnie's shoulder. "Any further and it's an automatic loss."

Mitch gritted his teeth. "Did the old lady talk yet?"

"What old lady?" Arnie asked.

Masters started to sweat, finally. "The old lady in the jail."

"I didn't say it was an old lady," Arnie said.

Masters gripped the edge of the table with his free hand. "That's what they said on TV," he said.

Arnie looked up at him. "Yeah, I guess she's talked some," Arnie said, wiping the sweat out of his eyes. "Most people do."

"You ever talked to a really old lady?" Masters asked, trying to keep his effort from showing on his face.

Arnie looked up at the crowd. "Not lately."

"They don't say a goddamn thing," Masters grunted, and reached for his cigar.

Arnie knew what that meant. The guy was about to try something.

"She must have told them something," Arnie said, "because they're setting a roadblock for midnight to catch the other one."

Masters leaned in. "Circle the whole city, you mean?" He punched his shoulder forward.

"Calling up the National Guard for it," Arnie lied. "Any road he takes out of the city, they've got him."

"How do they know what he looks like?" Masters leered.

"They don't," Arnie said. "But they're gonna open up every car, looking for that little girl."

"What if he leaves before midnight?" Masters said.

"Well then, the bastard will get away, won't he?" Arnie said.

Masters gave a hearty laugh, looked up at Arnie, sucked in his breath, clenched the table, fought Arnie's arm up to even, then whacked it down hard on the other side, breaking something, a knuckle probably.

"All right!" Mitch shouted, and the crowd exploded.

Arnie stood up quickly and backed away from the table as Mitch's friends came up to congratulate him.

"You can take five minutes if you both agree to it," Rodney said.

"I need something to eat," Arnie said, looking around. "I need a hot dog."

"Take mine," Jake said from behind him.

"Thanks," Arnie said.

"Cost me two bucks," Jake said, for the benefit of anyone listening.

Arnie reached into his pocket for the cash. "Thanks," he said, and turned back to the table.

What kind of game was Arnie playing here? Jake wondered. Why doesn't he just take the guy downtown? But maybe Arnie thinks if he takes Masters in, the little girl will just die wherever she is. Jake conceded that that was a possibility, but he didn't know how losing to the guy was going to get him to reveal where he'd stashed the kid. And Jake was convinced Arnie would lose here.

FAY PICKED UP the phone on the first ring.

"Fay," the Chief said, "I think you better come see this."

She was so relieved to hear a familiar voice she didn't even ask what it was she was supposed to see. "I'm ready," she said.

"It's a parking garage downtown," he said. "I'll have a patrol car pick you up. It's the Cowboy. Bomb blew up in his face. The car should be there in five minutes."

Fay started to ask about Arnie, but the Chief hung up. Had Arnie chased the Cowboy into the garage and been blown up with him? No. No, she thought. Arnie is at the fairgrounds.

But somebody's there, somebody else. Why else would he want me to come? Those two little boys. That's who it is. Joshua and . . . what's his name? Richard? Yes. Wait a minute, are they blown up? No, she thought. Please God, no.

Fay knew Lizzie would come home to change before she went out, so she found a piece of paper and wrote her a note.

"Dear Lizzie," she began. "I have gone downtown to find the last two boys. If you need me, call the police and tell them I am with the Chief."

She started a new paragraph.

"Please don't leave with Paul before you see me." She underlined *please*.

"I know you are going, but I also know some other things about your trip, things I'd want to know if I were you, like where you get married. You asked me that, remember? So wait for me."

Fay thought a minute and then added. "Since I'm never going to see you again after tonight, I won't charge you a thing."

Then she skipped a few lines and signed it, "Love, Mom."

She taped the note to the center of the table, pulled the drapes apart, saw the patrol car approach, unbolted the door, locked it behind her, then ran out toward the waiting policeman.

Downtown, the Chief met Fay at the parking garage and walked her past the barricades and over to the scene of the explosion.

"It was a modified military device," he said.

"Somebody was trying to kill him?" she asked.

"That's what our guys think," he said. "The Cowboy probably saw the bomb when he opened the car door. Then, when he tried to defuse it, it blew up on him."

Fay wasn't close enough to see any really sickening details, but the acrid smoke still trapped in the garage burned her eyes and nose. She coughed hard and asked if there was any water.

"You don't have to go any further if you don't want to," the Chief said.

"Then why did you want me to come?" Fay asked, looking in her purse for a handkerchief.

"The attendant said the Cowboy was here earlier today,

driving a pickup truck. The truck sounds like the same one you saw at his house. And we know from the children you found that he took those other two boys somewhere . . ."

"And you think they might be right here."

"Yeah," the Chief said, slightly ashamed of how obvious it sounded. "Maybe he brought them here, jimmied a trunk open, and stuffed them in."

Fay shook her head sadly. "And you want me to tell you which car they're in."

"Be a damn sight easier than impounding every car that's here," he said.

"For you, maybe," Fay said.

"There's an extra ten grand in the pot now, you know."

"Yes, I heard," Fay said, surprised that the Chief would think money made any difference to her. "Whose money is it?"

"The name is Rafael Soares," the Chief said. "Ever heard of him?"

Fay reeled. No, she'd never heard the name before, but she knew who he was all right. The King of Coins. The financial wizard. Paul's father.

"No," she said, covering her mouth with the handkerchief.

"Big banker. From Brazil, originally," the Chief said. "Lives in California now, though. Big Catholic too, I guess."

"Why do you say that?" she asked.

"I don't know," he said. "Something about how he talked about the children."

"You don't have to be a Catholic to like children."

"O.K." He realized he'd never tried to talk to Fay without Arnie around to translate. "Can you find the kids or not?"

"I don't know," Fay said. "Where should I start?"

"I'd start at the top," he said, pointing to the elevator. "I'll come with you if you want."

"That's all right," she said.

"It's pretty dark up there," he said, stuffing his hands in his pockets.

"All right, then," she said, knowing he was only trying to help. "Come with me. But you can't be right there, you know, I'll need a little—"

"I can do whatever you want," he said, putting his arm around her as they started for the elevator. "You just tell me."

"And what if I can't find them?" she said, slipping out from under his arm.

"Then we'll seal the place. Bring in a computer and a phone bank." He frowned and scratched his head. "We'll file for the search warrants and open all the trunks."

"How long will that take?"

"Start to finish, two days," he said.

She nodded. "And the kids will die. If they're here. If they're not dead already."

"Well," he said, pressing the elevator button, "you see why I called you."

GAIL AND THE Mayor had been lingering over their decaf for quite a while now, discussing, among other things, whether the next cup should be real coffee. It was hard to know, they said, whether the rest of the evening held some event they'd need to be awake for or one they'd rather sleep through.

The dinner had been so-so. She'd had steamed mussels and a salad, and he'd eaten the battered trout, which was not what they'd called it on the menu, but rather his description of the treatment it had received in the kitchen.

The conversation had been lively, but was punctuated by abrupt and seemingly unbridgeable silences. He was relieved that no one had recognized him, had come over to the table to say hello. She suspected that several people *had* noticed him, but upon seeing her had decided that whatever they had to say to him could wait till tomorrow.

What they had in common was a deep-seated fear of leaving the restaurant. They had become terribly dependent on the structure it provided for them. Once they left this table, the future would close in around them like the dense foliage and treacherous undergrowth of a tropical forest.

Once they hit the highway, somebody would have to make a move, say whether to go home or not, together or not. If anybody brought up the rules, what they "should" do, there would be a discussion about it. And a discussion would be the end of the evening, and neither one wanted that. So they ordered more coffee. Real for Gail, decaf and a brandy for the Mayor.

Just then the Mayor spotted one of the policemen assigned to guard him talking to the maître d'.

"If you have to go, please do," she said. "I can call a cab or something."

"You can come with me," he said, as the sergeant approached.

"Sorry to disturb you, sir," the sergeant said, "but the Chief wanted you and Mrs. Wilkins to know."

"Know what, Sergeant?" the Mayor said, reaching for his newly arrived brandy.

Suddenly very afraid, Gail looked up at the young officer. "I'm not ready for this," she said.

"Oh no, ma'am," he said, sensing her fear. "They haven't found any more kids yet."

She was not relieved.

"I'm sorry, ma'am," the sergeant said.

"So what is it, Bill?" the Mayor asked, hoping to get back to Gail before she disappeared into the agony again.

"It's that Cowboy where we found the other kids," he said. "He's dead. A bomb blew up on him in a parking garage downtown."

"What was he doing there?" Gail asked.

"That's what I came to tell you," he said. "The Chief thinks he was hiding the other kids in trunks of cars. They're searching for them now. They've got that psychic—"

Gail reached under the table for her purse. "Peter," she said, "we have to go down there."

"Thank you, Bill," the Mayor said, standing up.

The sergeant thought he was being dismissed, but he wasn't sure. "If you need a ride, sir, I'll—"

"No thank you, Bill," the Mayor said, motioning for the waiter. "I have my car."

Gail put on fresh lipstick while the Mayor signed the check.

"Are you sure you want to go?" he asked Gail, as she closed her compact and dropped it back into her purse. "It could be . . ." He paused, wondering how to warn her. "It could be anything, I guess. It could be nothing."

"If Beth is dead in one of those cars, I want to see it," Gail said. "I don't want somebody calling me on the goddamn phone about it." She gulped down the last of her coffee.

"Well then," he said, "let's go."

*   *   *

ARNIE'S HOT DOG had helped. He had won the second round of arm wrestling fairly easily. And except for some routine swearing and name-calling, they hadn't talked at all. Maybe Masters was thinking, maybe Arnie's lie about the roadblock was having an effect.

Arnie was tempted to have a beer. He hadn't had one all day. In fact, as he thought about it, he had missed all kinds of things today, like meals and chairs and the finals of the U.S. Open on TV. Arnie thought there ought to be certain things in a day or it didn't count. Like if you didn't have a decent cup of coffee, or see a pretty pair of legs, or get to work the crossword puzzle in peace, then you shouldn't have to be a day older at the end of it.

Arnie walked back to the table, quite aware that not one person had slapped him on the back and said good luck.

"Want to double the stakes?" Masters asked, rolling up to the table.

"Can't do it," Arnie said, still standing, patting his wallet. "I can't afford to lose that much."

The crowd laughed.

But Mitch didn't like that attitude. "If you think you're going to lose," he pounced, "I'll save myself the trouble of beating you and just take your check right now."

"*You're* going to lose," Arnie needled, deciding he would have a beer after all.

"I never have before," Mitch said casually, setting the brake on his wheelchair.

"Why is that?" Arnie said, spotting the beer man and waving to him.

Masters took a wet cloth from Rodney and wiped his hands, then mopped his forehead. "I like to win," he said, and handed the cloth back to Rodney.

"It's just a game," Arnie said, pleased to see that his stall was making Masters nervous.

"Correction," Masters said. "Only boys play games."

Arnie didn't agree. Masters was still playing his games because he hadn't really won yet. From what Arnie knew about military life, when you really knew you'd won, you walked off the field and took a shower. You didn't parade around in your bloody battle dress; you wrapped a clean towel around your clean waist and drank a beer.

Masters was a pretty fair actor, but he was only playing

the part. The real hero went home after the game to the
party his mother had planned for him. The real hero took his
suffering in stride and refused to feel special about it.

Masters asked the crowd to step back a little, give them
some air, he said, then nodded to Rodney. "Let's get on with
this, huh? I've got a date."

"Goin' to a dance?" Arnie quipped, as the man handed
him the beer.

"It's none of your goddamn business where I'm going,"
Masters snapped, cranking his elbow into position.

Arnie collected his change and his beer, lifted up his
shirt, and undid his belt.

"Oh for God's sake," Masters barked. "What are you
doing now?"

"Am I making you nervous?" Arnie asked, fixing it. He
dug into his right front pocket for something.

"I told you," Masters said, tapping the table, making his
watch flop around like a freshly caught fish. "I'm late."

Arnie finally found what he was looking for, and slapped
his badge down on the table.

Masters scowled. "Get your ass in that chair, boy."

"Damn badge was stickin' right in my leg," Arnie said.
He popped the top off the can of beer. "I'm ready," he said,
and took a long deep drink, then set the can on the table and
burped.

Masters planted his arm on the table again. "I'm giving
you one minute or it's a default."

Arnie sat down, slid his elbow up to its place, then
clenched his fist repeatedly to pump up the blood in his arm.

Masters read the name off the badge, really beginning to
wonder if he might be in trouble here. His voice was like the
low rattle of a poisonous snake about to strike.

"Who are you, Campbell?" he rasped.

"I told you," Arnie said easily, stretching his fingers
wide. "I'm a cop."

They clasped hands.

"*Go!*" Rodney said.

Masters gave it everything he had, clamped his jaw shut,
drew his whole face into tight focus, and tried a quick stab.

Arnie forced himself to laugh and rode it out. "What are
you trying to do, old man? Beat me?"

"You asshole," Masters swore under his breath.

"Hey, watch it," Arnie whispered back. "There's people here."

"You fucking asshole," Masters mouthed. His face turned bright red, his cheeks puffed up, then exploded, showering Arnie with spit but otherwise having no effect on his defiant upright arm.

Arnie reached for his beer. "Want a drink?" he asked, wondering how much longer he could pretend not to be dying here. God, the man was strong.

Masters couldn't do it. He shook his head, relaxed his shoulders, resigned himself to another strategic siege, and asked Rodney to get him a beer.

Arnie inhaled and mashed Master's arm down an inch. "Is your wife's name Edith?" Arnie asked.

"Yeah," Masters hissed, his wrist stiffening into steel. "What of it?"

"A friend of mine knows her," Arnie said.

Masters yanked his arm back to upright. Rodney shouted his approval and set Masters' beer down on the table.

Arnie drove his arm down again. "She says your daughter is a real pretty blonde. How old is she now?"

"She died," Masters said, jerking back to upright and holding there.

Arnie knew he could take this first inch anytime he wanted to, so he did it again, just for effect. "What happened to the baby?" he challenged.

Mitch batted away a wasp drawn by the smell of beer and sweat. "What baby?"

"My friend told me Colleen had a baby," Arnie said.

Masters' cheek twitched at the name. "Who is this friend of yours?" he asked, bouncing Arnie's arm back to upright.

Arnie lobbed the name across the table like a grenade. "Fay Morgan."

Mitch knew the name. "Fortune tellers ought to be against the law," he spat.

"People need somebody to talk to," Arnie said, a pain shooting up from his elbow like a lighted fuse.

Mitch returned a smile from somebody in the crowd behind Arnie's head. "They can talk to their parents," he said flatly.

Arnie braced his left arm against his knee for support. "Maybe they're afraid of what their parents would say."

"Then they shouldn't do it," Masters said, taking another drink of his beer.

"Do what?" Arnie asked, as their arms shook together, dead even, over the center line.

Mitch looked him square in the face. "Do what they go see the fortune teller about."

Arnie reached for his beer. He wanted to win here. He knew it didn't matter, really. The department would pay him back the two hundred dollars if he had to write the check. But it was personal now. He was not letting Masters have the satisfaction of beating a cop. No way.

"Maybe she was raped," Arnie said, dropping the tough-guy voice he'd been using. "Maybe it wasn't her fault. Ever think of that?"

Masters noticed the change. "No such thing as rape, Campbell," he said.

Arnie let him have an inch. "That's bullshit, Masters."

"She was weak," Masters said, his knuckles white from the pressure, the black hairs on the back of his hand glistening with sweat.

Arnie leaned forward and lowered his voice. "She was a kid, Masters."

Masters' back stiffened. The muscles in his neck bulged. He wanted to kill this cop, he wanted to break his arm, twist it right off like a chicken leg.

"She was no kid." Masters took a breath, then spat out the words. "She was a slut like her mother."

Arnie jabbed Masters' arm back to upright. Slut, *Slut*, the man said. Arnie counted to eight. *He's calling his daughter a slut. A daughter who died!*

"Masters," Arnie snapped, his face red with rage, "you're finished," and with that, Arnie bashed Masters' arm flat down on the table. And won.

"Yeah!" he shouted.

The crowd was silent. Their hero had lost.

And only then, as she placed her icy fingers on his sweaty shoulders and planted a prim kiss on his cheek from behind, did Arnie realize that Vi Ewing had been watching the whole time.

"Arnie! Arnie!" she said, pinching his left arm, finding the exact center of his bandage.

"Ah-h!" he yelled, and sprang out of his chair.

"You were wonderful," she gushed, and slipped across to the end of the table to congratulate Masters.

"Well." She leaned down to Masters. "I'm just *so* grateful I could see this."

Masters didn't look up.

But Vi Ewing wouldn't quit. "We have two heroes, here," she announced to the crowd. "This detective has found eleven of the kidnapped children all by himself!"

There was genuine applause from the crowd.

"Good match," Masters said to Arnie, releasing the brake on his chair and extending his hand.

And as Arnie shook it, somebody snapped a picture.

"Isn't that nice!" Vi said.

Masters rolled back a little. "All right," he called out. "Everybody who came in my van, we're leaving right now."

"What about the money?" Arnie called to him. "You owe the tournament two hundred bucks!"

"He's good for it," Rodney answered and wheeled Masters around.

"Don't I get a trophy or something?" Arnie yelled.

But he didn't get an answer to that. Four men in wheelchairs, one V.A. chaplain, and Rodney fell in behind Masters and proceeded through the hole that opened up for them in the crowd.

Arnie started off in the other direction, but Vi caught his hand. "It just makes me feel so good," she said, falling in step with him, "to know there are such dedicated policemen in this city, people who really care."

Arnie sped up to get away from her, but she just trotted along as gracefully as she could. When they reached the exit, he pushed the door open, then held it while two men on crutches slipped by him.

"Good night, Mrs. Ewing," he said, and strode off down the sidewalk.

"Where are you going?" she asked, catching up to him.

He stopped her. "I'm on duty, Mrs. Ewing. If you need a ride home, there's an officer at the information booth."

"I want to go with you," she said. "If you're going to find those last three children, I want to be there."

"I can't take you," he said. "It's against the regulations."

She dropped her pleasant voice. "Maybe we'll just call the Mayor and see about that," she said.

"Do it," he said. "But until I get a direct order from the Chief of Police, you're not setting your little fanny anywhere near me tonight."

"I could report you for that remark," she said.

"Please do," he said. "I hope it makes the front page."

They rounded the corner of the building and Arnie stopped. Mitch and his gang were loading into the van.

"I'm gone," Arnie said, ducking down behind a dark Buick. "You do what you want."

WHEN THE ELEVATOR opened, Fay and the Chief saw that the top floor of the parking garage was empty except for a white Eldorado convertible and a dusty brown Pinto hatchback stuffed to the gills with somebody's whole life.

Fay stepped out onto the concrete. She didn't know how to go about this exactly, but she'd seen enough of these two cars already. The Eldorado, parked near the elevator, didn't even have license plates.

"Somebody probably just drove it up here, ran out of gas, and decided it was all for the best," the Chief said.

Fay walked ahead of him down to the next tier of cars. She ran her hand up the aerial of a black Lincoln and wondered what a skillet was doing in the back window of the tan Audi.

"It's not a new car," she said, and then she knew what it was. "It's a car they don't make anymore." She was staring at a license plate that read TOM-86.

"Like a Rambler?" he asked. "Or a Viceroy or a Valiant? Or do you mean really old, like a Packard, or a Studebaker, maybe, or an Alpine? Yeah! A Sunbeam?"

"What does a Dodge look like?" she asked.

"The old ones were real ugly, boxy little cars, in real dull colors like split pea or mud. With big wide strips of chrome along the side and—"

"That's not it, then," she said.

"Maybe we should just walk on a little further," he said.

"There's no use walking if we don't know what we're looking for."

Sure, he thought. That makes sense. "Want me to stand still or walk?" he asked.

"What's a Nash?" she asked, starting down the line of cars.

"They made the Rambler," he said. "And all of them were black and cheap like—"

"No," she said. "It's not black. What's a car that smells like gasoline on the inside?"

"I had a Ford that did that," he said. "But almost any old Volkswagen would too."

"It has rubber mats on the floor."

"Right," he said, admiring the wire wheels on a slick silver Corvette.

"It has a broken lock on the glove compartment, too," she said.

"What color is it?" he asked, thinking how much it would help if she knew something about the outside of this car.

"I don't know," she said. "It's dark."

He thumped the zippered cover of a little Fiat convertible. "The car is dark? Or it's too dark in here to tell?"

"Both," she said, hesitating behind a blue sedan.

"Is that it?" He jumped.

"No," she said. "I like the looks of it, though."

"It's a '72 Volvo," he said, coming up beside her. "It's a helluva car. Drives like a tank. Rides like a dream. I took one out for a test drive once, used car, and the whole exhaust system fell out on the highway."

"What did you do?" she asked, moving on to the next tier of cars.

"Went real slow," the Chief said. "Cars won't hardly go at all without the exhaust. Limped up into a gas station, called the dealer, told him as soon as he fixed it, I'd buy it. Got a real good deal, too."

She laughed. "I bet you did."

"Never had another lick of trouble with it."

"It's a bird," she said. "It's the name of a bird!"

"Falcon!" he said, starting to look for one.

"No," she said.

"Firebird?" he asked, trying to remember if they'd passed one.

"No."

"Lark," he said. "Skylark!"

"No," she said.

He walked on. "Hawk?"

"No."

"Phoenix?"

"No."

"Thunderbird!"

"Uh-uh," she said.

"Fiero?"

"Is that a bird?" she asked.

He was flat out of birds. "Are you sure it's not a horse?" he asked. "There's a whole lot more horses than birds. Colt, Mustang, Pinto, Pony, Charger, Bronco—"

"Stud," she said. "They ought to name one Stud."

He laughed. "Sell a million of 'em, I bet," he said, stopping to read the sign in the window of a red Mercedes turbo. RADIO ALREADY STOLEN, it read.

"The guy's lying," the Chief said.

"What do you mean?" she asked, walking over to the window on the passenger side.

He pointed. "See those wires coming out of that hole for the radio?"

She peered into the dark car.

"They're fake," he explained. "The guy's got one of those lift-out radios, what-do-you-call-'ems, portables. Thing goes in the trunk at night. Then he just stuffs these wires in here to look like his radio was ripped out."

Fay straightened up. "Chester," she said, turning around slowly.

"Yes, ma'am?"

"We found them," she said quietly.

She pointed in the back window of the car parked next to the Mercedes. "They're right there in the backseat of that—"

She grabbed the door handle and shook it hard. "They're under that thing, that blanket, whatever it is," she said.

But he was already at the other side of the car yelling into his radio for help, and rocking the car back and forth as hard as he could.

"Joshua!" she screamed. "Richard! Wake up!" But if the boys were under the tarp in the rear seat, they weren't moving.

The team arrived quickly from the street level, broke the window, opened the door, released the parking brake, and rolled the car out. Then, when they had enough room, they opened the back doors and lifted the two boys out onto the waiting stretchers.

Fay backed up. She couldn't move. She hadn't really thought they could find all twenty-seven children alive, but the prospect of finding two of them dead paralyzed her.

"Fay!" the Chief screamed. "They're alive!"

Her knees buckled. She turned quickly and clutched the door of the Mercedes for support.

In another minute, as the boys were loaded into the ambulance, the Chief came up beside her, but he could see how shaky she was.

"It's all right," he said. "He must have given them some kind of sleeping thing. They're going to make it."

She wasn't responding.

"Fay," he soothed, "you found them!"

"No," she said, turning around carefully and reaching for his hand. "You found them, Chester."

"No, no," he said. "I would've walked right by. You did it." He thought she should be excited. "You did it!"

"What kind of car is that?" she asked, still dizzy, still empty.

"It's a Dart," he said.

"Is that a bird?" she asked, wiping her eyes.

"Yeah," he lied, taking her arm and easing her away from the car. "I used to see those Darts all the time as a kid. Little-bitty things. Fast, though."

Fay smiled, shook her head, and held his hand as they walked to the elevator. "You ought to be real proud of yourself, Chester."

"Yeah," he said softly. "Thanks." He looked down at his shoes. "I wanted to do *something*, you know?"

She squeezed his hand. "I know."

11:00 P.M.

 AS GAIL AND THE MAYOR DROVE UP TO THE PARK-
ing garage, the ambulance carrying Richard
Isaac and Joshua Beckstein careened out the
exit, its siren wailing.

Gail saw Fay standing on the sidewalk, and jumped out
of the car. "Who is it!" she screamed.

"We found the two boys!" Fay called, hurrying toward
her. "They're alive!"

Gail stopped cold.

Fay kept talking, pointing to the upper tiers of the
garage. "They were asleep in the backseat of a car."

That was not what Gail wanted to hear. She wrapped her
arms around herself and held on tight. "But no Beth," she
said.

"Gail," Fay said, determined to reassure her, "if these
two are alive, then Beth is alive! All we have to do is find
her."

Gail looked away. "Did you check the rest of the cars?"
she asked.

Fay reached out to her. "She's not here, Gail."

"Did you look?" Gail demanded, backing up even further.

"They're looking right now," Fay said.

"They should break into every car up there," Gail cried.
"Tear them apart!"

"Gail," Fay said more firmly, "Beth is not here. She's

344

with the other man. But Arnie knows who he is and he's tracking him down right now."

"What other man?" the Mayor asked, coming up to them and putting his arm around Gail.

"There's another man involved, an older man in a wheel-chair. Beth is with him."

"Why?" Gail asked, grabbing the tail of the Mayor's sport coat, wadding it up in her hand like an old Kleenex.

"Why does he have her?" Fay asked, not wanting to answer that question.

"Why *Beth*?" Gail asked. "Why did he take my little girl, of all these children, of all the children in the city? What did I do?"

"Gail," Fay said quickly, "Arnie has been after this man for the last two hours, so any minute now we'll hear something. I know it."

"No," Gail said, reaching out for Fay's hand, "you don't know it. You're just trying to make me feel better."

"Nobody's ever gotten away from Arnie," Fay said. "Ever."

Gail closed her eyes and took a deep breath, hoping the air would hold her up. But it was no use. As Fay watched helplessly, another of the thin threads of hope, by which Gail had been suspended all day, snapped.

The Mayor slipped his arm around Gail's waist to support her. "Do you want to go home?" he asked. "I'll take you wherever you want."

"Just don't leave me."

"No," he said. "I promise."

"I'm going home too," Fay said. "If you want me to come over, just call."

Gail nodded, her hands clasped even tighter to her face now, and the Mayor led her around the car, placed her in the seat, and buckled the seat belt over her.

"I have some Valium at my house," Fay said to him when he came around to get in his side of the car. "If she needs it."

The Mayor nodded. "What do you think we should do about Marvin?" he said. "He's still in jail."

"I don't think we should do anything until she tells us to," Fay said. "If she wants him out, I'm sure you can arrange that."

"All right," he said, "we'll see you at the house, then."

Fay waved as they drove off, then joined the young officer who had arrived to take her home.

THE TWENTIETH CARD in the Tarot deck is called Judgment. The picture is a rather routine Bible-school presentation of the Last Judgment. An angel blows a trumpet and the souls rise from the ground and ascend into heaven. But since souls are so hard to draw, most decks make do with naked bodies, arms raised high, standing in open coffins.

Most of Fay's clients felt comfortable with this card, felt as if they'd seen it before, knew what it was, and weren't all that worried about it. It was just another one of the Bible's bribes. If you're good, then after you're dead (we can't say when, but we'll call you) we're going to have a great big dance, and everybody comes nude and you'll be just sick if you're not invited, so behave yourself.

But even people who believed in the Last Judgment on some spiritual level, even the folks who were looking forward to it, didn't really think it would happen—physically, that is, so you could see it, record it on film, teach it in history class, that kind of real.

Some churches did hold, Fay remembered, that on the Day of Judgment the physical bodies would arise to be reunited with their souls, but she couldn't see why anybody would go to those churches. What's so good about a heaven where, one of these days, you're going to get your embarrassing old body back?

There were some people who liked to play with the idea, though. One client, a math teacher, actually assigned the problem to his classes. There are this many square feet of standable surface on the earth, and at least this many people who have ever lived. Now, if all those people were to rise up all at once, would there be enough room for them? The correct answer was "Yes."

But generally the Judgment card was not ever the subject of much discussion around Fay's table. She was glad of that. What she had to say about it might make some people very uneasy.

For there really was, according to Fay, such a thing as Judgment Day. But it wasn't the same day for everybody, and some people might have more than one. Then too, some people might miss theirs altogether, like not hearing the alarm one morning. *Exactly* like not hearing the alarm. Judgment Day was a sort of celestial wake-up call.

But it didn't have to come in the morning, of course. You could be washing your hair or your car, or eating lunch, or reading. It could feel like a breeze or sound like a sigh. You might even think it was you who sighed, but it wasn't. It was the angel's trump. And the message was, if you want to rise, this is the time. The ground is loose around your feet, the currents are right. You're cleared for takeoff. Go.

Go where, the angel didn't say. How to fly? No, the angel couldn't help with that either. Nor could the angel speculate about whether you'd miss your old friends or your comfortable shoes, or if, aloft, you'd be a little airsick, and if so, for how long.

All the angel said was *come*. It's time. Time for a change generally; time to move on. Or maybe even time to quit. You could get a considerable lift out of that. Or time to push, or win, or play in the right league.

But you had to go the minute the angel called. Later on, after you'd thought about, planned for it, strapped on your parachute and said your good-byes, the wind would have changed. Whatever altitude you'd gain then would be difficult to maintain.

Fay wasn't sure what made some people hear this call to rise above the rest. But she knew how to recognize them. They were lighter, they laughed more easily, their clothes moved with them when they walked, their talk was simple, straight, and clear.

The judgment that was made on these days was not whether you had been good, or obeyed the rules, or lived in peace with God and the world. The judgment was: Could you accept your rightful place in the company of the blessed? Could you, as they used to say in Bible days, rejoice and be glad?

As Fay drove home, however, she was afraid that Gail was feeling that hateful old vengeful style of judgment. She had been judged and found wanting. For her sins, her little girl had been taken away.

Fay knew that if Arnie were unsuccessful, if he failed to find Beth, or found her too late, she would have to be the one to tell Gail, to try to stand between her and the abyss until the angel got there.

For yes, there were times—and this might very well be one of them—when senseless earthly tragedy interrupted the natural flow of things, threatened the very life of someone the angels had been watching.

When that happened, the angels couldn't afford to wait for the right time. They had to swoop down, cut the ropes, lift her up and hold her safely aloft until she woke up in a year or so, and realized the worst was over.

ARNIE AND JAKE had no trouble following Masters' metallic gray van through the city.

Jake ran a check on the plates and when the operator came back with the information, she said the Chief had been looking for them for an hour and what the hell was their location?

Jake told the operator they were tailing a possible suspect who had a possible police radio in his car so they couldn't say where they were, but they didn't need any help right now.

"Find out what the Chief wants," Arnie said. "It could be a message from Fay."

"Pick up passenger in car following you," the operator said.

Jake whirled around in his seat to look.

"Who is it?" Arnie asked.

"Gold Oldsmobile," the operator answered. "Orders from the Chief on request from the governor."

"Goddamn fucking radio," Arnie said.

"Who is it?" Jake asked.

"The Mayor's wife," Arnie said.

"How do you know?" Jake asked.

"I ran into her at the fairgrounds," Arnie said. "I told her to get lost."

"Forget it," Jake said, putting the radio back in its cradle. "We just never found a convenient time, that's what."

When Masters turned into the huge County Rehab Center, Arnie pulled in at the doctors' entrance and turned off his lights.

Three orderlies came down the front steps.

"I can't see a thing," Jake said, training his binoculars on the van.

"Maybe I'll go watch," Arnie said.

"He knows you," Jake said, handing him the binoculars. "I'll go." And before Arnie could object, Jake opened the door and slipped across the grass to the gravel driveway.

What was Jake going to do, Arnie wondered, pretend he was the gardener? But as Arnie watched through the binoculars, Jake developed an artificial leg just at the edge of the driveway, and gimped his way right toward the van. The guy's got a lot of nerve, Arnie thought. Why doesn't he just get in the van while he's at it?

As Jake approached on the passenger side, Masters saw him, assumed he was a recovering veteran, lowered the passenger window, and called out. "You're lookin' good, boy!"

Jake gave him an appreciative thumbs-up signal, and continued on around the van.

Arnie watched as the first paraplegic went up the ramp in his wheelchair, followed by the orderly carrying the man's Thermos bottle, the giant stuffed panda he must've won on the midway, and the banner he had waved in the game.

The second one wore a baseball cap and had a lap full of popcorn boxes. The third one looked either asleep or sick, Arnie couldn't tell which.

The knock on the window made Arnie nearly jump out of his seat.

"What the—" He snapped his head around and reached for his gun.

"I told you I wanted to come," Vi said.

He rolled down the window. "What the hell are you doing?" he barked.

"I'm coming with you," she declared. "The governor has made me a special deputy. There is a direct order from the Chief of Police."

"I didn't get it," he said.

"Call them on the radio."

He looked in his rearview mirror and wondered how he thought he could catch Mitch Masters if he couldn't spot a gold Oldsmobile pulling up behind him and blocking his exit.

"Go move your car," he said.

"What are you following *him* for?" she asked. "He's just that man from the tournament."

"Right," Arnie said. "Go move your car."

She crossed her arms. "Not till you promise to—"

"Lady!" he screamed. "If you really want to see what you're going to see by being with me tonight, then you deserve it! Go move your fucking car!"

He turned away from her to watch as a man in green work clothes closed the back door of Masters' van, then walked around and climbed into the passenger seat next to Mitch.

Where was Jake? Inside the van maybe? Couldn't be, Arnie thought.

Vi tapped on the passenger window. "Where do you want me?" she asked.

"Get in the back," he said, putting the car in gear. "And stay down."

"You think you can scare me, don't you?" she said, closing the door behind her.

"I said you could get in," he muttered. "I didn't say you could talk."

Masters' van pulled away from the ramp. Still no sign of Jake.

"He's going around the back!" Vi pointed, as if Arnie couldn't see that for himself.

"Please sit back," Arnie said, feeling her breath on his neck. "It makes me crazy when people—"

Masters had cleared the main building now, but instead of going toward the highway was proceeding further into the grounds of the institution. When Arnie reached the main building, he stopped, just to give Jake one more chance to appear.

"Aren't you going to follow him?" she inquired.

"Please, Mrs. Ewing," he said, as nicely as he could, "shut up."

"Wouldn't it be easier if you called me Vi?" she asked, sitting back in the seat.

"No, Mrs. Ewing," he said. "It wouldn't," and he turned onto the road Masters had taken.

Was Jake unconscious in the back of the van?

"Do we think he's the kidnapper?" Vi asked, leaning forward again.

"Do we think I'm here for the scenery?" Arnie mimicked her coy tone.

"But he's a wonderful man!" she protested. "He's done all those things for all those brave people."

"Right," Arnie said. They drove past the administration building, then the old dormitories, then something that could be a greenhouse, then the low white modern structure Arnie knew to be the now-unoccupied children's unit. Each building had safety lights installed on the roof, and each parking lot had one tungsten lamp posted in the center of it, but the roads were completely dark and too narrow by modern standards.

"Didn't this used to be something else?" Vi asked.

"Mental hospital," Arnie said.

He followed the van past the playground, the ball diamond, the cafeteria, and the shop; then stopped far back as Masters turned off onto a smaller road marked by a little sign.

"Where is he going?" Vi asked.

"If I knew that," Arnie sighed, "I'd already be there waiting for him."

"But how do you know it's him?" she asked.

"Look," he said, turning around to face her, "we have to make some kind of deal here."

"Fine," she said, looking out the window.

"You *don't* ask me any more questions, and when we get there, you *don't* get out of the car. You *don't* interfere, in any way, with what happens."

"What does that mean?" she sniped.

Arnie exploded. "This guy is a killer! That's what it means! A fucking killer! And I watched you cozy up to him at that ballgame—"

"I didn't know he was the kidnapper!" she said.

"You don't know a goddamn thing," he snapped. "You don't know how dumb you sound, and you don't know how stupid you look. And maybe you just don't care, but you should care. Like you should've cared when your boys were missing, and you should've cared a lot that some other lady took the time to find them. But no. All you care about is your own damn self, and how much attention you can get, and how much hypocritical bullshit you can sling, and how many people will buy it. Well, I for one won't. I'm sick to death of you, and the last thing I thought I'd have to tolerate is being locked up in a car with you. But here we are, so I'm just warning you to shut up or I'm going to kill you before he even has a chance."

He took a breath.

She sat back in her seat. "What did I ever do to you?" she pouted.

But Arnie didn't answer. He pulled onto the smaller road, and followed it for about a quarter of a mile, then stopped. Two hundred yards ahead of him a clearing opened; he saw Masters pull up to the far end of a building that could be, from the steam pouring out of the stone chimneys, the laundry. An eerie orange glow came from a wall of basement windows on the right side of the building.

Arnie pulled off the road and stopped under a clump of low-hanging trees.

"Who found my boys?" Vi asked, tentatively.

Arnie loaded his pistol. "It was another one of the mothers around the table this morning."

Vi was genuinely surprised. "How did she do it?"

Arnie reached in the glove compartment for his flashlight. "She crawled through a cave," he said. "The whole fire department was out there trying, but she did it, she saved them."

"I see," Vi said, nodding to herself. "Have they found her children yet?"

"She only has one child," Arnie said, getting his handcuffs out of the pocket on the door. "A little girl named Beth. And no, we haven't found her yet. She's the very last one."

Vi Ewing's voice cracked. "And you think this man has her?"

"Yes," Arnie said, "I do."

She bit her lip. "I'm sorry."

"Yeah," Arnie sighed, reaching for the door handle, "so am I."

BUT BEFORE ARNIE could get out of the car, the front passenger door flew open and Jake slammed himself into the seat.

Jake was panting hard. "Move it!" he gasped. "He's coming this way!"

Arnie slammed the car into reverse, flung his arm over the seat, looked out the back window, and mashed on the gas. "Hold on," he said to Vi.

"What did he do?" Arnie asked, as the car slid onto the road, and Arnie turned around and leaned his head out the window to see where he was going.

"He just dropped off the other two guys," Jake said, beginning to recover his breath.

"Didn't pick up anything?" Arnie asked, as the car sped backward out the little road.

"Just a box of shirts," Jake said.

Arnie jerked the steering wheel hard and the car bumped up onto the main road, then sprang forward with a lurch.

"O.K.," Jake shouted. "Step on it! If we beat him to the gate, we can—"

But Arnie's hands fell from the wheel.

"What are you doing?" Jake yelled.

"I'm thinking," Arnie said, sliding his foot onto the accelerator and depressing it gently.

"If he sees us on this road—" Jake argued.

"I don't think he's *going* anywhere," Arnie said, and gave the car a little more gas.

"The kid's not in the van, if that's what you think," Jake said.

"I think Beth is right here," Arnie said, turning into the children's unit and driving to the far side of the lot.

"But why would he—" Jake started to object.

"He could've gotten anybody to bring those guys home, couldn't he?" Arnie said.

"Sure," Jake said, as he saw Masters' lights turning onto the main road.

"So if he came here," Arnie finished, "then this is where he wants to be. And my guess is it's this building right here." He pointed to it.

He turned off the ignition. "It's wheelchair accessible, it has toilets and beds. It's perfect."

"But wouldn't somebody see him?" Vi asked.

"It's empty now," Arnie said. "Thank God. It was a terrible place for kids. I used to bring them out here from—"

He stopped. Masters' van came down the road, turned into the children's unit parking lot, and drove up to a ramp on the west side of the building.

"That's the kitchen," Arnie said.

"O.K.," Jake said, checking his pistol. "How do you want to do this?"

"I'll follow him in," Arnie said. "You wait for him on the outside."

"What do you want me to do?" Vi asked carefully.

"As soon as he leaves his van, call for a backup and an ambulance. But tell them no sirens."

"You mean talk into the radio?" she asked.

"Yes," he said, and looked over at Jake. "It's this black thing in the middle up here."

She sat up to look.

"And don't get out of the car," he said.

She nodded and whispered *good luck*, but they didn't hear her.

Arnie and Jake darted across the dark lot, then ducked down behind a concrete turtle and watched as Masters opened the door of the van and activated the ramp that would level his wheelchair onto the loading dock.

Arnie slipped through the low shrubbery and positioned himself just under the loading dock, then waited for Jake's signal that Masters was opening the door.

Then, when he heard Masters' wheels clack over the aluminum floor strip, he hauled himself up and raced for the door, and caught it before it slammed shut. Arnie remembered the layout of the first floor and knew it would take Masters about five seconds to get to the elevator in the lobby. Arnie counted to five, then drew his gun and eased the door open.

It still had that schoolroom smell, crayons and vomit. He stepped inside, pushed the button to unlock the door for Jake, then closed it behind him noiselessly.

He ran past the steam table, grateful for what little light was coming in through the windows, skirted the dining room, the chairs and tables stacked against the wall, then rushed along the hallway with its construction-paper pumpkins and cutout witches still riding their brooms across the bulletin board.

He had always hated this building. Something about it made kids shit on the floor and slit their wrists in the bathroom. He'd always thought if he had to do some hard time, he'd rather do it in a real prison.

He stopped just inside the door to the lobby and listened as the elevator doors closed, then opened the door and watched as the indicator lights came on. Arnie's memories of this place were so clear. Second floor, Mike Evans fingerpainting. "God Going to the Store," he called it. Third floor, adolescent Sandra with her thing for setting fires. Four, the infirmary. Masters was going to the infirmary!

Arnie bolted for the stairwell. As he reached the fourth-floor landing, he heard Masters' wheels turn the corner. Arnie waited a moment, then opened the door a crack and saw Masters wheel into the last room on the left.

Sticking close to the wall, gun drawn, Arnie crept down the hall. Two doors away, he stopped cold.

A bed creaked.

Masters' voice. "Hey, lollipop," he crooned, as though it were a warm summer morning and just the two of them in the whole wide world.

Sheets turned back.

"Did you have a nice sleep?" he asked.

A chain hit the floor.

"I told you I'd come back," he whispered.

Then the bed creaked again, springing back louder this time, lighter. Like he picked her up.

Arnie made his move.

Six quick steps and he was in the doorway, feet spread wide apart, holding the gun with both hands, pointing right at Masters' head.

"Police!" he shouted.

But Masters didn't respond. He lifted the little girl's head up to his face. "Lollipop?" he faltered.

"Hold it, Masters!" Arnie roared.

And this time, Masters looked up.

And the limp little head fell back onto his chest.

Arnie couldn't see Masters' face, only the outline of his seated body, backlit by the dim yellow safety lights outside the window. He was making no attempt to escape. But it was Beth, all right. Lying across his lap, shoes off, her legs dangling over the side of his chair, a loose arm falling into the single stream of light not obscured by the wheelchair.

"Who is it?" Masters asked, his voice barely audible, disembodied in the darkness.

"It's Detective Campbell," Arnie hissed, still holding the gun on the man. "I want the little girl."

Masters stroked her fine silky hair.

If he had harmed her, Arnie couldn't see it. There was

no blood, her clothes seemed perfectly intact. Her shoes were side by side on the little nightstand beside the bed.

"This little girl?" Masters inquired, from what seemed like miles away.

Arnie cocked his pistol. "Put her back on the bed, please."

"It's not what you think," Masters remarked.

"How the fuck do you know what I think!" Arnie bellowed, his fear for Beth mounting by the minute. "Put the kid on the bed!"

"She's just resting," Mitch explained.

"She can rest on the fucking bed!" Arnie yelled. "Or I'll blow your head off, and don't tempt me!"

Slowly, almost mechanically, Masters turned his chair to face the bed, laid her down, and pulled up the sheet.

"Now, back up," Arnie barked. "Over there!" He pointed to the radiator across the room.

Arnie moved to the bed and bounced it with his hand. "Beth? He shook the little girl's shoulder. "Beth! Wake up!" Her neck was cold.

Arnie pulled his handcuffs out of his pocket.

"Goddamn you!" Arnie was hysterical. "You—"

"I didn't kill her," Masters said, his hands folded in his lap.

"You brought her here, you chained her to this—" Arnie slammed him back against the wall, then cuffed the chair to the radiator.

"I don't have a gun," Masters said as Arnie frisked him.

"If you did, I'd kill you," Arnie snapped, stepping back.

"Yes," Masters said. "So would I."

Arnie reached for his walkie-talkie. "Jake!" he screamed. "Get up here! Fourth floor. Hallway to the right, last door on the left."

He threw his gun on the bed, then bent over Beth, felt behind her ears, then her temples, but the signs were all there. He checked her wrist. Or not there.

He stepped back, still facing the wall, a wave of rage swelling up in him. He had to get her out of here.

He picked up the weightless child, and turned to Masters. "I hope there's a God," he spat. "I hope you burn in hell."

Then he rushed out of the room, down the hall, and stepped into the elevator.

The bright overhead light hurt his eyes. He folded the cold child up to his chest and closed his eyes. But the tears came anyway, bitter liquid pain running down his face. He clutched her even tighter and sobbed helplessly, her small heart so still, his massive one a stabbing savage in a mean, dark cave.

He knew it. Beth was dead.

As the door opened, Jake was just running into the lobby.

Arnie stepped out of the elevator, and Jake saw the little girl, her yellow overalls wet from Arnie's tears.

"Oh no," Jake said.

Arnie couldn't talk. "That goddamn . . . this poor . . . her shoes . . ."

And then they heard the shot.

Fourth floor, hallway to the right, last door on the left.

FAY HAD MADE herself a grilled cheese sandwich and a cup of coffee, and for once, both of them actually tasted as good as they smelled. She was scrubbing the inside of the coffeepot when Arnie called. In her hurry to get to the phone, she carried the coffeepot with her, leaving a trail of suds across the floor.

"Fay," he said, "sit down."

"It's all right," she said, so glad to hear his voice. "Tell me."

"We found Beth."

She had been waiting for those words, but they didn't sound right. Her throat caught, her hand squeezed tight around the handle of the pot.

"Fay?" he asked. "Did you hear me?"

She dropped into the chair, soapy water sloshing out of the pot as it hit the arm.

He tried to say it gently. "She's dead, Fay."

"No, Arnie," Fay cried. "The other two boys looked dead too, but they weren't, they were just—"

"No, Fay," he said, forcing the words out of his mouth. "Whatever he gave her to sleep, he gave her too much."

"Oh my God," she whispered, holding her stomach.

"And Masters is dead too."

She doubled over, head on her knees.

"Fay?"

She coughed. "I'm here."

"The ambulance is taking Beth to the morgue right now."

"Oh no. Sweet Beth," she cried.

"As soon as I get home," he said, "we'll go over to Gail's together."

She pulled herself out of the chair. "I think I better go over there right now, Arnie," she said weakly.

She lifted her head and looked around the room, trying to find something to hold on to. "Arnie," she stuttered, "did he hurt her?"

"No," he said quickly. "He didn't touch her. She just went to sleep, that's all."

She wiped her eyes. "Did you shoot him?"

"No," he said. "I chained his chair to the radiator in the room where I found them. But when I picked Beth up off the bed, I left my gun, and he—" He paused, his chest heaving. "The guy threw his body out of the wheelchair, dragged himself across the room, pulled himself up on the bed, got the gun, and blew his brains out."

Fay stared at her feet.

"Fay?"

"Yes, Arnie." Her head was so heavy.

"Vi followed us out here. I sent her home."

"All right," Fay said. "I'll tell Peter. What about Marvin?"

"The Chief is taking care of it," Arnie said. He stopped. "So . . . I'll be home in twenty minutes. Unless you think I ought to call Gail right now."

"No."

"O.K.," he said, "but can you tell her that I—"

Tell her what? That I tried real hard but I didn't get there soon enough? That maybe if I had . . . what? That if things had been different, it wouldn't have worked out this way? What?

"That you're sorry," she said, "Yes, I will. Are you all right?" she asked him.

"No," he said. "I'm not. I'll see you in a little bit." Then he remembered. "They told me you found those two boys, Fay. That's real good." His voice cracked. "I'm real proud of you."

"Thanks," she whispered. And whatever else she might

have said to him stuck in her throat. But she couldn't hang up. She pressed the phone into her shoulder.

"I'm so sorry, Fay."

"I know, hon," she managed. "It wasn't your fault. Please don't think it was your fault."

"I know," he said, "I just feel so . . ."

"Come home," she said. "Just come on home."

"I'll be right there."

"Good," she said.

Slow motion, it all felt like slow motion. She lowered the receiver into the cradle. Water, it felt as if she were wading through thick, dark water. She picked up the coffeepot and took it back to the kitchen. Then she stood in the middle of the living room and tried to think if there was anything she should take with her, anything that would help. Then, finding nothing, she got her raincoat out of the hall closet, slipped it on—it took forever to get it on—and walked out the door.

Her arm shook as she pressed the buzzer at Gail's apartment. Peter answered the door.

"Beth's dead," Fay whispered, still standing in the hallway.

But he had already seen it on her face. He stood there, his arms stiff at his sides. He sniffed, his head twitched involuntarily.

"How?" he mouthed.

Gail called from the kitchen. "Peter?" She was talking to her father on the phone. "Who is it?"

"I'll tell her," Fay said, stepping into the room.

"Jesus God," he said.

Fay shook her head. She was glad Gail was in the kitchen. She took his hand. "You stay out here, huh?"

"Sure," he said, closing the door. "Sure."

As Fay walked down the hall, she heard the end of Gail's conversation. She called him Daddy, she told him not to worry. She told him there wasn't anything he could do but get a good night's sleep. Then she said she loved him, and hung up the phone.

Fay stood in the doorway, Gail sat at the kitchen table, facing the other way.

"Gail?" Fay said carefully, taking one step in.

"I'm all right," Gail said, wetting the dish towel in her

mouth and dabbing at a spot of raspberry jam somebody had spilled on the table.

Fay walked up behind her, put her hands on Gail's shoulders, then leaned down and kissed the top of her head.

Gail wrapped the dish towel around her hand and pulled it tight. She tried to laugh. "Daddy thinks the Communists did it."

Fay kissed the side of Gail's face.

Gail unwound the dish towel, then quickly wrapped it around the other hand.

"I told him I knew for a fact it was the Republicans," Gail said. "He almost hung up on me." She stared at the refrigerator.

Fay knew this was the worst sentence anybody ever had to say. She pressed down gently on Gail's shoulders, hoping to absorb some of the anguish when it hit.

"Gail," Fay said quietly, "Beth didn't make it."

"What?" Gail turned around, as if she hadn't heard it, her eyes begging for mercy.

Fay kept hold of Gail's shoulders. "Arnie found her." She forced herself to go on. "But the man had given her a sleeping medicine and—"

Gail grabbed the table.

"—it was too much," Fay finished.

"Beth is dead?" Gail asked, praying to have misunderstood.

"Arnie is so sorry," Fay started.

"Beth is dead?" Gail screamed.

"He got there as fast as he could, but—"

"My Beth is dead?" Gail wrapped her arms around herself and dug her nails into her flesh.

Fay grabbed her as the convulsions began.

"BETH," she cried. "BETH!" And then the real scream tore through her, as though a savage claw clenched shut around her heart and tore it out raw and whole.

"B—E—T—H———"

Gail shook uncontrollably, knocking Fay into the table, knocking the table away from the wall. Fay held on to her as the tears poured down her face, but soon her hair was wet too; her arms, her whole body was crying. And then suddenly she began to shrink away, to disappear into the hole where her heart had been. Fay grasped the back of her neck, and they both fell back into the wall.

"B————E————T————H————"

"Peter!" Fay called for help.

He ran down the hall, grabbed Gail out of Fay's arms, circled his arms around her like an army, and squeezed tight.

"You're all right," he said. "I've got you." He held her hand. "It's all right. You're going to be all right."

He patted her back. "We're right here." He massaged her neck. "I'm not going to let go." He squeezed tighter. "You're all right. It's all right," he said, over and over again until something, some ancient, blood-level survival instinct said to her to stop.

Gail lay limp against him, and Fay rose from the floor. It is one thing to say that we are all connected here. It is quite another thing to hear the sound it makes when we are ripped apart.

Gail pushed away from Peter and stood up.

"Where is she?" Her voice cracked. She reached for his hand.

"The ambulance is taking her to the morgue right now," Fay said.

That word. Morgue.

"I have to change," Gail said.

"You look fine," Fay said.

"I want to change," Gail said, and she stumbled numbly toward the door.

Peter started after her, but Fay caught him. "I think it's all right," she said. "We'll hear it if she needs us."

Fay opened the refrigerator and pulled out the bottle of ice water, then went to the cabinet for two glasses. She poured them each a glassful, and they sat down at the table. She told him that Vi had been there with Arnie, and that Marvin would be at the morgue. She told him the name of Gail's minister, and the name of the funeral home. She found Gail's address book, and made a list of the relatives she knew Gail would want someone to call.

When he asked for more of the details, she told him Mitch Masters had killed himself. Peter said he thought that, in a while, Gail would want to know that.

Then Fay went into Beth's bedroom, where Gail was standing in front of the little girl's closet. Fay took her hand and said she didn't have to do this now. But Gail said she wanted the undertaker to have everything he needed when he picked her up.

Fay said a dress would be nice, and Gail reached for the white one Marvin's mother had sent Beth for Easter. Fay opened a dresser drawer and held up socks until Gail nodded at the pair with the cats on the toes.

And then Gail couldn't stay in the room any longer. The smells, the baby powder, the shampoo, the vaporizer, the tennis shoes, the smells from the beginning, the diapers, the milk, the baby-food carrots she'd spat up for so long, the smells, the smells. She had to get out quick. She had to close the door to keep the smells in.

As they passed the bathroom, Fay stuffed Kleenex into Gail's jacket pocket, and they met Peter at the front door of the apartment. It took both of them to get Gail down the stairs.

Once they were on the street, Fay said she would come along if that would help, but Gail said no. Then she reached out and Fay held her as long and close as she could, and then Peter took her arm and led her to the car.

As she watched them drive away, Fay prayed. For divine grace, for holy comfort, for the blessing of the pure in heart. And then she turned and walked down the street, toward her own doorway and the black Rolls-Royce parked in front of it.

12:00 A.M.

 FAY SAW HIS LANGUID ARM FIRST, DRAPED OUT the open window of the satiny Rolls, smoke curling lazily from the cigarette he held loosely between his fingers. She crossed the street about four cars ahead of him and stepped onto the sidewalk.

She knew she shouldn't stop, knew he wouldn't get out of the car, and knew that talking to him through the window would only make her feel worse. But she was going to do it anyway. From now on, there was nothing she wouldn't do to keep from losing Lizzie.

She walked in front of the car. He saw her, all right, but he didn't sit up, of course.

"Paul?" She tried not to bend toward him.

He gazed up at her, his voice as smooth and rich as an amber liqueur. "We wondered where you were," he said.

Fay straightened her shoulders. "If you're waiting for Lizzie," she said, "she's not coming with you."

Paul slipped further down in the seat, leaning his head back against the headrest. "If she weren't coming with me," he explained, perfectly pleasantly, "I wouldn't be waiting for her."

"Where is the boat going?" Fay asked.

"Wherever Dad says," Paul said. "It's *his* boat."

Fay nodded. "How long will you be gone?"

"Till we get back, I guess," he said, enjoying the elegance of the truth.

Fay stood there fuming, wishing she had a bottle of red

nail polish to drip down the side of his car while she thought of what to say next.

But Paul was completely at ease. "I heard you found those other two boys," he said, flicking the cigarette butt past her into the street. "I wanted to congratulate you."

"Was it your father who put up the reward?" she asked.

"I think so," he said. "He likes to do things like that." He glanced out the window to Fay's front door. "He'd probably double it if you asked him to. Means nothing to him one way or the other."

"Did you tell him it was me who was finding the children?"

"Maybe I did," Paul said. "I forget."

Fay had the whole picture now. "So he's buying Lizzie for you, is that right?"

Paul laughed.

Fay went on. " 'Just give the old lady a check.' Is that what you told him? So she won't miss her daughter?"

"Don't take the money, then," Paul said, still laughing. "Doesn't matter to me."

"What about your other girls?" Fay asked. "Do you just hand their mothers the money in cash?"

"Cash?" Paul choked. "Please." He still couldn't stop laughing.

Fay had to get to Lizzie. Why had she wasted all this time talking? Did she think there was something else to learn? Did she think she might have imagined all this? Did she think he wasn't really the Devil and was maybe just a handsome Brazilian rogue of a boy?

She hurried around the car and across the sidewalk. No way was he taking Lizzie away from her. No way.

FAY OPENED THE door.

"Mom?" Lizzie called. "Is that you?"

Please God, Fay prayed, help me. I have to make her see who he is. See what's going to happen if she leaves with him.

"It's *me*," Fay called back.

Lizzie came to the doorway of the hall, pulling a silver slip over her head. "What's up?"

"Up?" Fay repeated. She started for the closet, then decided to leave her raincoat on for the moment.

"With the kidnapping," Lizzie said, smoothing the slip down over her ribs and hips.

Fay pitched her purse into the chair. "It's not good," she said.

"You didn't find Beth yet?"

Fay stopped. Her purse had knocked over the needle-point pillow. There was her mother's loaded pistol, the one Fay had hidden there two hours ago when she was afraid of those boys on the street.

"Whose gun is that?" Lizzie asked.

"It was Mother's," Fay said, picking up the pistol and stuffing it into her coat pocket.

"What did Granny need a gun for?" Lizzie asked.

"Snakes," Fay said. And she walked past the girl into the kitchen.

Lizzie followed her. "Snakes?" She laughed.

Fay flicked on the kitchen light and stood there watching as a water bug scrambled back into the sink for safety.

"Beth is dead," Fay said, finally. "Arnie found her dead."

"Mother?" Lizzie asked from behind her.

"What?" Fay crossed the room to the refrigerator.

"What are you doing *here*? Why aren't you with Gail?"

"Where do you think I've *been*?" Fay asked, jerking the refrigerator door open.

"I just *asked*," Lizzie said, leaning against the door-frame. "You don't have to scream at me."

"I'm not screaming at you," Fay said.

"Yes, you are," Lizzie said. "Does Arnie know you have a gun?"

Fay bent down to look at the bottom shelf. "Yes," she said. "What happened to the rest of that pound cake?"

"I ate it," Lizzie said, and turned to go.

Fay whirled around. "You gave it to *him*, didn't you."

Lizzie sighed. "I ate it, Mom. Me, Lizzie. I ate it."

Fay saw Lizzie's patronizing look. "You have no idea, do you." She slammed the refrigerator door.

"I'm real sorry about Beth," Lizzie said. "I tried to say that, but you—"

"No idea," Fay said.

"It's not your fault, Mother," Lizzie said. "You did the best you could. You found all the rest of the children."

Fay shook her head. "That's not what I'm talking about." She opened the door to the pantry.

"I said I was sorry," Lizzie said. "I don't know what else to say. I have to get dressed."

"You're *not* getting dressed," Fay said.

Lizzie stopped in the doorway and took a deep breath. "I have to get dressed, Mother. We're going out on the boat again." She paused. "I thought I told you that, but I guess with all this stuff going on today . . ."

Fay closed the pantry door. There was nothing in there that would help. "Do you know where this boat is going?"

Lizzie looked away. "No, Mother."

"Well, I do," Fay said. "And I know who Paul is, and who his father is, and you're not going."

"Not going?" Lizzie asked, her back stiffening in surprise.

"No," Fay said.

Lizzie studied her mother a moment.

"I'm serious," Fay said.

No, Lizzie thought, you're tired and weird. And she turned abruptly and walked back toward her bedroom.

Fay walked to the sink and picked up a not-too-dirty glass and filled it with cloudy water from the tap. The gun felt good in her pocket, the barrel long and cold against her thigh, the handle grip hard and round on her hip. Men knew about this, she thought, men grew up playing with guns. They knew how good it felt to have one on your side.

When Fay got to the doorway of Lizzie's room, the girl was staring into her closet. But the good cheer Lizzie had felt, anticipating the party, had left her. Beth, across the street, was dead. And her own mother was walking around the house with a gun in her pocket.

"You really *know* where the boat is going?" Lizzie asked, over her shoulder.

"Yes," Fay said, leaning against the doorframe, "I do."

"Did Paul tell you?" Lizzie stepped into a pair of silver strip sandals.

"No," Fay said. "I saw it."

"Oh." The girl nodded. So it was a vision. One of her mother's little trips. Well, no wonder she was acting so strange.

"You go to California," Fay said.

Lizzie knew she had to be careful. "I see," she said. She

didn't want to insult her mother. "You think he's kidnapping me. Is that right?"

"I know it," Fay said, "and it's not the first time, either."

"It's the first time for me," Lizzie said, admiring her legs in the mirror. "What else?"

Fay took a sip of water. "At the end of the trip Paul asks you to marry him," she said.

"What do I say?" Lizzie asked, disappearing into her closet.

"You say yes," Fay said.

"So what's the bad news?" Lizzie asked, pulling out a pale voile wisp of a dancing dress. "Does his daddy hate me?"

"He buys you a convertible," Fay said.

"His mother poisons me?" Lizzie asked.

"She has the archbishop of Portugal bless the orchids for your wedding."

"You mean I actually marry him?" Lizzie grinned, stepping carefully into the dress.

"In San Diego," Fay said, finishing her glass of water.

"Do we have babies?" Lizzie asked.

"I only know of one," Fay said, watching as Lizzie struggled to zip the dress. "But there could be more, I guess. Want to know her name?"

"No," Lizzie said quickly. She turned around. "I'd like to think it up." She stopped. "If that's O.K. with you."

Fay bit her lip, and watched as Lizzie put on the gold hoop earrings. Think it up. Did people actually think they *made up* their children's names? Did they really believe that a creature as complicated as a child could arrive on the earth without a name? Could let someone else decide its name?

"I don't know why you're so worried about all this," Lizzie said, walking into the bathroom and opening the medicine cabinet. "Just because you saw it, doesn't mean it's going to happen."

Fay took a breath.

"But even if it does," Lizzie went on, "it sounds like a pretty nice life."

She found her mascara and a tiny pot of cream blush and closed the cabinet door. "Did you tell me all of it?" Lizzie called out.

"I left out the part where you never call me and I never see you again," Fay said, walking up to block the bathroom door. "You don't invite me to your wedding, and you don't let me see"—Fay stopped herself from saying Katie's name—"my granddaughter."

Lizzie applied the mascara carefully, slowly stroking both sides of her long lashes. "Why would I do that?"

Fay cleared her throat. "I don't know," she said. "Maybe you're ashamed of me. Maybe I'm not good enough for you anymore."

Lizzie started to work on the other eye.

Fay went on. "Maybe you find out I was right, only you don't want to admit it, so you just don't call me."

"Right about what?" Lizzie leaned toward the mirror to inspect her work.

"That he's going to hurt you," Fay said. "He does something terrible, only—"

"So people hurt each other," Lizzie said. "They get over it."

"—only I can't tell you what it is," Fay finished, "because I haven't seen that part yet."

Lizzie had to laugh. "Well, maybe you could call me right before it happens and . . ."

Fay didn't think that was funny. She tried to explain. "I want you to be married."

"Right," Lizzie said.

"I want you to have a family," Fay pleaded. "But I want it to be your family. Not his."

"Mother," Lizzie said, dabbing the blush just under her cheekbones, "what if I like it?"

"You'll hate it," Fay said. "You'll hate how they live, you'll hate the way they talk—"

"If I hate it, I'll leave," Lizzie said. She was finished in the bathroom now.

"He won't let you leave, Lizzie," Fay said.

"No, Mother," Lizzie said, pointing to Fay's stance in the doorway. "It's not Paul who won't let me leave, it's you."

Fay backed up. "Lizzie, please," Fay said. "Have I ever stopped you from doing anything?"

Lizzie walked toward her dresser.

Fay answered her own question. "No," she said, "I haven't. I've given you everything you ever wanted."

"No, Mom," Lizzie said over her shoulder. "You gave me everything *you* ever wanted."

Fay took a step toward her, genuinely confused. "What did you *want*?" she asked.

"I don't know," Lizzie said, picking up her gold evening bag. "Right now, I just want to go."

Fay's heart stopped. "Is that what you always wanted?" she asked. "To leave me?"

"Maybe," Lizzie said, checking herself once more in the full-length mirror. "I don't remember."

Fay couldn't breathe for a second. Could that be true? All Lizzie ever wanted was to leave? No, no. Lizzie had been happy here. All Lizzie needed was a better explanation. "I had to keep you here," Fay said, "so you could grow up."

"Well," Lizzie said quietly, putting a tissue in the little purse, "you don't have to do that anymore." And she closed the clasp.

And they both heard the front door open.

"Lizzie?" Paul called.

"I'm coming," she sang out, starting toward Fay.

"No," Fay said, grabbing her by both arms. "I can't let you go. I can't let you leave with him."

Gently, Lizzie pried her mother's hands loose, then held them in hers. "Mother," she said, "this is crazy. You're all worked up over nothing. It's just another party."

"Please," Fay said. "I wouldn't do this if I didn't think there was a real—"

"No," Lizzie said. "I promise. I'll be back in the morning."

And then Fay saw it. Looked right into Lizzie's pale green eyes and saw it. When Paul was finished with her, his father would hire the lawyers, bribe the judges, and take Katie away. Lizzie would lose her daughter not because Paul wanted to raise the little girl, but just because his father liked to win.

Someone knocked on the bedroom door.

"Lizzie?" It was Paul.

Fay froze as the door opened. She had to tell her.

"What's going on in here?" Paul asked.

"Lizzie . . ." Fay began.

"Mother thinks you're kidnapping me," Lizzie said, casting a careful sideways glance at Fay.

"That's not a bad idea," he said, opening the door even wider behind him. "You look wonderful."

Lizzie smiled at him. "Thanks," she said, then turned to

Fay and gave her a light kiss on the cheek. "I'll see you in the morning, Mother."

Fay looked up at her. How could she tell her? *What* could she tell her? That she would lose her child? Lizzie wouldn't believe it. Nobody ever did.

"Lizzie," Fay tried again, "if it's just another party, then you don't have to go. There are lots of parties."

"I'll be all right," Lizzie soothed.

"No," Fay pleaded. "You won't!"

Lizzie took Paul's arm. This was almost funny. "You'll be O.K., Mom." She grinned and patted Fay on the shoulder. "Arnie will be home soon."

And Paul and Lizzie turned together and walked out the door.

Fay stood there listening to their footsteps down the hall. She couldn't wait for Arnie. Paul was *not* going to get away with this. Walk off with her daughter? Walk off with her granddaughter? Just because he was young and rich and always got what he wanted? Not a chance in hell.

"Lizzie!" she screamed, and ran after them.

Paul was just opening the front door.

Lizzie stopped. "What?" she asked.

Fay drew the gun and braced herself against the door to the hall. "Get out of the way," she said.

"Mother!" Lizzie screamed.

Paul bolted out the door, dragging Lizzie behind him. "Get in the car!" he shouted, and pushed her toward it, then ran around the front of the shadowy Rolls.

Fay charged through the living room and out onto the sidewalk.

"Mother!" Lizzie cried, from the front seat, her hands pressed up against the closed window. "Don't do this!"

"Lizzie!" Fay screamed, but the engine roared to life. Fay ran back behind the car, but she didn't know where to shoot. The tires? The windows? What if she missed the tires and hit the gas tank? What if she blasted the windows and the broken glass hit Lizzie?

"Lizzie!" she screamed again, but the tires squealed, the car sprang forward and pulled away from the curb.

"Stop!" she screamed, and ran out into the street. But the car didn't stop. She raised the gun high above her head, fired two shots into the heavy black air, then ran up the street after them.

The Rolls ran the light at the corner. She couldn't see Lizzie inside it now.

Still, she followed, still screaming. "You don't know what he's going to do!"

And then she felt her legs slow down. They knew, even if she didn't, that it was useless.

"He's going to take . . ." She stopped. She had to stop. "K—A—T—I—E—!" Fay cried.

And then, in a desperate rage, she flung the heavy pistol toward the tiny red taillights now taking a left turn three blocks away.

Lizzie was gone.

Fay didn't move. She stood over the yellow line down the middle of the street, folded her trembling arms around herself, and stared straight ahead. If any cars came, they'd just have to go around her. If anybody had heard the gunfire, they'd just have to get up, turn on a light, and worry about it. Fay wasn't going anywhere until she felt like it. Where was she supposed to go? Home? Why? Because she'd left the front door open? Who cared? So she could change clothes? Sleep? Eat? Work? What was the point?

She closed her eyes. But there was nothing to see there either. She already knew what would happen. Arnie would come home, they would go to Gail's, then to bed. Maybe he would quit the police force tomorrow, maybe he wouldn't. Maybe they would go to Wyoming tomorrow, maybe they wouldn't. But Lizzie would not come home.

She wiped her forehead on the sleeve of her shirt. She couldn't leave that pistol on the street. She opened her eyes and started up the street to find it. Behind her, somewhere down the block, a car screeched to a stop. She assumed it was Arnie.

"Miss Morgan?" a young police officer called, running toward her from the station on the corner.

"I'm all right," she yelled back to him.

"Fay!" It was Arnie's voice, shouting as he chased up the street.

"I'm all right!" she yelled even louder, angry at both of them for finding her here.

"I heard the shot," the young officer said.

"I lost my mother's gun," Fay said, stooping down to look underneath a beat-up Buick. "Let me have your flashlight."

"Fay?" Arnie asked, coming up to join them now.

She stood, took the young officer's flashlight, and turned to face Arnie.

"They got away," she said.

The young officer wanted to seem in charge. "Miss Morgan called me about an hour ago," he said to Arnie. "Told me there were some robbers watching her apartment."

But Arnie knew Fay hadn't been chasing robbers.

She walked on up the street.

"Where are you going now?" he called.

"She says it's her mother's gun," the young officer said, as they followed her. "I guess they tried to steal it."

"There it is," she said, pointing under the custom Jeep.

"I'll take care of this," Arnie said to the young man.

"It's Rodgers, sir," he answered.

"O.K. Rodgers," Arnie said. "Thanks."

"That's the lady who found all those kids, isn't it?" Rodgers asked.

"Yeah," Arnie said. "See you later."

"Anytime," Rodgers said, deciding reluctantly that it probably wasn't a good idea to ask her for an autograph right now.

"I DIDN'T HIT them," Fay said, as soon as the young officer was out of earshot.

"Good," Arnie said.

Fay wiped the gun on her skirt. "I wanted to, though. I wanted to kill him," she said.

He shook his head. "It doesn't feel as good as you think," he said. "The minute you know they're dead, you start to wonder what else you might have tried."

She nodded, then shuddered to think how dangerously close she had come to it. Dead in the street, the Devil would have won for real.

"Want to walk?" he asked.

"I want to change clothes," she said, studying the gun in the glow from the streetlight.

He stooped to pick up a soft-drink can lying in the gutter. "I want to throw this away," he said, "and go in there and quit." He pointed to the station. "Then I'll come down to your house."

"You're really going to quit?" she asked, but it was more an echo than a question.

"I'm going to try," he said. "Want me to walk you down to your house first?"

"No," she said, "I'll be all right." And she walked off, carrying the pistol loosely at her side.

Arnie watched her go. If there were bullets left in that gun, that was *her* business. Maybe, if he were an ordinary cop, he'd have taken it away from her. But he could see it made her feel better. And after this day, she deserved to feel better. Besides, he laughed to himself, he'd like to see somebody *try* to take anything else away from Fay Morgan tonight. She wasn't going to shoot anybody. She was just going to put the gun back in the closet where it belonged.

As Arnie watched Fay, she watched Paul and Lizzie boarding the boat.

"Why did you do it?" Paul asked, taking her arm. "Why did you save me?"

Lizzie spoke softly, privately, ignoring the crowd that was waiting for them. "I wanted to be with you," she said.

"She wanted to kill me," Paul said, with no malice, but a world of wonder at the actual fact of it.

"She loves me," Lizzie said, stepping onto the gangplank.

"Is that what happens to people who love you?" he asked, accepting a glass of champagne from the steward.

She laughed as the truth came to her. "If it is," she said, "does that scare you?"

"No," Paul grinned, tilting the glass toward her in a silent toast. "It's good to know, though."

Fay swallowed hard, and walked up to her door. She felt the vacant chill as soon as she stepped inside the apartment. Was it just Lizzie who was missing? No. She closed the door behind her. It was everything Lizzie had held in place just by living there. History, hope, the length of love, the promise of a child.

She walked to the closet, hung up her raincoat, then put the gun back in the box on the floor. Fay could just hear her mother clucking over this.

She closed the closet door, walked to the bathroom, and washed her face. She looked awful, and felt even worse, like a cracked, cheap plastic carryall, abandoned in the back of somebody's closet.

She changed into faded trousers and a flannel shirt, then slipped on a pair of moccasins she and Lizzie had bought ten years ago on a trip to the Blue Ridge.

As she passed the closet, on her way back into the living room, she stopped. She missed her mother, actually missed the nosy old hen. Missed her smell, her hair. Missed how she thought she knew everything, missed how mean she could be when she was right. Maybe, just maybe, way off in the distant future, way beyond where Fay could see right now, maybe Lizzie would miss *her* that way.

No, Fay thought. That was hope. Fay didn't believe in hope. Fay believed in phone calls.

Arnie was standing on the sidewalk when she came out into the living room.

"I want to sleep at my house tonight," he said, opening the door. "Want to come?"

"I want to go to Gail's first," she said, running her hand along the back of the old upholstered armchair.

"I just checked," he said. "They left the morgue about ten minutes ago. So they're not back yet."

He lifted the paper sack he held in his left hand. "I bought us a beer," he said.

"Good," she said, pushing her hair back away from her face. "A beer would be real good."

"I thought we could lock up," he said, "then sit out on the stoop and drink it."

"Good," she said.

He waited while she retrieved her purse from the chair, then closed the door behind her and locked it.

Fay sat down on the raised concrete stoop and stretched her legs out in front of her.

"How do you feel?" he asked, as he sat down beside her.

"I don't have any feelings left," she said.

"They'll be back."

"I can wait," she smiled, running her hand down his arm.

He set the sack between his legs, pulled out one of the cold beers, and flipped the top.

"Thanks," she said, lifting the rush of cold foam to her mouth and licking the side of the can to catch the runoff before it ruined her pants.

"I saw what was going to happen to Lizzie," she said finally, "but I couldn't tell her."

"It sounds like you did the right thing, Fay," he said. "It's over. Don't worry about it."

She stared into her beer. "How can it be over? Things don't ever end, Arnie. Tell me one thing, one thing that was ever over."

"Well," he pondered, then opened his beer. "For starters"—he took a long drink—"this day is over."

He put the bag off to one side for the cans when they were empty, set the beer down on the stoop, and reached into his pocket for a fresh pack of cigarettes. Slowly, he unwound the gold strip around the top of the pack, tore off the folded foil square, and tapped the pack against his hand.

"Did you resign?" she asked, wishing there were a breeze, or just one breath of air she didn't have to take by force.

He lifted the pack to his mouth and pulled one cigarette from the trio his tap had forced out of formation. Then he put the pack back in his pocket and reached into the other pocket for his lighter.

"I filled out the papers," he said, then shrugged. "Sooner or later, somebody's bound to find them."

Good, she thought. So at least they didn't have to leave for Wyoming *tomorrow*.

She pushed her hair back from her temples. "How can it still be so hot out here?"

He smiled as the thought hit him, then flicked the lighter, cupped his hands around the flame, lit the cigarette, and inhaled. "You never did smoke, did you?"

"No," she said, gazing out into the darkness. "I never did."

He blew the smoke out in front of them in one long curl, reached for her hand, and squeezed it.

"That's too bad," he said quietly. "Be just the thing."

ABOUT THE AUTHOR

MARSHA NORMAN, a native of Louisville, Kentucky, won the Pulitzer Prize for her play *'night, Mother*. Three of her six plays premiered at the Actors Theater of Louisville, where she was playwright-in-residence for two years. Marsha Norman has received grants from the National Endowment for the Arts, the Rockefeller Foundation, and the National Academy and Institute of Arts and Letters, and has written for film, including the screenplay for the motion picture of *'night, Mother*. This is her first novel.